SONGBORNE GATES

BOOK 2 OF THE DELIBERIA CHRONICLES

S. LYNN HELTON

ISBN (Paperback): 978-1-7348581-4-3
ISBN (eBook): 978-1-7348581-5-0

Scripturio Books
www.ScripturioBooks.com
24.04.03

Acknowledgments

Many heartfelt thanks to my beta readers.
You continue to help me with great ideas
to improve my stories!

CHAPTER 1

Shyvoan Naivaschld had heard them all, all the tales of how her red hair meant that she was cursed, an agent of bad luck, or some other form of foolishness. At least she had normal brown eyes, they told her, instead of the rare green or even rarer blue that would have truly meant she was cursed, according to those old tales anyway.

Sitting nearby, the chatty aspirants—the warrior-trainees—directed periodic sidelong looks her way as they worked on their weapons, looks that told her they persisted in sharing the gossip about her. Although none of the other warriors gave her a second glance.

Probably got stories from Neasha before the troop left on this scouting trip. If only her sister wouldn't continue to mention Shyvoan's supposed ill luck to everyone every chance she got, people might actually forget about it. But Neasha had been reminding everyone of it as long as Shyvoan remembered, and she showed no sign of letting people forget the supposed curse.

Shyvoan frowned and focused her attention on smoothing the kalsh oil onto her sword. The oil, when combined with the berevo wood from which the weapon was made, both strengthened the weapon and helped it hold its edge longer.

Her thoughts drifted as she worked at the familiar task. *Not cursed, and not magic, either.* The magic in her family line had ended with her mother. Neither she nor Neasha had inherited the slightest bit of magic. As a child, she had been disappointed. But no longer. She had no desire to be a mage. *A mage was even more of a target than everyone else.*

Shyvoan set aside the oily cloth she had been using and held her sword at eye level to peer at it in the murky light of near sunset. *Good, only one small spot that needed more attention.*

The warriors' spears and swords were all crafted from berevo wood, but her sword included a little something extra. It had been somehow infused with dragon scales, a technique long lost. Passed down in her family for decades, the weapon brought her no magic, but the dragon-scale-infused sword needed little care beyond the occasional oiling and polish. Unlike the regular berevo weapons that the other warriors carried, which were a uniform gray-white color that seemed to catch the light at every opportunity, her darker sword blended better into the surroundings.

Shyvoan shot a glance at the aspirants. They spoke almost loud enough for her to make out the words, but at least they seemed to be trying to keep it quiet. Scouting and chatter did not make a good combination.

At a sudden silence, she looked up from her task, first scanning around their hidden camp for any threat. Then she spotted the troop's commander, Troop-Lead Meara Eadaschld, crouched on the far side of the group of youngsters. With the mottled gray-brown leathers she wore, and her brown skin and hair, the Troop-Lead was a challenge to spot in the dim light.

Shyvoan smiled to herself. *Troop-Lead probably had to remind them to chatter quieter. Youngsters.* Not that she herself had many more years than they did. Only a few. But she had already survived almost five years among the Shields, the warriors and scouts of their people. *Far removed from the aspirants.*

Leaving the group of aspirants, now subdued and talking in voices too quiet for Shyvoan to hear more than a hint of a murmur, Troop-Lead Meara next approached Shyvoan.

The tall, stocky woman crouched next to her and leaned close to Shyvoan's ear. "I know you just got back, but Teigye's spotted a strange light on watch—"

Shyvoan grinned. "Of course I'll check it out." She kept her voice as low as Troop-Lead Meara's had been.

The Troop-Lead grinned back at her. "Never one to sit still for long."

"Not if I can help it."

Although she had returned less than an hour earlier from a scouting run, Shyvoan was ready to go out again – and she was the one most often asked to. She was no mage, but her companions in the warriors, her squad-mates, had commented time and again over the years that they enjoyed better luck in her vicinity, when she joined patrols or scouting parties. In spite of the reputation of her red hair. Her groups came back alive, seemed to heal faster from any wounds, got better information from their forays. Not from anything she was aware she did, though.

Troop-Lead Meara handed Shyvoan a small jar containing a varicolored gelled tincture in shades of brown and green—called simply 'the color' by the warriors—that helped them blend in with the woods. Made by the best herbalists among the denizens, the stuff looked like mud, but had no odor and protected them from biting insects. The warriors all wore leathers made from hides from tarandeer—the people's beasts of burden and sources of milk, meat, and hides—which already blended well with the trunks, stems and twigs of the plant life around them. But skin did not blend in as well, especially Shyvoan's, light brown as it was. Even with her freckles.

Shyvoan murmured her thanks and spread the color on her face, neck and ears, the parts of her skin that might show after she put her gloves and cap back on. She wore her bright hair in tight braids wrapped around her head – she had not yet loosened them after she returned. Her cap hid her hair well.

"Which way?" She returned the jar and pulled on her cap and gloves.

Meara indicated a direction behind Shyvoan with a slight motion of her head. "Maybe near the land's edge."

"Is it moaras then?" Shyvoan referred to the Maheaja-Folk that lived in the sea.

"Teigye said it didn't seem like anything we've heard of them doing." Meara shrugged. "Take Buok with you. His bow'll give you that little extra, if you need it."

Shyvoan nodded acknowledgement. He would watch while she got close. She looked around for Buok Daheaschld, one of her squad-mates. The man already watched her and Meara. When his gaze met Shyvoan's, she gave him a quick nod. He answered it with a nod of his own, stuffed the last of his meal into his mouth in one big bite, and gathered his gear, pulling a cap much like Shyvoan's over his short, shaggy black hair. Buok still wore the color on his light brown skin from his scouting duties earlier.

A few minutes later she and Buok met with Teigye Klaidschld, another of their squad-mates at the edge of the camp. Although his darker-brown skin and hair tended to blend well into the surrounding woody foliage, he too wore the color on any exposed skin. It mixed raggedly with the narrow, short beard that edged his jawline. Cleanshaven, Buok did not have that problem.

"Can't tell you much," Teigye said, his voice little more than a whisper. "I saw a flash of light, sort of purple, off that way." He gestured the same direction that Meara had. "Looked big but didn't last. There and gone again faster than saying it, and the wrong way and color for sunset."

With a nod and a pat on the shoulder to express thanks, Shyvoan led the way into the dusk-shadowed forest.

Shyvoan and Buok slipped through the trees with little effort. They both had learned the game trails this direction and so had no need to take the time to find a good path. The normal sounds of the forest at sunset surrounded them: dusk birds muttered and chirped, insects sang, a couple of wild canids sounded their raspy barks in the distance. A sporadic breeze rustled the leaves, and they adjusted their movement patterns so their own slight sounds blended into the wind. Close to a quarter hour later, they peered out at the shore from a screen of dense brush.

Twilight lingered in the sky, but darkness already gripped the land. The Shallow Sea beyond the land's edge reflected the sky in broken bits and silhouetted two figures on the beach, a stretch of bare land more rocks than sand. The figures appeared human, but that could be a semblance to draw the warriors in. One figure stood and the other crouched next to the first.

With a gesture for Buok to stay hidden and find a vantage to attack from, if needed, Shyvoan edged through the trees to come out at a spot that would not indicate the camp's direction.

After she heard the faint call of the Nightsinger—a tiny bird that sang only during the hours of darkness—repeated in a distinct pattern that meant Buok had found an advantageous position, she eased out of the brush. She deliberately rustled it to see what the figures would do.

The crouching figure did not move, but the standing one spun around to face her. The standing figure dropped a hand to its side, as if to grab a weapon, but then stopped. No weapon was there.

Shyvoan studied what she saw of the shore. No sign of any strange lights and the Shallow Sea held none of the telltale ripples that signaled that any moaras lurked beneath the small waves and waited to attack. Those aquatic Maheaja-Folk preferred deeper water anyway.

Shyvoan walked closer to the two figures, her pace slow and deliberate, her left hand near the hilt of her sheathed sword. As she approached, details of the figures became clearer, even with the light fading.

The two figures looked like human males. They wore odd clothes, some sort of loose cloth. Belted shirts that reached almost to their knees and loose trousers beneath, very unlike her own snug leathers. The best Shyvoan could tell, the colors of the strangers' clothes were not the forest browns, grays, and greens that they should have been. These clothes stood out starkly against the backdrop of the rocky shore, even in the dim light. *Blues and purples?*

Both strangers had light skin, much like her own, although the standing man's looked darker than his companion's. His hair also looked darker than his companion's.

Shyvoan stopped a few steps away from the men. From that close, she saw that the standing man stood less than a half-head taller than she did. The crouched one glanced at her, his expression disinterested. His gaze slid past her face and back to his feet. Both men had a few days' growth of beard.

Seeing the crouched man better, Shyvoan frowned. His cheeks looked hollow, and his hands trembled. *Ill?*

Both men wore rings. The standing one had a single ring on the thumb of his left hand. It had some kind of stone in it. The crouching man wore a similar ring, also on his left thumb. But he also wore a ring on the third finger of each of his hands. Shyvoan gave them a second look. *They match. Interesting….*

She looked around again. The men had small packs with them, but she saw no sign of how they had gotten there. No wreckage from a boat and there had been no tracks in the dirt-sand near the forest's edge. The customary briny odor of the Shallow Sea drifted into her face with the breeze but without the additional acrid bite that came with the moaras' presence. *But if they had somehow transformed into humans, or had magicked themselves to* look *like humans, would that odor cling to them?*

The standing man took a slight step toward Shyvoan but when she clasped the hilt of her sword he stopped and held his hands out to the sides.

He stepped back and said something.

"I don't understand you," Shyvoan said.

With a perplexed look, the man said something else. The words had a different sound to them this time.

Shyvoan shrugged. "Still don't." She placed one hand flat on her chest. "Shyvoan."

The man peered at her and repeated what she said. His accent was strange but intriguing at the same time.

Shyvoan nodded and repeated her name, before she pointed at him and gave him a questioning look.

He placed his hand flat on his chest, mimicking her gesture. "Devrand."

She repeated the word. *Hope that's his name and not his people's word for man, or even the word for his people.* She turned her questioning look to the crouched man, whose gaze seemed fixed on his feet.

She looked back to the other and pointed to the crouching man. "Devrand?"

The standing man looked startled, then laughed. He shook his head and pointed to himself. "Devrand." Then he pointed to his companion. "Jarthan."

Shyvoan gave him a slight smile. *Good. The words were most likely their names, then.* Behind her back, she made the signal for caution but not current danger. *Hope Buok sees that in the fading light.* Then she scrutinized Devrand and Jarthan. *What would be her best course of action?*

True they looked human. But it would need a mage to say for certain whether they were of the Maheaja-Folk. Although she had not seen it herself, some tales claimed that a few of them—very few—had ways to appear human. Until they attacked.

Doubtful that they could be moaras. Shyvoan had never heard that any of those water dwellers functioned well on land for so long a time.

Devrand studied her in return. After a few minutes of this, Shyvoan made her decision. She'd chance that they were human, as they looked. At least she didn't see any of the telltale signs the mages had told them to look for: a hint of light in the eyes, the hair that looked unreal up close, too many or too few fingers and oddly jointed.

She extended her right hand in proper greeting, with fingers together and her thumb tucked into her palm. "I give you greetings."

Devrand studied her expression a brief time, before he imitated the gesture. He gave her a quizzical look.

Shyvoan stepped close enough to touch her fingertips to his to complete the greeting. At the touch of his fingers on hers, a strange sense that something had gone out from her crawled across her skin. A few seconds later, the sensation vanished. *Must have been a wild imagining. Not a surprise under the circumstances. Finding a couple of strangers at the land's edge with no visible way to have gotten there.*

"And there, now we've officially met. I think, anyway." She pulled her hand back with a slight smile.

Devrand's quizzical expression deepened, and he took a step toward her, his hand still extended but now lifted toward her face. Shyvoan did not move but watched him closely. *Might this be part of how these strangers greeted people? And what was that scent? Burnt wood?*

She glanced around but saw nothing burning. *Odd.*

With a light touch, he swiped a finger along her jaw and came away with some of the color. He squished the stuff between his fingers as he watched how it spread and coated them. He took a quick sniff and gave her that quizzical look.

She laughed lightly, dug a rag out from a pouch on her

belt and wiped the color from his fingers.

The Nightsinger signal came from the forest behind Shyvoan, this time the signal that they should leave. She glanced at the sky, surprised at how dark it had grown. They needed to get back within the wards of the camp. She'd just have to take Devrand and Jarthan there and let their mages make sure they were the humans they appeared to be.

If they were not, she and Buok would have the whole camp to help them hold the strangers, or eliminate them, if they needed to.

She clasped Devrand's sleeve and gave it a gentle tug before she pointed back the way she had come.

"We need to go," she told him, although he would not know what she said. "It's not wise to be without wards in the night, if you can help it."

She tugged on his sleeve a second time.

With a nod, Devrand clasped Jarthan's shoulder and pulled him to his feet. The other man sagged a moment then stood on his own but slumped and avoided looking at Shyvoan.

Devrand said something to him and Jarthan grabbed the two packs from where they sat at their feet. Devrand clasped Shyvoan's arm in a light grip and headed the direction she had indicated. Unfortunately, he grabbed her sword arm.

She shook him off with a frown. When he gave her a confused look, she flapped her hand at him to get him to move further away and pointedly placed that hand on her sword's hilt.

He looked abashed, then nodded and scooted around to her other side, drawing Jarthan with him. With another wave of her arm, followed by a slight push, she indicated that they should follow, not walk next to her.

Was that a flash of anger in Devrand's expression? Maybe not accustomed to following? The expression vanished, leaving her wondering if she had seen it at all.

She led the way back across the rocky shoreline and into the surrounding forest, entering at almost the exact point she had left it earlier. Buok's Nightsinger call told her he followed.

As she led the strangers along the wider game paths, she was pleased to note that they moved with almost as little noise as she and Buok. *Could they be scouts, too? Perhaps from somewhere on another of the islands in the Shallow Sea, someplace her people had no knowledge of. Maybe they had come to join with them against the Maheaja-Folk. But then how had they gotten there?*

Shyvoan wrestled with these concerns the entire trip back to the camp and she tried to ignore the twitching sensation in her back and shoulders. She could tell that the strangers kept back a couple of steps from her, but that did not help her unease. *Still, Buok watched them.* He was fast enough and skilled enough with the bow, even in the near dark, to put an arrow in both before they did her any real harm.

As they approached the hidden camp, Shyvoan spotted one of the watchers in the trees and whistled the signal that let the other warrior know that she returned with something that might be important.

A few seconds later, she heard the Nightsinger call go out that communicated that information to the camp. She heard the two men behind her pause at the sound and glanced back at them to motion them to keep moving.

Another couple of minutes and they reached the first of the wards surrounding the camp – concentric rings formed by three special token-sticks, each of which stood about knee-high, placed in the ground at an equal distance from each other and activated by a mage. Troop-Lead Meara stood several steps further into the small grove, just visible through the trees.

Shyvoan stepped to one side and motioned the men toward the camp as she watched the wards, which she saw as faint, thin lines on the ground. How they reacted could tell her something about the two strangers. She followed them as they approached the Troop-Lead but stayed far enough back that her presence would not influence the wards.

The strangers passed all three ward lines without setting off any alarms and without showing any signs of discomfort. The troop's mages would confirm, but it looked like the two men were the humans they seemed to be.

The men stopped in front of the Troop-Lead and Shyvoan joined them.

"They don't seem to know our language," she told Troop-Lead Meara, who gave her a surprised look. "And I couldn't understand anything they said. I saw no sign of the light and found nothing to indicate how they came to be where I found them."

Becoming aware of Devrand's scrutiny as she spoke, Shyvoan gave him a sidelong look. He smiled and turned to look around.

"Take them to see Uasal," the Troop-Lead said. Uasal Breanschld was the troop's most-accomplished mage. "Then grab some food and join me and we can talk more."

When Shyvoan joined the Troop-Lead in her tent, she took the seat that Troop-Lead Meara indicated near the tiny brazier, glad of the warmth. She took a few bites of food then told her what had happened and what she had noticed. Partway through her narrative, Buok joined them. When she paused to eat some of her meal before it got too cold, he added something she had not noticed.

"From my vantage in one of the trees near the shore, I spotted an odd mark on the ground a few steps behind the strangers," he said.

At Shyvoan's surprised look, he added, "You probably wouldn't have seen it from where you stood, even if the sun stood high."

Troop-Lead Meara waved at him to continue.

"It looked like a narrow line across the area, perhaps

two or three feet long. It cut through the rocks there, right down to the dirt and sand beneath, from what I could see. Maybe some magic."

The Troop-Lead frowned. "Should have Uasal take a look at that, then. But at first light. I don't like the feel of this night."

"Any warnings from the watches?" Shyvoan said.

Troop-Lead Meara shook her head as she stood. "It could just be these newcomers." She headed to the tent's flap. "Finish your meals and get what rest you can. I'm setting heavier watches and might need you two to stand a watch, too."

Shyvoan and Buok exchanged uneasy glances, then did as directed.

CHAPTER 2

Troop-Lead Meara kept the strangers in a small tent of their own, near the center of the camp, and set a couple of warriors to watch their tent throughout the night. As she headed to her own rest, Shyvoan passed the Troop-Lead and Uasal where they stood in deep conversation. They glanced several times at the strangers' tent. Shyvoan glanced there, too and saw only the closed tent. *Wonder what that's about.*

The next morning seemed full of shortened tempers and more yawns than usual, Shyvoan right there with the others. Everyone else must have had as uneasy a night as she had. While she ate her bland but filling breakfast in the near-dawn light, Shyvoan watched the tent the strangers occupied. She wanted to monitor them. *Also see them in the light of day.* But then Troop-Lead Meara brought Uasal over, the mage smoothing some of the color on her pale skin while she walked.

"I need you to show Uasal where you found the strangers last night," Meara said.

With a nod, Shyvoan gulped the last of her meal and

hunted out Buok to come along.

Buok and Shyvoan led the way and retraced their path through the woods. As they walked Usual shared the little she had discovered about the strangers. "They're most definitely human. I feel they've traveled far. And, most curious, they carry the faintest hint of a strange magic about them."

"Not Maheaja-Folk?"

"No. Not anything I've encountered before."

When they reached the land's edge, all three of them crossed the rocky shore area to the odd spot Buok had seen the night before. The area, when they arrived, looked as Buok had described it. Shyvoan and Buok backed away to let Uasal do her magic while they kept watch.

After several minutes, Buok leaned close. "The woods are very quiet this morning," he observed.

"That almost sounds like a pass phrase." Shyvoan shared a slight grin with him, then sobered. "And yah. Think something's coming?"

"It has that feel to it," the archer said. "But no one's seen any signs that they've found us."

"That's odd," Uasal muttered.

"What, that they haven't found us yet?" Buok said.

"That, too," the mage said. With a serious expression, she pushed her long tail of yellow-brown hair back over her shoulder. "But this is very odd. There's magic here, but it's unlike any I've ever encountered. Or even heard of."

She stood and brushed her hands off on her leathers. Although unskilled with most weapons, she dressed like all the warriors. If it came to battle with Maheaja-Folk, she would use her magic, at least as much as she could.

"I can't even tell what it does," she complained. "But it's faint and fading fast. In another couple of hours, the only thing left will be that line to mark that it was ever here."

Shyvoan moved closer to scrutinize the line.

"Almost looks like it cut right through the rocks," she

said.

"It did. Let's get back."

Uasal led the way back to their camp and set a fast pace. Her skill at woodcraft nearly matched Shyvoan's and Buok's, so they moved with no more than a whisper of sound.

The bustle about the camp surprised Shyvoan when they returned. It looked like everyone hurried about, no one out scouting. She parted from the other two and sought out Troop-Lead Meara.

"I'm giving you charge of our two guests," the Troop-Lead said as she approached. "We've got to move camp. The northern scouts came back right before you did and reported signs some Maheaja-Folk are moving toward us."

"Back to the denizens' lodgment, then?"

"We all know the lodgment's time is limited. And it's looking like we'll have to get them moving before the change of seasons, but we'll not head back yet. The troop will split into the squads to finish seeing to the possible paths through this area. Should make it harder for the Maheaja-Folk to find us as smaller groups."

Shyvoan nodded her understanding and turned toward her own small tent. Meara stopped her with a hand on her arm.

"Liphye will get your things together. I need your attention on our two guests. I'm splitting your squad for now. You'll have those two along and a couple of others to support you. Continue to investigate paths for moving the denizens through. You're one of the squads who'll angle inland. Also watch those two. See if they've any connection to the Maheaja-Folk." The Troop-Lead waved a hand toward Devrand and Jarthan, who sat near the remnants of the camp's small fire.

Jarthan's attention seemed to be on his own feet, but Devrand watched the activity around them with interest. After a minute, he placed a hand on Jarthan's shoulder and gave him a little shake before he leaned close and spoke to him.

Shyvoan watched them, concealed by the controlled chaos in the camp. *What was their relationship?* They did not look like brothers. The previous night, the way Jarthan had toted both their packs, it seemed that perhaps they were master and servant. But there seemed to be something more there.

With a mental shrug, she made her way through the chaos and sat next to Devrand, in a place from which she still saw Jarthan. This close, she now saw that Devrand's hair was auburn and Jarthan's a gold-brown. Devrand's eyes were an unusual blue-green color. When Jarthan glanced at her, she saw that his eyes were green. Then she noticed how the others in the camp went out of their way to avoid coming too close to the two. Probably because of that notion that green or blue eyes meant the person was cursed, although neither of them had the damning red hair that she did.

"We're moving out. All of us," she said, although, of course, they would not understand her.

Jarthan did not look at her, but Devrand gave her a quizzical look.

With a sigh, she tried to mime packing gear and walking elsewhere. She could not tell if the message got through, but she heard snickering behind her.

"Is this a new game?" Liphye Maivschld teased as she dropped Shyvoan's two packs at her feet. "Can I play, too?"

Shyvoan spared a glare for her friend and squad-mate. "Please, join in any time. They don't speak our language and I have no idea how to teach it to them."

Liphye planted her hands on her hips and eyed the two men. Devrand studied her in return and his lips quirked in a slight, calculating smile as he did so. Shyvoan glanced at her friend but saw nothing to warrant the expression. Liphye stood a little taller than Shyvoan, with black hair and dark brown eyes and skin. She had a ready smile, but right then wore a slight frown.

"Think we've got any clothes that don't scream 'Here I am!' and such to everyone in sight?" Liphye said after a few minutes.

Shyvoan surveyed the clothes both men wore that morning. She'd been so occupied looking at Devrand's face, she hadn't paid any attention before. It looked like they had tried to blend in, but they both wore greens far too bright for the forest, and solid, rather than the mottled coloring everyone else in the camp wore. And the low shoes both men wore looked like some kind of soft leather, nothing like her own sturdy books of tarandeer leather or the goat-hide leather shoes most non-warriors wore.

Without thinking about it, Shyvoan reached out and fingered the cloth of Devrand's sleeve. She found the fabric thin, nowhere near as sturdy as the cloth she knew, made from yarns spun from goat hair. *Be surprised if his shirt didn't tear at the first sharp twig.*

Then Devrand's hand covered hers.

She looked up sharply at his smiling face, an alluring smile unlike the one he had given Liphye. She jerked her hand back, disconcerted at a momentary tug at something inside her. She forgot it in the next instant.

"I need to stay and watch these two," she told Liphye. "Orders. So, you see if you can find something better for them to wear. I suppose even a cloak would help."

"Definitely would," Liphye said and headed back into the chaos.

A tap on her arm drew Shyvoan's attention back to Devrand. He pointed the direction Liphye had gone, with a questioning look for Shyvoan.

"Oh, that's Liphye. My friend."

At the confusion in his expression, Shyvoan sighed.

"Liphye," she said.

He repeated it a couple of times before he started pointing to various objects around them and giving her questioning looks.

Before Liphye returned with her arms full of clothing, Devrand could name everything around them. Jarthan had glanced at her from time to time, and he mouthed the words, but never vocalized any of them.

"Here you go." Liphye dumped the clothing in Devrand's lap.

He looked startled, then laughed and looked through the pile, tossing clothes to Jarthan as he picked out some for himself.

"I'll catch up to you on the walk," Liphye said. "Lots to do." She hurried back into the bustle of preparations.

By the time everyone was ready to go, Devrand and Jarthan had both changed into their new clothes. In their usual squads—mostly—the warriors and aspirants trickled out of the area, headed various directions. Devrand submitted to having the color smeared on his exposed skin, but with a sour expression. Jarthan had no expression at all.

Devrand's new clothes were slightly too big for him, but he somehow made them look as if they had been made for him. Jarthan's seemed to hang on his frame, although when she looked closer, Shyvoan saw that they were not that much too big. They just gave that impression.

She grabbed her two packs and motioned for her charges to come with her. Buok joined them.

"Troop-Lead says Uasal is with us," he told Shyvoan.

With a nod of understanding, she found them a place in the brush close outside the outer ward-ring. There they hunkered down to wait for the mage, who needed to dismantle the wards behind the troop.

As Shyvoan and her two charges watched from their bushes, Buok took himself off to cover the mage from a different direction. The scouts had not reported any Maheaja-Folk close, but that did not mean they abandoned caution.

From the corner of her eye, Shyvoan saw Devrand

giving Uasal's actions his intent attention. But when the mage joined them, he ignored her.

With Buok flanking them and sometimes ranging ahead or behind, Shyvoan led her squad along the wider game trails to help avoid leaving traces of their passage in the surrounding brush. As they moved inland and roughly eastward, the trails narrowed as the trees grew closer together. Shyvoan looked for wider trails but did not spot any. *Won't bring any denizens' carts through here.*

Although the squads kept in contact with various birdcalls, Shyvoan and her companions saw none of the others until midday, when Shyvoan's squad and two others met in a hidden clearing for food and to share anything they had spotted in their travels. Fortunately, no one had encountered any of the Maheaja-Folk.

As they prepared to leave again, Liphye drew Shyvoan to one side and leaned close.

"Keep an extra wary eye on those two," she warned. "I think that Devrand's up to something."

Shyvoan eyed the two men where they sat and watched everything around them.

"What've you seen?"

Liphye shrugged. "Nothing overt. But look at how Devrand pays such close attention to anyone talking."

"Trying to learn our language."

"Perhaps. But it almost looks like he already knows more than he lets on. Maybe better watch what you say around him, just in case."

After Liphye returned to her squad, Shyvoan watched Devrand a little longer. With his intent expression, it seemed clear he listened to the talk around him. As for what he might understand….

Shyvoan gave a mental shrug. *How could he learn very much so fast?* Perhaps he simply responded to the facial expressions of the speakers. He could probably tell from those when they joked or talked about something serious. If he imitated them unknowingly, that could look like he knew what they said, although he did not.

The afternoon crawled. Clouds filled the sky and made the shadows beneath the trees even darker. The game trails Shyvoan and Buok found narrowed further and looked less traveled. They took extra time to cover traces of the squad's passage.

Perhaps three hours after the midday meal, while Buok scouted around their path, Shyvoan heard the particular daybird call that he used to indicate trouble.

She warned Uasal with a quick hand-sign and hurried her charges into a concealed hollow. She drew her sword and crouched in the brush at the edge of the hollow, Uasal at her side.

The mage pulled something from a pouch at her waist and sang sonant magic under her breath, the wordless song just loud enough to interfere with Shyvoan's attempts to listen for approaching danger. She recognized the tune as the magic that bolstered nearby warriors for battle, a magic that all the troops' mages knew.

Shyvoan cursed to herself at the sounds that formed the magic while at the same time appreciated Uasal's intent. She edged away from the mage, all senses alert.

A few seconds later, she heard the twang of a bowstring and a cry of pain. The cry was not human.

Shyvoan eased toward the sounds, her motions as quiet as she could manage… until she heard the distinctive whistle-shriek produced by darts used by one type of Maheaja-Folk, and not the one that had cried out. *That meant at least two of them were attacking.*

Shyvoan slipped the small buckler that she had carried on her back onto her right arm and charged ahead.

She broke from the bushes and dropped to the ground, narrowly avoiding impalement on the single horn in the forehead of a stocky goat-like unicorn; goat-like if the goats she knew stood tall enough to look her in the face when she was standing. Short brown hair covered the unicorn and rags of velvet of the same color hung from its brown horn. Its eyes were orange, with the vertical slit pupils characteristic of the Maheaja-Folk and also the wild creatures of the islands. A bloody cut ran along its side.

Shyvoan rolled to the side to evade the creature's attempt to spear her on its horn. Then an arrow struck the creature in the shoulder.

Good news, Buok was still in the fight.

Darts from the gray-skinned hob atop the unicorn's back tracked Shyvoan as she rolled across the ground, but they all missed her.

She jumped to her feet and charged the Maheaja-Folk pair.

The unicorn spun faster than she expected, and her sword clattered against its horn, then sliced right through.

The creature screamed and turned angry, reddened eyes on her before it tried to butt her with its head.

She dropped and rolled again and scrambled to her feet to run around the pair.

Typically, unicorns would also kick out with their cloven hind hooves, but when enraged like this one, they seemed to forget that attack.

Another arrow struck the creature and it screamed, more in anger than pain, it sounded like. Shyvoan understood some cursing in its scream. A few glimmery sparks sprouted from its truncated horn but fizzled without doing anything.

Shyvoan caught some darts from the hob in her buckler before she charged her from the side as the unicorn turned to try to face her head-on.

Shyvoan's sword took the hob in her side and arm before she drew her own sword. The hob leaned enough away that she took only shallow slices, but she overbalanced herself and toppled from the unicorn's back, an expression of astonishment and dismay on her face. The expression seemed focused on Shyvoan's sword.

A figure darted out from the bushes and ran to the unicorn, hands outstretched.

"Devrand," Shyvoan shouted, but he ignored her.

He deftly avoided the sharp hooves and headbutt attempts of the creature and placed both hands on its side.

It froze in place before it crumpled to the ground.

The other three of their squad stepped into the bloodied glade, although Jarthan stopped at the edge of the surrounding bushes. Buok shot the unicorn, ensuring it would not rise again.

The bleeding hob lay on the ground and cursed them all, but with no strength of magic behind her curses. Uasal stood with her arms uplifted, facing the hob, and her lips moved in near-silent song. *No doubt blocking the hob's magics.*

Shyvoan kicked the hob's blowgun out of reach and grabbed for her sword while she flailed at her. Buok stepped closer with a nocked arrow pointed right at the hob's nose and she froze, staring at the sharp point with crossed eyes.

Shyvoan searched the hob and removed anything weapon-like that she found. Uasal stepped close and wrapped sonant magic around the hob, singing the tones in a low voice to form visible restraints. She added more magic to bind her wounds. After the hob shrieked at them that they would die, Uasal gagged her with a strip torn from a bandage, rather than more magic.

"Just these two?" Shyvoan said to Buok.

He nodded and slipped into the surrounding brush to check one more time.

Devrand made the waving-hand motion at the hob and unicorn that Shyvoan had learned meant he wanted to know the name of something.

She pointed to each and labeled them for him then grabbed his arm to get him to look at her.

"And just what was that you did?" She pointed to the unicorn and them mimed placing her hands flat on its side.

He gave her a blank look.

"Something to do with what I told you about earlier," Uasal said. She pointedly tilted her head toward the hob, who watched them with an intent expression.

Shyvoan released Devrand and instead grabbed the hob's bonds and hauled her to her feet. She scrutinized the hob a minute or two but saw nothing of particular interest.

Like most hobs, she resembled humans in that she had arms, legs, torso, and body at roughly human proportions, although she stood less than two-thirds Shyvoan's height. Again, like most hobs, her face had a squashed look to it, the features flatter than a human's and her ears looked too large for her head. Her gray skin was darker than most hobs Shyvoan had seen, and her long unkempt hair a yellow-white – a common color for them. Her eyes with their vertical slit pupils were much the same color as her hair.

"Take her along?" she said to Uasal.

After a moment's consideration, the mage gave a sharp nod. "We've got her contained. The Troop-Lead might have some questions for her."

"Good point." Shyvoan grabbed the hob's restraints while Uasal dug out a pouch of special powder that mages in every troop carried and sprinkled it over the body of the unicorn. She waited until it did its magic, and the body sank into the ground before she took charge of the prisoner again, grabbing hold of the magical bindings to guide her along.

Shyvoan took her squad back to their original path. Before they had gone too far, Buok eased up behind the hob, towering over the creature at almost twice her height, and blindfolded her with a strip of cloth. Shyvoan gave him a nod of approval, and he slipped back into the brush to continue scouting ahead and around them.

CHAPTER 3

SOMEWHERE AT SEA

In an area of deeper water, far beyond the outer bounds of the Shallow Sea, an unnatural shadow fell across a section of waves. The waves there stilled as the water became like a sheet of glass and reflected the clouds, a perfect mirror. In the center a thin shadow reached toward the sky from the flat surface, a line that hung impossibly in the air. The center of the line bulged from side to side and stretched into a massive, shadowed oval. The water where the oval touched it turned a different shade of blue and the oval brightened into a different sky, a different sea.

A four-masted ship, large and made of dark wood with a reddish tint, sailed through, passing from one sea to the other. The oval snapped shut behind it.

And the gale hit.

~ ~ ~

After the storm subsided more than an hour later, many of the crewmembers gathered on the deck to look at this new world. Gyasi K'rond joined them and gazed at the water that surrounded them. Purple-blue water, with a greenish hint to it, and no land in sight. He gave the *Deliberia* and its crew a quick scrutiny and found the first intact while the latter looked dazed, just as he felt.

He eased across the deck to the ship's rail and clutched it as his legs tried to buckle from a lingering unsteadiness after the wildness of the storm. Like the rest of the crew, he went barefoot on the deck and wore loose trousers, gathered at his ankles, under a hip-length tunic. Unlike the others, Gya's tunic was patterned, covered with swirls in yellow and orange, a splash of bright colors against his dark brown skin.

Alorsha Tavano—owner of the sailing ship *Deliberia* and Gya's teacher in magic—joined him. She also clutched the rail, like she needed it to hold herself upright, and her golden-brown skin held a hint of gray to it. Wind teased her straight black hair into her eyes, a problem Gya did not have with his pale-yellow hair close cut.

"I'll be all right," Alorsha said, when he gave her a concerned look. "I think. But there's something about the magic in this place…. Join me."

Gya scrunched his face, his expression doubtful, but nodded. "I'm still not very good at this."

"And that's why you're practicing it, apprentice," Alorsha said with a stern look that morphed into a smile.

She slid her right hand over to touch the side of his left on the rail. Touch helped her guide him in the magic. Together they reached out to the magic of this new world through the magic that resided in the taiawood that comprised the ship. The world's magic had already begun to seep into the wood.

"It feels weaker than we've seen before," Gya said. "Or is it my lack of expertise with this?"

Alorsha shook her head. "It's not any lack on your part."

She dropped down to sit on the deck and watched the crew at their jobs, while Gya leaned on the rail and looked out over the water.

"Will we be able to get enough of the magic?" Gya said after several minutes.

"I'm not sure. I hope so—"

"There's something there!" Gya jumped back from the ship's rail, nearly tripping over Alorsha, who pulled herself to her feet with a grip on the rail and peered over the side.

Wrinkling her nose at a sudden acrid briny odor that wafted up from the waves, Ship's Master Saevalde Eztevo joined Alorsha while Gya edged only close enough to peek over the rail.

"I've never seen the like," Saevalde murmured as she tucked strands of her brown wavy hair back into the short braid at the back of her head.

The three watched the activity in the water. Creatures unlike any they had seen before swam swirls around each other a few feet out from the ship's hull. They only somewhat resembled fish.

Sunlight flashed off scales as their tails broke the surface. Large fins that looked like wings extended from their sides and waved in the water. Above the fin-wings, they had narrow torsos with two arms, hands with dexterous fingers that held weapons, shoulders, neck, and head. The tops of their heads and down their backs seemed covered with short, sleek fur. Their sharp-featured faces had two large eyes and a wide mouth and small, pointy nose. They had two small flaps in the same locations on their heads as their observers' ears.

Gya sidled closer to the rail and rested a hand on it to steady himself as he counted at least twenty of them. They moved around so much, though, that the number could be wrong. He guessed if one stood on the deck with them, it would be shorter than him and the others, maybe not even reaching taller than Alorsha's shoulder.

The creatures swam closer to the ship and stopped a foot away from the hull. They stuck their heads out of the water and stared at the ship several long minutes, before they turned their gazes to the three at the rail, who gazed back at them. Gya tried to guess what the creatures might be thinking. *Were they angry? Or perhaps those expressions didn't mean anger at all. For them.*

After the two groups stared at each other for many long minutes, one of the water creatures shouted something as it looked from one to another of the three at the rail. The deep voice led Gya to think that one might be male.

Some sort of water-people, not creatures. But why wasn't the world's magic working through the ship's magic so he and his companions could understand the water-person's words?

"The *Deliberia* must not have gleaned enough of this world's magic yet for conversing," Alorsha muttered, apparently having similar thoughts. "Maybe *they* can work some magic to allow us to speak with one another."

She leaned over the rail and shouted to the water-people, "We don't understand you."

The one who had spoken said something more and exchanged looks with the others in the water. After they spoke together a short time, the first reached out and placed a hand on the ship's hull just above the waterline.

Gya jumped as a surge of strange magic flowed through the ship and his hand. Alorsha jumped too, and just shook her head at the concerned look from Saevalde.

This time when the water-person yelled to them, the three on the ship understood the words. "Go back where you came from. We want no more of you Human-Folk here."

Alorsha exchanged glances with her companions and leaned over the rail again. "We'd gladly go back, but we can't. We don't have the magic to open another passage right now. Also, we seek two of our own that we would take with us."

The water-people exchanged looks and muttered to each other in soft voices, soft enough that those at the rail could not understand what they said over the sounds of the water and ship.

"This could get ugly. Think I'll alert Mikolus," Saevalde murmured and left to find the Ship's Captain, the person in charge of the weapons-work for the crew and guarding them and the ship.

"Should I get our offensive potions?" Gya whispered to Alorsha.

"Not yet. But make sure you're in contact with *Deliberia*'s magic. If we must defend, we can use that at first."

Together, the two mages drew out some of the ship's magic and held it ready. Then they waited.

After several more minutes of what seemed to be an argument, the water-person who had spoken to them slapped the water in a gesture that looked like frustration and swam away from the group, diving deeper into the water. A different person looked at them and seemed to study them for a minute.

"We need to talk about this," the person shouted to them. This one sounded female. "We will return."

Then the water-people swam away. While most of them dove deeper and out of sight, a few lingered at the water's surface and caught some small, silvery-blue fish. They swallowed them whole before they followed their fellows.

Saevalde and Ship's Captain Mikolus Ludek joined the two mages at the rail. Gya paid little attention to them as testing the magic the water-people had slipped into the taiawood occupied him. It had a different feel to it than the little ambient magic he sensed. *Curious.*

"Everyone knows to keep their weapons close at hand," Mikolus said, his gaze on the sea below them. "Just in case."

"Can you work that wayfinding magic of yours to be finding our direction, lass?" Saevalde said to Alorsha.

With a nod, Alorsha led the way to a short pole

attached to the rigging. She pulled the chain she wore around her neck over her head and hung it from the end of the pole. Then she knelt and placed one hand on the deck. Gya felt her connect to the taiawood's magic and give the lightest touch to the magic in the stone from her mage ring that she often wore as a pendant on the chain.

The pendant swayed back and forth several times before its motion altered so it swung in a small circle. Bit by bit, the circle flattened until the pendant swung back and forth to make an arc that formed close to a half-circle that pointed at the bow of the ship at one end and the port side toward the stern at the other.

Gya retrieved the box that held Alorsha's compass and set it on the deck beneath the swaying pendant. He handed Alorsha a folded piece of paper, a pen, and a small jar of ink that he pulled from a pocket.

Alorsha knelt next to the box and removed the lid to reveal the engraved square metal plate that covered the inside bottom of the box and the short-handled metal spoon that sat atop it. She moved the spoon to the smooth circular center of the metal plate and turned the box to line up the spoon's handle with one of the sets of lines that ran from the circle to edge of the plate.

"Ranging a little east of north to southwest," Gya murmured, comparing the pendant's arc to the compass.

Alorsha nodded as she drew the triangle that represented the pendant's arc and labeled the direction on her paper.

"Haven't seen it swinging quite that far before," Saevalde said as the pendant continued its motion.

"Something with the magic in this world," Alorsha said. "It's weak and hard to work with. I think that's the best idea of Devrand's location that we're getting right now."

"If he and Jarthan are far off, that covers a big area," Mikolus muttered.

Saevalde nodded her agreement. "We'll sail in the direction midway between the two ends of the arc. Good enough for starting, anyway."

"Has he started pulling magic to himself?" Gya said.

Alorsha shrugged and shook her head. "Doesn't seem like it, but my sense of his magic feels vague. I'll try again in a few hours. The *Deliberia* probably just needs to absorb more of this world's magic to have enough to help with the direction and sensing his magic. Or so I hope."

CHAPTER 4

Shyvoan and her squad rejoined the rest of their troop after sunset but while light still lingered in the sky, after they met a runner sent back to direct them to the troop's location. Shyvoan left her two charges under Liphye's watchful gaze and reported to Troop-Lead Meara while Uasal and Buok took their prisoner to the side and arranged for guards for the hob.

After she filled the Troop-Lead in on the attack, Shyvoan grabbed some food and took it to her two charges. She waved Liphye off for the moment. She settled on the ground next to Devrand and shared out the food with him and Jarthan. She gulped hers, not tasting it, and shifted around so she faced Devrand.

He gave her a questioning look as he chewed.

She again mimed what he had done to the unicorn and its resulting collapse and gave him an exaggerated look of inquiry. "What did you do?"

His questioning look deepened and he continued eating.

Shyvoan scowled at him and sent one of the aspirants

who happened to be nearby to get Uasal.

When the aspirant returned with the mage, Shyvoan indicated to Devrand that he should watch.

She turned to Uasal. "Would you please do a small bit of flashy magic for us?"

Uasal looked from her to Devrand and back again, shrugged, knelt on the ground, and cupped her hands. Shyvoan pushed Devrand to lean close. Uasal sang a few tones under her breath and a sparkling green flame the length of her smallest finger appeared in her hands. With a gesture, Uasal made it float in the air a finger-width above her hands.

Shyvoan pointed at the flame. "Magic," she told Devrand.

After Uasal dismissed the small magic and returned to her own meal, Shyvoan mimed again what Devrand had done to the unicorn and pointed at him.

"Magic? Is that what you did? What and how?"

With a blank look for her, Devrand sat back with a sigh. Then he gazed at her a long time.

Trying to figure out what to tell her? Or still trying to figure out what she was saying?

For a moment, his unusual blue-green eyes drew her closer, then she pulled back.

"Talk to me." She pointed at his mouth and pointed to herself to try to get her meaning across.

"Magic?" he said. He shrugged and repeated himself.

Shyvoan sighed. She eyed the small camp around her and tried to ignore the man's presence right next to her. No one had raised any tents for the night, although the air felt damp and cold. They would move on again at first light, the Troop-Lead had informed everyone.

With another sigh, Shyvoan pulled a blanket from her pack and handed it to Devrand.

"Sleep," she told him and pointed at some of the other warriors nearby who had already rolled themselves in blankets and seemed asleep. She pulled out another blanket and tossed it to Jarthan before she went in search of Liphye to borrow one of her blankets. In passing, she asked Buok to keep an eye on the two strangers.

"Already doing it," he said with a smile and continued with his meal.

The next day was much like the previous, except no attacks this time. Shyvoan's squad traveled with one of the others this time, too, which provided some relief from her constant vigilance over the two strangers.

Not that she stopped watching them.

They moved further to the north and east again, further into the forest, and the land underfoot became rough and hilly. The strangers traveled in the middle of the squad, and she most often took the rear. The two kept to themselves and their interactions interested her.

For the most part, the two traveled without conversation. When they did talk, their body language looked most like superior giving instructions or orders to an inferior. Certainly, Jarthan took charge of both their packs and did all the things one would expect to see a person's servant or underling doing for them.

But at other times, Devrand seemed considerate of the other man, making sure he drank and ate, and pulling out a second cloak to put under the one from the troop when the air grew colder.

Shyvoan wondered at it. Master and servant who had been together so long they had developed a friendship of sorts? Maybe two people of different stations drawn together for some reason? Lovers maybe. Although if that were the case, she guessed they might be in the midst of a disagreement.

She shook her head at her fanciful imagination.

But one thing she did notice as the day wore on. Devrand's reactions did not look much like those of someone who listened to learn words in a new language. His interest was too intent and when one of the warriors grumbled about shepherding them around and muttered that maybe they should just leave them for the Maheaja-Folk, Devrand's quickly hidden reaction looked like he had understood the warrior's words. Shyvoan recognized both alarm and anger as they crossed Devrand's expression, before they slipped away, and he again assumed a bland look.

When they stopped for the evening, after the tents had been raised—the Troop-Lead planned for the troop to stay there a full day, if possible—Shyvoan cornered Devrand away from the others, including Jarthan, but not out of sight of them.

When he gave her his bland look, she had a sudden urge to shake him.

Instead, she took a slight step back, hoping that would help her resist the urge better, and glared at him.

"Time for answers," she said. "And I know you can understand me. At least some of what I'm saying. Time to start telling us about yourself. About what you did back there."

For a moment, she considered taking some drastic action to get something other than that bland expression from him. Then he smiled at her, a bright smile that for some reason made her feel warm and welcome.

With one finger, he wiped off a bit of the color that she had missed along her jawline.

At his touch, that strange tug again plucked at her. Hadn't she felt that before? But the thought slipped away from her.

He gave her a slight bow.

"I did not answer you before because I needed to become more certain of the language, needed to determine more of you," he said. His words held a hint of an odd accent, but she understood him. "I needed to be sure you were not working with our foe."

"Wha...? We'd never ally with Maheaja-Folk. How could you think such a thing possible?"

"We are from a great distance away," Devrand said.

"We had no idea what it is like here."

Shyvoan studied him with a frown. *It might be possible.* But every human she and the others had encountered, on every one of the islands, had been under threat from the Maheaja-Folk.

"Just where do you come from? Tell me of your foe."

"A great distance away, as I said. You would not have heard of it. Our foe, she is cunning and determined. She has long hunted us."

With the curiously stilted way he spoke and the unusual way he phrased his words, he must not yet be comfortable speaking her language.

"She? Only one, no others? And will she follow you here?"

"She has others who do her will. And she is how we came to be here, in this place. The magic…." He trailed off as footsteps drew near.

Liphye joined them. "For not knowing our language, you seem to have a lot to say now."

Devrand gave her his bland look and no other answer.

Liphye matched him stare for stare before she turned her attention to Shyvoan. "Troop-Lead wants you. And you're to bring him along. I'll spell Buok and watch the other one."

With a nod of acknowledgement, Shyvoan led the way to Troop-Lead Meara's tent. Devrand trailed a step behind her, his manner docile.

As they passed Jarthan, Devrand signaled something to the other man, who glanced at her before he hunkered down further by their packs.

The Troop-Lead met them outside her tent and led them to the far side of the camp away from the others, but still within the ward-rings. Before she could say anything, Devrand spoke.

"I thank you for taking us into your care," he said with a slight bow. He smiled at the Troop-Lead's astonished expression.

"I have a small ability to be able to learn things about others, a small magic if you will. I have been able to learn your language this way, but it is not an immediate thing." He bowed again and brushed his fingers across the back of Troop-Lead Meara's hand. "I regret any concern my silence has caused you."

Shyvoan watched the tension slip away from the Troop-Lead as she returned Devrand's smile.

"Interesting. I'm sure our mages would like to hear more of this small magic. And any others you might have. As you know, magic's been slipping away from us for many years now."

Because she watched for his reaction, Shyvoan saw Devrand's surprise, but he covered it well.

"Devrand had just been telling me how he's being hunted," Shyvoan said. "He and Jarthan."

The Troop-Lead nodded. "They *do* especially hunt any of us that show any magic. Makes my decision that much easier. Shyvoan, you and your usual squad will return to the denizens' lodgment. Gather reports from as many other squads as you happen across and take all the information to the Elders Council. The denizens need to get ready to move again. More scouts have reported signs of the Maheaja-Folk and we know what that means."

Shyvoan nodded. Maheaja-Folk had attacked humans all her life and for many years before that. Human settlements had become temporary things by necessity. The warriors were out now to discover what the Maheaja-Folk were up to, if they could, and clear the way as much as possible for the next inevitable move for the denizens.

"Take Devrand and Jarthan with you. They're more denizen than warrior and would do better with them than staying with the troop. Plan to leave right after the morning meal and make speed. I'm sending a few missives with you, too."

Without waiting for a reply, the Troop-Lead returned to the center of the camp and spoke with other warriors.

"Is this small magic what you did to the unicorn?" Shyvoan said as she and Devrand followed the Troop-Lead's path at a slower pace.

He shrugged.

"So, then what *did* you do?" Shyvoan persisted. "Try to learn their language, too?"

He lightly touched the back of her hand and her agitation eased. "I tried to learn anything about it," he said. "I had not seen a unicorn before."

Shyvoan stopped, incredulous. "What? How's that possible. They've been at the forefront of the attacks for decades."

Devrand shrugged again and headed toward Jarthan. "Not where we come from," he called back over his shoulder, just loud enough for her to hear.

~ ~ ~

Shyvoan puzzled over Devrand and Jarthan enough that night that it interfered with her sleep. The next morning, she grumbled at everyone who tried to speak with her, until they avoided her sour mood.

Her wondering persisted as she prepared for their departure after the morning meal. That Devrand's hiding a lot. But is what he's hiding something harmful to us? Or is it just him not wanting to share some things about himself?

Buok, Liphye, and Teigye, Shyvoan's usual squad-mates, would accompany her and their guests. Everyone's packs included more food than anything else. As a mender-in-training, Teigye also carried some healing supplies. Devrand relented and agreed to carry a pack like the others, but he took the lightest of the packs and left Jarthan to carry one the heavier ones assigned to them. Shyvoan noticed that both Devrand and Jarthan were now cleanshaven. *Must have gotten a shaving knife from someone.*

The squad set out as planned and Shyvoan pushed their

pace through the morning, with periodic rests that allowed them to maintain the pace. As they traveled, she changed who she walked with several times, trying to get Jarthan alone, but somehow Devrand always managed to stay within hearing, so she had no chance to question the other man as she wanted.

When they stopped for food and more rest around midday, Shyvoan asked Buok and Teigye to occupy Devrand's attention for her. They managed that by starting an intense discussion that bordered on an argument, right next to him.

Shyvoan slipped to Jarthan's other side and leaned close so only he could hear her.

"Do you also know our language now, like your companion?"

With a sidelong look for her, he held her gaze longer than he had before and nodded once. He glanced at Devrand, and Shyvoan saw apprehension in his expression before he dropped his gaze to his feet.

"I'm not supposed to talk with you," he said, his voice so soft that she at first wondered if she had heard him.

"Shall I go, then?"

He gave a quick shake of his head.

"Are you two really hunted?"

A nod.

"What hold does he have on you? Can I free you somehow?"

"You can't," he muttered. "Wouldn't do any good. He's the only way I'll ever get home."

He shifted away from her right before Devrand's attention wandered to them. *Almost like he had known the other man was going to turn around.* Shyvoan busied herself with fiddling with her boot. She hoped Devrand had not seen her talking to Jarthan and hoped that she had not made things worse for the man.

When she looked up, she found Devrand's gaze on her. She gave him a questioning look and he returned the expression with a dazzling smile.

"Tell me more about how your magic's been slipping away," he said.

"You mean yours hasn't?" Teigye said, hope clear in his expression. "Where you're from you've still got the magic? Will your denizens come too, to help us?"

Devrand winced, an expression that flashed across his face before it disappeared.

"No." He held up a hand against Teigye's eagerness. "That's not at all what I meant. I thought perhaps something might be learned from how your magic's been slipping away. Perhaps it's different."

"Seems your magic's pretty strong," Buok said. "It brought you here from 'a great distance', as you tell it."

Devrand frowned and shook his head with a sad look on his face. "We didn't bring ourselves here. She who hunts us was closing in and this escape presented itself."

"There's a magic that'll send people to faraway places and such? Just floating around where you came from?" Liphye said.

"Not just floating around. It was a unique moment," Devrand said. "And I've some questions for you, too. Perhaps we could exchange an answer for an answer."

"Perhaps." Buok eyed the younger man.

"What's your question, then?" Liphye said.

Devrand frowned. "To repeat myself, how has your magic been slipping away?"

Liphye, Buok and Teigye all exchanged looks. Liphye shrugged and smirked at him. "Don't know. We're none of us mages."

"And what of her?" Devrand indicated Shyvoan. "And that sword."

"I don't know that you get another question yet," Liphye said.

"*He* asked me several." Devrand pointed at Teigye.

"I'm no mage either," Shyvoan said. "Although magic did run in my family. My mother was the last of the line with it. The sword's been passed down in the family for years."

"There's your luck," Teigye said.

Shyvoan grimaced and waved a hand in negation. "No mage has determined that it even exists. There's no magic about me."

"Even so, I'd rather scout with you than anyone else. People come back alive when they're with you," Teigye muttered.

Shyvoan tried to ignore Devrand's gaze on her. She didn't want to discuss her 'luck'. *Not at all.* She shoved the last bit of her meal in her mouth to free her hands to gather the few things she had scattered about when they stopped.

"If we can find them, I hope to sleep this night with one of the other squads, at least, if not another troop," she said when she finished chewing. "Let's go."

With a few grumbles, the others gathered their things and they set off again.

As they walked, Shyvoan frequently found that her gaze rested on the two strangers. *What secret—or secrets—did they hold so close? What magic dropped a unicorn with a touch?* That had to be what had happened. It had to be more than Devrand trying to learn about the Maheaja-Folk.

And finally, can we turn that magic to our benefit? Maybe they could stop running from the Maheaja-Folk and turn the war back on them.

CHAPTER 5

By nightfall, they had not yet encountered any of the other squads nor another troop. However, Buok reported that he had seen signs of them, so they opted to continue a little longer, despite the potential hazards of traveling at night.

But after another hour, Shyvoan called a halt. Buok pointed out a single cadno tree, large enough to accommodate them for the night.

"In a tree?" Devrand said as he waited his turn to climb.

"No one with us to set up the ward-rings, so it's the safest spot we'll get for the night," Shyvoan told him. "Many of the Maheaja-Folk, especially those who prefer the deepest parts of the night, have an aversion to the cadno."

She watched him clamber up the trunk. Fortunately, the cadno had a rough trunk, with many knots that helped with climbing it. Once Devrand had climbed high enough, she turned to Jarthan. *Would he be able to make the climb?*

"I'll take those." Shyvoan held out a hand for the packs

Jarthan carried. After a moment's hesitation, he handed them over before he studied the tree.

"Buok can drop a rope to help you climb," she offered.

He gave her a slight smile. "Sorry, just lost in a memory. I haven't climbed a tree since Al—" He coughed. "In a long while."

His smile turned wistful, and vanished as he turned back to the tree and began to climb. He moved slowly but seemed to have no problem otherwise.

Shyvoan watched him until he settled himself on a high branch. *Wonder what that smile was about. And what had he almost said?*

She startled when a rope dropped next to her; she had been so lost in thought. Pushing aside her wonderings, she tied the packs to the rope and added her own to make her climb easier. She tugged once on the rope to signal that her squad-mates should pull it up and followed the others into the tree branches.

~ ~ ~

A light tap on her arm woke Shyvoan some time later. Liphye leaned close to whisper in her ear.

"Some of them are sniffing around the base of the tree," she said. "Jerffu, Buok thinks."

Shyvoan frowned. "They're less leery of the cadno than most." She kept her voice as quiet as Liphye's.

Shyvoan felt more than saw Liphye's nod. "I'll wake the others. Oh, and here." She pressed one of their small crossbows into Shyvoan's hands along with several bolts. "Just in case." She eased her way around Shyvoan and higher in the tree, almost silent as she moved.

Shyvoan stretched out along her branch and prepared her crossbow. Leaning to one side, she peered through the branches between her and the ground. She heard the faintest cry of the Nightsinger, Buok's signal that he was alert and ready.

At first, she saw little in the gloom. She saw the ground in several places and shadows of the other trees, so the moon had risen. At the best of times, it provided little light. This was not the best of times.

Shyvoan took care to focus her gaze a little to the side of the areas where she hoped to notice motion. She kept her breathing slow and even as she listened for any movement below.

A hint of motion to her left caught her attention. She squeezed her eyes shut for a few seconds and looked again, hoping to see better.

Another motion, offset from where she had seen the first, and a figure edged further into an area visible through the gaps in the tree.

Shyvoan had not seen one from above, but she recognized the jerffu, a dog-like Maheaja-Folk with a short snout, no visible ears, and finger-long claws on its front paws. Its shaggy fur and the scales on its head would have a reddish tint if seen during the day, which seldom happened.

This was bad, as jerffu commonly accompanied—

Shyvoan froze when she saw the shadowy form of a farlith from the corner of her eye. It vanished when she looked directly at its location.

She eased the crossbow around to aim for the farlith and looked at the jerffu so she could spot the other Maheaja-Folk from the corner of her eye.

The jerffu raised its head and seemed to look right back at her.

Then a brilliant yellow-white flash exploded in her face.

She heard her shot go off and a cry of pain. The branch beneath her cracked and dropped her to the ground.

She landed hard, driving all the breath out of her. For seconds that stretched far too long, she could not catch her breath. *Can't just lie here…. Have to*—

Sounds of fighting close by cut through the disorientation and she rolled away to get time to stand.

Something rushed at her, that corner-of-the-eye farlith, and she drew her sword. She swept it out toward the thing, to keep it away. She hoped.

The farlith reacted with violent flailing as it seemed to try to get away from the sword. Her sword sliced through it.

With a shriek that made her ears hurt, the farlith was torn in two before it vanished.

At the same time, the sword went icy in Shyvoan's hand, painfully frigid, and she dropped it.

She rolled again, scrambled to her feet, and winced at pain that shot along her leg.

Without thinking, she grabbed her sword again and found it only cool to the touch. She peered into the gloom to see how the fight progressed.

Another of the shadowy farliths appeared at the corner of her vision and she swung her sword that direction. She did not hit that one.

She spotted Liphye and Teigye fighting one of the largest jerffus she had ever seen. Its head reached above the level of her waist. From the looks of it, though, they would prevail. Another jerffu lay motionless on the ground at the base of the tree.

Another farlith to her side and she swung the sword again. She missed again.

A terrible cold tore through her from a spot on her upper back. She tried to turn, tried to bring the sword around. But she moved so very slowly. So slowly that it might not matter.

She turned.

Slow. So slow.

A shadowy form there at the corner of her vision. Its arm, if it could be called an arm, reached out behind her.

That must be what I felt.

She needed to swing the sword. She brought it around, her movement so very sluggish.

The farlith flowed away from her.

The cold crept through her.

Was that someone behind the farlith? Hard to tell for certain with only sidelong glances.

Darkness crept along the edges of her sight, but she glimpsed the farlith at the corner of her vision.

Fuzziness, fogginess wrapped her.

Bit by bit, she slid toward a cold, gray sleep.

Was that Devrand standing behind the farlith?

Need to get away…. Don't touch it. Get away.

Devrand reached out with both hands and plunged them into the farlith from behind.

The farlith shrieked, worse and louder than the one hit by the sword.

It looked like Devrand sucked the shadow into himself.

Shyvoan's sword fell to the ground.

She followed it.

~ ~ ~

Something touched her and Shyvoan rolled over swinging… nothing. Her hand held nothing.

"Easy, easy, I'm not the foe."

She groaned at the battered ache that emanated from her chest.

"Shyvoan?"

She slit her eyes open and startled when she found Teigye's face right in front of her in the dim moonlight.

He startled too, at her sudden motion, and laughed.

Someone grabbed her under the arms and hoisted her to her feet. She groaned again as standing reawakened the pain in her leg.

"We've got to get going." Buok's voice came from behind her. He supported her until she stopped wobbling, then let her go.

She looked around the base of the tree and scrutinized the aftermath of the battle.

"How long was I out?" she said as Jarthan climbed

down the tree to join them on the ground.

"Several minutes," Liphye said. "That was a lucky swing with your sword to get that farlith off you." She grabbed her pack from the ground and shrugged her arms through the straps.

Shyvoan glanced at Devrand. He met her gaze with his bland one. *Starting to hate that bland gaze.* She spotted her sword not far from his feet and stumbled there to grab it.

"After that, the others just left," Teigye added, oblivious to the exchanged glances. "We got all the jerffus, though." He gestured at the three that lay unmoving in the clearing.

Shyvoan paced a couple of steps, restless with a sudden sense of urgency. At least the motion seemed to be easing the pain in her leg. "We've got no mage to bury the bodies," she muttered with a frown.

"True, that. And so, we need to get going," Buok repeated and held her pack out to her.

"Why is that?" Devrand said. "Other than the stink, of course." He waved a hand in front of his face, his expression one of disgust. The stench of the dead jerffus hung in the air, something Shyvoan had been able to ignore until then.

"As soon as any of the Maheaja-Folk pass close enough to this spot, they'll know others of their kind have been killed," Liphye told him. "And not just from the stink."

"And they'll come for us," Buok said and headed off the direction they had been traveling.

"Even the cadno won't be enough to hold them off," Teigye added before he followed the archer.

Shyvoan settled her pack on her back with a soft groan and gestured Devrand and Jarthan ahead of her, following the others. She followed them then, only limping a little, with Liphye bringing up the rear.

"So, what is it about the cadno?" Devrand said to Shyvoan in a quiet voice as they picked their way through the near-dark forest in Buok and Teigye's wake. Jarthan had dropped back to follow right behind them.

"I don't know," Shyvoan said, also keeping her voice quiet. "I've heard various things from our few mages. The wood interferes with the Maheaja-Folk's magic, one said. Another said the touch of it burned them. And I've heard that it acts like poison to them."

"So, you make arrows and bows, maybe other weapons out of it? Something more effective against these enemies?"

Shyvoan shook her head. "We use other trees for the weapons: the flexible aliso is for making bows, and the strong berevo is for swords and spears. Cadno trees are extremely rare. That one's the first one I've seen in many years. And the last wasn't even on this island. They're better used for a sanctuary, when one finds one, than chopped down and cut up for other things. There's only ever one when you see one. We don't know how to even grow another. At least, that's what I've heard."

Devrand chuckled. "Not a farmer, are you?"

Shyvoan smiled. "Not at all. Warrior-trained from the time I could first follow instructions. We have a few who are farmers. But we don't usually stay somewhere longer than a year, at the most."

"So, you're hunted, too," Devrand murmured as he moved ahead of her, seeming lost in thought.

She did not think that he directed that comment at her and so did not respond. But she found it curious.

He had said he and Jarthan were hunted by 'her'. Next chance she had, when they were not trying to move with no noise, she intended to dig out more information about that.

They proceeded slowly the rest of the night, especially after the moon set, but put a good bit of distance between them and the site of the small battle.

Sounds of creatures scurrying and sometimes distant Maheaja-Folk voices haunted them through the forest, along with the normal night sounds. They managed to avoid encountering any more Maheaja-Folk.

As the sky brightened with the coming dawn, Buok returned from scouting ahead. His grim expression sent a shiver of warning through Shyvoan as she met him a little apart from their charges.

"I've found some of our people. One of the smaller troops," Buok said, reluctance evident in his tone and demeanor. "It's bad."

"Battle?"

Buok shook his head. "Looks like most of them were killed as they slept. Maybe a couple were able to fight. It wasn't enough. I don't think anyone made it out."

Shyvoan frowned at the ground. "Last night?"

"Looks like it."

"Whose command?"

"Lusaschld's. And he's one of them there."

Shyvoan pictured that Troop-Lead. Oshean Lusaschld had been an older man, experienced, with a ready smile and a booming laugh when something funny caught him unaware. She had liked him, although she had not known him all that well.

She sighed. "Guess we'd better take a look. Do what we can."

"We'll want to be quick," Buok reminded her.

She nodded. "I know." She met his gaze. "We've still got some days of travel."

"At least two," he agreed. "Even pushing it."

She sighed again and shook her head.

He patted her shoulder and touched two fingers to the hilt of her sword in a gesture to invoke good luck.

"We'll make it," he told her.

She nodded, not wanting to contradict him. *Not sure I believe that, though. Regardless, hope he's right and I'm not.*

With a quick word to the others about what Buok had found, she followed Buok through the forest to the small glade the other troop had sheltered in.

As Buok had said, it was bad. They stopped at the edge of the glade and Shyvoan surveyed the carnage. Blood everywhere. Looked like Buok had counted correctly: the entire small troop and the Troop-Lead, thirteen men and women. Blackened marks on the ground showed where the ward-rings had been, with the token-sticks only piles of ash. Much of the camp looked magic-burned.

She and Buok shared a look before he headed back to get the others. She eased closer to the carnage to see if anything could be salvaged, to see what she could gather to return to any family among the denizens.

Shyvoan struggled against nausea until Buok moved out of sight, then dashed into a nearby clump of brush and emptied her rebellious stomach. After a few minutes to catch her breath, she returned to the site of the gruesome massacre. She had been in many battles by then and had come across the results of Maheaja-Folk attacks all too often, but this one was particularly horrid. Most of the bodies looked savagely shredded. *Maybe jerffus?*

She picked her way into the camp, still fighting her nausea from the heavy death-miasma that seemed to hang in the air, although she had nothing left in her stomach to void. She looked for any small items to carry back to these warriors' families. As usual, the Maheaja-Folk had only killed. They did not seem to have taken anything away.

When Buok returned with the rest of their group, Shyvoan had two separate piles of items at the edge of the camp. One held personal items to return to families and the second held a few things her squad could use.

After they adjusted to the horror of what had happened there, and with some visits to bush clumps to deal with nausea, the others helped Shyvoan sift through the camp. Buok and Teigye gathered the bodies together, wrapped each person in a cloak and laid them out side by side at the far edge of the camp. They did not dare take the time to bury them. And they could not burn the bodies; that would draw all the Maheaja-Folk who were anywhere nearby.

After a few minutes, Liphye, and surprisingly Jarthan, joined them to help. Shyvoan did too, after she had finished with her two piles of goods. Devrand stayed with the gathered items. He wrapped the few keepsakes for the families and stashed them in a bag. The other pile, food and water and some clothing items, he stuffed into a pack, after he picked out gloves for himself.

When they had all finished their tasks, they collected the new bag and pack, then lingered at the row of wrapped warriors. None were left with their weapons. Teigye, Buok and Liphye carried those in bundles, so none were left for the enemy.

"Seems like we ought to say some words," Teigye said.

Shyvoan nodded. "I don't know what to say."

Buok stepped forward. "Travel on, fellow warriors. You've fulfilled your duty and we'll take it from here."

After they left the devastated camp, the group increased their pace. Among the warriors' bodies, Shyvoan had seen that a few of the Maheaja-Folk had been killed. When more came for their dead, they would see that humans had been there and be even more keen on hunting them.

Tired of the forest and tired of trying to slip a small group through, Shyvoan wanted nothing more than to be done with it. So, she pushed their pace and changed their travel to a few hours of walking followed by a few to rest followed by traveling again. It left her tense and worn and with little time or inclination to try to get more information out of her charges, much as she wanted to.

In this manner, they arrived at the denizens' lodgment close to two and a half days after they left the site of the massacre.

CHAPTER 6

IN SIGHT OF THE SHALLOW SEA

A change in the *Deliberia's* motion underfoot drew Gya's and Alorsha's attention away from their magic work in the hold.

"Good enough for now." Alorsha patted the timber they had strengthened using the taiawood's own magic. "Better see what's going on."

Alorsha led the way as she and Gya hurried through the ship's passageways and up ladders, greeting crewmembers as they passed. When they arrived on the main deck, they headed for Saevalde, who greeted them with a nod as she handed off control of the ship's wheel on the aft raised deck to a nearby crewmember.

"We're at risk of running aground if we continue on our current course," Saevalde said. "Any chance your pendant might point us a different way now, lass?"

Alorsha shrugged. "Let you know in a minute."

Gya and Saevalde followed as Alorsha returned to the main deck, to the pole she used for her wayfinding magic. The pendant traced a smaller arc than it had when she last checked, the previous day, but it still indicated the same rough direction.

Saevalde pointed the same direction the ship's bow did and swept her arm toward the starboard. "Shallow waters coming up all that way."

Then she nodded toward port. "Some there, too, but from what we can see so far, their edge is angling to the north."

"So, we sail around the shallow area and maybe still roughly go the direction we need," Gya murmured.

"Roughly," Saevalde concurred. "For the time being, anyway."

"Is that our best course, then?" Alorsha said.

"Aye, lass. At least from what we know right now. We can only hope we come across deeper waters that'll be letting us head back more the direction we really want."

Alorsha and Gya lingered at the rail after Saevalde left to make the necessary course correction. Before long, the *Deliberia* turned to port to sail along the edge of the shallow waters.

Without warning, Gya pounded one fist on the ship's rail, but looked abashed when Alorsha peered at him.

"How have you handled the frustration?" he said. "Chasing Devrand. All the obstacles. Not catching him or even learning why he does this?" Gya waved a hand in the air. "This running to another world. Grabbing magic."

He slumped against the rail. "Why'd my friends and brother have to die?" he whispered. "Devrand should be held answerable."

Alorsha sighed and turned to lean her back against the rail, her elbows propped there too. "Not always well – to answer to how I've handled the frustration. Other than that, I've not got any great insights. Just keep improving in my magic and prepare for a confrontation that I *do* believe will come. Be ready for it."

She patted Gya's shoulder and headed to her cabin, muttering, "I *have* to believe I'll get Jarthan back."

CHAPTER 7

The squad paused where the forest gave way to a sheltered valley. From their vantage, Shyvoan saw a sliver of the Shallow Sea beyond the low hills across the valley and, more clearly, the more-than-usual activity in the denizens' lodgment.

"Looks like they already got word," Buok muttered.

"Maybe," Liphye said. "But we all knew we'd be moving soon anyway. Maybe the Elders Council decided to get started on it without waiting to hear back from the scouting troops."

Shyvoan followed her fellow warriors into the valley. "Buok, Liphye and Teigye, you three take Troop-Lead Meara's missives to Leader Finnschld and give her a full report on our scouting. After Finnschld's done with you, unless she says otherwise, get your own belongings ready for the trip and help others."

The three warriors nodded their understanding and Shyvoan matched their nods. That should give them time for their own pursuits in the lodgment. Buok must be eager to spend time with his spouse again and would likely hurry to her when he could. The petite woman understood and braved his time spent at warrior duties, but would no doubt be glad to have him back and close for the upcoming journey.

Shyvoan turned her attention to the strangers. "Devrand and Jarthan, you'll come with me to see the Elders Council. And I'll inform them of what's happened."

"Leader Finnschld?" Devrand said.

"That's Shield-Lead Keavye Finnschld," Liphye said.

"She's the warriors' leader, the Shields' high-commander," Buok added.

"You'll know her when you see her," Liphye said. "She's about my height, very wiry, with pale-yellow hair, cut short, and light-brown skin."

"And she walks like she's stalking something. All the time." Teigye grinned.

At the edge of the lodgment, Shyvoan split off from the other warriors and, with a wave at the two warriors who acted as watchers at the lodgment's edge, led her two charges further into the transitory town.

Everywhere she looked, people worked to pack their belongings and convert their tent-homes back into narrow traveling wagons.

Devrand and Jarthan followed at her heels, and she saw startled reactions to the two men from most of the people they passed. Had to be to their eye colors, since nothing else stood out about them as particularly remarkable, dressed much like her as they were.

She watched the two men, too, for their reactions.

Devrand gazed around at everything. He looked interested and often like he studied his surroundings. Even Jarthan looked around some.

Shyvoan led them toward the center of the lodgment, where the denizens' elders lived and were to be found most of the time. *Surely, at least one of the elders would be there, even with all the bustle.*

"What are the looks we're getting?" Devrand sidled up

to her.

She gave him a startled look. "Ah… no one told you?"

His turn for the startled look. "Told us what?"

Shyvoan stopped right there, in the middle of the lane and pulled the two men close. She pointed at Devrand's eyes, then Jarthan's.

"These," she said. "Eyes of those colors supposedly mark you as cursed, bringers of bad luck. Something many believe, or aren't certain they don't believe.

She grabbed some loose strands of her hair and pulled them free of her cap to show him. "Same with this. Red hair like mine, green eyes, and especially blue, all mark the cursed. I'm just lucky my eyes came out the normal brown, so everyone's told me."

Devrand stared at her, disbelief clear in his expression. Jarthan chuckled softly but sobered and dropped his gaze when Devrand glared at him.

Shyvoan tucked her hair away and grabbed Devrand's arm to pull him along the lane again. Jarthan followed, as usual.

"So, what of these houses? Tents?" Devrand said after a few minutes of wending their way along the lane.

"What of them?" she countered. "They can be set up and taken down with little difficulty when we need to move again. Just get a new tent when you need more room."

She looked at him sidelong and realized she still held his arm. She dropped it with a frown.

Jarthan edged close. "How long have your people lived like this. Ready to pack up and move with little notice?" he said in a quiet voice.

Shyvoan shot him a startled look at this boldness in speaking, something she had not witnessed before.

"I'm not certain," she said. "It's been like this all my life. I think maybe something around a couple hundred years, more or less."

After that, they walked in silence the next few minutes,

until Shyvoan stopped them in front of the green at the center of the lodgment, around which five large tents sat, in the process of being dismantled back into wagons.

"Feayon!" Shyvoan called a greeting and waved at the elder. The short man with unruly gray hair, a precise mustache, and pink-tan skin stood in the center and directed the chaos. He waved back and a moment later joined them as he brushed his hands against each other. He clasped Shyvoan by the shoulders and pulled her close for a minute.

"You made it," he said with a delighted smile. "We've lost so many of the warriors we sent out, we feared Troop-Lead Meara's troop numbered among them.

"She sent me back, along with a few of the others. The rest should be on their way, probably not too long behind us. We'd hoped to meet some of the others on the way back, but… well… it's not good. We only encountered Troop-Lead Lusaschld's troop – after Maheaja-Folk had already killed them all."

Elder Feayon studied his hands for a long time and let out a heavy sigh.

"It's not good all around. We've lost close to a quarter of the warriors who went scouting. We probably should have done this well before now." He waved a hand at the packing.

Shyvoan shrugged. "At least we're doing it now. It looked like east to that island across the way is a good direction. I'm sure Troop-Lead Meara put all the details in the missives she sent to the Leader."

Feayon nodded. "I'm sure. Meara's very thorough." He turned to Shyvoan's companions with a wry grin. "And I've let you be remiss. Who are these two? Are they from that island?"

The hope in his gaze crumpled when Shyvoan shook her head. "From much further, to hear them tell it," she said. "This is Devrand and Jarthan. And the tale of their arrival is a strange one."

"Come sit then, and tell me." Feayon included Devrand and Jarthan in the gesture and led the way to one of the half-assembled wagons. He pulled a jug from the back and some baked-clay cups and indicated some wooden boxes nearby for everyone to sit on. After he poured everyone's drinks, he settled on a box of his own, with a questioning look for Shyvoan.

She took a long drink and told Feayon about the previous several days in detail, starting with the men's arrival on the shore. Devrand watched her during her narration, his expression intent, while Jarthan seemed to find the ground at his feet far more interesting than what she said.

"I'd hear more about who's hunting you," Feayon said to Devrand and Jarthan.

Jarthan did not look up. Devrand took a sip of his drink and grimaced. Clearly, he disliked the kuchal, the fermented milk. He shuddered slightly and smiled at Feayon.

"I don't think you have anything to worry about from our pursuer. She'll likely ignore everyone but us, unless you happen to get in her way."

Jarthan started to say something but subsided when Devrand squeezed his shoulder. Devrand's knuckles whitened with his grip and Jarthan winced but wiped his face of any expression when he saw Shyvoan looking at him.

"Your consideration in warning us about her is appreciated," Feayon said in a bland voice. "Nevertheless, we'd benefit from knowing more about her, just in case."

Devrand frowned and shrugged. "Not much to tell. As I told Shyvoan, she's hunted us a long while."

"What type of Maheaja-Folk is this 'she'?" Feayon said.

"She's not," Jarthan blurted out, then fell silent at a look from Devrand.

"A human would side with Maheaja-Folk against her own?" Feayon said, his voice full of disbelief.

Devrand shrugged.

"He's never said she's sided with them," Shyvoan pointed out. She turned to Devrand. "In fact, you've been rather vague on that part."

Devrand shrugged again and remained silent. Shyvoan exchanged a look with Feayon. Was he as uneasy about this as she was? Did she trust Devrand that this mysterious 'she' would not have any interest in anyone else? Did they need to know more?

The sound of her name being called interrupted her unsettling considerations. An aspirant ran up to her, then saw who kept her company and gave Feayon a quick bow.

"Your pardon, Elder Feayon. I come from Shield-Lead Finnschld." The aspirant glanced at Shyvoan before he turned his attention back to Feayon. "The Leader wants to see Warrior Shyvoan."

"Of course," Feayon said. "I'll just continue this interesting conversation a while with our two visitors." He shooed Shyvoan on her way.

"I'll tell the Leader you're on your way," the aspirant said and ran off again.

Shyvoan finished the last of her drink and followed the path the aspirant had taken. She glanced back once at Devrand, who met her gaze, watching her.

As she made her way through the lodgment, Shyvoan judged that everyone might be ready to leave in a few days. *Wonder if that's the plan.*

"Troop-Lead Meara recommends that you continue to act as escort to our two guests, but in effect be their guard," Shield-Lead Finnschld greeted Shyvoan when she found the Leader amid the bustle to pack the warriors' compound.

"They're currently with Elder Feayon," Shyvoan reported.

Leader Finnschld acknowledged the information with a nod. "You needn't take up your guard duties for several hours. I'll join Feayon and speak with the newcomers at length."

After she scrutinized Shyvoan, her expression severe, she added, "I suggest you take yourself off to grab a few hours of sleep, if you can. I'll send someone along later to help you get yourself packed. We plan to leave in two days." The Shield-Lead sent Shyvoan on her way, their meeting that brief, the kind of meeting Leader Finnschld preferred.

Shyvoan walked back across the lodgment to reach her small tent-home near the far edge. Most of the other people who lived in the same section were fellow warriors and had already packed their own homes, so hers stood out. *No doubt the others are part of that chaos at the warriors' compound, helping pack that up.*

Shyvoan considered her home for a minute. It would not take her long to convert it back into the little travel wagon. She could rest afterward, inside the wagon, knowing she had nothing left to do to get ready to leave.

She yawned, stretched tired muscles, and decided to do it that way. If she hurried, she could still get a couple of hours or more of decent sleep.

~ ~ ~

Someone called her.

Shyvoan grumbled an incoherent response and rolled over. She bumped into the side of her travel-wagon, which led to more grumbling.

"Shyvoan?"

"Give me a minute."

Grumbling only to herself now, Shyvoan pulled on a shirt and pants before she peered out of her wagon. What she saw brought a smile to her lips.

"Renan!"

Renan Darreschld, a shaggy-haired man, and a warrior like Shyvoan, returned her grin. "I was coming to help you get packed, but—"

"But I beat you to it." Shyvoan slipped on a pair of shoes and climbed out of her wagon. He caught her in a quick embrace, then stepped back and studied her face.

"You look a mess," he said.

"Thanks."

They both chuckled.

"Was it bad where they sent you?" Renan said after their merriment died down.

"Bad enough. Way more attacks than we saw even just last month. And those Maheaja-scum wiped out Lusaschld's troop. Him, too."

"I heard."

They both studied the ground for several minutes and scuffed their feet in the dirt.

Shyvoan broke the melancholy silence first. "And what of your troop?"

Renan shrugged. "Not as many attacks as you, from what I heard at the compound." He grinned at the look Shyvoan gave him. "Yah, Liphye told on you. You know she thinks we belong together."

They stared at each other, and both laughed. "Yah, we *did* have fun together, but any longer and we'd have driven each other insane," Shyvoan said.

"So very true. And what's this I hear of the two new men in your life." Renan's gaze held a glint of mischief.

Shyvoan waved her hand in the air, fending off his teasing. "I'm sure Liphye told you all about them, too."

"Well, I don't know if she told me *all* about them. So, what's your opinion of them? Could they bring help?"

Shyvoan frowned. "I doubt it. They're hunted themselves. So, at best, I think they'd just bring more trouble."

He scrutinized her expression. "And you suspect it's worse than that?"

"Yah. Maybe. I don't know. The one is very good at being evasive. The other hardly talks at all and seems under the first one's thumb, but it's not clear how or why."

Shyvoan leaned closer and dropped her voice. "And I think the first one has magic. Maybe more than any mage currently alive. But he tries to hide it, denies it in spite of his actions. And he seems a little too eager to conceal those actions." She dropped her voice further. "I think he maybe pulls magic from others."

"What?"

"Well, something like that." Shyvoan told him what she had seen with Devrand and the farlith and unicorn.

"And that might be how he learned our language. Though how Jarthan learned it then, I don't know. But I think Devrand somehow pulled that knowledge from me. And maybe others in our troop, too."

"And I heard you get to continue guarding them."

Shyvoan nodded. "Probably the whole luck thing."

Renan gave her shoulder a commiserating pat. "Sounds like they plan to keep us all close to the denizens when we move," he said. "So, you'll have the rest of us to help out with the guarding thing."

Shyvoan nodded and turned around at a sound of footsteps approaching.

"And this must be the famous pair," Renan murmured.

Buok and Liphye approached, flanking Devrand and Jarthan.

Jarthan glanced at Shyvoan, with a quick, slight smile for her while Devrand's attention lay elsewhere. Devrand's gaze fixed on Renan as they approached, and he scowled.

Shyvoan gave him a questioning look, but he did not respond. *Now what's he unhappy about?*

When they were close enough, Shyvoan made the introductions.

Yah, the look Devrand gave Renan was very unfriendly. But why?

"And here are your charges safely returned to you," Liphye told Shyvoan with a grin. "None the worse for wear after speaking with the Elders Council and the Leader."

Jarthan grimaced and looked away. Devrand frowned.

"The Leader has assigned them their own travel-wagon," Buok said. "It'll be along soon, along with one of the tarandeer to pull yours."

"Ours are on their way, too," Liphye said. "We need to stick together, you know."

"Leader Finnschld asked if we'd agree to stay in our usual squad. She's further dividing the warriors' troops into small squads that move around among the denizens as we travel and share watch and scouting duties," Buok said. "That last will be much as we're already used to."

"With few exceptions, she's letting everyone pick their squad-mates, if they want," Liphye added. "Letting the squads rearrange themselves, even across troops."

"Generous of her," Shyvoan said. "I'm sure with what's happened everyone wants to keep friends and family in sight when they can. Although, if those who take her up on it haven't worked with their squad-mates much, the rest of us'll have to keep an extra eye out until they've settled in with how to work together."

The other warriors nodded.

"Where are we traveling?" Devrand spoke up from his perch on a wheel of Shyvoan's wagon.

"East to the next island," Liphye said. "That's part of what we were doing out in the forest. Checking the paths that way and such."

"There'll be some trouble getting the wagons through some of those areas," Shyvoan said.

"True, that. So that'll be the other thing the various squads will help with," Buok said. "Clearing paths. But disturbing the forest as little as possible to avoid attracting the Maheaja-Folk's attention."

"Wonderful," Renan said, with an expression of disgust. "I leave my woodcutting family so as a warrior I can do more woodcutting."

Shyvoan and Liphye chuckled, and Buok gave him a commiserating pat on one shoulder.

"Why not just confront these Maheaja-Folk and get them to stop?" Devrand said. "Make them stop, if you have to."

"That's been tried," Buok said. "They killed every delegation that we sent. And we can't match their magic. Even when the attacks started, our magic had been dwindling for a long time. And no longer any way to renew it."

Devrand looked at him with interest. "Renew it? There used to be a way to do such a thing?"

Jarthan watched Devrand with an intent expression but looked back to the ground when he noticed that Shyvoan had seen.

"So the mages say," Renan said. "But no one's seen a dragon in around two hundred years. Maybe longer."

"Dragon?" Devrand repeated.

"Yah, you know big, scaly reptile with wings. Supposedly not always the friendliest, even with those they associated with. Don't you have dragons where you're from? Where is that, anyway?"

Devrand's face lost all expression. "As you said, no one's seen a dragon in about two hundred years. *I* certainly haven't." He hopped down from the wheel and walked a short distance away, apparently engrossed in watching the activity further along the path where several families struggled with some independent goats.

"Well, look at mister high and mighty," Renan muttered. "Not much for answering questions, is he?"

"Not that we've seen," Liphye said. She leaned close to Shyvoan and lowered her voice. "And that's something else both the Elders Council and the Leader want you to work on. Getting some answers out of them."

Shyvoan nodded her understanding.

"Now, better see what's up with the wagons. Everyone's in such a flutter, I'd not be surprised if they went to the wrong part of the lodgment." Liphye waved to Buok and Renan to join her. "We'll be back soon."

Shyvoan turned back to see what Devrand was up to and came face to face with Jarthan.

Did he hear what Liphye said? He was so unobtrusive that she had forgotten he was there.

After a moment of exchanging stares, he gave her a slight nod.

"Be careful around him," he said in a voice so soft that she strained to hear him. "He's more dangerous that most think."

Devrand called his name and he hurried to join him. Shyvoan followed at a slower pace. Just what they needed, something else dangerous. And what exactly had Jarthan's words meant?

~ ~ ~

The two days before the denizens planned to leave stretched into three. Shyvoan kept busy with preparations. She tried to help the denizens be ready in time, but many of them shied away from her, as usual. In the end, she supervised fellow warriors more than helped denizens who did not want to be too near her. Probably her *dear* sister Neasha continuing to remind them of the bad luck curse Shyvoan supposedly carried. Keeping fresh in everyone's mind the story that their parents died because they had run back to find a wandering Shyvoan when she was little more than a toddler.

Shyvoan had little opportunity to try to corner Devrand for answers and the man proved adept at avoiding such a situation. Shyvoan did notice that he was accomplished at appearing to help without doing any of the hard work. Jarthan got those tasks, which he did without complaint.

Finally, the morning arrived that the denizens began their exodus from the valley, headed to the island east of their current one.

Shyvoan's squad was near the front, where they helped

the civilians get their wagons moving, found stray children and goats, and in general tried to make the whole thing go as smoothly as possible.

Shyvoan's squad—squads being no more than six in number—contained the same individuals that had arrived in the lodgment with her: Devrand and Jarthan, Buok, Liphye and Teigye. Although her two charges were not warriors, Meara had chosen to count them as part of Shyvoan's squad.

After they left the valley behind and entered the woods, the wagons spread out and formed smaller groups that each had an assigned squad. The squad's tent-wagons formed an even smaller group within their assigned denizens' group. Buok's spouse drove the tent-wagon that was theirs, while aspirants drove the others. The denizens' groups would travel together near the others while taking slightly different paths through the woods. The larger group that Shyvoan and her squad-mates were part of took a route that first ran southeast.

About midafternoon, Shyvoan's group spotted the Shallow Sea through the trees, their sign to turn to the east. Devrand walked near Shyvoan, but with some distance between them so he did not actually walk with her. She watched him as he observed everyone nearby, his expression calculating.

After some time, his attention turned to the sea and stayed there. She drifted closer.

"Looking for something in the water? The moaras can be worse than their cousins on the land. Did you encounter them when you arrived?"

With a startled look for her, Devrand shook his head.

"I've not encountered these moaras. I assume the cousins you meant are the Maheaja-Folk?"

"They are *all* Maheaja-Folk," she said. "The moaras are the water-dwellers. There are others who favor the land and some the air. Those are the cousins I meant."

His expression turned thoughtful "Are we back to

exchanging questions and answers?"

Shyvoan shrugged. "If you like."

Devrand matched her shrug. "Then why do these Maheaja-Folk attack you?"

"That's probably a question best asked of the Elders Council." She held up a hand when Devrand looked annoyed and about to object. "Hold on. I *will* answer the best I can. Somewhat around a couple hundred years ago is when the first attacks came, so I understand. Before that, we and the Maheaja-Folk basically ignored each other. Except for the mages. It's said they and the dragons had some kind of arrangement connected to humans knowing magic or learning magic, something like that. But over time the dragons got fewer and fewer."

"So, you don't know why they attack?"

"Should be my turn for getting an answer, but I'll give you this one. No, I don't. I'm not sure anyone knows the truth of it. Except them, of course, and they don't act inclined to sit and chat. They just seem to want to kill us. All of us. So, we move around. Trying to survive."

Devrand nodded. "All right, your turn to ask a question."

"What are you looking for in the water?"

His gaze returned to the glimpses of the sea that came between the trees.

"Our hunter is on a ship. She comes via the water."

Shyvoan gaped at him. She had not expected to hear *that*. "But… how? Does she have a pact with the moaras? They've always been quick to destroy any boats we've tried to use."

"She won't have encountered these moaras before," Devrand said. "They destroy all boats? But how are all of you going to reach this other island, then?"

Shyvoan nodded. "They destroy them without fail. But you said 'ship'. On a ship, she won't even be able to get close to you here. It's named the Shallow Sea for a reason. Between all the islands we've been on, the sea is only a few feet deep, at most. Shallow enough that at low tide we can walk to the next island. That shallowness extends far out around each island, too. No ship designed for deeper waters can get close. And most of the moaras dislike the shallower waters, so they seldom get close to land. That frees us, at least, from having to worry about them. Too much, anyway."

"I think we're back to you again for a question," Devrand said with a smile. He reached out and brushed a strand of her hair back from her face. She stared at him a short time as she collected her thoughts.

"Tell me more about this 'she' who hunts you and Jarthan."

Devrand grinned. "Not exactly a question."

"Implied."

He glanced at her sidelong. "I'll grant you that. She's determined and resourceful. She's gotten too close too many times to count. She's unlikely to give up the hunt."

"She *is* a human, isn't she?"

"And there's a question." Devrand grinned.

"Well?"

"She is. And I've known her a long time." He turned his gaze back to the sea, his expression thoughtful.

They walked in silence for several minutes. Devrand divided his attention between the glimpses of the sea and the others who traveled with them.

"I'm surprised she hasn't shown up already," he muttered, his voice almost too soft for Shyvoan to make out the words. Then he glanced at her and spoke aloud. "Why haven't you banded together with others to fight the Folk?"

"We have. We do." Shyvoan waved a hand in the general direct of the entire group of denizens. "This is everyone we've come across. Those who've survived. But there *could* be more people where we're going. We can hope so anyway."

CHAPTER 8

ALONG AN EDGE OF THE SHALLOW SEA

The *Deliberia* came to an abrupt halt. The sudden cessation of motion propelled Gya and Alorsha hard against the edge of the table where they worked in her cabin. It also tossed the leaves and stems of various plants they worked with, and a couple of jars, to the floor. With a groan, Alorsha pushed back from the table and glanced at Gya.

"Probably bruised," he said. "But otherwise, fine. What *was* that?"

Alorsha shrugged. "Come on."

They descended to the main deck from Alorsha's cabin and workroom in the elevated aft deck and eyed the crewmembers gathered along the rails. The sails above billowed in a steady breeze, but the ship did not move.

"Did we hit something?" Alorsha called to Saevalde, who also leaned on the rail.

"I'd not be saying 'hit'. Better take a look, lass."

The two mages joined the Ship's Master and peered over the side. At the waterline, a myriad of what looked like vines, pale blue-green, gripped the *Deliberia*, wrapping it and holding it tight. The ends of the vines formed thin stems that resembled fingers, several branching from the thicker stems that disappeared beneath the water's surface. As they watched, the thin stems thickened and divided at their tips into smaller stems as they crept further along the hull and closer to the deck.

Alorsha tapped Gya's hand and together they reached out through the *Deliberia*'s magic to the vines.

"Feels like the magic the water-people slipped into the ship so we could talk," Gya said.

Alorsha nodded.

"So, have they decided and be returning to talk?" Saevalde said.

"Maybe they don't want the ship to continue that direction for some reason?" Alorsha muttered, still focused on the magic.

"But they're plants, right?" Saevalde said. "As coppice-mages, you can be doing something with their magic?"

With Alorsha guiding, the two mages drew out some of *Deliberia*'s magic and pushed against the growing vines. To no effect. So, they reached into the vines' magic, grasped it, and tried to direct it away from the ship. It just gave way before their need before it swirled back around to its own purpose. Something about the *Deliberia*'s magic reaching to the vines' made the vines shine with a bright green glow.

When Alorsha and Gya pulled back from the magic, they found that Mikolus had joined them.

"Interesting," he said as they watched the glow fade.

"They're the water-people's doing," Alorsha told him and Saevalde. "Their control of the vines is impressive and I'm not sure we can break it. Or what the consequences would be if we do. Their purpose is to hold us here."

"Can you tell why?" Saevalde said.

"Not so far, but we'll look again. But first…." Alorsha headed to the raised deck at the bow, the others keeping pace with her, and peered ahead. Toward the horizon that direction, the water looked different from what they had seen so far.

"An even shallower area?" Gya said.

"Seems likely. The lookouts above called down possible land out there. At the edge of visibility. Islands maybe."

"Right before we were stopped," Mikolus added.

Alorsha met his gaze. "They don't want us to get there?"

"Might be."

"Some of them seemed none too happy about us being here earlier," Saevalde added.

"But they also said they'd return. This could be their way of keeping us from going too far before we can talk again."

"Might be," Mikolus repeated.

Alorsha made a face at him. "You're no help."

He smiled at that. "Not at the moment, no. But I'll make certain everyone's ready in case we need to defend ourselves."

Alorsha nodded and clasped his arm. "I know you will. Gya and I will have our magic ready, too."

Gya nodded.

After Mikolus and Saevalde returned to their tasks, Alorsha and Gya stared over the side several minutes at the encroaching vines.

"It somewhat resembles seaweed," Gya said. "Gone a little crazy on the growth though."

But that growth had slowed. The vines reached about halfway up the ship's side but did not look to be growing any further.

"Now my head aches," Gya said.

Alorsha nodded. "Mine, too. Something from the contact with the water-people's magic in the vines, I'd say. It seems we and it aren't suited. Perhaps we'll try again later. For now, we'd best sort out those leaves and stems again."

Gya made a face but nodded his agreement and followed her back to the cabin.

CHAPTER 9

The first night away from the lodgment, it seemed that every denizen had forgotten how to set up the camp. The warriors spent much of their time trying to make sure everyone was set and had eaten before the night advanced too far.

Shyvoan drew first watch that night. After the camp had settled, peace permeated the surroundings. She heard only the normal sounds of normal night creatures as they moved about and the occasional distant barks of wild canids as they hunted.

Shyvoan had once seen a pack of the long-legged, shaggy brown animals—with their erect pointed ears, bushy tails, and long muzzles—take a couple of the young of the people's animals, the goats and tarandeer. The canids only tried that sort of thing when they formed a pack, something they did in the spring.

She could tell by the barks that these hunted alone. *And it wasn't spring, anyway, so no concern there.*

She shivered in the cold. *Have to pull out a heavier cloak for next watch.* The summer days were rapidly fading, and it would only get colder now.

Close to the end of her uneventful watch, as she paced, she caught a glimpse of a greenish light out in the Shallow Sea, which she happened to be able to see from her current vantage.

She whistled the short Nightsinger tones that conveyed both a non-urgent alert and that she moved out from her post to check something. After she heard the replies from both sides that indicated the warriors on watch there would cover her area too, she eased into the trees and headed for the shoreline.

The night creatures she had heard earlier, those nearby, fell silent as she passed. She followed a faint game trail that brought her to the edge of the trees after several minutes. A narrow rocky shore stretched before her to the water, similar to the one where she had first encountered Devrand and Jarthan.

She slipped into a brushy area and took a good long look at the shore and sea. No moonlight yet, so everything was murky. The air had that damp feel to it that meant they might see fog before morning.

Nothing moved on the shore, nor in the water nearby. She turned her attention further out into the water, to the deeper areas. *Hope it's not any moaras.* While they did not like the shallower water, and liked even less coming ashore, many had magic that could reach from far out.

And some *would* come ashore, if only for a short time.

Something lurked far out in the water. Making a guess at how far out, Shyvoan judged it had to be large, larger than any moaras she knew of, although fantastic tales sometimes passed among the people.

She made her way as close to the edge of the water as she dared. *Hope any nearby moaras aren't paying attention.* She hunkered down in a group of larger rocks and watched the thing she had spotted.

She could not make out its shape; it was not much more than a shadow on the water. She watched it for close to half an hour. It never dipped below the surface during that time. *And nothing showing like a tail or fins.*

Not that she would necessarily be able to identify such things at that distance.

Could that be the ship of Devrand's foe?

Shyvoan shrugged to herself. Unwilling to stay away from the camp any longer, she headed back when it seemed clear the shape was not coming any closer to shore.

After she woke her relief to take over watch duties, she picked her way through the rather haphazard camp to the neat compound the warriors had arranged. Shyvoan found Leader Finnschld awake in her tent.

Not too surprising. The Leader seemed to manage on just a few hours of sleep any given day.

The Troop-Lead gestured her to the one small stool and handed her a mug of warmed kuchal.

"At this rate, we might see snow, I expect, sooner than we might think," Leader Finnschld said.

Shyvoan sipped her drink with a nod. "Feels like we'll have fog before too long. But otherwise, it's quiet out there right now."

"We can hope it stays that way. But you didn't come to exchange pleasantries."

Shyvoan told her about the light and the shadow she had seen out on the water and her suspicions about it.

"Would this foe of the stranger's be foe or friend of ours?"

Shyvoan shrugged and drank the last of her drink to give her time to consider that.

"Devrand is clearly not telling us everything. It makes me uneasy, but he's given no other sign of anything to worry about. I can't say about this foe. We don't even know if what I saw was her."

The Troop-Lead nodded, her expression thoughtful. "I'm reassigning your squad. I want you to stay along the southern edge of our caravan. Keep an eye on the water.

Let me know if you see that whatever-it-was again."

"Devrand and Jarthan, too?"

Leader Finnschld pondered that. "I'm inclined to say no. I do prefer having you, or at least someone from your squad, keeping an eye on them. But I don't want to split you up that much."

"Might I suggest Renan?" Shyvoan said with a grin. "I'm pretty sure he and Devrand disliked each other on sight. So, if Devrand's up to something, Renan'll likely spot it."

The Troop-Lead studied her and nodded again. "As you say. I'll inform Renan. You'll let your squad know of their new duties in the morning. And keep what you saw to yourself and your squad-mates. No need to alarm our guests, if it *is* their enemy. And who's to say their enemy would be ours, too. Now go get what sleep you can."

With that dismissal, Shyvoan hurried back to her own tent wagon. As she climbed in, a sensation that someone watched her prickled her skin. Hand on the hilt of her sword, she turned to survey the other tent-wagons near hers and saw the flap twitch closed on the one that had been assigned to Devrand and Jarthan.

Interesting. And which of the two men had been watching her?

~ ~ ~

A furor startled Shyvoan from a sound sleep. She grabbed her sword and boots and clambered from her wagon.

All around her in the moonlight, she saw others doing the same, some in their leathers. *Should've slept in my leathers, too.*

Nothing was amiss in their section, but she heard the sounds of fighting to their north. With a look, she gathered her fellow warriors to her with the intention of heading to the ruckus, but the Nightsinger call that meant to stay at post brought them up short.

So, instead, they spread out, their backs to the wagons nearby and scrutinized the trees that surrounded them, weapons held ready.

Several times Shyvoan peered in the direction of the sounds but saw nothing from her vantage. The others shot glances that direction too, but no one said anything. Shyvoan longed to run help, but if she did so and the Maheaja-Folk attacked here, it would be a slaughter of her people.

After a long half-hour or so, the sounds stopped. Before too much more time passed, an aspirant came running with instructions from the Shield Lead.

"You're to double the watch," the aspirant gasped as she tried to catch her breath. "And have the others get what sleep they can."

"What's happened?" Liphye said.

The aspirant shook her head. "Can't tell you much. I only know a small group of Maheaja-Folk attacked. The warriors got them all, but there were some wounded."

After they exchanged worried looks among themselves, Shyvoan and her squad-mates followed the directive the aspirant had brought them. Liphye joined Buok, who had already been on watch, while Teigye and Shyvoan returned to their beds. In passing, Shyvoan saw Devrand peering out of his tent-wagon. When he saw that she saw him, he gave her a slight nod before he ducked back inside.

Shyvoan climbed into her own wagon and changed into her leathers before she settled back to try to get more sleep, if she could.

~ ~ ~

In the morning, Shyvoan caught Buok early, before the others were more than half-awake and shared their new duty arrangement from the Troop-Lead.

"I'll get our guests settled with their new guardian," he

said, "so you can tell the others."

Shyvoan nodded her agreement. "First, I'm off to find out more about what happened last night."

Buok grinned. "Ahead of you, there. I've got the details. A couple of the denizens apparently decided it would be daring and fun to sneak out into the woods outside the ward-rings. None of the watch saw them go and only learned they were out there when they heard the screams. Neither of the young men survived the Maheaja-Folk attack and several warriors who went to their aid suffered severe wounds. They did get all the Maheaja-Folk, though."

Shyvoan frowned. "I fear this might mark just the first of many attacks to come."

With a nod and a shrug, Buok headed to their guests' tent-wagon. While he occupied Devrand and Jarthan, Shyvoan told the other warriors in her group of the new duty arrangement and shared with them, and their two flanking groups, what she knew of the previous night's attack.

When whole caravan headed out again, much later in the morning than Shyvoan would have preferred, Buok guided their guests' wagon ahead of their spot and turned them over to Renan.

Throughout the day, Shyvoan spotted Devrand hovering near the edge of the caravan from time to time. When his gaze met hers, he smiled, and something about the smile bothered her. But nothing she could point to.

Many times, he did not notice her regard and she watched how he interacted with the other denizens. Several of the women seemed taken with him, despite his 'bad luck' eyes, while many of the men reacted, at first, more like Renan had. After a time, though, he seemed to charm them, too. Jarthan hovered nearby, but always in Devrand's shadow and did not interact with anyone that Shyvoan saw.

Also throughout the day, Shyvoan periodically ventured

south of the caravan's main trails to watch for the thing she had seen in the night. The first time, she saw no sign that it had moved, and the same when she ventured that direction after the midday meal.

Keeping her actions casual so as not to alarm anyone who might watch them, she took Buok, Teigye and Liphye one-by-one near the shore to get their opinions. After they returned, they compared notes.

Buok's vision at a distance was the best of the group. "Definitely some kind of large boat."

"Seemed like it wasn't moving, though," Teigye said.

"It might not look like it," Liphye countered. "But it could be pacing us."

Shyvoan sent Teigye to Troop-Lead Meara with the updated information. He returned with instructions to continue their current activities, report if anything changed, and see the Troop-Lead that evening.

Nothing changed the rest of the day. Shyvoan caught Devrand eyeing her with a quizzical expression and tried to avoid his gaze. The object she had spotted on the water seemed to draw no closer and did not seem to move otherwise, either.

They reported to the Troop-Lead as ordered and shared their observations before they headed back to their part of the camp for the evening.

After they had finished eating, Devrand joined Shyvoan by the fire.

"Am I now an undesirable?" he said in a low voice.

Shyvoan gave him a startled look. "Not that I'm aware of. But you do realize that we have duties to perform."

He waved a hand in the air, like he brushed off that statement. "Well, of course." He looked around at the others who sat nearby and leaned close to Shyvoan. "Walk with me? So we can talk?"

Shyvoan studied his face but could not read his intentions in his expression. Maybe she might actually learn something from him. She agreed.

He stood and held out a hand to help her to her feet. She took it although she did not need it and caught the expression on Liphye's face. Her friend waggled her eyebrows at her, with a sidelong glance at Devrand. Shyvoan returned her friend's look with a mock glare and led the way away from their small campfire and along the paths within the larger camp.

"You have something to tell me?" Shyvoan said after they passed out of hearing of their companions and paused in a spot where their conversation would be unheard by anyone else over the general noise in the camp.

With a chagrined look, Devrand rubbed his hand along his jaw.

"I… well, we got off to a bad start," he said. His tone lacked the usual confidence and touch of arrogance that Shyvoan had become accustomed to. Shyvoan made a sound of agreement.

"So…." Devrand gave her a half-bow and smiled. "Hello. I'm Devrand Charnov. I'm something of a mage and have come here, with my cousin, from a great distance. If you're interested, I can tell you something of that."

Shyvoan laughed in spite of herself. "Hello, Devrand Charnov. I'm Shyvoan Naivaschld. I'd certainly be interested in hearing more about how you came to us."

They continued through the camp, their pace slow as they talked.

"Unfortunately, I truly cannot tell you much. I don't know as much as I would wish. As I've said, we're hunted. And we escaped through that magic passage, which brought us here. We didn't know where it would bring us, just that it would take us away from the one hunting us. When we arrived, I had no way to know at first whether you were allied with her."

"So, she *does* have humans with her. And that's why you pretended you couldn't understand what we said."

"I wasn't pretending. This language we're speaking is

not one I knew before. As I've said, we're from very far away. When you first spoke to us, I had no idea what you were saying."

Shyvoan considered that. "How far away? And you understood us before you let us know that you did, didn't you?"

"Yes, I understood before I let you know. I wanted to learn more of you." He gave her an intent look that hinted that he might mean just her personally. She turned away and watched those they passed as she walked, surprised to see that no one reacted anymore to his unusual eye color. Certainly it could be seen in the brightness from the multiple campfires.

"As for how far away," Devrand continued. "I truly can't say. I don't know the distance covered. But aside from common things like people, tents, fires, things like that, nothing here is like where we came from."

He eyed a nearby campfire as they passed it. "Are all of you always prepared to pack up and flee, if these Maheaja-Folk come attacking?"

"We are. We've lived like this for a few generations. We find a place to settle for a while—I think the longest was a little longer than an entire year—then flee again when the Maheaja-Folk find us. Until we again find a place where they're not encroaching. Another island."

"And this Elders Council is your rulers?"

Shyvoan nodded. "As much as we have any. They'll settle disputes and make decisions that affect all of us, but otherwise we all pretty much go our own way."

"And the warriors and mages?"

"Any who follow the warriors' path, and the mages, are part of the Shield. As Shields, we defend the denizens, and we all answer to our Troop-Leads and ultimately to the Shield-Lead. We have few mages left now. They support our efforts to keep everyone safe."

Devrand nodded and seemed lost in thought.

"What of your cousin?" Shyvoan said a few minutes

later, breaking into his thoughts. "He looks unwell, and you treat him like a servant. At best."

Devrand nodded and a flicker of sadness crossed his features. "Yes, he's not well. I care for him, and he serves me in return." He turned to look at her. "It's the way of our people."

Shyvoan frowned. "If he's unwell, I'd think you'd be more considerate of his health, then. But he's the one doing all the harder work—"

Devrand held up a hand to stop her. "His affliction has affected his very being, that which makes him himself. Our healers told me that he needs the work to stay more himself. Or he might lose himself entirely."

Shyvoan's frown deepened. "I've never heard of such a thing."

Devrand shrugged. "Maybe it's not something that ever afflicts your people." He waved both hands at the people around them.

They walked several minutes in silence as Shyvoan considered that. She started to ask another question but stopped herself. Devrand's soft chuckle drew her gaze.

"Go ahead. Ask." He ran a gentle finger along her wrist and leaned close, his gaze holding hers.

After a moment, she looked away with a soft laugh. "I forgot what I wanted to say."

He laughed with her.

"So, you're a mage?" she said.

"I am. Although, much as with your mages, I have little magic to work with. But that leads me to something I wanted to mention to you…."

He paused then, as a small group sauntered past them with smiles and cheerful greetings. More than one woman's gaze lingered on Shyvoan's companion as they passed.

Devrand watched the group until they had moved far out of earshot.

"I've been thinking about that magic passage. With

enough magic, I believe it would be possible to open another one. That could be a way to get your people far away and safe from these Maheaja-Folk. Sounds like we just need to find one of those dragons again to get enough magic."

CHAPTER 10

"And how would he open such a magic passage?" Elder Padrigean demanded, her expression closed, when Shyvoan met with the Elders Council and the Troop-Lead to tell them of Devrand's idea. The Elder's short gray curls bobbed against her brown-black skin with the emphatic nods with which she punctuated her words.

Shyvoan shrugged. "I didn't ask for details. Yet. He might not have any yet. He did say he'd need more magic to do it."

Elder Grannye threw up her hands in disgust, her perpetual frown in full force. Her long white braid flew back over her shoulder with the intensity of her gesture. A flush reddened her pink-tan skin—normally even lighter than Feayon's—with her agitation. "We *all* need more magic. But that's not happening. This is just unhelpful taletelling."

"He pointed out that we need to get magic again somehow from a dragon," Shyvoan said.

"Whether or not that's how the magical families got their magic, it doesn't really matter," Leader Finnschld said. "No one alive's seen a dragon. We don't even know where to find one, if they even still exist. And I can't see the Maheaja-Folk letting someone go look for one, or better yet, giving us an idea where to look."

All the elders exchanged significant looks and nods. But then Elder Earlu, one of the quietest of the elders spoke up, at the same time scratching his knuckles along the bristly white beard that stood out against his golden-brown skin. "There might be something in the old writings."

He inclined his head toward Elder Feayon and gave him a questioning look.

"Bah," scoffed Elder Duveasa, the youngest of the Elders Council. She waved her hand in negation and shook her head at the same time before swiping strands of her white-steaked dark hair out of her eyes. "You two and those old writings. If we can even read them, they were written when the people lived very far from here. Nothing in there's going to be of any help."

She leaned toward Shyvoan and gave her shoulder a few condescending pats. Her red-brown skin contrasted with the mottled-brown of Shyvoan's leathers. "We appreciate that you're keeping us apprised of the stranger's thoughts. You can just tell your young man that we need to concentrate on things that we in fact *can* accomplish. But thank him."

"He's *not* my young man," Shyvoan sputtered. "I'm only watching him because it's my assigned duty."

The elder patted her again. "Of course, dear. Better go keep an eye on him, then."

Shyvoan looked at all the others and received nods and frowns, except from Elder Feayon. He turned his head slightly—so she could see one of his eyes that none of the others could—winked and darted his gaze back toward where his tent-wagon sat.

Shyvoan stood to give the group a slight, stiff bow. "With your permission, I'll return then to my *watching* duties." She whirled around and stomped away, before she said something she should not.

Out of hearing of the gathering, she met with Buok. Liphye and Teigye had stayed behind since their watches started soon.

"Most believe trying to find a dragon is a waste of time. But I suspect Elder Feayon disagrees. He seemed to be telling me to visit him in his tent-wagon."

After a noncommittal grunt, Buok said, "And what of you? Do you believe this Devrand can really make a passage to take everyone to safety? We still have unanswered questions about him."

"I don't know what I believe," Shyvoan said and watched the gathering of leaders for signs that the meeting was ending. "I'd love to find a way to ensure everyone's safety. And the thought that we might be able to renew our magic…. I want to believe it's all possible. But at the same time, it seems too fantastic. Yet…."

"Yet?" Buok prompted when she did not finish.

"Yet." Shyvoan smiled. "We're charged with our people's safety. Anything that might improve that should be investigated thoroughly."

Buok chuckled. "True, that. I'll help keep an eye on our charges while you see what investigating you can accomplish." He tilted his head toward the leaders' meeting, which was clearly ending. "See if Elder Feayon has something useful."

Shyvoan nodded. "See if you can maybe talk with Jarthan without Devrand around. There's something odd between those two. Might be information we'd want."

With a nod, Buok headed back to their small camp at the edge of the larger temporary encampment. Shyvoan headed the opposite direction, to Elder Feayon's tent-wagon, and stifled a yawn as she went. If she didn't get back to her own tent-wagon soon and catch a bit of sleep, she'd be worthless when they traveled on the next day. Hopefully, whatever Elder Feayon wanted to talk with her about would be short.

She met the elder outside his tent-wagon and he placed a finger on his lips. "Bide a moment," he whispered and crawled inside his tent-wagon.

Shyvoan put her back to the wagon and sidled into the shadows next to it to be less visible. She waited several long minutes while she listened to the muffled rustling from within the wagon and the occasional muttered curse. Then the elder clambered back out of the wagon and looked around for her. When he spotted her, he joined her in her shadowed area and pressed a thick scroll into her hands.

"Read through that," he told her, still whispering. "As I remember, it talks of the dragons. But don't let anyone know you have it. It's only supposed to be for mages. And while you're from a mage family...."

"Not being a mage myself, I shouldn't have it, let alone be reading it."

"Right you are."

Shyvoan turned to leave, but then turned back. "I didn't know that you're a mage."

Elder Feayon shrugged, his movement slight. "Not much of one anymore. Haven't got the concentration or the voice anymore to properly sing the magic, not even to help bolster the ward-rings. So, I keep the scrolls." He gave her a gentle push. At the same time, he handed her one of the small baked-clay light-pots the menders and mages often used. "Off with you now. If you're to read and get some sleep, too."

Shyvoan hurried back to her own tent-wagon, carrying the scroll and pot behind her back under her heavy cloak. From the questions the others threw her way when she returned, she could tell Buok had told them of the leaders' thoughts. To avoid answering those questions, and avoid Devrand, she made much of how she hoped to sleep soon and wanted some time alone. She slipped into her tent-wagon and pulled the flap closed tight behind her.

She removed the pot's lid and pulled out one of the light-leaves tucked inside. Setting the lid aside, she dropped the elliptic white leaf in the special oil contained within the pot. A glow grew in the oil as the leaf rapidly disintegrated and less than a minute passed before she had light bright enough to read by. The light would last for about an hour. She had no idea why or how it worked; she only knew that it did.

She set the pot on a flat spot and unrolled the scroll carefully to read it.

She did not get far in her task before fatigue drug her eyelids closed one too many times. She put the lid back on the small pot and tucked it in a corner of her tent-wagon on the wooden boards that made up the wagon's bed. She took a quick look around through her tent flap—all quiet in the encampment—before she scrunched back inside her wagon and tucked the scroll away at the end furthest from the door, by her feet.

The next she knew someone called her name, from right next to her ear. Grumbling, she sat up and blinked in the bright light that filtered through her tent canvas. Looked like it might be later in the morning than she would have liked. She poked her head through the flap.

"What?"

Teigye bounced with impatience. "We let you sleep as long as we could, but you really need to get up. We need to go."

With a groan, Shyvoan waved acknowledgement and hurried through her few preparations. She skipped her morning meal until they were traveling. She tucked the scroll away, safe and hidden in her bedding, then guided the tarandeer who pulled her wagon into place behind Devrand and Jarthan's wagon.

Typical of its kind, Shyvoan's tarandeer stood close to five feet tall at her shoulder with short dark-brown hair that covered her body and short tail. The hair shaded to an even darker tone on her large, elongated head, in particular around her muzzle, ears, and wide-set eyes. Long sturdy legs that ended in broad, deeply cloven hooves supported her muscular torso. Small, simple antlers grew atop the tarandeer's head between her tall, inward-curved ears.

After Shyvoan maneuvered her wagon into line, an aspirant hopped into the seat to take over guiding the sturdy tarandeer. That freed Shyvoan to again hover at the edges of the caravan and keep watch.

That afternoon, Devrand joined her, having somehow evaded the watchers supposed to keep him away from the southern edge of the group.

"When were you going to tell me about that?" he demanded as he pointed through the trees at the distant shape on the water.

Shyvoan studied the shape. Still far out in the sea, no further away nor closer to them than before.

"Why should we have?" she shot back. "Sure, it's probably your hunter's ship, since we know of no one foolish enough to be out on moara-infested waters like that. Nor of anyone who could even build something like that. But it's out there and we're here and I doubt they can even see us."

Devrand shook his head, like he disagreed, but he did not say so. "Still—"

"Still, what? We're keeping an eye on it. It hasn't come any closer than that. I doubt it can. Likely the water's too shallow, even out that far. It *is* called the Shallow Sea, after all."

Devrand squinted at the supposed ship while a variety of expressions ranging from alarm to annoyance chased each other across his face. He settled on a frown.

"I suppose I see your point," he allowed, his tone begrudging.

Shyvoan gave a curt nod. "Then I'll get back to my duties, and you'd better return to Renan."

"Back to my own personal guardian," Devrand muttered, but did return to the bulk of the caravan.

Shyvoan returned to her watching.

~ ~ ~

That evening at dusk, as most of the caravan settled in for the last meal of the day, the Maheaja-Folk attacked again. This time the attacks came at two different spots around the ward-ring, neither near Shyvoan and her group. They stayed watchful.

From their spot at the southern edge of the encampment, Shyvoan saw the flashes of magic from the attack on the western edge. They seemed to be crossing the wards somehow.

She paced and alternated her attention between the woods nearby outside the ward-ring and the flashes of the attack. She itched to go help, but the flashes died away a short time later. While she and Buok and Liphye remained vigilant as they ate their now-cold meal and paced their edge of the encampment, Teigye ran to the command section to report in and get details of the attacks.

Before he returned, Devrand approached, coming from the western part of the encampment. When he met Shyvoan's gaze, he joined her.

"What were you doing there?" she demanded.

He shrugged. "Taking a look at the Maheaja-Folk's magics, helping bolster the ward-rings."

"You can do that? Why haven't you done it before?"

"It's not a use of magic that I knew before. I needed time to learn how it works."

"So now you'll be helping with the ward-rings."

"As I can—"

"Shyvoan!" Teigye ran over, interrupting him. "It's Renan. He's wounded."

Buok sidled over next to Devrand to indicate to Shyvoan that he would guard him. "Go. We've got things here."

Teigye led Shyvoan back through the encampment to

the command section, which was also where they cared for the sick and injured. He had nothing to tell her about Renan's injury as they jogged there but filled her in on the details of the attacks.

"The attacks happened at the same time, with only three Maheaja-Folk at each, as far as anyone saw. Archers managed to get all of them, but the attacks seemed mostly to be testing our ward-rings, although one tent-wagon got a bit scorched."

"And what was Renan doing there?" Shyvoan said. "His squad's back near ours."

Teigye chuckled. "Well, he and his new lady friend hadn't seen each other in a while. She's been off on scouting trips. Seems that they were off duty and so…."

Shyvoan sighed. "Of course."

When she found Renan among the wounded, she saw that his injury was less serious than the others in the section. He greeted her with a grin, thanked Teigye for bringing her so fast, and shooed both his hovering lady friend and Teigye off.

Shyvoan crouched in front of him and studied the burns across the left side of his face and shoulder and down that arm.

"The way Teigye acted, I thought you'd be at death's door."

He grinned and winced. "Sorry about that. I needed to talk with you."

She settled all the way to the ground. "In that case, you'd better talk." She grinned back at him.

"I was near the western attack. Your friend Devrand hovered around the area. And I swear I saw him slip outside the ward-rings and sneak up behind one of the Maheaja-Folk, a hob, and hit him in the back with both hands. Then the hob just crumpled. And right then is when I got hit with this from one of the others." He gestured at his burns.

"When I could look again, Devrand was nowhere in

sight. And arrows skewered that hob, same as the others. Looked like they're what killed him."

"First, he's not my friend," Shyvoan snarled.

Renan leaned slightly away and held a hand between them. "All right. Sorry."

"Second, thanks for telling me. How certain are you that it was him?"

Renan scrunched his nose. "Fairly. It was dark, but who else would have gone outside the ward-rings?"

Shyvoan nodded. "Keep this to yourself for now. I need to think about this."

"You'll tell the Leader, though, won't you?"

"I'll tell Troop-Lead Meara and let her decide. So please don't let anyone else know what you saw."

After Renan agreed, she left him, passing his lady friend on her way back with some medicine. She and Shyvoan exchanged tight smiles and nods as their paths crossed. Shyvoan next stopped by the Troop-Lead's tent-wagon to let her know what Renan thought he had seen.

"And I'd like to talk with that hob that we captured a few days ago," Shyvoan concluded her report. "Ask a couple of questions, if I may."

Troop-Lead Meara frowned and shook her head. "You can't. The morning that we all departed the lodgment, the hob was found dead where we were holding her."

"Maheaja-Folk? To keep her from talking?"

Meara shrugged. "It's possible. But she hadn't a single mark on her." She gave Shyvoan a significant look.

Shyvoan frowned at the ground. "You think Devrand…."

"Perhaps. Especially with this information from Renan. But even with what you saw with the unicorn, we don't have something definite that we can attribute to him. Neither Uasal nor Buok saw clearly what happened with the unicorn. Even you didn't, truly. It's entirely possible the man stabbed it." Meara sighed. "But either way, you and your squad stay alert. Let them know what Renan saw, and about the hob, but keep that from anyone else. And if you see anything else…."

"Of course." Shyvoan nodded her understanding. She returned to her squad and shared what had happened to Renan, what he thought he saw, and what she had learned about the hob. After that, the squad returned to their usual evening pattern of activity, but voluntarily set a double watch.

When Shyvoan looked for Devrand, Buok told her, "He went back to his tent-wagon a while ago. And I've arranged for new guardians for the man while Renan recovers."

Shyvoan thanked him with a nod and returned to her own tent-wagon to read some more of the scroll and get some sleep before her own watch later.

CHAPTER 11

AT THE SHALLOW SEA'S EDGE

Gya leaned against the rail and glared at the seaweed, or whatever it was, that clutched the *Deliberia* in such a tight grasp. Three days so far held in this spot, no matter what he and Alorsha tried. Three days during which *that Devrand* got further and further away.

He clenched a fist and pounded it against the rail. *Why does nothing we think of work?*

The magics they had worked together, both going through the *Deliberia*'s magic and not, had produced nothing more than glows of various intensities from the vines and had hardly shifted the plants. Alorsha had even climbed in a tender and had some crewmembers lower her far enough to touch the plants with a hand, to touch their magic. But she could not get them to budge.

When Mikolus attempted to cut them, one detached from the ship long enough to slap him out of the tender and into the sea. The vines let him climb a rope ladder back aboard the Deliberia but clasped the tender he had used, tied it to the ship's side, and held it there.

Alorsha joined Gya at the rail. "Any change?"

Gya shook his head and together they wordlessly stared at the vines.

A wet plop that sprayed him with drops of water drew Gya from his pondering. A net of wriggling silvery-blue fish had landed on the deck behind him. Much larger than the ones they had seen the water-people eat days earlier, they otherwise looked like the same type of fish. Gya looked up in time to see a large, scaled tail go back over the rail into the water. *One of those water-people, judging from the size.*

He and Alorsha exchanged glances.

"At least they're concerned that we don't starve," Gya offered.

"And now I get to see that these get cleaned," Alorsha muttered. She waved some crewmembers over to the netted fish and left to direct the matter of the fish bounty.

CHAPTER 12

As the caravan traveled, Shyvoan grabbed every opportunity to read the scroll. And reread it. The best times she found were the times she did not have watch duties and after everyone else either left to attend to their duties or slept. While interesting, much of the scroll spoke of things she was sure made sense only to a mage. It was vague too, maybe deliberately so, about how dragons were involved in renewing mages' magic.

The days passed, each differing only from the others by the timing of the attacks from small groups of Maheaja-Folk, which brought injuries and damage to the denizens and warriors before they either killed the Maheaja-Folk or drove them off. The caravan lost ten denizens to the attacks and half as many warriors, with several other warriors injured. The Leader sent squads out to hunt the Maheaja-Folk, but they never encountered any on those forays.

The caravan moved slower than Shyvoan had hoped, and the elders looked dissatisfied with their progress. Nevertheless, they made progress.

And the ship seemed no closer.

One evening close to a week after the large caravan had headed out, Shyvoan found Devrand staring out at the Shallow Sea from the edge of the trees that marked the beginning of the shoreline. The shape still lurked out there.

Shyvoan studied it. Was it larger? Had it gotten closer? Maybe. Then again maybe not. Was it a ship, as Buok had said? Or was she just convincing herself that it looked like it?

"I can't understand why she's come no closer than she is now. She's never held back before from coming after us as soon as she could. I know they have tenders, small boats to take them through shallower water. Certainly, one of them could have brought them close enough to come ashore," Devrand said when she joined him.

"They could be having problems with the moaras that we can't see from here," Shyvoan said.

"That must be it." He turned to eye her. "Have you learned anything that can help find the dragons? That elder did give you something to look through that might be helpful, didn't he?"

"No one's supposed to know about that," she said.

He only smiled. She met his gaze a moment before she turned away. "No, nothing helpful. A lot of talk of speaking with dragons, getting magic from dragons but without details. Also, a sort of diary of a journey to meet with a dragon, but even that's very vague."

"Vague in what way?" He brushed his fingers across the back of her hand. "Tell me what you can remember."

As if his touch had given her the ability to see the scroll right in front of her, she spoke like she read from it.

"'The path was hard to find next to the stream, but once on it, we saw it clearly. Some magic at work, without a doubt. White vesnaflurs verged on the path the entire way. We followed the path for six days, heading out at dawn each day, although it had not seemed we would need to go so far. In places, we had difficulty keeping our footing, scrambling and sliding to make progress. Always the sun rode on our backs, no matter whether morning or afternoon. The sixth day we came to the threshold and within the stone the dragon met with us as we had all agreed.'"

Shyvoan blinked. She felt like she just woke from a deep slumber. *Is that a scent of burnt wood?* She gave Devrand a quizzical look.

He smiled back at her. "A little help for you to recall the words better."

"I still don't see that it helps."

"Some parts of what you recited might help. We can tell there's a long path, flowers—"

A scream overrode Devrand. They both spun in the direction it came from.

Shyvoan drew her sword and tugged on Devrand's sleeve. "Come on."

He resisted. "I'm no warrior. Shouldn't I just stay here?"

"*Here* is outside the ward-rings. Come on!"

So, they ran toward the sound.

They burst out of the tree cover to chaos along the southern edge of the encampment. Shyvoan pulled Devrand across the ward-rings and pushed him toward a couple of mages who worked at a ward token-stick. Then she turned back to assess the fray.

Perhaps ten hobs attacked half that number of warriors. The hobs used no magic for some reason but attacked with short swords and those horrible little darts. Shyvoan counted another two warriors down, and some denizens pulled them to safety.

Something's off…. The hobs are actually inside the rings!

That was what the mages worked on. That section of the ward-rings had been breached.

She charged into the conflict and aimed for the closest hobs, who recoiled from her sword. A minute or so after she joined the fighting, more hobs, atop unicorns, charged in from the southeast.

The next many minutes were a blur of shouts and screams, curses and blood. Shyvoan heard the distinctive sounds of arrows, and the hobs began to drop. Minutes later it was all over.

After she dropped the Maheaja-Folk she battled, pain shot through her and yanked her attention to the numerous cuts she had taken. She cleaned her blade and sheathed it before she stumbled away from the carnage to find one of the menders.

Devrand found her first and slipped an arm around her, over her protests, to guide her further into the encampment to a temporary refuge set up by the menders.

The next many minutes Shyvoan endured poultices and stitching followed by bandaging. All the while, Devrand hovered nearby to fend off others until the menders finished with her. Then the rest of her squad pushed past him to assure themselves of her condition. None of them had escaped unscathed, but she seemed to have taken the worst damage of the squad.

Beyond that, the news was less positive. The squad that traveled close behind theirs had been devastated, with only one survivor. The menders were uncertain she would make it. Four denizens dead, and three other warriors, with many more injuries, among the denizens, too. And a mage had been killed.

Shyvoan dropped her head to her hands as she took it all in.

"Why do they just chip away at our edges like this? There seem to be plenty of them to attack outright."

"Probably just for this reason," Devrand said.

"What?" Shyvoan looked at him and he waved an arm all around them.

"They're not just attacking you; they're attacking your will to fight. Sapping it. Slowly, but certainly. Planning something big would be my guess. Perhaps soon, too."

"And so now it seems that you're such an authority on these things?" Teigye said.

Devrand shrugged. "Never said I was. It just looks like what they're doing, is all." He walked off, headed back toward his tent-wagon.

Liphye helped Shyvoan to her feet and the squad strolled back to their part of the encampment.

"I saw the strangest thing," Liphye said in a hushed voice, just loud enough for the four to hear. "During the fighting. I swear I saw that Devrand pop up behind one of the hobs on its unicorn. I didn't see any magic or anything, like their magic, but then the hob and unicorn dropped to the ground. When I looked again, Devrand was nowhere in sight."

"Similar to that first attack after we had found the two strangers," Buok said.

"So, you *did* see that too?" Shyvoan said, relief clear in her voice.

Buok gave a curt nod. "But I wasn't sure what it was I saw."

"Renan also saw him do something like that," Shyvoan reminded them. "Devrand's said it's to learn about them by that action, but I have to wonder...."

"Looked to me like he killed them both," Liphye said. "Not that I'm complaining. It looked like they were getting ready to charge and those horns are cursed difficult to avoid when they do that. Even so, either very brave or very stupid."

Shyvoan nodded, finding it increasingly difficult to stay awake. Probably one of those concoctions the menders had her drink for the pain. When she stumbled, Liphye slipped her arm around her waist to help her along.

"We can talk about it more after those medicines the menders gave you wear off," she murmured.

Shyvoan nodded in agreement. Or thought she did anyway. Right before she began a long, pleasant slide into velvety darkness.

CHAPTER 13

Her world shook and jostled her from side to side. Shyvoan reached for the comforting velvet darkness she had been enjoying but it eluded her and slipped away, giving way to the brightness of daylight shining through the canvas of her tent. A jolt rougher than the previous ones woke the pains in her body and she groaned as events of the previous day came back to her: the attack, and the stitches that followed.

The flap of her tent opened, and she cursed at the increased brightness and the headache aftermath of the menders' concoctions.

"Seems like she's back with us, just as the menders said," Teigye said in a bright tone.

Shyvoan mumbled some curses at his cheerfulness and crawled to the end of the tent-wagon as she fought to keep from tumbling over from the jostling. She peered around the smiling Teigye.

"I see we're already moving again. How late is it?"

"Not very. We only started out again less than an hour ago. Oh, and here." He held out a warm mug. A slight bit of steam rose from its contents in the cool morning air.

Shyvoan made a face and Teigye chuckled. "It's not the strong one that gave you the headache you're suffering from. Seems that this is enough to take the edge off all your pains. So the menders said. Although they did say you could have one more dose of the other instead, if you needed."

Shyvoan reached for the mug. "No thanks. This will be fine."

Teigye hovered while she drank it. She gagged at the bitterness but knew she would be grateful for its effects.

"The Leader said to ride today as much as you can," Teigye said and took back the now-empty mug. "Rest and recover." He grinned at her before he closed the flap. "If you can take the jostling."

"And if the boredom doesn't make me crazy," Shyvoan muttered.

She managed to take the jostling and boredom until close to midday before she decided that she was done with them. She struggled into her leathers, wincing as the movements tugged at her wounds. She winced again when she saw the many slices in her leathers. *Have to get those taken care of soon.* After she checked to make sure the scroll remained hidden and secure in her bedding, she grabbed her sword, scrambled out of her tent-wagon, and dropped to the ground behind it.

She stood motionless until she got her bearings and caught her breath from a stab of pain, then moved out of the way of the wagon that followed hers. She eased between moving wagons to the southern edge of the caravan. *No signs of anything amiss.* That was good.

A warrior from one of the other squads on that edge waved at her and pointed further back along the caravan's path. *Must be where I'll find the rest of my squad.*

With a nod of acknowledgement for the warrior, Shyvoan moved out of the paths of the wagons at that edge. Rather than walk back along the caravan and have to walk back again to her current location, she found a shady spot next to a tree and leaned against its trunk. She kept watch all around while she waited for her squad to make it to her spot.

She was glad she had decided to do so when it took close to an hour for them to reach her.

"Hey, she's back among the living," Liphye called to her.

"Told you she wouldn't stay in her wagon all day," Teigye said.

"True, that," Buok said. "It's good to see you up again."

Shyvoan smiled at them but frowned at Liphye's next words.

"Devrand's been asking after you," she told Shyvoan.

Teigye elbowed Shyvoan gently in the side. "Think he's got a thing for our Squad-Lead?"

Shyvoan groaned and glared at him.

"Could be," Buok joined in the banter. "He ignored all the denizen women who've been making eyes at him. Must be someone else has his attention."

"Might be fun to tryst and such with a man from far away," Liphye said with a wicked grin. "Maybe he'll know some new, diverting—"

"Liphye!" Shyvoan growled at her friend, who just shrugged.

"No, Shyvoan's right," Teigye said as he patted her shoulder. "She ought to at least wait until she's no longer held together by menders' stitches."

Shyvoan took a swing at him, but he danced out of reach and laughed all the while. The others joined in and after a moment, Shyvoan did too.

"Maybe I'll beat you to him. Those exotic looks—" Teigye broke off when everyone stared at him. He shrugged and grinned.

"We don't really know him," Liphye reminded him, sobering. "Might not be wise—"

Teigye waved a hand at her objection. "The getting to know is half the fun," he declared. But then he nodded. "Yah, I hear you."

They rejoined the caravan then.

"I suppose I'd better find him and see what he wants," Shyvoan said, her lack of enthusiasm for the idea clear in her tone. She did not feel ready to play word games with him yet. But maybe better to get it over with.

"Don't do anything I wouldn't," Liphye called after her.

"That's a pretty short list," Teigye said. "Just don't pull out your stitches."

Shyvoan sighed and waved a dismissive hand back at them.

She had not located Devrand, or Jarthan for that matter, by the time she worked her way to the center of the caravan where the Elders' wagons were. It seemed many people had seen Devrand recently, but none knew where he had gone.

Shyvoan saw Elder Feayon driving his own wagon and waved to him. He nodded to her, but when she started toward him, he waved her off with a significant nod toward the other Elders who traveled close. She nodded back. Maybe she would get a chance to speak with him sometime later. She wanted to talk about the scroll.

She had taken a few steps back into the mess of traveling wagons when she heard her name. She spotted Troop-Lead Meara waving to her and made her way to the older woman.

The Troop-Lead looked her over critically. "Don't overdo it," she said. "But it's good to see you getting around as well as you are."

"Thanks in part to some stuff from the menders."

Troop-Lead Meara barked a laugh. "No doubt. Walk with me a bit."

They walked in companionable silence for several minutes.

"Anything more you can tell me about your charges?" the Troop-Lead said, breaking the silence that had fallen between them. "This Devrand seems able to endear himself readily to people."

Shyvoan nodded. "I've noticed that. Except for Renan, from what I've seen."

"Yah, him. Perhaps one or two others. Including his cousin Jarthan, I'd say."

"Agreed. And Devrand's very evasive whenever I try to learn something from him. Although I might have gotten one thing."

"Tell me it's what he's doing running into battles to touch Maheaja-Folk," Troop-Lead Meara said with a wry, sidelong glance.

"Yah, that. I doubt he's told me all of it, but he said it was to learn something of them. He says they don't have unicorns where he came from. And I suspect he did something similar to learn our language."

The Troop-Lead raised her eyebrows in a questioning look. "Explain."

Shyvoan took a moment to compose her thoughts so that what she had pieced together would, she hoped, make sense.

"I'm certain that he knew nothing of our language when Buok and I first encountered him and Jarthan. I just saw in his expression that he didn't know what we were saying. And he said some things that I couldn't understand. But then, a few days later, he conversed with us with no hesitation. Not even any fumbling for words. I think he drew the knowledge of our language from me somehow. Like he said he learned of the unicorn."

Troop-Lead Meara frowned and pondered that for several minutes. "Kind of supports his contention that he and his cousin come from very far away. I've never heard of magic like that. Could be handy. He's more forthcoming with you than with anyone else."

"Wonderful," Shyvoan muttered.

"I can assign others to guard and watch him and his cousin, if you prefer."

Shyvoan considered that and shook her head. "If I'm the one who can get information from him, I'll just keep working at that, then."

"If you can get him off away from his cousin, someone else in your squad can have a try at that one. Maybe he'll talk if Devrand's not around."

"Maybe…." Shyvoan drew the word out long.

Troop-Lead Meara nodded. "Yah, I know. Not too likely. But it's worth a try, anyway. I don't like that these two have so many secrets from us. Do what you can to remedy that. Even if you need to act as enamored of him as some of the others."

With a scowl at the thought of that, Shyvoan nodded.

"And before too long, stop by supply to trade in those leathers for more intact ones." Meara pointed at the worst of the slices in Shyvoan's leathers. "That's not the way to be prepared for the next attack."

Shyvoan nodded again and headed straight to the supply wagon. The warrior there took one look at her and sighed.

"Another whole set," he said. "You're the fifth one today."

"Sorry?"

The other warrior chuckled. "Hey, not truly your doing, right? Hold a moment." He climbed into the wagon and returned after a few minutes with a set of leathers.

"These should be your size. And not much breaking in left for them."

Shyvoan gave them a dubious look. "What happened to their original owner?"

The warrior gave her shoulder a slight squeeze. "Nothing bad. An aspirant who discovered being a warrior wasn't for her. I think she's helping herd the goats now. Here, let me help you up so you can change. Just leave your old ones near the opening. We can use them for patches."

With the man's help, Shyvoan clambered into the moving wagon. With much wriggling, and some hisses when she pulled at a wound, she changed from her sliced leathers into the new ones.

After she climbed back out of the wagon, she endured several minutes of inspection from the other warrior.

"They'll do you," the man said. "A little loose in the shoulders and the legs are a little short, but you'll tuck those into your boots anyway. Still, if anything bothers you, come back and we'll see what we can do."

Shyvoan stretched her arms out to both sides then over her head, crouched, and stood upright again.

"I'll remember that, but I think they'll be fine."

"Good. Then off with you. Back to what you need to do next."

After she thanked the other warrior, Shyvoan plunged back into the chaos of the moving caravan and again tried to locate Devrand.

An hour later, still unsuccessful, she returned to her squad's section of the caravan and filled them in on what Troop-Lead Meara had suggested. Liphye volunteered to speak with Jarthan.

"Who can say where it might lead," she said with a grin. "When he smiles, he's rather appealing."

Shyvoan groaned and lightly punched her friend's shoulder. "So, you're no longer meeting up with that strapping woodcutter?"

Liphye shrugged, with a saucy grin, and Shyvoan shook her head.

A commotion further ahead in the caravan drew their attention. Buok headed that direction to take a look while Shyvoan dug out some food.

Before Buok returned, the caravan had drawn to a halt. Shyvoan heard the murmuring of many voices as speculation ran through the denizens and warriors alike, but at least she heard no sounds of fighting.

That has to be a good sign, anyway.

Buok returned, his expression more relaxed than Shyvoan had seen in a while.

"The front of the caravan's reached the edge of the eastern shore," he told them. "The Elders Council ordered a halt and we'll set up camp here while we determine the pattern of the tides and send a couple of squads to scout the other island again."

Shyvoan nodded. The last scouting party to that land had been around the time the denizen's lodgment had been set up a couple of seasons previously, after they had come to this island from one further west.

Without any further need of discussion, the squad split to arrange their portion of the encampment and help the denizens in the near vicinity. This encampment would be less haphazard than previous ones, since they could be there several days.

Her squad-mates would not allow Shyvoan to do any heavy work, so she supervised and answered what questions she could when denizens had concerns.

Devrand and Jarthan joined them as the aspirant who drove their tent-wagon moved it into its position in the circle around their section's central fire. With a wave, Devrand sent Jarthan to the tent-wagon and he approached Shyvoan.

"You're looking much better," he said in a low voice when he came close. "I asked about you, but they wouldn't tell me anything. And later, I tried to see you, but you were gone. Where did you go?"

Mindful of Troop-Lead Meara's directions, Shyvoan gave Devrand a delighted smile.

"My squad-mates told me you had asked after me. I tried to find you."

He smiled back. "Well, here I am now."

She gave him a sidelong glance. "I have to make sure we're all set here for camping a few days, but then let's meet. We can continue that discussion the attack so rudely cut off. Somewhere quieter." She looked around meaningfully at the many people within hearing range of them.

Devrand brushed his fingers across the back of her hand. "Yes, let's do that. Let's share the evening meal together."

An interesting tug pulled at Shyvoan, inclining her to agree, and a burnt-wood scent wafted past her and was gone. Since she had no objection to it, she told him to meet her at her tent-wagon later.

With a satisfied smile, he nodded. "I'll bring the meal, so you needn't worry about anything."

After he disappeared into his tent-wagon, Shyvoan drew her squad close and let them know the plan.

"Sounds good," Liphye said. "With Devrand out of the way, I'll give Jarthan some more pleasant company for the meal."

"And we two will go about our regular duties." Teigye drew his expression into an exaggerated pout and gestured at himself and Buok.

"Fine with me," Buok said. "I'm not much the 'get them to talk with me' type."

Liphye gave Teigye a punch in the arm. "If he won't talk with me, you can try some wiles next."

"Want to wager who's successful?" Teigye gave her a big grin.

"You got it," Liphye said.

~ ~ ~

When the rest of the squad gathered at the fire for the evening meal, along with several denizens whose wagons also traveled with their group, Shyvoan took herself to her tent-wagon. She anticipated no need to blend into the woods, so she tossed her cap atop her bedding and rebraided her hair to contain the tendrils that always seemed to escape. After a moment's consideration, she left the two braids hanging down her back rather than pinning them up around her head as usual. *Strange to leave them hanging almost to my waist.*

When she climbed out of her tent-wagon, Devrand already waited for her. He carried a small bundle and a jug and wore his own clothes instead of the ones from the troop's stores. Should she have changed out of her leathers? A moment later, she chided herself for the silly thought. This was no assignation.

She glanced at the gathering around the fire and found everyone's gazes on her and Devrand. She scrunched her nose at the rest of her squad and turned her attention back to Devrand.

He gave her a slight smile. "We seem to have attracted a lot of attention."

"Is that a problem?"

He laughed. "No. Still, I think we'd rather not risk being overheard, am I right?"

Shyvoan nodded and led him away from the gathering by the fire. "We need to stay inside the ward-rings. But I'm sure we can find someplace less busy."

They did find a spot near the ward-rings, but on the other side of several of the tent-wagons from everyone else. Shyvoan spotted one of the warriors who kept watch beyond the rings, but he stood far enough away that their conversation would not carry to his ears – as long as they kept their voices quiet.

Devrand handed her the jug and unwrapped his bundle to reveal food wrapped in a blanket. He spread the blanket on the ground, set the food atop it and sat, with a gesture for her to join him.

"I figured we can eat and talk. The food's nothing different from what everyone's having tonight, but I managed to get that drink you people seem to like."

Shyvoan settled across the blanket from him, and they shared out the food. After a few bites to tame the worst of her hunger, Shyvoan gave Devrand a questioning look.

He swallowed hastily. "I've been thinking about what you recited to me from the scroll. I believe there are clues in there."

"Is that why you were asking about me?"

"Part of it, yes." He ran his hand along his jaw and cleared his throat. "Anyway, about what the scroll had to say. A long path—"

"Six days long, if we believe the writing."

"You have reason not to?"

Shyvoan shrugged. "I suppose not. Just suspicions. This is a thing mages have kept secret. Would they just write it out openly?"

"True. But I don't think I'd call this particularly open." He took a bite of his food and washed it down with a sip of the kuchal. He made a face at the drink, as he had before.

Shyvoan laughed. "You don't have to drink it if you dislike it so much."

"I believe I'm starting to get used to it. And I'm tired of water. But back to the scroll. A long path, with flowers on its edges. Are you familiar with those flowers? Do they grow in a certain place?"

"They're pretty common. Although I've never seen a path lined with them."

"With the way your people relocate, I doubt it's even on this island. How old is the scroll? And do you keep track of the islands your people lived on before?"

"Both of those are something Elder Feayon should be able to help with. So… path, flowers…. Difficulty keeping their footing. Why?"

"A muddy path? A steep path? A path full of rocks? Or roots? Going up or down a mountain?"

Shyvoan pondered that and thought of no other explanation.

"And you said, 'always the sun rode on our backs'," Devrand said after another couple of bites of food.

"The vesnaflurs bloom in the spring," Shyvoan said as

she thought out loud. "That could mean they traveled south. At that time of year, the sun is further north in the sky than now, the end of summer. If they always faced south, the sun would always be on their backs."

Devrand nodded. "So, we have a direction to go."

"It's no good without the place to start from," Shyvoan pointed out.

"The scroll also said threshold and within the stone," Devrand said after a couple of minutes of thought. "Do your dragons live in buildings or tents? Maybe big, spacious ones? So, they could have thresholds?"

Shyvoan laughed at the thought. "I have no idea. But maybe it just means an entrance."

"But entrance to what? 'In the stone'...."

Devrand turned his attention back to his meal and finished eating, his expression thoughtful the whole while. Shyvoan ate the last bit of her meal, too, and watched his expression for any clue to what he was thinking.

"We can hope your elder might have the answer to where to start from," Devrand said, breaking the silence.

Shyvoan nodded. "Gives me a few questions for him, anyway. And I have some for you."

Devrand looked up from his cup and gave her that bland look of his.

"What are they? Are we back again to exchanging questions and answers?"

"If we have to be."

Devrand scrutinized her expression and shrugged. "Ask your questions."

"When you touch something, like hobs and unicorns, you do more than learn of them, don't you?"

Devrand gazed at her many long seconds, then shook his head. "I just wanted to learn of them. I can't say why they dropped afterward."

"Can't or won't?"

He shrugged.

"So, you're claiming whatever you did isn't what killed

them? Can you do that to anything?"

"What does it matter if it did kill them? They attacked. They've been attacking your people for how long?"

"Can you do that to anything?"

Devrand frowned. "I was just learning of them."

"So, can I expect to drop dead sometime? That *is* what you did to learn our language, isn't it? Learned it from me somehow."

Devrand's expression morphed into something that resembled chagrin. "It *is* similar to how I learned your language. From you and from your Troop-Lead Meara. But if it was going to do something like that to you—if that's even what did it to the hob and unicorn—I'd think it would have already happened."

Shyvoan glared at him. Somehow, his answers seemed off, but she could not pinpoint what or how.

He reached out to her, faster than she would have suspected he could move, and placed his hand over hers on the blanket. She had started to pull away, but at his touch, she stopped. A hint of a burnt-wood scent floated past.

"What did you do?" she demanded.

"Nothing much at all." He leaned close to gaze into her eyes. "I can strengthen what's there. Things like feelings. You didn't want to pull away from me."

Shyvoan glared at him. "So, this is your magic?"

A sudden flush of desire swept through her and vanished in the next instant.

"I can't create something that's not there, but I *can* strengthen what's already there. Think about that."

He stood and walked away.

CHAPTER 14

Shyvoan sat there a long time after Devrand left and tried to get her thoughts in order. What she'd learned was worrisome. He had not denied that he had killed the hob and unicorn with his magic. True they were the enemy. But something about the way it worked bothered her.

And his last words were just annoying. True, yah. But just because she had the glimmerings of some inclinations that direction did not mean she intended to follow through on any of them. Certainly not with his help through magic.

Could that be what's going on with all the others he interacted with, everyone who seemed enamored of him?

After she ran these thoughts around her head a few times, she grew disgusted with the whole topic and decided to let Troop-Lead Meara know what she had learned. After that, she would see if she could talk with Elder Feayon.

She might not like Devrand, might have fond thoughts of shoving him back where he came from—if she could—but she could not deny that if he *could* make this passage thing and take her people away from their enemies, she needed to ensure he had all he needed to do it.

She gathered the blanket and remnants of their meal then dropped everything off behind her tent-wagon on her way across the encampment. She avoided her squad-mates, not yet ready to share with them her talk with Devrand.

~ ~ ~

Troop-Lead Meara scowled after Shyvoan shared the details of what Devrand could do. "Keep this new knowledge to yourself for the time being. Just say the word if you'd rather hand off his guardianship to other warriors. I'll allow another squad to take over."

Shyvoan shook her head in refusal. "Very few seem resistant to his charms, magic-enhanced or not. My squad is among those few, so we should keep this duty, no matter how distasteful."

A brief smile touched Troop-Lead's lips at Shyvoan's last comment. She nodded. "Continue on, then. But know that I'll keep another squad nearby poised as backup, should you need it."

Shyvoan smiled her agreement to that and left to seek out Elder Feayon.

She found the elder seated in the shadows of his tent-wagon. He looked like he had expected her to visit that night. He patted a spot next to him on the sideboard of his wagon and passed her a small cup of kuchal.

"You look like you need it," he said in a low voice.

"Thanks," she murmured. She drank it in one gulp and refused more.

"I've got some questions about that scroll," she said, keeping her voice as low as his.

He nodded at her to continue and filled the cup for himself from a jug that sat next to him.

"Do you know how old the scroll is?" Shyvoan said.

Elder Feayon sipped his kuchal while he gave that some thought.

"I believe Turea wrote it. She was an elder when I was

a young man. But I don't think it came from her memories. I suspect she copied from an older scroll. To preserve the information, I'd guess."

Shyvoan sighed. "So, while the scroll seems to detail a journey to meet a dragon, there's no telling where to find that path that it describes. Does anyone keep track of the islands we've lived on before?"

"Not in any kind of an official sense," Elder Feayon said. "But between us, we elders have much of that knowledge." He winked at her. "Part of being an elder is holding the people's past knowledge against such an instance as this."

Shyvoan covered her eyes with her hands and massaged her temples as she tried to ward off an impending headache. "It seems we need dragons to renew our own magic—"

"That *is* where our magic came from to begin with. Someone wanting to be a mage would seek out a dragon to get magic from it. Then the magic stayed in their family for several generations but became weaker and weaker with each generation. As you know from your family."

He tilted his head toward her sheathed sword. "And those families had some heirloom item that they passed down. Perhaps to take to the dragons again when they needed to renew the magic in the family line."

"Perhaps? You don't know for certain?"

Elder Feayon shook his head, his expression sad. "I'm the last to hold magic in my family, and for some reason no heirloom item was passed to me. The dragons were long gone before I realized I should go renew the magic. I don't actually know how that works."

Shyvoan looked up at a sudden thought. "What if it's not the dragons who were long gone? What if we left wherever they are? We've been moving ahead of Maheaja-Folk attacks for years. To find the dragons, maybe we need to go back to where they live."

She groaned. "And that won't be a quick journey. We

move the denizens' lodgment… what? Around once a year, sometimes twice? Going to a new island in each of those moves."

"We move that frequently now," Feayon said. "But in the past, we changed lodgment locations less often. Before my time, but I remember my parents complained about the change, about moving more frequently. So somewhere around eighty years ago is when we started moving around once a year. Before that, from what I overheard, we stayed in place for two years and longer. And *much* longer if you go back far enough."

Shyvoan glanced over her shoulder to the west, not seeing the trees that stood there but instead seeing a chain of islands that stretched an unimaginable distance.

"That could be hundreds of islands in our past to search for dragons." She slumped and dropped her head to her hands. "Are we doomed to keep running from the Maheaja-Folk until they kill us all?"

Elder Feayon patted her shoulder. "I know it seems overwhelming. Maybe get some rest and you'll have more ideas to help in the morning. And I'll poke through some of Turea's other writings—that woman liked to write— and see if I find anything else. Maybe you should review that scroll, now that you've seen the description of the path, maybe see if she tucked anything else of use in there."

"A lot of it doesn't make any sense," Shyvoan complained.

Elder Feayon chuckled. "And for that I apologize. As you've no doubt guessed, it's not intended to be read by a non-mage. You don't have the background for those parts, is all. Regardless, something might jump out at you."

He nudged her off the board. "Sleep is what you need now, though."

With a nod, Shyvoan headed back to her tent-wagon. Sleep sounded good, and she ached. Liphye met her before she reached her tent-wagon.

"Devrand looked rather annoyed and such when he returned," Liphye greeted her.

Shyvoan shrugged but could not stifle her grin. Devrand being annoyed did not bother her much. *His easy assumption that everyone would become enamored of him needs some disruption.* "At least I'm not the only one," she said. "I did learn some things from him, anyway. Told the Troop-Lead. How about you? Any luck getting anything from Jarthan?"

Liphye shook her head. "Not really. He confirmed much of what we've already learned from Devrand. He seemed to enjoy my company, but also kept looking around nervously, like he feared being caught."

"By Devrand, I'd wager."

"Yah. One thing he let slip, though. I've got the name of their hunter!" Liphye bounced on her toes in her delight, with a large grin for Shyvoan.

"And? Are you going to share?"

Liphye leaned close. "Her name's Deliberia."

"Good. We've got a name. Maybe I can shock Devrand with knowing that and get more out of him."

"But you did get something from him tonight?"

Shyvoan nodded. "And the Troop-Lead wants to keep that information close, for now."

Liphye threw her hands up in disgust. "Of course. We just need to watch the guy, right?"

Shyvoan grinned. "Right. But I can tell you that it's definite he's got some magic. And it's very different from what we know from our mages."

Liphye looked thoughtful and gave an abrupt nod. "Explains some stuff." She chuckled when Shyvoan tried to stifle a wide yawn.

"You head on to your bed. I've got watch in a few. But you get out of duty this night. Sleep and heal."

Shyvoan waved her thanks and climbed into her tent-wagon. She spent some time going back through the scroll as she tried to find anything else of use. She fell asleep long before the watch changed.

~ ~ ~

The next couple of days Shyvoan avoided Devrand, although she kept an eye on him from a distance. As did her squad-mates. Most of the warriors kept busy with either watch duties around the encampment or scouting on the other island across the strait.

Shyvoan was on light duty and so spent her time—when not keeping an eye on their charges—around the edges of the encampment, watching the tides and reporting on them. Others tested the waters between the two islands and determined that, as expected, they would be able to cross with the tent-wagons only during low tide.

The denizens were in high spirits in anticipation of the end to their journey. Although from what Shyvoan heard from the warriors who had first scouted the new island weeks earlier, the first suitable place for the more permanent lodgment lay still a few days of travel inland from the shore.

Shyvoan had found nothing further in the scroll from Elder Feayon and so had returned it that morning. Elder Feayon had nothing for her then but asked her to stop by after the evening meal. Shyvoan had no duty assignment for several hours and so ambled to the edge of the encampment nearest the crossing between the two islands.

She could just make out a couple of warriors on the other island's shore and waved back when they waved a greeting.

Devrand found her there an hour later as she watched the tides and pondered finding dragons.

He took a seat on a large rock a short distance from her.

"I'd ask that you people leave my cousin alone," he said by way of greeting. "Your badgering has him quite upset."

Shyvoan gave him a sidelong look. "Him upset? Or is it

you? What's your hold on him?"

Devrand frowned at her. "I take care of him. He's ill, as I've told you."

"So you've said."

"Do you dislike me so? Others seem not to share your opinion."

"And how much have you 'strengthened' their liking for you into adoration?"

He shrugged. "I've been thinking about your dragons. The parts about 'scrambling and sliding' and 'within the stone' could mean a highland area, maybe mountains. 'Within the stone' could mean inside a cave."

Shyvoan considered that. "Makes sense. Unfortunately."

"Why unfortunately?"

"I think the last island we were on that had anything that even resembled highland areas, let alone mountains, was back around the time I was born. That would be twenty-five or more islands back to our west. And I'm not sure those areas could fit the description, even as unclear as it is."

Devrand frowned at that. "Your people have always traveled to the east? Going from island to island ahead of the Maheaja-Folk attacks?"

Shyvoan nodded, with a questioning look for him. *Where is he going with this?*

"Why always east? And what makes moving to a different island safe for you for a time? Don't the Maheaja-Folk show up again eventually?"

"They do. And I don't know. We've always gone to the east. At least as far as I know."

"Could they be driving you that direction? Herding you like your denizens herd their goats?"

Now Shyvoan frowned. A disturbing thought, especially since it makes a sort of sense.

"Maybe driving us away from the dragons," she said.

"Maybe. So why?"

"They don't want us to be able to renew our magic, maybe. Without magic, we're really no match for them. We've only survived as well as we have because they don't attack in any great force."

"And that seems odd, too. If they can continue to attack with a few of their creatures, why not wait, attack in greater force, and overwhelm you? Something else to think about." He walked a few steps back toward the bulk of the encampment and looked back at her. "Find me if you want to talk more about how we get to those dragons."

Shyvoan watched him walk further into the encampment, greeting many of the denizens as he passed. Has he enthralled most of the encampment? If so, what might he do with such power over nearly everyone?

And why did she so strongly suspect that his intentions might not mesh with the denizens' and warriors'?

She slid her sword from its sheath and brushed her fingers along the dragon-scale infused blade. It seemed strong against the Maheaja-Folk and their magic. *If needed, could it be strong against Devrand's magic too?*

CHAPTER 15

Not long after a sunrise obscured by thick clouds, the first of the denizens' wagons crossed to the new island. The tide would not yet be at its lowest for about an hour, but the water was low enough for the tarandeer and wagons to cross. They would have about two hours of good crossing, not nearly enough time to get everyone to the new island. Keeping an eye on Devrand and Jarthan—who had both wanted to witness this first crossing—and watching the first group head into the water, Shyvoan sighed. *Going to be a long several days to get everyone over there.*

An odd sound drew Shyvoan's attention from the wagons, a kind of whining whistle. She had never heard anything like it before.

She scrutinized her surroundings but spotted nothing amiss, or even different. The sound grew louder which made it easier to tell the direction: back toward the encampment.

Shyvoan signaled to her squad-mates to stay with their charges and the people crossing and jogged back to the main encampment. She felt much better than she had the day before, but a full-out run might have torn open some of her wounds again.

No sounds of distress or fighting, so that's reassuring. Yet that strange sound seems ominous.

When she arrived at the encampment, as drizzle began to fall, she found the denizens milling around with anxious expressions as they looked for the source of the sound. The warriors she saw also looked around for the source but stood with weapons ready rather than milling aimlessly.

Shyvoan paused and closed her eyes to better concentrate on the sound. It grew louder then softer, like the source approached and retreated again. *No, not exactly.* It sounded more like it circled the area, and at about tree-top height.

"'Ware the sky," she shouted to the warriors nearby and plunged into the encampment looking for an open area.

The sound changed and rose in pitch, coming closer from behind. She turned to look and managed to trip over a rock, which sent her scrambling sideways to regain her balance. Fiery pain sliced across her cheekbone. It narrowly missed her eye and knocked her further off-stride.

She raised her sword, blinked against the drizzle in her face, and spotted something moving fast in the storm's gloom. She heard a few pings as something impacted on her sword's blade and the thing flew past.

Without the rain in her eyes, she saw what attacked her: a hob riding atop the Maheaja-Folk bird called an arcasi. She had not seen an arcasi before, but all warriors learned about the various kinds of Maheaja-Folk that the people had encountered over the years. Arcasi looked much like hawks, but much bigger, big enough for a hob to ride. Their feathers were supposed to be as strong as dragon scales, with sharp edges and tips. They attacked by shooting those feathers at their target.

This one flew toward the center of the encampment, where the Elders Council camped, with other elders grouped nearby.

As Shyvoan ran after it, she ignored the blood she felt running down her cheek and the pull of her stitches at her motion. She shouted as she ran and gathered warriors with her, especially archers. Hopefully, some warriors were closer to the elders' tent-wagons than she and her companions were. If only she were more skilled with a bow.... Although the archers nearby had not managed to hit the Maheaja-Folk.

The arcasi shot more sharp feathers at her and the other warriors. Only a couple of them grazed anyone, causing wounds no worse than one on Shyvoan's cheek.

The hob shouted something, and the bird rose higher in the air. It hovered there for a moment before it dove at the elders' wagons ahead.

Shouts of warning came from several of the warriors. Shyvoan shouted with them. She saw the elders start at the sudden noise, then the deadly feathers sliced through them. They hit the members of the Elders Council and several other elders nearby.

An archer near Shyvoan managed to hit the hob in the leg. The creature shouted what sounded like curses as he guided the arcasi around for another attack.

Shyvoan and the warriors without bows ran to the stricken elders and began moving them to shelter while they urged others who had not been hit by feathers to take cover themselves.

More archers shot at the attackers and more arrows struck them. More feathers rained down and hit more of the elders and some of the warriors.

Another volley of arrows skewered both arcasi and hob and they fell, crushing one of the wagons.

Shyvoan turned her attention to the wounded. All the elders of the Elders Council had been hit with multiple feathers and none looked in good shape. The other elders who had been hit with feathers had taken far fewer. The warriors worked to stop the bleeding until menders could get there. One warrior ran off to hurry them.

Shyvoan found Elder Feayon propped unconscious against the wheel of one of the wagons while two warriors worked on him. Feeling useless—she could do no more than they—Shyvoan moved closer to the hob and arcasi to look at them.

Both were clearly dead. Careful of the sharp edges, she grasped one of the arcasi's feathers and pulled. At first it resisted her tug, but then it popped free of the bird.

The feather reflected the dim light with a gray-white sheen. It was lighter than she expected, and sturdier. When she tried to break it by stomping on the flat side, her action dented the shaft a little and nothing more.

"Looks like they'd make good daggers," a voice said in her ear. "What *is* that thing?"

"It's an arcasi, Devrand. First one I've seen. They're supposed to be pretty rare among the Maheaja-Folk."

Devrand knelt and scrutinized the bird and hob, but touched neither one.

"Would only take a few of those birds to devastate a camp like this one," he muttered. "Good thing they're rare."

He looked at the menders who worked on the elders' injuries. "Risky flying all the way to the center of the camp to attack."

"They made it here."

"True. And a shame." Devrand inclined his head Elder Feayon's direction as the menders who had worked on the elder sat back with sorrowful expressions. "Which one's his wagon?"

Shyvoan fought back tears. They might not have been related, but grief gnawed at her the same as when her own grandfather had died years before. "What?"

"Can't ask him any more about the dragons. Maybe there's something in his stuff."

"How can you—"

"How can you not?" Devrand snapped. "This is the future that faces all of us unless someone finds a different solution. You can't deny that they're likely to kill everyone."

Shyvoan glared at him, annoyed that he was right. *But even so.*

Devrand pulled on her arm to get her to stand. "If you won't help, tell me which one's his and I'll grab whatever I can."

She turned toward Elder Feayon's wagon and met Troop-Lead Meara's gaze as the commander entered the area with more warriors. Devrand turned to see what had caught her attention and frowned.

"Fine, then," he said and walked away before Troop-Lead Meara got any closer.

The Troop-Lead watched him with narrowed eyes then, with a slight nod to Shyvoan, turned to survey the battle's aftermath. Shyvoan saw her expression slide into sorrow as the menders laid out another of the elders before they moved to help with the last three from the Elders Council.

At a slight gesture from the Troop-Lead, Shyvoan joined her.

"What part did that man have in this?"

Shyvoan shook her head. "None that I'm aware of. He came after it was all over. At least as far as I know."

Troop-Lead Meara nodded, but with a deep frown. The menders left yet another of the elders.

"Are we to lose them all?" the Troop-Lead murmured.

"One useful thing Devrand pointed out," Shyvoan said. "They flew across half the encampment to get to this point."

"A deliberate attack on our Elders Council," Meara said after some thought.

"It looks that way."

For several minutes, the Troop-Lead watched the

activity around them in silence. The menders moved the still-living elders to their own section of the encampment to better care for them out of the drizzle and the warriors took charge of the dead, their own and the two enemies.

"Are they watching us then?" Meara said in a low voice. "Figuring us out? It's what we've tried to do with them."

"But we've never spotted even one of their scouts. Whenever we encounter any Maheaja-Folk nearby, they're attacking. How are they watching us?"

Troop-Lead Meara met Shyvoan's gaze, her demeanor serious and her expression worried. "You may share this with your squad-mates, but no one else. And make certain you're not overheard. The Leader's been considering the possibility for some time that they have put spies among us somehow. So be extra vigilant. And report anything suspicious to me or Leader Finnschld."

Shyvoan suppressed a shiver of apprehension and nodded her understanding. She hurried after the menders and caught one who was not involved in the care of the elders to have him look at the slice she took from the feather.

He peered at her and sent her off to the menders' section, where a different mender there cleaned the wound and spread a healing poultice on it.

"You were fortunate," the mender said. "It's not too close to your eye and it's not bad enough that we need to stitch it. Use the poultice on it morning and night until it's healed, and it might not even scar." She handed Shyvoan the small jar. "Oh, and if you can avoid using any of the color—at least for a couple of days—that would help."

Then she sent Shyvoan off, away from the ongoing bustle around the injured elders.

Shyvoan made it back to her squad in time to see the last of that tide's wagons finish their crossing. They would have many hours before the next group crossed, but they also were not on that duty.

After she ensured no one dawdled behind, and no

other warriors lingered nearby to overhear, Shyvoan shared what the Troop-Lead had said, and the details of the attack.

None of the others looked happy when she finished.

"I wager our problem is Devrand," Teigye said. "Always sneaking around. Maybe he sneaks out of the encampment to meet with his Maheaja-Folk buddies."

Buok shook his head. "Can't be him. Our own troop mage said he's human. Maheaja-Folk don't work with humans."

Teigye frowned but allowed that he spoke truth.

"And that's the problem with this idea," Liphye said. "We've never caught one spying on us. And considering the length of time we've been hostile, we should have caught *one*, you'd think. We know their abilities and such, including ones like the arcasi that none of us had seen before today. We *know* they can't turn themselves invisible. Nor can they change their shapes to look human, except for the moaras. And even *they* can only do that for a few minutes at most, so it's said. So how can any Maheaja-Folk be spying on us?"

"How did they know where to go to take out the denizens' leaders?" Shyvoan countered.

They all fell silent at that, lost in their own thoughts.

~ ~ ~

After the solemn ceremony to bury their dead, after she said a final good-bye to Feayon, Shyvoan sat that night by their fire and stared into it, brooding. None of the elders on the Elders Council had survived the attack, so that left only the Shield-Lead of their original leadership.

The denizens who remained on the near side of the strait planned to meet that evening to choose who among the other elders would fill the empty places on the Council. The second group of denizens had crossed the water between this island and the new one, and carried the news of what had happened with them.

That night's decision about the elders would not be binding until they heard from the rest of the people, those who were already on the new island.

Shyvoan ate her meal, with long pauses between bites, but did not taste it. When someone sat next to her, she did not even look to see who it was.

"I got the elder's scrolls," Devrand whispered into her ear.

She turned a cold look on him. "Did you even wait until they had taken Elder Feayon away?" She kept her voice as quiet as his.

"What does that matter? He's no longer around to object *or* help, and we need any help we can get if this is to work."

Shyvoan stared at him many long minutes before she gave a curt nod. "Can you read our language? To know what's important in those scrolls you've pilfered? Did you learn that too when you pulled how to speak it from us?"

Devrand frowned and shook his head. "No. So I need your help. Just as you're going to need mine if we're to make a passage that leads away from here."

He reached for her hand, but she pulled it away from him. "Granted. But don't try any more of that enamoring on me."

He gave her that annoying bland look and said nothing.

She finished her meal, very conscious of his gaze on her. "Don't you have something else to do other than watch me eat?"

"Not really. I've already eaten. And looking through the scrolls doesn't do me any good."

Shyvoan glanced at their surroundings. No one paid them any particular attention, but enough people were nearby that she did not want to bring any scrolls out by the fire. "Not here," she told Devrand.

"I'll get the scrolls and meet you someplace less visible, then," he said. "Your wagon?"

"Behind the wagon will do fine. That's still within the ward-rings and close enough if there's another attack, but shadowed and out of the way."

With a nod, Devrand moved off.

Shyvoan touched her cheek. It ached, and the poultice did nothing for that. But otherwise, the wound felt less angry. *Hopefully, the Maheaja-Folk don't put anything like poison on the arcasi's feathers.*

After a time, she wandered to her wagon and dug out her light-pot. When she slipped behind the wagon, she found that both Devrand and Jarthan waited there, already seated on the ground. Devrand sat with his back propped against one of the wagon's wheels, and Jarthan slouched on his far side. At Devrand's other side lay four scrolls, the thickest the one Shyvoan had already read through and only recently returned to the elder.

"Jarthan?" Shyvoan said.

The man glanced at her with a half-smile before he turned his attention back to the ground, as usual.

"He might have some useful thoughts," Devrand said. "And I know he'll not say anything." He glowered at his cousin, who shrank further under the expression.

With a shrug, Shyvoan sat next to the scrolls by Devrand and situated the light-pot so it would give light but not be readily visible to anyone beyond the three of them. As she settled it, both men gave it quizzical looks but neither said anything.

Devrand handed Shyvoan a scroll. "I think look here first. It has a separate note in it. Maybe it's meant for you."

Shyvoan unrolled the scroll and a scrap of paper fell out. She grabbed it and brought it into the light from the light-pot. It had two words on it.

"Rashean Anyeschld," Shyvoan read. "Why would Feayon have Mender Rashean's name written in here."

"Who's Mender Rashean?" Devrand said.

"She was a mender when she was younger. Now, she still helps them mix herbs into creams and things like that.

She's no mage. And she's also… well, she takes a different view of things, different from most anyway."

Devrand gave her a quizzical look but did not say anything.

Shyvoan tucked the note in her belt pouch and turned her attention to the scroll. After a few minutes of trying to make sense of it, she sighed. "I can read all the words here, but it's not making sense to me. Something that concerns herbs, though."

"Probably why Rashean's name was with it, then."

Shyvoan grabbed a second scroll and skimmed through it to get a sense of what was there.

"And what's that one?" Devrand said after several minutes of silence as she read.

"Stories, the best I can tell. I do see mention of dragons, so maybe a closer reading might reveal some—"

She fell silent at the sound of someone approaching. A moment later Leader Finnschld stalked around the end of the wagon and peered at them.

"And have you found anything useful yet?" she demanded when no none said anything. "You *are* still looking into the dragons, aren't you?"

"I—" Shyvoan stopped, uncertain how much to say after Elder Feayon had warned her to share the details with no one.

The Leader smiled and settled to the ground next to her. "Feayon kept me informed of what you were up to," she told Shyvoan while she ignored the two men. "With him gone, I expect you to keep me completely informed."

After a moment, Shyvoan found her voice. "Of course. What did Elder Feayon already tell you?"

Leader Finnschld's smile had a feral edge to it. She shared it with Devrand. "Why don't you tell me what you've discovered so far. And share your guesses, too."

Shyvoan told her about the first scroll and the small part that seemed useful, the description of the path. She shared their guesses about the probable features of the area where the path would be found and the note with Rashean's name. The Leader glanced at the herb scroll and agreed with their conclusion.

"Although any conversation with Rashean will have to be approached with care," she said. "Remember, she's sometimes easily flustered and upset." She paused, lost in thought, then nodded as she seemed to decide something. "I'm afraid you'll have to speak with your sister and her spouse about talking with Rashean. Rashean is fond of them, and they might be able to help. And if it'll help you, be sure to let your sister know you're doing this on my orders."

Leader Finnschld glanced through the other scrolls while the others looked on. When she finished, she held the one with stories out to Shyvoan.

"This one might give you some ideas about dealing with a dragon, assuming you're able to find one to do so. And your duties will now include figuring out how to do so." She gave Shyvoan a stern look. "Keep the knowledge to as few people as you can but bring your squad-mates into this."

The Leader still held the last scroll as she stood. "I'll keep this one," she said. "It's not related to what you're working on. Nothing in here you need to see."

She eyed the three with a stern expression a few minutes longer before she strode away.

Shyvoan studied her feet as she tried to control the uneasiness that gripped her from Leader Finnschld's abrupt visit. She shouldn't have tried to keep secret from the Leader what she had been looking into with Devrand. How could she have been so foolish? So far, she had escaped any penalty. Now she just got to wait to see what the repercussions of her actions would be.

Devrand's voice interrupted her recriminations.

"You have a sister?" he said.

Shyvoan glanced at him and caught Jarthan also looking at her, curiosity clear in his expression.

She nodded. "Yah. Neasha's not a warrior like me, nor a mage like mother was. She takes more after father. Interested in herbs and other plants and has some skill with them. Her spouse, too. Although with their family now they don't spend as much time with the herbalists as they used to. Neasha and I've never been close."

She shrugged. "We don't look much like sisters. She's not got the freckles that I have and her hair's brown. What of you? Did you leave family behind when you had to run? Someone who cares for you?"

She saw Jarthan's sudden stricken look before he turned away. Devrand's face remained expressionless.

"Some family," he said, his tone flat. "Relatives who helped raise me. A few people like that." He looked lost in memories for a moment before he shook them off. "So, we need to speak with your Neasha and her spouse."

"Not tonight. They've got their family to take care of. And Rashean's likely already asleep."

With a nod, Devrand handed Shyvoan the remaining scrolls as he stood. Then he grabbed Jarthan's shoulder and hauled the other man to his feet.

"Until tomorrow, then."

CHAPTER 16

BEYOND THE SHALLOW SEA

Gya slumped on the ship's rail in a moment of dejection. Three weeks, more or less, they'd been in this world already. Why couldn't he and Alorsha find a way to break free of the vines that held the Deliberia? And what was the continuing difficulty in her wayfinding magic for locating Devrand and Jarthan? More of the world's magic had seeped into the taiawood of the ship but it did not seem to help with either problem.

He stared at the dark smudge of land in the distance to their north, almost invisible in the twilight gloom, and let his thoughts wander while he hoped a new idea would come. When it didn't, he turned around to lean his back against the rail and watch the crew at their tasks.

He watched Alorsha again work her wayfinding magic for the direction to Devrand and Jarthan. The arc the pendant inscribed was shorter than the first one so many days ago, but still gave a wide area of possibilities. Saevalde joined her and they spoke, Alorsha shaking her head and giving the pendant a glare.

A strange groan from the starboard side shivered

through the ship, drawing the attention of everyone on the deck.

"What could that be?" Alorsha's voice carried clearly in the sudden cessation of activity.

She and Saevalde hurried to the starboard rail, along with many of the others who were on deck. Gya followed, too, and looked over the rail as the others were.

At the waterline, where the ship met the water, a mob of the water-people had gathered, two deep. They formed a curved line that looked like it might go around the ship. Those closest to the ship rested their hands on the vines, which peeled back from the *Deliberia*'s hull. Then they placed their hands on the ship's hull.

"More of those water-people here," one of the crew called from the other side of the ship.

Gya looked for the two they had spoken with so many days ago but could not tell if they were there.

"What is this?" Alorsha called to the gathering as Saevalde left her side.

Gya watched Saevalde hurry across the deck then he turned back to the water-people. *Probably going to get Mikolus.*

One of the people within touching distance of the ship looked at Alorsha. The others had their eyes closed and seemed to be concentrating.

"We take you to the conclave of the moaras, we sea-dwellers of those your kind call the Maheaja-Folk," the person said. "The conclave would offer a pact." She closed her eyes, too, as the last of the vines slipped beneath the waters.

In eerie synchronization, the water-people turned to face the ship's bow, each with one arm outstretched and that hand on the hull at the waterline.

Alorsha placed both hands atop the rail and drew on the magic in the taiawood. Gya followed suit when he felt what she was doing.

Was this some sort of attack? With the magic, he and

Alorsha were prepared if it was.

The wind in the sails died away. Not that it had been of any use earlier while the vines had held them. The ship turned to starboard, its motion smooth and slow.

Gya caught his balance as the ship continued to turn and picked up speed. The water-peoples' magic encased the ship and spun it. But oddly, he did not feel the motion – at least not until he looked toward the horizon.

Then he clenched his eyes shut and gripped the rail. Please let the spinning sensation and nausea subside soon!

"Do we allow this?" Mikolus's voice came through his disorientation.

"Don't think we can stop them," Alorsha murmured. "Be ready for anything when we get wherever we're going."

"Of course."

Gya heard the Ship's Captain's footsteps recede and dared to slit his eyes open. He could no longer tell whether they were spinning. A blue fog surrounded the ship and formed a kind of bubble centered on the *Deliberia*.

A glance over the rail showed him the water-people where they had been before, doing what they had been before. A hint of water was there, too, but a different color than before.

"How long will it take to get there?" Alorsha called to them.

Without opening her eyes, the water-person who had spoken before said, "As long as it takes. Rest for the conclave. We take you there."

Alorsha exchanged a look with Gya.

"Wonderful," he muttered.

CHAPTER 17

That night, vague feelings of some dire change looming, some alteration in the making plagued and disrupted Shyvoan's sleep. She gave up on any further sleep less than an hour before dawn, used the poultice on her cut face before she dressed in her leathers and cap, and stepped out into the quiet encampment.

Liphye had watch and Shyvoan greeted her friend in a low voice. "I need to meet with everyone as soon as your replacement comes at dawn," she added.

Liphye nodded acknowledgement but kept her attention on her surroundings.

Shyvoan next built up the fire, just enough to warm some kuchal and the leftover stew from the night before. Liphye joined her, after she had passed the watch duty to someone in the squad near theirs and dished up some stew for herself.

"I told the others to join us," she told Shyvoan, who nodded, her mouth full.

Buok and Teigye stumbled from their tent-wagons minutes later, grabbed food and drink, and hunkered down close by.

Shyvoan finished her last few bites and told the others about everything she had not shared with them before, the scroll from Elder Feayon and its possible clues, the two new scrolls, the need to talk with Rashean.

"Dragon hunting, who would have thought?" Teigye said when she finished.

"I don't think you'll want Devrand with you when you talk with Rashean," Liphye said.

"We can occupy him with reading the scroll of stories word for word," Teigye said with a grin. "Slowly. Maybe a couple of times. With pauses to debate what it all means."

"Leader Finnschld thought that might have some helpful information about dealing with dragons," Shyvoan said. "Also go over the other scroll from Elder Feayon, the one he first gave me. Maybe all of you will see something I missed. I'll take the herb scroll with me."

"I hope it'll be one of Rashean's good days," Buok said. "She knows much."

Shyvoan retrieved the scrolls from her tent-wagon and handed them to her squad-mates. While she cleaned up after the meal, they looked through the herb scroll and came to the same conclusion that she had: something to talk with Rashean about.

Shyvoan slipped away then, as Devrand emerged from his tent-wagon.

First to her sister. She herself had spoken little with Rashean and was uncertain the older woman would know her if she just arrived there without warning.

On the other side of the encampment, Shyvoan located Neasha's tent-wagons. The family had two tent-wagons to accommodate Neasha, her spouse Glin Orinschld, and their two young children. Both Neasha and her spouse were working at the fire when Shyvoan approached, but the children were nowhere in sight. *Maybe still asleep.*

Glin greeted her with a slight wave of his hand, which drew Neasha's attention to her approach.

Neasha glanced at Shyvoan, narrowed her eyes, and returned her attention to her task. "I see you're well. Of course. Despite all the attacks."

Shyvoan shrugged and exchanged a look with Glin. "You're all well?"

Neasha shrugged. "Yah. Though travelling with the littles is a challenge. Not that you'd know. I'll be happy to get to our new lodgment on the next island."

Shyvoan nodded at the mention of her niece and nephew, both under the age of five. Neasha had mentioned before what a handful they were. "How soon do you get to cross?"

"Not for another two days, sounds like. I don't suppose the great warrior could manage to get her older sister a better spot? Get us across sooner?"

Shyvoan frowned. "You know I've got no say on such things. That's not part of my duties. But it's about one of those duties that I'm here. Leader Finnschld wants me to speak with Rashean."

"And you need one of us there to vouch for you to her. Of course." Neasha brushed her hands against her legs, the motion abrupt. "So of course, I'll drop whatever I'm doing to cater to my warrior-sister's needs."

"Neasha." Glin's tone held a note of warning.

"No, it's fine." Neasha waved a dismissive hand in the air.

"You're busy. I'll take care of it." Glin gave his wife's shoulder a light squeeze.

Without looking at either of them, Neasha nodded and Shyvoan caught a glimpse of the sly smile on her sister's lips. While he brushed stray ashes from his red-brown skin and black hair, Glin led Shyvoan away from the little camp and toward the herbalists' section of the encampment.

"Sorry," he muttered after they passed out of Neasha's hearing range.

"*You* don't have to apologize," Shyvoan said. "It's nothing different from what I've heard most of my life.

Practically the whole time she raised me after our parents were killed. Until I left to become a warrior. But no more of that, please."

Glin nodded. "Rashean should have finished her morning meal. Should be a good time to talk with her."

The herbalists were busier than Shyvoan expected. She hovered off to the side while Glin dove into the bustle in search of Rashean.

After a couple of minutes he returned, with the woman in tow. While Rashean was no more than about twenty years older than Shyvoan, somehow, she always pictured her older, as one of the elders. Rashean had that air about her, although her straight black hair had no white in it and her golden-brown skin showed few wrinkles.

Glin led the way to a quieter area off to the side.

"Rashean, you remember Shyvoan, don't you? She's Neasha's younger sister," Glin said.

Rashean peered at Shyvoan. She did not look in her eyes but rather studied the rest of her in a long, slow perusal. She then smiled. "Of course, dear. The bad luck that isn't. Connected to Neasha and Glin." She nodded her head at Glin.

Shyvoan kept a pleasant expression on her face. "I'm glad to see you again. I wasn't sure you'd remember me. I hope you can help me with something."

Rashean's gaze drifted off to the side, but she replied readily. "I'm good with the plants. Is it something about those?"

"I think so."

"This is good then, Rashean?" Glin said. "You talking with Shyvoan."

"It's good. I see her connection. You can go back to Neasha now." She waved a hand in a vague gesture.

With a slight smile for Shyvoan and a light pat on Rashean's shoulder, Glin took himself off.

After he had gone, Shyvoan gently clasped one of Rashean's hands and put the scroll into it. "Here."

The woman turned the scroll over in her hands a couple of times. "Feayon's" she said. "So sad."

"Yah. He was helping me with something, and I hope you can help further."

Rashean dropped down to sit right where they stood. "Sit, sit."

Shyvoan joined her on the ground and watched as she eased the scroll open.

"Ah, it is," Rashean said.

Shyvoan tried to wait patiently while Rashean read through the scroll, but she could not help shifting around. After several minutes, Rashean patted her on the knee.

"Always all the energy. Always off to something new," she said and gazed at Shyvoan's right shoulder. "I remember this. The mages said it wouldn't work and hid it away as too dangerous. If not workable, then why any danger?"

Shyvoan puzzled over that. "Is there anything in there that would relate to dragons?"

Rashean lifted her gaze to meet Shyvoan's for an instant and looked away again. "A dragon to make you a mage again?"

"What? No, I've never been a mage." Shyvoan wrapped her arms around herself as Rashean's words brought back the bitterness of finding that she would never follow in her mother's footsteps. Would never wield the magic. She could not even manage to sing the right notes for the simple drinking songs that the warriors enjoyed, let alone the precise tones needed for the sonant magic.

"They used to do it," Rashean continued, oblivious to Shyvoan's distress. "Go to a dragon, come back with magic. So I've heard. But the dragons are long past. And this is something else. Although…. Maybe. A connection. Everything's connected, over time."

"I don't understand," Shyvoan said.

"Of course not." Rashean patted her knee again. "The

connections can be used. When we are in a place, make it a home, we affect it. Every place. They all connect to us and we to them. These herbs." She pointed to some drawings on the scroll. "Strong enough to use the connection."

"What do the connections do?" Shyvoan said.

"Connect," Rashean said and laughed. "It's what you do." She poked Shyvoan in the shoulder.

"We have connections to the dragons?" Shyvoan said.

"Yah. The magic."

Shyvoan groaned. "But we have little magic left. The mages can barely hold the ward-rings. And I have none."

Rashean rolled the scroll and whacked Shyvoan on the knee with it.

"Listen. Family connections to dragons. Homes connected to homes. Faster journeying."

Shyvoan considered that for a few minutes and shrugged. "Do you have these herbs? The strong ones to help with the connections?"

Rashean nodded. "Yah, yah. I will gather them for you. Come back for them when I say."

"What am I supposed to do with these strong herbs when you get them?"

Rashean grinned. "Find dragons."

She stood, dropped the scroll in Shyvoan's lap, and tottered back to the herbalists in that unusual gait she had.

Shyvoan stared after her until she no longer saw her in the bustle. "Sure. Find dragons, she says," she muttered to herself. "Simple as that."

When she returned to her squad's camping group, Shyvoan found them huddled with Devrand, clustered around the two scrolls. Jarthan lingered nearby, as usual, but did not look at her when she joined them. He looked more unwell than he had before.

Devrand looked up as she sat between Liphye and Buok.

"About time you returned. So share what you've got from that other scroll," he demanded, but kept his voice low.

Shyvoan shrugged. She pulled the scroll from her belt and placed it with the others.

"More confusion than anything else." She also kept her voice low.

Teigye chuckled. "If you've come from Rashean, that's not surprising," he murmured.

"I thought this Rashean was supposed to clarify things," Devrand muttered. "Give us something to help."

"And she very well might have," Shyvoan said. "I just don't see how it fits. I don't understand what she told me." She shared what Rashean had said and done. Perhaps with more of them trying to decipher it, they might make sense of it.

But when she finished and looked from one to the next, she met with head shakes all around.

She sighed. "How about all of you, then? Anything new from the scrolls?"

Teigye drew himself up into an exaggerated pose of someone prepared to impart profound knowledge. "We have learned that one must be respectful when dealing with a dragon," he said in a pompous tone, but continued to keep his voice low so no one else could overhear. "The dragons in the stories do like mountains, so that seems to fit with the path description."

"The stories also implied that it's an older dragon a mage should deal with," Liphye added.

"So, a dragon elder, then," Shyvoan said. "Makes sense, I suppose. But did you find anything about how one 'deals' with a dragon?"

They all shook their heads. "The scrolls become vague on that point," Buok said.

"It might be that it depends on the specific dragon," Devrand said. "Much like with people, maybe each has its own likes and desires. Figure those out, use them to get what we need."

"Seems like except for being huge, lizard-like creatures,

they're otherwise much like us," Teigye said.

Shyvoan considered what they had said. "All right. So, we deal with the dragon. Somehow. Any further clues about how to find it? Or them?"

"Has anyone talked with that hob you captured?" Jarthan said and received several surprised looks.

"I don't see talking with her doing any good," Liphye said. "She'd have no reason to tell us anything useful."

"True, that. Just the opposite, I'd think," Buok added.

"It's not an option anyway," Shyvoan said. "Troop-Lead Meara told me the hob was found dead right before everyone departed the lodgment."

"Probably her own people. To keep her from talking," Devrand said.

Shyvoan scrutinized his expression. With that bland gaze of his, she found no sign that he knew anything of what had happened, in spite of the Troop-Lead's suspicion about his involvement.

"That arcasi *did* fly almost directly to the Elders Council section," Liphye pointed out. "Looks like the Maheaja-Folk are getting information somehow."

"Maybe sneaking around somehow," Teigye said.

"Perhaps we shouldn't speak so openly about this, then," Buok said.

Shyvoan nodded. "I wouldn't want to risk word of what we are interested in getting out." She leaned in and motioned the others to do the same. "But the way the encampment's set, I don't see that we can find a secure place to talk. We'll just have to take extra care that no one overhears us. Especially after I get whatever it is Rashean'll have for me."

With nods all around, they dispersed, each going their own way to whatever duties or activities they had for the day. Shyvoan took all the scrolls back to her tent-wagon and tried to get some sleep while she waited to hear from the herbalist.

That afternoon she had still heard nothing, so she

busied herself helping denizens prepare to cross to the new island. A sense of urgency had her in its clutches, a need to rush as many of the people as she could to safety on the new island. But why did she feel so? At least the need took her mind off the confusion around trying to find a dragon. For the most part.

How are we going to travel all the way back to the west far enough to reach the islands where the dragons might be?

~ ~ ~

Rashean had still sent no word by the time Shyvoan's night watch came. As she kept watch, she paced more than usual and tried to connect the separate bits of information that they had. When she could not make any connections, she figuratively threw her hands up in disgust. *Must still need more pieces.* At least over the course of the day they had been able to get more of the denizens across during each low tide than the previous day.

Her watch passed slower than she wanted and, except for the turmoil in her thoughts, without any disruptions. When she turned the duty over to one of the warriors from a neighboring squad, restlessness kept her from sleep. So, she paced through the encampment, her steps quiet as she surveyed the activity around her.

Without meaning to, when she rounded one of the tent-wagons Shyvoan startled a man and woman who strolled hand in hand and rounded the tent-wagon at the same one. Later a pair of women almost collided with her as they walked with arms wrapped around each other's waists, laughing together, and paying little attention to anything other than each other. In each case Shyvoan simply exchanged nods with the couples and moved on.

She smiled at her memories of being occupied in a similar manner not that long ago. Too bad she and Renan weren't compatible otherwise. The times with him had been fun.

She was not yet ready to seek out another partner. After all this was resolved would be soon enough. Her duties would be lighter again, which would give her time to get to know someone other than those in her squad. *Good plan*, she decided and returned her attention more to her surroundings.

From the look of the encampment itself, they might have close to half the denizens across to the other island already. *Good news.*

Shyvoan had no destination in mind but found her steps taking her toward the herbalists. When she arrived, she saw a light in the tent-wagon that she thought was Rashean's. After she watched for a brief time, Shyvoan approached.

Rashean threw open the flap right before she got there.

"Your connection is almost right," she greeted Shyvoan. "You're just a little early. Sit and wait a bit."

The older woman gestured at the footboard and disappeared into the tent-wagon again. Shyvoan sat where instructed and waited.

Not quite a quarter-hour later, Rashean climbed out of her tent-wagon, deftly maneuvering around Shyvoan. She sat next to her and handed her a rolled scroll and a small pack.

"Herbs in the bag," Rashean said. "Should be enough. Better be."

"And this?" Shyvoan said as she unrolled the scroll.

Rashean did not respond at first, just watched Shyvoan with an intent expression.

Shyvoan scrutinized what she found on the scroll. Some sort of drawing. It looked like nothing more than random shapes connected by lines. Many random shapes. A smaller squiggle sat next to each larger shape that was connected to others by lines.

After she watched her for a time, Rashean leaned over and placed her finger on one shape toward the right that was connected to only one other.

"Sixteen days ago," she said. With a meaningful nod for Shyvoan—although Shyvoan did not know what she meant by it—Rashean climbed back into her tent-wagon and doused the light.

Shyvoan sat there and stared at the tent-wagon's flap for several minutes. After she heard soft snoring coming from within, she headed back across the encampment, her confusion that much worse.

In the morning, the squad and their two charges gathered at the side of their small fire. They made sure no one was close and sat near enough to each other to brush arms when they moved, to be able to talk in low voices. In the openness of the encampment, it was the best they could do for a secure place to talk. Shyvoan brought out the scroll from Rashean and shared what the herbalist had said.

"Connections," Jarthan murmured when she had finished. Everyone stared at him. "Sixteen days ago, we were at that tent-town, that lodgment of yours." He met Shyvoan's gaze. "This is a map."

Devrand snatched it from him and examined it.

"Homes connected to homes," Liphye said. "She's saying there's a connection between the places we've raised our lodgments."

"She said they all connect to us," Buok said. "And that the connections can be used."

"Used," Shyvoan repeated.

"But used how?" Teigye said.

Shyvoan held up a hand against more questions as she tried to pull together a thought she had glimpsed. A hint.... *They were connected to places they had lived and those were connected.... Rashean had said 'faster journeying'....*

"I think she means we can somehow use the connections to travel to those places," Shyvoan said. "And use the herbs she gave us to make it work somehow."

"Seems like we need a mage, too," Teigye muttered.

"Sounds like the sort of thing that needs a mage to make it work."

"But how do we use the herbs?" Liphye said. "What are we supposed to do with them?"

"There can be magic in plants," Devrand said.

"We used to know someone who would know how to use them," Jarthan said at the same time.

Devrand glared at Jarthan, and the other man retreated into himself again.

"Is that Deliberia who could do that?" Shyvoan said, curious to see their reactions to her knowledge of the name.

Both men gave her such incredulous looks that she almost laughed at their expressions.

"No, it's not." Devrand scowled.

"*Deliberia*'s the ship's name," Jarthan said and again subsided under Devrand's disapproval.

At mention of the ship, Shyvoan sighed. She had forgotten to keep an eye on it.

"That ship we'd been watching?" Teigye said.

"Know of any others?" Liphye teased him.

Teigye glowered at Liphye. "It's not there anymore."

Shyvoan cursed to herself. How could she have forgotten about the ship?

Devrand whirled on Teigye. "When did it leave? Which way did it go?"

Teigye shrugged. "No idea. It just wasn't there anymore yesterday morning when I looked."

"Why didn't you say something?" Shyvoan said.

"I told Troop-Leader Meara. I figured you knew."

Shyvoan turned to Devrand and Jarthan. "You said they hunt you. Why would they just leave? Where would they go?"

"How should I know?" Devrand shot back. "Someone should have mentioned it earlier."

"You didn't notice?" Liphye challenged. "If they hunted you, I'd think you'd be paying attention to that."

Devrand glared at her. "I've been concerned with other things. She hadn't moved. Why should she?"

Shyvoan caught a glimpse of the slight smile on Jarthan's face before he noticed her attention on him. *Smiling at Devrand's agitation?* But then the expression disappeared, and he returned her scrutiny with no expression at all.

"Getting back to this scroll from Rashean," Liphye said. "It looks like we need to return to our former lodgment on this island and start from there. Right?"

"Why not wait and start from the new lodgment on the new island?" Teigye said. "We ought to still connect to the one here, if we're understanding Rashean right and believe her."

"If we are, it sounded like the connection to where we live takes time," Shyvoan said. "I suppose we could wait a while at the new lodgment—"

"There's nothing to say the Maheaja-Folk will give you that time," Devrand broke in.

"True, that," Buok said. "Better to go back after everyone's across to the new island and travel from there. I doubt the Maheaja-Folk would expect such a move, either. So, our chances of getting through without being attacked should be good."

"It'll take several days to get back there," Teigye warned.

"Less if we were to ride tarandeer," Devrand said.

The squad-mates stared at him.

"What?" he said. "Many of those tarandeer are certainly big enough and look sturdy enough to ride. That'll get us there faster, even going through the woods."

"None of us rides the tarandeer," Shyvoan said. "They're for meat and clothing, our leathers, pulling the wagons, and other things, as needed."

"And carrying things," Teigye added.

Buok made a show of examining the trees around them. "Doesn't seem that riding would work well in the woods," he said. "The game trails are narrow for the most part and the tree limbs low."

"But are all the islands wooded like this?" Devrand said.

The squad-mates considered that.

"Some of the old tales speak of open grassy areas," Teigye ventured after a few minutes. "I suppose riding could make the going faster there."

"And how would riding them work anyway?" Liphye said. "No one's done it before."

Devrand and Jarthan exchanged glances.

"Should be able to teach them some," Jarthan murmured. "Just nothing fancy."

Devrand frowned and shrugged. "I suppose."

"What do you mean?" Liphye demanded.

"Where we're from, we don't have tarandeer," Jarthan said. "But we have creatures that are somewhat similar. We learned to ride them to get places faster than just walking. The same skill should work here."

"They're needed to pull the tent-wagons," Liphye said. "Even if we were to consider riding them."

"We're all going to look like fools, if we do try this," Teigye said.

Shyvoan agreed with Teigye's assessment. To herself.

"Should at least consider it," Devrand said.

"Perhaps," Shyvoan said.

With nothing further to say at that time, they all went their separate ways. Teigye indicated by hand signals that he would keep an eye on Devrand.

Shyvoan grabbed the other scrolls and slid them, along with the one from Rashean, into the pack of herbs and slung the pack on her shoulder. *Just keep it with me.* She would rather haul it around with her than leave it lying somewhere, even in her tent-wagon.

She grabbed a little to eat and headed across the encampment to let the Troop-Lead know the latest information.

When she told Troop-Lead Meara the idea of riding tarandeer, the woman's first reaction was laughter. Shyvoan grinned in response.

But after the Troop-Lead sobered, she nodded, her expression thoughtful.

"I know that the Leader has considered in the past the possibility of riding tarandeer," she told Shyvoan. "She hadn't done anything toward that, but perhaps now's the time."

Shyvoan looked around. As Devrand had mentioned, some of the tarandeer were sturdier than most, without a doubt. But as Liphye had said earlier, they needed them elsewhere. She mentioned this to Troop-Lead Meara, who nodded and told her to give her a few hours.

So Shyvoan returned to helping denizens get ready to cross to the new island the next low tide. As she looked around the encampment, she estimated they might still need a couple of days to get everyone across, although they were making progress getting more people across each low tide. *If only the low tides lasted longer.*

Late that afternoon, an aspirant sought out Shyvoan and told her that Leader Finnschld wanted to see her entire squad, plus their charges, right after the evening meal.

Evening found Shyvoan standing face to face with one of the tarandeer, its wide muzzle mere finger-widths from her own nose. A folded blanket sat on its back, tied on with ropes at either end that stretched around its body. The ropes closest to its front legs had a curious loop knotted on, one on each side.

The animal gazed at her, placid and unsuspicious of their plans, and blinked its wide dark eyes, its round pupils large in the fading light. Shyvoan stared back. *How's this going to work?* She had driven one to draw her tent-wagon but riding one had to be a very different thing. *Didn't it?*

"We picked out the sturdiest ones for you. And the calmest," the Leader said. "Based on what Devrand has told us, we picked tarandeer that are already accustomed to carrying something on their backs, but that also have pulled wagons and so know how to be guided using reins."

"But what about those wagons, then?" Teigye said.

Leader Finnschld smiled. "We've shuffled some of the tarandeer around, and in a couple of cases have rigged two to draw some wagons. So everyone will still get where they need to be." She nodded to an open area to the side of the command section. "We cleared that area for you."

She stepped back and folded her arms. Troop-Lead Meara came over and joined her. Shyvoan grimaced. *Just what I need, commanders watching every move as we try out this insanity.*

Devrand and Jarthan each led a tarandeer to the cleared area and motioned the others to follow and bring their tarandeer. Each of them took two of the squad to work with. Shyvoan and Teigye ended up with Jarthan.

First Jarthan led his tarandeer over next to one of the tent-wagons, then demonstrated how to get on the animal by climbing on the end board and swinging one leg over it to settle astride on its back. He the slid his feet into the rope loops. The tarandeer looked startled when he settled on its back and minced sideways away from the wagon. It danced a few steps before it settled and stood still on stiffened legs while its skin twitched.

"What signal have they been trained to for walking forward?" Jarthan said to her and Teigye.

"Two shakes of the reins, like so," Shyvoan demonstrated the motion in the air.

Jarthan copied her motion and after a moment the tarandeer walked forward a few skittish steps. It looked back at Jarthan several times.

"Pull back on the reins to stop," Teigye added.

After a few more steps Jarthan did so and the tarandeer stopped. It turned its head, with a sidelong look for him, but otherwise did not move. Jarthan swung his leg over its neck and slid the short distance to the ground. He looked at Shyvoan and Teigye. "Your turns."

He helped them practice mounting and dismounting several times. Then he helped Leader Finnschld and Troop-Lead Meara try it a few times when they joined them.

Shyvoan glanced at the others and saw Devrand taking them through the same steps. *Looks like he's a good teacher. Wouldn't have expected that.*

Jarthan mounted his tarandeer again. Next, he had Shyvoan and Teigye mount their own and practice signaling the tarandeer to walk and to stop after a few steps. He did the same with his own.

"To turn, what signals do you give them when they pull the tent-wagons?" Jarthan said after they had repeated the motions several times.

"A tug on the rein that's on the side you want them to turn toward," Shyvoan said.

Jarthan followed her directions and guided his tarandeer around the cleared area. It still acted skittish but followed the signals. He stopped in front of Shyvoan and Teigye and gave them a nod.

Follow my lead," he told them. He led them around the cleared area as they practiced walking forward, turning both directions and stopping. Devrand, Buok and Liphye joined them after a few minutes.

The tarandeer grew less skittish as they repeated the same actions but still seemed less than pleased with the new arrangement.

Liphye grinned at Shyvoan. "Who'd have thought it? Riding tarandeer!"

Shyvoan grinned back.

After close to an hour of this, Devrand and Jarthan had them all dismount. When Liphye slid to the ground, she groaned.

"Ugh, my legs."

Shyvoan discovered what she meant when she also dismounted. Pain shot down the outside of her legs, through her inner thighs, and settled in her hips to make it hard to walk. Her stitches even ached. *Have to remember to have the menders remove them soon.* Leader Finnschld and Troop-Lead Meara joined them and spoke briefly with each person. They spoke with Shyvoan last.

"What's your assessment?" the Leader said to her.

"It's possible," Shyvoan said. "It could work in areas we don't have to worry that low branches will knock us off. The tarandeer *do* walk faster than we do." She winced as pain again shot down the sides of her legs. "It'll take some work to get used to, though. And to get the tarandeer settled with the idea. How much time would we want to give it?"

"Not much. I want you on your way as soon as we get the last tent-wagon across to the new island. So, it's going to be something to work at on your journey."

Shyvoan nodded her acknowledgement.

After Leader Finnschld left, Troop-Lead Meara leaned close. "I'll take care of getting all your tent-wagons across and settled in the new lodgment. Don't worry about any of that. Make sure you have plenty of weapons."

With that cheerful caution, she headed off after the Leader.

CHAPTER 18

The next day the new Elders Council and Leader Finnschld pushed the pace to get the last of the people and tent-wagons across to the new island. Per the Leader's instructions, however, Shyvoan and her squad-mates spent their time preparing for their own journey back to site of the lodgment on the current island. Their preparations included more practice riding the tarandeer, and Shyvoan visited the menders to have them remove her stitches, a process that made her twitchy with the sensation of the thread pulling from her skin.

At the last minute, Leader Finnschld decided they should take the strongest of the mages with them, rather than one of their own troop mages, so Aivean Saivschld joined them, with her own tarandeer supplied by Troop-Lead Meara. A slight woman with light-brown eyes, pale brown hair, and skin several shades lighter than Liphye's but not as light as Shyvoan's, Aivean almost always wore a brimmed hat everywhere she went – uncommon attire for a mage who worked with the warriors. She was a few years older than Shyvoan.

The mage eyed the tarandeer that Meara brought for her with a troubled expression before Devrand took her aside to give her the basic knowledge and some practice riding.

Still aching from the unaccustomed riding, the group was ready to go when the evening's low tide came. They saw the last of the tent-wagons off across the water before they turned back west.

They rode for more than an hour to put some distance between them and the encampment site. At the same time, they used the ride to test how well riding through the forest worked before they stopped for the night. After she set the ward-rings around their small camp, Aivean brought out a jar of liniment from the herbalists to help ease everyone's pains from riding.

After that, with too many trees that grew too close together and low-hanging branches that threatened to sweep them from the tarandeer, they chose to walk more than ride. Even walking most of the time, and taking extra time and care to mitigate the hazards of riding in the trees when they did ride, the group came to the site of the lodgment in less than half the time it had taken to cover the distance with the tent-wagons.

Shyvoan stayed with Devrand, Jarthan, and Aivean, and the tarandeer—the others' and their extra pack tarandeer—while the others scouted around the large open area. When they returned with news of no sign of Maheaja-Folk, the group decided to make their camp on the far side of the cleared area that had held the lodgment.

They set up camp and entered the cleared area to try to figure out how to make the connection work. Shyvoan brought the pack of herbs and scrolls to the center of what had been the lodgment.

Aivean, Devrand and Jarthan paced the area and talked about magic while Shyvoan dug in the pack and pulled out a few packets of herbs.

Liphye and Teigye sat with her and together they

examined the packets, and the scroll from Rashean, when Shyvoan pulled that out, too. Buok hovered nearby and observed their activity while he also kept watch of the area in general.

"What are these little squiggles?" Liphye pointed to them on the scroll from Rashean.

Teigye held out one packet of herbs. "Maybe this." He pointed to a small mark on the corner of the packet he held, a small squiggle.

Shyvoan and Liphye leaned close to examine it, then looked at the scroll.

"Here." Shyvoan pointed to a matching squiggle that was several large blobs along the crooked line that ran from the blob they thought meant the site of the lodgment where they now sat.

"And here's this one." Liphye pointed to another squiggle and large blob further along the line and showed the matching squiggle on her packet of herbs.

They continued matching packets of herbs to the various marks on the map Rashean had drawn. After that, they lined them up from closest—what they believed to represent the current island—to furthest away, the last island along the line, which like the first had only one connecting line.

Devrand, Jarthan and Aivean joined them as they finished lining up the packets.

"So, we know which herbs go with which old lodgments." Shyvoan pulled the last herb packet from the pack. Her fingertips brushed something different in the bottom and she pulled it out, too.

Another scroll, not very big. She placed the last packet in its spot in the line before she unrolled the scroll. She recognized the squiggles from the herb packets and map, but nothing else on the scroll.

Aivean's eyes widened when she caught sight of the scroll. "Oh, I didn't know Rashean knew that!"

"Knew what?" Liphye said.

"A quick way to write notes," Aivean said. "I'd thought that only mages use it, but she's not a mage. Interesting."

Shyvoan handed her the scroll and they all watched her study it.

She seemed surprised to be the center of attention when she looked up after long minutes of reading, and her cheeks turned pink.

"Uh, I think I see how this is supposed to work," she said.

"So, we can travel from here to the previous lodgment using this connection idea rather than walking or riding the whole distance? And without having to wade through the water, too," Teigye said.

Aivean nodded. "I think so. Let me ponder this some more and reread the scroll. But yah, I think so." She headed back toward their camp.

After he exchanged bemused looks with the rest of the group, Buok followed Aivean while the others helped Shyvoan return the packets and scrolls to their pack. She placed the packets in the pack in an order that had those for the closest of the old lodgments at the top. Then she and the others returned to their camp.

Early the next morning—another cloudy day—after everyone packed to travel, Aivean led them to the westernmost edge of what had been the lodgment. She found a spot at the edge of the cleared area where two trees grew tall and close together, so close that only one of them at a time, as they rode or led their tarandeer, could pass between them.

"I believe this'll work," Aivean said. "May I have that first packet of herbs?"

Shyvoan handed it to her and stepped back a couple of steps.

"You've figured out how to connect to the previous lodgment?" Liphye said.

Aivean nodded. "At least, I think so." She opened the packet, dumped a little of its contents into her hand, and spread out the bits of herbs with a finger. "Look here. This flower when in full bloom looks much like that 'squiggle' on the map next to the island before this one." She pointed to some purplish bits of petals. "It grew all over the place back at that lodgment. But not so much here."

She pointed to the green leaf bits. "These are more common here, but not so much back there."

"Now let's see if I've understood correctly." She turned toward the two trees and crushed the herbs further in her hands. She blew the herbs from her hands between the two trees and sang the sonant magic with a string of soft, low tones.

The herb dust floated between the two trees and shimmered in the gloomy light. Then it drifted to the ground.

Aivean's expression fell.

"What went wrong?" Teigye said.

Aivean turned to look at them, her shoulders slumped. "I can't do it. The gateway should have held, but I don't have enough magic." She brushed loose tendrils of her hair out of her eyes and tucked them under the edge of her hat. She looked ready to cry.

Jarthan elbowed Devrand in an uncharacteristic move and nodded in Aivean's direction. Devrand scowled at his cousin, but the expression vanished a moment later.

"I can help with that," Devrand said, his tone odd.

Shyvoan peered at him. *Odd that he sounds resigned and bitter. Wonder why?*

Aivean glanced over her shoulder at Devrand and gave him a wide smile. "Yah, I welcome your help."

Devrand stepped up to her side and placed one hand on her shoulder. Shyvoan noticed he positioned his fingers so he touched her skin at the edge of her collar. She recalled his touch on her own face and the sensations from that touch. *His magic must require touch of skin to skin.*

Aivean repeated her actions after she got a nod from Devrand.

This time when the herb dust floated between the two trees and shimmered, it hung suspended there as Aivean sang. The shimmer faded and the dust turned opaque. Shyvoan no longer saw anything between the trees; it looked like fog hung there and blocked the view.

Bit by bit, the shimmer reappeared and brought with it the sight of another place between the trees.

"That does look like the lodgment area before this one," Liphye said as she peered into the shimmering dust.

Devrand turned away from Aivean and gestured Jarthan closer. "We should go," he said. He took the reins of his tarandeer from his cousin. "No telling how long the gateway will stay open."

He led his tarandeer between the trees, Jarthan and his tarandeer right on their heels.

The rest of the group could now see them in that other place. Devrand beckoned them forward, his motion urgent. One by one the rest of the group led their tarandeer through the opening.

Shyvoan went through last. When she passed between the trees, a strange tingling trickled across her skin as the dust touched it. The next step, she walked on the grass of their previous lodgment on a different island.

A wave of fatigue crashed over her, and she struggled to stay standing. The others struggled also, even the tarandeer.

"We're fine," Teigye answered her unspoken question when their gazes met. "Just wearied."

Aivean nodded. "The gateway magic must draw from each person who goes thr—"

"We need to close it," Jarthan shouted.

Exhaustion forgotten for the moment, Shyvoan whipped around and saw two hobs approaching the gateway from the other island.

Aivean scrambled to the gateway, Devrand right with her. He clasped her hand as she faced the two trees that framed the gateway on this side, too. She sang a soft, wordless song, different from the one to open the gateway, and made a throwing motion toward the dust shimmer before she blew hard into it.

The dust wavered and the group saw the hobs rush toward them. Then the dust flew away from where it had hovered, dissipated into the air, and all that could be seen between the two trees was more of this island's old lodgment area on the other side of them.

Aivean dropped and Devrand half-caught her before they both sank to the ground.

The others scrambled to them, but Aivean's eyes already fluttered open again. She smiled at Devrand, then her expression turned somber.

"It takes a lot, it seems," she said, her voice low and soft with fatigue.

"We should find a better place than this and set up camp," Buok said.

When no one argued, they moved a short distance away, out of a direct line to the gap between the trees in case the Maheaja-Folk could open the gateway.

Fighting their exhaustion, they set up a concealed camp and Aivean managed to set the ward-rings before she collapsed into a deep sleep. Devrand was not far behind her, and the others rested, too, but remained on guard in case the magic somehow drew the Maheaja-Folk of this island.

After an hour or so, Shyvoan's lethargy eased enough that she felt more herself again. When she saw that Jarthan was awake, she shifted to a spot next to him.

"He can enhance someone's magic somehow?" she said in a soft voice to keep the words just between the two of them.

Jarthan glanced at her and gave a slight nod.

"What else can he do?" Shyvoan said.

"I think you know," he said, with a sorrowful expression.

Shyvoan frowned but nodded. "Is that his hold on you?

He's drawn something from you?. Or enhanced some bond you have?"

"Something like tha—" Jarthan broke off as Devrand stirred and rolled over. Devrand glanced at Jarthan, then gave Shyvoan that bland look.

She returned his look, and he flashed her a quick smile. Shyvoan got the impression that he was delighted by something. The next moment, the smile slipped away.

"I've a feeling that we can expect this for every gateway we travel," Devrand said and waved a hand at the group in general.

"Still far faster than if we walked and rode the whole distance," Buok commented.

"Just getting across each island to the next would take days alone for many, if not most of them," Liphye said. "And with the number of islands we'll likely need to cross and such...." She shrugged.

"But still slower than I had hoped," Devrand said. "I don't suppose there's any place on this island that might conceal a dragon?"

"No one ever saw a dragon while we were here," Shyvoan said. "I know if someone had, the mages would have been all over it to renew their magic."

Devrand nodded. "Of course." He clambered to his feet and gestured Jarthan to join him.

"I won't cross the ward-rings," he tossed back over his shoulder as Shyvoan had been about to tell him not too.

She frowned. Does he now have some bond to me that he can know what I'm going to say?

With that uncomfortable thought stuck in her mind, she turned to setting their camp better.

Aivean slept the morning away and her motions were sluggish when she was awake in the afternoon. Devrand was little better. The others recovered faster and seemed almost back to normal by evening.

The next morning, Shyvoan felt even better and judging from the way the others moved, they seemed to also. Some sluggishness lingered, though.

When Aivean woke, she looked around with an expression of confusion for a few minutes before her expression cleared. She met Shyvoan's gaze with a slight smile.

"Are you up to doing the next gateway this morning?" Shyvoan said to her.

Aivean frowned. "I believe so. I feel a little strange, still, but think I can do it. Especially if Devrand helps again." She shot him a smile, which he returned.

"Certainly," he said.

As she had done before, Aivean selected two trees that grew close together toward the western edge of the area that had been the lodgment. Shyvoan pulled out the herb packet with the squiggle that matched that for the next island on the map and handed it to the mage. Aivean pulled out a pinch of the herbs, returned the packet and did as she had before: blowing the herbs between the trees and singing. But this time, Devrand stood with her right from the start, with his fingertips resting against the skin of her shoulder near her neck.

The gateway formed and they again stepped through. Right after the last of them passed through the gate, Aivean closed it the same way she had closed the previous one.

Shyvoan expected the exhaustion this time but even so, it took its toll. *Hopefully, this won't hold true for every single gateway.* Or they might find themselves unable to move at all after they managed to get through that last gate.

CHAPTER 19

After their fifth trip through a gateway, they decided to spend an extra day at the old lodgment sites, hoping that would help with the exhaustion. The next few gateways that they traveled in this pattern their hopes seemed fulfilled. At least both Aivean and Devrand said it made a difference.

Shyvoan was not as certain. She seemed to always carry with her a lack of energy. But that could also be the anxiety that had never left her. She had hoped it would vanish when they found that the gateways worked, but instead it lingered and ate away at her.

She took to pacing endless hours around their camps, supposedly on watch—which she was—but also trying to work off the tension that dug its claws into her.

Their tenth gateway, their fifteenth day on this odd journey, brought them to their first island that was not mostly forested. The trees that had served as their latest gateway stood in an isolated small clump of trees several minutes' walk from the old lodgment.

From the area that had held the lodgment, they saw

several other clumps of trees, but this island looked to be largely covered in knee-high grasses.

"Doubled watches," Shyvoan said.

The rest of the squad-mates looked at their surroundings and all nodded.

They headed across the large open area that had held the lodgment to another clump of trees to the west and made their camp there.

Buok set off to hunt for some of the rodents that used to live in the area. When they had lived there years previously, the people had regularly hunted the robust-bodied, short-limbed, long-tailed animals for food. Shyvoan left her tarandeer in the camp and set off to scout their surroundings. She warned the others not to expect her back for several hours as she wanted to take a good look around them. What she did not tell them was that she was even more uneasy here. *But why?* If a reason other than each trip taking them closer to a dragon was the culprit, she planned to find it.

She stayed alert as she explored, but made little attempt to blend in. Her leathers were more suited for the shadows and tree trunks than meadows of autumn-tan grasses.

She startled a couple of rodents on her walk. That should bode well for Buok's chances. But she heard no birds. *Odd.*

Here and there she spotted some plants that might be vesnaflurs. The leaves, at least, looked sort of the right shape. The plants were not numerous and none of them grew close enough to each other to line any sort of path.

Shyvoan stopped at the edge of another small clump of trees to look and listen. Of course, her passage could have startled the birds silent, but after she had held her position long enough for them to sound again, none did.

She would have been around fifteen years of age when the people lived on this island. She *did* somewhat remember the area, although at that time she had been far more interested in her weapons training, and the boys near her age. She had not studied scouting until the next year or so, when they had already been on another island, one with many more trees.

This island seemed too quiet. While the air had become cooler as they moved more into autumn, she would have expected to hear bugs in the grasses, warmed as they were by the sun. And the birds, of course.

Shyvoan stayed there another half hour and watched and listened. Still no sounds of birds or insects. The longer she held still, the more certain she became that something differed somehow. The normal smells of warm grasses and trees seemed muted. The colors, too, seemed less vibrant than in her memory.

Scoffing at herself, she continued her circuit. *Perhaps memory just painted everything stronger.*

Her steps took her toward the southern shoreline, where the tall grasses gave way to coarse sand. Nothing like the rocky shoreline of her most recent home island.

She crouched in the grasses and looked across the beach and out into the water. No sea birds hovered along the shore, although a few crabs scuttled across the sand.

The water nearby looked deeper than that which circled her last home island. Slight waves shifted some floating seaweed.

An out-of-place shape far out on the sea caught her attention. To the southeast, a shadow darkened the water at the horizon.

Shyvoan squinted in the reflected sunlight and watched for close to a half hour, then cursed when she was certain.

She finished her circuit, faster than she had originally intended. *Have to get back to the camp with the news.*

She arrived back at camp more winded than she would have liked. The fatigue still plagued her, clearly, and drew on her.

Startled looks greeted her. She smiled, glad to see that Buok had returned. He and Liphye sat off to one side of the camp while they cleaned several rodents.

"Did you know your *Deliberia* follows us?" Shyvoan demanded of Devrand.

She caught a quick flash of a pleased expression on Jarthan's face, then Devrand scowled at him, and he dropped his head.

"Did I know?" Devrand placed emphasis on the last word. "No, not *know*. Expect? Well, yes. She *is* hunting us, as I believe I've mentioned."

Shyvoan stalked over to him. "Yah, you did mention that. So how does she hunt you through magical gateways and across water that holds no tracks?"

"If I knew how she followed me, don't you think I'd have done something to hamper it?" Devrand's glare was all for Shyvoan. But beneath his bravado, she glimpsed a hint of worry.

"Did it look like she was trying to come ashore?" Jarthan said and ignored the glare Devrand turned on him. *Was that a hopeful note in his voice?*

She shook her head. "Not that I saw in the time I watched the ship. It seemed to be sailing west, but no closer to the shore, to us."

"Could your hunter know where we hope to go?" Liphye said.

Devrand shrugged, his expression troubled. "I don't see how."

"If you have something connected to the ship or your hunter, I could see if I can learn something," Aivean suggested. "I've got a good feel now for these connections that Rashean introduced us to."

"Yes!" Jarthan said.

"No," Devrand overrode him and gripped his arm.

The two men glared at each other, and something went out of Jarthan. Shyvoan could not be certain, but it looked like his illness, whatever it was, suddenly flared and he wilted. Devrand caught him and took him to their piled bedding where he settled him under a blanket.

Shyvoan and her squad-mates drew aside, while Aivean

joined Devrand and fussed over the two men.

"What was that?" Teigye whispered.

"I'm not sure," Shyvoan whispered back. "Devrand's got some hold on his cousin. I suspect using his magic somehow."

"From the looks of that, I suspect he's the cause of Jarthan's illness." Buok nodded his head toward the two men and kept his voice low.

"What can we do about it?" Liphye said. "Looks like he's got our only mage enamored with him."

They all glanced at the others, to see Aivean wrap her arms around Devrand. She appeared to be comforting him in his apparent concern over his cousin.

"Wonder if they're even really cousins," Teigye muttered.

"Maybe once we reach the dragons, learn how to renew magic from them, we can do something," Liphye said.

She grinned at the skeptical looks and shrugged. "It could happen. Maybe all of us could get magic from a dragon."

Teigye grinned back at her. "I can just see that. Me as a mage."

The others chuckled and separated to take care of all the duties around the camp.

That night, after they finished the evening meal, Buok sought out Shyvoan.

"Walk with me," he said, his voice not much above a whisper.

They paced to the edge of the ward-rings Aivean had set and stared out into the darkness.

"Have you felt it?" Buok said.

Shyvoan gave him a sidelong look. "Possibly. Depending on what you're talking about."

He gave a curt nod. "A number of things. Certainly, the lack of birds…."

"I haven't heard any insects, either. It's early enough in the fall that we should still hear some."

He nodded again. "And everything feels off somehow. I'm not sure how to describe it."

"The colors seem duller than I remember," Shyvoan said.

"I thought so, too. And I can't feel completely rested. There's always a crumb of fatigue that won't go away."

This time Shyvoan nodded. "Any ideas?"

"Something the Maheaja-Folk have done, or are doing, I'd say."

"Makes sense. Humans haven't been here for years. Do they change an area to suit them better?"

Buok shrugged. "Never much studied them for anything like that."

"And as far as I know, we're the first people to ever go back to where we lived before. To venture back into the lands the Maheaja-Folk again have sole claim to," Shyvoan said.

"Yah, the first I've heard of, too."

Shyvoan sighed. "This journey feels too long already, and we've not reached the halfway point yet. Maybe we can learn more of the Maheaja-Folk, though."

Buok nodded. "I've got first watch. With Liphye and Aivean. I'll start here, for now. Get some sleep, if you can."

With another nod, Shyvoan returned to the camp to rest before her turn at watch. Devrand had insisted on joining the watches, so he would share her watch. But at least Teigye would too. She found Devrand's regard increasingly disquieting the longer they traveled. Unlike Aivean, whose interest in him was clear. His interest in the mage, though, seemed casual at best.

The next day was much like the previous, except for any gateway traveling. Midmorning, Devrand and Aivean took themselves off, to see the shore they told everyone else. The rest exchanged knowing looks. Aivean certainly had more in mind than just a look at the water.

Jarthan stayed in the camp but responded to any

attempts to talk with only grunts. So, the others let him be and just made sure he had food and water near where he lay wrapped in blankets.

Buok and Shyvoan shared their concerns with the others and found they had noticed much the same thing. Liphye and Teigye headed to the north to try to get more rodents and look for anything more to learn of the Maheaja-Folk.

Shyvoan stayed in the camp while Buok decided to scout around the area again. With only herself and Jarthan there, maybe she could get him to talk.

With little trouble, she managed first to get him to eat and drink. He looked awful, pale and ill, as Devrand had claimed.

She leaned close while he nibbled at the food. "Anything you can tell us about your cousin would help," she murmured. "And how can we help you?"

He shook his head. "He's not my cousin," he whispered.

Shyvoan scrutinized his face. "Then what's the hold he has on you? Tell us how to help."

"You need to stay out of what's between us." He leaned close, with an urgent look for her. "Your best choice is to get us away as soon as he can make the passage. You don't want us staying with your people."

He turned away and would not respond to any further attempts at conversation.

After that, Shyvoan spent her time pacing the ward-ring while she watched for anything untoward. She paid little attention to Jarthan, except to notice that he seemed to have fallen asleep. *Surely, that would help him.*

Buok returned before any of the others and reported nothing of any concern. He brought a couple of rodents with him and cleaned them while Shyvoan rested again. Before too long, Liphye and Teigye also returned, followed by Devrand and Aivean. Teigye and Liphye brought back more rodents and some tubers they had found so the evening meal featured a delicious meat stew.

Again, they set watches of three people each for the night, but nothing disturbed them. In the morning, Aivean and Devrand opened the next gateway.

After she stepped through, Shyvoan stopped and stared. There seemed to be no color and little light there. Could they have somehow stepped from day into night? It looked that way.

She blinked then, and the place looked normal. Or as normal as everything had been looking. The colors still looked dulled, and the light seemed dimmer than it should have been. She moved out of the way to give Devrand and Aivean room to follow her through the gateway and close it behind them.

Shyvoan met Buok's glance with a questioning look and he nodded. He led the small group through the densest forest Shyvoan had ever seen to a depression filled with smaller trees than those they had just traveled through.

"This was the lodgment site when we lived here," he told them.

"How can that be?" Teigye said. "I don't remember a forest here. Seems like I ought to remember *this*." He waved a hand at the tall trees that surrounded them, with questioning looks for Liphye, Shyvoan and Aivean. They all shook their heads.

"True, that," Buok said. "It wasn't like this when we lived here."

"We suspect the Maheaja-Folk have changed the places we left behind. Beyond what would have happened with the plants and animals moving back in," Shyvoan said.

"Why haven't we seen any of them. Your Maheaja-Folk?" Devrand said. "I would've thought we'd encounter them on this journey. Certainly, if we hope to meet the dragons."

Shyvoan pulled her pack off her tarandeer to begin setting up camp. The others followed her example.

"Agreed," she said while she worked. "It's odd that we've not encountered even one of the Maheaja-Folk."

"It's also odd how the islands have changed," Liphye added. "Has anyone else noticed the smell?"

Shyvoan paused to pay attention to the air. She *had* noticed the odor but had discounted it. The air smelled odd, and scratched her throat when she breathed in.

"They might be changing the places to be unappealing to us," Devrand said. "Or perhaps harmful."

Shyvoan frowned. "Great. At this rate, are we going to be able to make it to the end of Rashean's map then, before we enter an area we can't survive?"

"As opposed to surviving dragons," Teigye muttered, but then grinned at Shyvoan.

"Can we somehow speed up our journey?" Liphye said as she worked on a small fire pit. "Maybe go through gateways more often again? Or skip ahead somehow?"

Aivean dropped some twigs and branches she had gathered nearby and frowned. "I don't know. I feel tired all the time, which makes the magic hard to do. Even with Devrand's help." She gave him a brilliant smile at that.

"Would using more of those herbs at a time make a difference?" Liphye said. "Strengthen the magic some?"

Aivean shrugged. "I'm not sure. Let me think on it."

They finished the camp setup and separated to hunt and scout. Devrand teamed up with Shyvoan to look around.

"Want to see if the ship's there again," he told her and led the way south.

"You really believe it could arrive as fast as we do with the gateway?" Shyvoan said as she caught up to him.

He shrugged. "No telling where she's involved. She's quite determined."

"And why is that?" Shyvoan demanded. "And what's the hold you have on Jarthan. Who's not your cousin."

Devrand stopped and eyed her. "I see Jarthan's been speaking out of turn. Can't have that." Before she could react, he clasped her hand.

"You don't need to worry about such things," he told her and rubbed his thumb across the back of her hand in a soothing motion. His voice deepened and its calming tones washed over her. "We'll find the dragon and get the magic to make a passage to travel away."

Something had been on her mind…. But she didn't need to worry about it.

"That's right," he said. "I'll take care of Jarthan, as I have been, so you needn't worry about him either."

"Of course," she murmured.

"Now we need to see if that ship might have arrived." He brushed a hand across her cheek before he led the way again.

Shyvoan stood there in the dense forest a few minutes longer. Something had changed, but what? And what was that scent of burnt wood?

She shrugged to herself. When they got to the dragons, got the magic to make the passage, no doubt everything would become clear.

CHAPTER 20

After a day's rest, Aivean used more of the herbs for the next gateway first thing after the morning meal and reported afterward that it did make a difference. She rested most of that day and managed to open the next gateway that evening, again using more of the herbs from the gateway's packet. To allow her the most rest possible, the others covered watches, so she did not have to stand one. The next morning, she was able to open the next gateway.

They journeyed this way through the next ten gateways before Aivean clearly needed a longer rest, as did most of the others. Jarthan looked especially haggard. But Devrand looked little worse off than when they had started, although he did show signs of some fatigue.

The strangeness of the lands they visited for so short a time as they journeyed from one gate site to the next stayed much the same as when they first noticed it. The colors became duller, more washed out, and the light dimmer, but not so much as to cause them much concern. Yet anyway.

The air, too, stayed much the same. The odd odor grew

stronger and Shyvoan could taste it, too. But it seemed to offer no harm to them.

They set up their camp more extensively than they had been and sought out a nearby stream to clean clothes and themselves. A heavy forest blanketed this island, much as they had seen on most of the recent islands.

Although warmer than it should have been for the time of year, nothing unusual about the water otherwise caught Shyvoan's attention. Still, they boiled some to drink, to be cautious.

They all took turns to rest and clean up, and spent several hours at these tasks. After she had watched for an hour or so and cleaned up, Shyvoan stretched out atop her bedding. The air was cool, but still warmer than they would normally have for autumn.

Hope we can keep to this pace: two gateways each day, with sometimes the extra day for rest, like this day. Assuming she had counted correctly, this island numbered twenty-four in their journey, not counting the island they had started from. So, they were somewhere around twenty-four years into their past, at least regarding the lodgments. She would have been a couple years old when the people lived here.

Shyvoan did not fall asleep but did feel better after a few hours of rest and thought. After she rested enough, she paced around their small camp and scrutinized their surroundings. She saw no sign that the lodgment had ever been there, yet Buok assured her it had.

The trees looked strange; unlike any she had seen before. Thin dark trunks that grew in clusters, with the first branches far above her reach. Many of their leaves had fallen, with the rest colored a deep red-brown, so she could not guess what they looked like in spring and summer. The leaves were small, about the length of her longest finger, and oval. Although the damp air clung to everything, the leaves on the ground crunched underfoot.

With a hand signal to Liphye, who was on watch, that she was going to scout around, Shyvoan headed into the surrounding trees, aiming for the southern shore. As she passed them, she checked on their tarandeer. The animals seemed dissatisfied with the plants available to eat, but still nibbled at them.

She stopped and looked closer. *Yah, the tarandeer are a bit thinner than when we started out.* Too late now, but maybe they should have left them behind after they had crossed the island back to where they made the first gateway.

She sighed. Although they had traveled far, they still had far to go. The anxiety continued to nag at her, made all the worse in that nothing particularly bad had happened. Only faded colors, warm water, and strange-tasting air.

At least Shyvoan heard some birds on this island. Not many, and she did not recognize their calls. But it was better than those islands silent of birdcalls.

Perhaps half an hour after she left the camp, Shyvoan came to an area of brush rather than the trees. She paused to study it. The branches were almost bare of leaves, with myriads of small barbs on them. The bushes grew close together. *Trying to make a path through won't be pleasant, even wearing good leathers.*

Clouds had gathered but did not look like the type to threaten rain. Shyvoan turned east to follow the line of brush a while and looked for a way through.

After an hour of this, as she started back, she spotted a narrow path that led into the brush. With the bushes reaching the top of her head , her visibility would be limited.

She fixed her buckler on her arm, drew her sword, and edged along the path.

It wound back and forth several times but headed the general direction she wanted. After several minutes of this, she heard rustlings to either side, then behind her.

She whirled around and discovered the branches moving, closing in the path behind her. That quickly, the path out of the bushes vanished.

She turned again and found her path ahead still open.

Alert and uneasy, she continued and did not look back again at more rustlings. *Probably just more branches closing the way behind.*

She continued this way another quarter of an hour before she abruptly stepped out of the brush onto a narrow beach of gray-green sand.

On the sand, not two paces in front of her, stood one of the unicorns.

She raised her sword but paused when it spoke.

"Wait."

She crouched in preparation, although whether to attack or run, she had not decided. "What?"

"Bide a moment," it said. It formed the words with an odd accent, but Shyvoan understood it, and its voice sounded masculine.

"You can speak our language?"

It—he shook his head. "But you can understand me. Here. The air."

"Oh."

"You should not be here. All your kind are supposed to have been driven to the east. And are forfeit."

Shyvoan shook her head. "Why?"

"It's been decided. Either you or us. They decided us and so you are driven. And eliminated."

"Can you tell me where I can find a dragon? Then I'll be happy to go away."

The unicorn half-reared and backed away from her, upset clear on his goat-like face. "No! You must not. Not again."

Then he charged across the sand, headed east.

Shyvoan watched until he moved out of sight and chided herself for letting him capture her whole attention. Still, nothing else was there. The sand stretched to the water of the Shallow Sea, unbroken by rocks or any sea creatures like crabs.

The sea itself stretched to the horizon, also unbroken.

Maybe they had lost the pursuing ship. *Hope so.*

Her journey back to the camp was long and arduous. After she found no path back through the brush, she cut her way through. While her dragon-scale blade sliced through the branches with no difficulty, they grew back at an alarming rate. She all but ran and hacked her way to get through the brush back to the forest.

Hot and tired, scratched and grumpy, Shyvoan limped into camp. Before she answered any of the questioning looks that greeted her, she headed to the stream to clean up again.

When she had finished and returned to where the others gathered, she felt much better, although still confused by the encounter with the unicorn. She shared what had happened with the others over their evening meal.

They tried to guess why the unicorn had warned them off and what the 'not again' meant as it related to dragons. But no one proposed any idea that anyone considered at all probable. They did set double watches for the night. If one of the Maheaja-Folk knew they were on the island, more might be close behind.

While rustlings and sounds of nocturnal animals disturbed the night, nothing approached their camp. By mutual agreement, though, they packed the next morning and moved to the western edge of what had been the lodgment site. When Aivean created the gateway, Devrand stood with one hand touching her, as usual, and the other clasped around Jarthan's wrist.

Shyvoan exchanged looks with her fellow warriors and stepped forward to object, but Jarthan met her gaze, with a slight shake of his head. She frowned but did not interfere. She caught a quick, triumphant look from Devrand, which vanished the next instant.

Then the gateway formed and Aivean urged them all to hurry so she wouldn't have to hold it for long.

After everyone passed through and she closed the gateway, she sank to her knees, eyes closed.

"We'll camp here," Buok said and began setting up a quick camp off to the side, away from the direct path of the gateway. After Teigye had a small fire going, Devrand brought over some herbs from Aivean to heat in water.

"She said these will help," he told everyone. "But if we can now manage a longer rest, it would be a good idea."

He took the hot drink to Aivean, acting attentive and concerned for her while he ignored Jarthan, who huddled nearby.

Shyvoan grabbed a blanket—the air was much colder than the previous island—and draped it over Jarthan's shoulders. With a half-smile for her, he pulled it close.

For the first time on their journey, they raised the tents they had brought. The cold seemed to warrant it. Two of the tents were each large enough for two people to sleep within, if they didn't mind close quarters. The third could hold three, likewise in close quarters. Shyvoan, Liphye and Aivean took the largest one. Devrand and Jarthan took one of the others, leaving the last one for Buok and Teigye, who bantered good-naturedly about who snored the loudest as they got their gear settled within.

Everyone changed into heavier clothing and heavy cloaks and gathered near the fire. Buok pulled out a thick stick and a small knife and began carving something out of the wood. Liphye pulled out some wooden dice and, when none of the others acted interested, played a dice game against herself.

No one seemed much inclined to talk, so they otherwise huddled there while Aivean drank a second cup of her herb mix, and made Jarthan drink a cup, too.

"I'm afraid I'll not be up to making the next gateway for a while," Aivean said after she finished her drink. "Perhaps as early as tomorrow evening. I'll need to see how I am tomorrow."

"Let us know how we can help, if we can," Liphye told her.

Aivean nodded. "My thanks. I think I'll go get some

more sleep right now." She gave Devrand a sharp look. "Jarthan should too."

With a slight nod for Aivean, Devrand helped Jarthan to his feet and to their tent. Aivean retreated to the tent she would share with Liphye and Shyvoan, which left the four warriors gathered at the fire. Buok reached out to his pack nearby and pulled out a skin of kuchal.

"I feel a need for a swallow or two," he said. "Anyone else?"

After they had shared the skin around a couple of times, he set it aside again.

"I was just adding it up," Teigye said, "and we've still only managed to travel a gateway a day, even with those days of doing two."

"Are we in a particular hurry?" Liphye said.

She received shrugs from the others.

"I have a sense that we ought to get there as soon as we can," Teigye said after a few minutes of silence. "I can't say why, though. Maybe just nerves."

"Or wanting to get back to your new friend in Renan's squad," Liphye teased. "He seemed taken with you."

"Well, yah," Teigye said with a grin.

"I've also felt anxious," Buok said. "And the sense of urgency." He looked at Shyvoan. "I don't like what the unicorn said to you. Driven and eliminated."

"They've been attacking us for a long time, and we've survived," Teigye said.

"But not thrived," Buok said. "The Elders Council is all new, inexperienced. We've lost more people the last island than ever before."

"The arcasi have reappeared," Liphye said. "Those things are nasty."

"Tell me about it," Shyvoan muttered and fingered the faint scar that ran across her cheek from the arcasi's feather.

"I believe they *do* mean to get rid of the people," Buok said. "One way or another."

"Seems like this passage that Devrand says he can do could be our people's best chance," Teigye muttered.

"So, we *do* have some urgency to this," Shyvoan said. "True urgency, not just a vague sense of it. Anyone know any of those herbs that our troop mages used to help them keep going when their reserves got low?"

"Wasn't that what Aivean was drinking earlier?" Buok said.

"No, that smelled different from what I remember our troop mages drinking," Liphye said. "But much the same effect, I think."

"While I'm no herbalist, just a mender-in-training," Teigye said, "still, I can look around while out scouting. Maybe we'll get lucky and find some that will sustain her."

Shyvoan nodded. "We can hope. Can you describe what we might look for? Maybe the rest of us can keep an eye out, too."

Teigye shrugged. "There are three that I remember. Anla is a low-growing plant with clusters of white flowers. Large leaves and tiny flowers, about the size of the tip of your smallest finger." He held up his finger to demonstrate.

"The second, heagyn, is a thin vine that likes to cling to the evergreen trees. Its flowers are a light green, lighter than the leaves. Each flower has many tiny petals and overall is about as wide as your thumb is long. The flowers for both of those plants can be seen even this late in the season, although they'll probably be shriveled. The shriveled flowers are fine, though, and it's the flowers we'd want. The herbalists would dry them anyway, and this way they're already at least partway there."

He looked from one to another of them, his gaze questioning, but no one had anything to say.

With a slight nod, he continued. "The last plant, rastenye, is another low-growing plant. It's got oddly shaped leaves, almost triangular. No flowers. We'll want leaves from that one."

They all agreed that they would try to find some, too, and separated to see to the various camp, scouting, and watch duties.

Shyvoan looked in on Aivean, who slept peacefully. Then she headed to the next tent to check on Jarthan.

As she reached for the tent flap, Devrand flipped it to the side and clambered out. He pulled it closed behind him.

"I'm sure he'd appreciate your concern," he told her. "He's asleep. And likely to be that way for a time."

"You're drawing something from him, aren't you?" Shyvoan accused. "To help with the magic for the gateways."

He studied her and brushed a finger across the back of her hand. "So very persistent," he said. "I could wish that interest was for me."

Shyvoan backed away and shook her head against a fogginess that swept over her. "I…. What about Aivean?"

He shrugged. "What of her? We haven't committed to each other, made any promises or anything like that. Haven't you just been with someone you desired, only for the pleasure? No obligation?" He gave her a long, slow look from head to toe.

Shyvoan stared at him as she fought to clear the haze from her thoughts. This was *not* what she had come to talk about. But then she nodded. It was true, she had.

He stepped close and looked into her eyes, his beautiful, exotic blue-green eyes filling her vision. "Why keep prodding at me, then?" he said in a whisper. "Do you really wish to be at odds with me? When we could accomplish so much together. And have a magnificent time…."

Shyvoan stepped away and shook her head again. "I don't know how you do that," she muttered, "but stop. I know we need you if we're to get our people to a lasting safety. Otherwise, leave me be. I already told you not to try any more of that enamoring on me. And I'll work to see you don't take over anyone else, either."

He stepped back too. "If you wish," he said. "No more enamoring."

"And what of Jarthan?" Shyvoan said. "He should be able to speak for himself, should be free of you if he wants."

Devrand's smile took on a nasty edge. "Jarthan is not your concern. He goes with me, stays with me, and will be free of me only when I am done with him."

He brushed past her but looked back over a shoulder. "Just remember you *do* need me. You won't reach your precious dragons without my help. You might not want to push me too much."

Shyvoan glared after him, fists clenched, as he walked to the other edge of the camp and dug in the food packs. She hated that he was right.

~ ~ ~

The next morning, they moved their camp a couple of hours away from the first one, traveling to the north rather than toward the western edge of the former lodgment site, then settled in for the day again.

"I hope to be able to open the next gateway this night," Aivean told them. Toward that end, she rested in camp as much as she could.

Shyvoan, on the other hand, stayed away from the camp most of the day. Every time she caught Devrand's gaze he smirked at her. So, she scouted and picked leaves and flowers. Anything to help speed the time when they could be rid of him. While she foraged, she spotted some areas that looked more elevated than the rest of the land around them, but nothing like the highland areas or mountains that she expected from the scroll.

Of the various leaves and flowers that Shyvoan brought back later that afternoon, only the leaves were the right plants. Being autumn, they were at least partially dried already.

Aivean smiled in delight when she saw the leaves. "You found chathea, too!" She promptly crushed those leaves to make a tea for herself. So Shyvoan went back out to gather more—against a possibility that they might not find them on other islands—and as much as she could find of the other plants Teigye had told them about.

That evening while they ate, Shyvoan tried to speak of what has passed between her and Devrand and found that she could not. She shot a glare at him, and he smirked.

After the meal, they packed what they had unpacked for the day's camp and hiked through a forest of spindly trees back to the former lodgment site.

The gateway they had come through had been further to the east of the former lodgment than previous gateways, so they had not surveyed the site earlier. They found that area covered with sharp-bladed grass that sliced any exposed skin in reach. The grass stood tall, almost as tall as Shyvoan.

They were forced to circle the area to save themselves and the tarandeer from a multitude of cuts. They had discovered the grass cut right through tarandeer fur, so pushing a way through was not an option.

Close to midnight, they reached the far side and Aivean chose her two trees by the meager light of the moon.

While Shyvoan waited for the others to cross through the gateway she scrutinized the moon. She had the oddest sense that something was wrong with it, but she could not put her finger on it. Unable to figure it out, she crossed through the gateway last of all except for the three who held the magic for it. They followed on her heels and closed the gateway at once.

The group found themselves at the edge of another grassland area, grasses again as tall as Shyvoan. But these, at least, had no sharp edges.

They walked a quarter of an hour away from the site of the gateway and made camp, complete with tents again. As

Shyvoan crawled into her bedding she realized what had been wrong with the moon. *It's full. And it's been full every night for the past two weeks.*

After that realization, sleep was long in coming to her.

In the morning, the first topic of discussion was the moon. Shyvoan had not been the only one to notice its oddness. But they reached no conclusion about it, although Shyvoan favored Teigye's suggestion that the strange air might have altered how they saw things. She did not like that explanation, though. It created a host of new concerns. *Better just double-check everything. Likely the best to do to counter such a thing. If that's even what's going on.*

After she finished the second cup of her chathea tea, Aivean said, "I'm ready now to open the next gateway."

So, they packed the camp and made their way to the western edge of what had been the island's lodgment site. Like the previous island, this one had some areas more elevated than the rest of the land, but again nothing that could be considered mountainous.

When they reached the western edge of the former lodgment, the best Buok determined with the changed plants, they still stood in a sea of tall grasses. At least they had discovered the chathea plants for Aivean's tea growing in some of the less dense areas of grasses, so they had gathered a good supply of the leaves along the way.

Teigye tried to bend as much of the grass as he could, hoping to see further. They all agreed they glimpsed the tops of trees somewhere ahead. But at some distance.

"And that's well beyond the edge of the lodgment site, I'm sure," Buok said.

"Don't suppose you can make a gateway between blades of these grasses?" Liphye said to Aivean.

The mage frowned as she considered the grass that had gotten taller as they traveled. It now reached above the top of Buok's head, and he stood the tallest of them.

"It's probably tall enough," she said. "I doubt it's sturdy enough, though. I can see the magic of the gateway pushing sideways, and when the blades give too much, completely breaking apart."

"You're sure this is the edge of the old lodgment?" Liphye said to Buok.

"As certain as I can be," he replied.

"Could we twist the grasses together?" Teigye said. "Ought to make a stronger bundle that way."

"Are those trees too far for the gateway to work right?" Shyvoan said at the same time.

"I think they are," Aivean answered Shyvoan first. "Twisting the grasses together is worth a try," she then told Teigye. "Let's find two clumps that aren't too spread out."

Everyone poked around the area while they tried to stay close at the same time.

"Here," Jarthan called after several minutes of looking.

When everyone gathered at his location, Shyvoan saw that he had found two thick, tall clumps of grass that had a gap between them a little wider than most of the gateways they had used so far.

"Will these do?" he said when Aivean did not comment.

"We can make them work," Devrand said. "If we can make the twists sturdy enough, anyway."

Teigye set to twisting together all the grasses in one of the clumps. Aivean watched, her expression uncertain.

"I don't know," she muttered. "The space might be too wide—"

Devrand clasped her hand and the worried expression vanished. "It'll work," he told her. "I'll make certain it will."

He gave Shyvoan a determined expression followed by a smirk before he turned away.

With a frown, Shyvoan turned to twisting the second clump. With Liphye's help, they managed a column of twisted grass that stood tall, but not quite Buok's height. He shrugged at Shyvoan's concerned look.

"I can crouch to go through," he said. "We'll certainly lead the tarandeer through this time, rather than riding."

Shyvoan nodded and pushed against the grass column. It swayed, but otherwise felt sturdier than she had expected. Sturdy for grass.

Across the gap, Teigye and Buok finished the matching grass column and tested it as Shyvoan had the other one.

Devrand stood a short distance back and peered between the two, then gave a decisive nod.

"They'll do," he stated.

He and Jarthan and Aivean took their usual positions to open the gateway. Aivean grabbed a little extra of the herbs for this one, then paused.

"As soon as it's open, everyone better hurry through," she told them.

With nods all around, they held themselves ready to dash through the gateway when it formed.

After Aivean blew the herbs between the grass columns and sang the tones for the sonant magic, the gateway magic gathered. Shyvoan peered at it. The gateway seemed to be taking a long time. The strain grew on the faces of all three until the gateway finally formed.

"Go," Devrand shouted.

As usual, Shyvoan was last through before the three who held the gate. When she reached the other side, she continued at the same pace to clear the gateway and paid little attention to her surroundings.

Buok and Teigye caught her in time to keep her from going over a rocky embankment.

She gasped at the suddenness, gave them a nod of thanks, and turned aside to look back at the gateway.

"There's been a gap of time between everyone coming through," Liphye told her, "though we were right behind one another entering."

After a couple of minutes, Jarthan stumbled through and hurried out of the way of the two behind him. Liphye told him the same thing when the others did not follow right away and he looked worried. Aivean and Devrand did make it through, with the time gap between them, and Aivean immediately closed the gateway.

They turned to survey their new surroundings.

They stood at the edge of a steep embankment that sloped down close to twice Buok's height before it ended in murky water. Shyvoan could not see below the surface of the water. A thin mist hovered at its surface and swirled in a faint breeze. The air here smelled different. Again. Shyvoan sniffed. *Kind of a rotten-sweet hint to it, like rotting fruit.*

The light was dim but still brighter than the moonlit night of the previous island.

"I don't think we want to try to go through that," Aivean said.

Shyvoan eyed the water another few minutes. While the mist swirled with the slight breeze, the surface of the water remained calm. Yet it did not reflect the sky, which was a uniform light gray, like clouds covered it. Clouds that held a faint glow in their depths.

Shyvoan shuddered. "I agree."

"Around it is, then," Liphye said in a bright, cheerful tone as she mounted her tarandeer.

"And without delay, I think" Teigye said. "Seems like we shouldn't stay in this place any longer than we have to."

No one argued with that sentiment.

Both Aivean and Jarthan needed help to mount their tarandeer but seemed stable enough once there. Aivean poured some water into two cups and dropped the chathea leaves for her tea into them. She passed one to Jarthan.

"Let it soak for about a quarter hour," she told him. "It won't be as good as it is when hot, but better than nothing."

He nodded and moved his tarandeer into line in front of Devrand.

As Shyvoan moved her tarandeer into line behind Devrand's, she noticed that Devrand looked unphased and unwearied, unlike the other two who had opened the gateway with him.

Buok took the lead. "Although we're now on an island that has not held the lodgment for around twenty-seven years, I still remember enough of the area, I believe."

"Assuming it's not changed too much," Liphye said.

"True, that. Assuming so," Buok agreed.

He led them back from the edge. Shyvoan nodded slightly. *A wise move.* The edge looked unstable. Then he led them through grasses and brush on a southerly circuit around the depression.

After a couple of hours, Shyvoan spotted the gleam of the sea from time to time through taller brush around them. Another half hour and they traveled through an area higher in elevation than the shore and covered with low brush mixed with the grasses, the sea clearly visible on their left.

Are those ripples in the water? Maybe.... But every time Shyvoan peered closer, nothing was there. She loosened her sword in its sheath, though, and positioned her buckler on her arm.

She smiled grimly when she saw that her fellow warriors also prepared. At least she was not alone in her concern, which might mean she was not imagining things.

"What is it?" Aivean said in a soft voice.

"Maybe nothing," Teigye responded, his voice as low as hers had been. "Just ready in case it's not nothing."

Aivean shivered and looked back at Devrand, her expression fearful. Shyvoan could not see the expression Devrand gave the mage in return, but Aivean spun away again.

Both Jarthan and Devrand closed the space between their mounts and the others. Shyvoan stayed back at the rear, senses alert as wisps of fog began to appear.

They hurried through the treeless area and into an area of wide spaces between the trees, whose lowest branches grew far enough from the ground to let them continue to ride. None of the warriors relaxed their vigilance in the absence of any sounds of animals, birds, or insects.

The whining whistle, when it came through the fog, startled Shyvoan's tarandeer, which shied to one side. She ducked and leaned the other way as sharp feathers whooshed by her. Several of them hit her mount.

She heard a cry from Aivean but was occupied trying to get free of her falling mount. She threw herself to the side and almost managed to get clear. Her tarandeer did crash down on her left foot, and its weight pinned her there. After that, it did not move again.

She pushed at it to free herself while she tried to look around at the same time.

She spotted two of the arcasi Maheaja-Folk circling around to come at the group again. Devrand shoved Aivean and Jarthan into some thick bushes nearby, all of them on foot. Two tarandeer milled about bleating in pain and one other lay motionless on the ground, like hers.

Shyvoan cringed and curled close to her downed tarandeer as she heard the arcasi fly past again, shooting more feathers.

None of the feathers hit her although they did hit all around her. Fear gave her strength to shove the tarandeer far enough to free her foot.

As she hobbled off to the side on her half-numb foot and drew her sword, she looked around to assess the situation.

Devrand, Aivean and Jarthan were out of sight. *Hopefully unharmed.* Buok stood partway hidden in brush, bow ready. Liphye and Teigye held similar stances to Shyvoan's left and right.

Not for the first time, Shyvoan wished she had more skill with a bow.

Shyvoan edged into some brush while she kept track of the two arcasi as the birds came at them again. She heard the other warriors releasing arrow after arrow at the Maheaja-Folk.

One arcasi faltered as several arrows found their way between the hard feathers. The second swooped at her.

She held her position and watched it, sword ready.

It shot some feathers at her, but she avoided them by leaning to one side then the other. The wind of their passage brushed her face.

Closer.

The arcasi screamed something at her and extended its talons as it swooped for her head.

She ducked at the last minute, before she popped up and swung her sword.

The dragon-scale blade sliced deep into the arcasi's body and nearly severed a wing as she continued her swing.

The arcasi fell and flopped around on the ground as it tried to get away.

Buok put an arrow into its eye, which ended its struggles.

Shyvoan looked around and saw that the other one also lay dead. Several arrows sprouted from its body.

She cleaned her sword on some nearby grass. Where the arcasi's blood had fallen the plants smoked and withered. She avoided those areas.

Aivean, Jarthan and Devrand crept out of their sheltering bushes and peered around.

"Is that all of them?" Aivean said.

"For now," Teigye responded as he gathered the arrows. "We ought to move soon, before more find us."

Shyvoan looked around the battle site. "We're down two tarandeer for certain, and those other two don't look too good."

"We've packed our weight in gear before," Liphye said with a grin. "Time to do it again."

Aivean checked over the two injured tarandeer and spread a poultice that Teigye handed her on their injuries.

"They'll either be better in a day, or there will be nothing further to do for them," he said.

While they were occupied with those two, Shyvoan, Liphye and Buok unloaded the dead ones. Then while Shyvoan and Liphye put together packs for carrying, Buok field dressed the larger of the two tarandeer.

Devrand studied the dead arcasi and grabbed a few of the feathers before he approached Buok.

"Do we have time for that? Shouldn't we be getting out of here?"

"Almost done," Buok said.

"We can use the meat," Liphye added and handed Devrand a pack. He promptly handed it to Jarthan. Liphye handed him another, with a devious smile.

Devrand glanced at Shyvoan and when their gazes met, he shrugged and settled the pack on his back.

The others also shouldered packs and they packed the rest of the gear—the bulk of all they had—on the uninjured tarandeer. Buok dragged the tarandeer he had field dressed and they set off the way they had been headed, leading the remaining tarandeer and moving at a brisk pace.

CHAPTER 21

Another couple of hours brought them around the small lake to the western side of the area that used to be the old lodgment site. They had pushed their pace, on the alert for more Maheaja-Folk, but had seen no sign of any others.

They found a shaded spot and paused for a short rest. Both Aivean and Jarthan sank to the ground right where they had stopped. Liphye handed them each a mug of water after she shed her pack and dug out a waterskin.

Buok moved off to the side to cut meat from the dead tarandeer, with Teigye's help.

"Do we have to be at the exact western edge of the lodgment?" Shyvoan said to Aivean after she shed her own pack. "Might this be close enough?"

Aivean used a finger to stir her tea and looked at their surroundings.

"It might," she said. "Although the closer we can position the gateway arch to a direct line between the previous and next, the easier it is to form and hold. A little further north would be better, if there's something suitable for the arch there."

"And how soon will you be able to form the next gateway. Can you do it still today?"

Aivean sighed and closed her eyes. When she opened them again, she gave Shyvoan a determined look. "I'll be able to do it," she said with a decisive nod. "I'm not much help with all the rest of this." She waved a hand toward Buok and Teigye. "And I've never been good with the battle magics, even the simple ones. But this I can do. I will. Until we get where we need to be."

She shot a glance at Devrand, who gave her an encouraging smile and nod of approval. Then he gave Shyvoan the now-familiar smirk.

Shyvoan raised her eyebrows at him and gave him one of his bland expressions, until he turned away. She then dropped down to sit close to Aivean.

"Have you thought about how we get back, after we've accomplished this?" she said in a soft voice.

Aivean smiled and nodded. "Oh, yah," she said, her voice just as low. "We've still got plenty of the herbs for each lodgment. After I've gotten the magic from the dragon, I'll be fine for getting us back. Better than fine. Who can say how many gateways I'll be able to form each day. I'll maybe be able to skip to further gateways, instead of us having to go back through each one along the way. That assumes I can form the connection well enough."

She grabbed Shyvoan's hand and gave it an enthusiastic squeeze. "Don't worry. After we get the magic, everything'll work out great."

Shyvoan was not so sure, but she answered Aivean's smile with one of her own and left the mage to her chathea tea.

They lingered there long enough for Buok and Teigye to cut as much meat as the group could carry. While they did that, Shyvoan and Liphye scouted the area, concentrating their attention further north, although Shyvoan also ranged further west too.

When Shyvoan returned to the others, she found

Liphye back before her. Buok had already wrapped and distributed the meat among everyone's packs, ready to head out again.

"I might have found a better spot for the gateway," Liphye said. "At least as far as its location. But the only tall things there are taller versions of these bushes." She waved a hand at the bushes that shaded them.

Aivean turned to eye the bushes. "They have sturdy central trunks and branches," she observed. "We can make it work. Just might have to reshape it some."

"Then we'd better get to it," Devrand said as he stood and grabbed his pack. He pulled both Aivean and Jarthan to their feet as well.

"Show us," he said to Liphye and gestured her forward.

She shot a glance at Shyvoan, who nodded. So Liphye shouldered her pack again and led them to the north.

Liphye's spot lay closer than Shyvoan had expected, and she easily spotted the two bushes the other warrior had been talking about. She pulled out her sword and began to slice off the scraggly branches between them that would interfere with the gateway. She wanted to be quit of this island as soon as possible.

The other warriors joined her, and they soon had an arch-shaped hole between the two bushes. Aivean stepped close to study the results of their efforts.

"I could wish for stronger side supports." She ran a hand over the branches that formed the edges of the arched space.

Devrand stepped to her side and took her hand. "It'll work," he said, but his expression did not match his encouraging words. He looked irritated and impatient, rather than supportive.

"Of course," she said with a tired smile.

Again, the three took their positions and Aivean created the new gateway. A short, quick run through the arch for everyone, and they stood on yet another new island.

From that time, they fell into the pattern they had tried earlier, but kept to it with more success. They took a gateway each morning and evening to speed their progress and Aivean and Jarthan rode tarandeer for the daytime journey from the one side of old lodgments to the other.

Neither of the two injured tarandeer recovered and instead got worse, and so provided them with yet more meat. They fished when the opportunity arose and smoked the extra meat and fish to carry with them.

For some variety, they collected late berries and tubers when they found them, to bolster the dwindling stores they had brought with them. When they found them, they also grabbed the leaves and flowers that Teigye had described, Aivean's chathea leaves too, although the latter plant had become harder to find.

Devrand often wore a frown of discontent and his dark mood hung over the entire group. Even Aivean seemed subdued as they plodded on.

At that pace, before long they reached the point beyond which Buok, the oldest of their group, had no information about any of the old lodgments, not even from his parents' tales. So, they spent some extra time to figure out the best place to set each gate to leave one island for the next. After some trial and error, Aivean found a way to use a pinch of the herbs for the next gateway to help locate the best place to conjure it.

Twenty days they managed this pace before everyone agreed they needed a full day of rest again. The gateway the morning of the twenty-first day brought them to a pleasant island much like the one they had just moved the people from. It seemed mostly forested, with a variety of trees that grew with a bit of space between them. The normal forest sounds murmured behind the faint sounds of their footsteps. The light was brighter than they had seen on most of the previous islands, although the sun was not visible – just a bright haze in the sky. The odor in the air was less than they had recently encountered, too.

They found a small glen a short distance south of the best location for the next gateway and set up camp, including the tents. Liphye tethered their four tarandeer nearby where they could reach a variety of foliage for food and a brook for water.

The usual camp setup tasks, with the ward-rings plus some much-needing cleaning took them into mid-morning. Then they all settled near the small fire to enjoy its warmth in the crisp autumn air and food eaten while stationary. After he finished his meal, Buok pulled out an unfinished wood carving to work on. Shyvoan peered at it as he worked. *A mother goat and kid?*

"So that's what, seventy gateways now?" Teigye said and leaned back to tuck his hands behind his head after he finished his snack.

"The gateway that brought us here was the sixty-ninth one we've gone through so far," Jarthan said in a quiet voice.

"So, we're where the people lived sixty-nine years or so in our past," Aivean said. "Incredible."

"Roughly, anyway," Shyvoan agreed.

"Is that far enough back to begin looking for a dragon, for that path the scroll described?" Devrand said.

"Doubt it," Buok said.

Liphye nodded her agreement as she idly tossed her wooden dice from hand to hand. "Everyone's always said that it's more like a couple hundred years since anyone's seen a dragon."

Teigye groaned. "So, is that the last of the islands that Rashean drew? Assuming we can return to two gateways each day when we set out again tomorrow morning, seems like that's still many days of gateways left."

"And when we get closer to that two-hundred mark, we might want to spend more time on each island to thoroughly search it. See if we can find anything that might lead us to a dragon or seems a possible place for one,"

Shyvoan said.

"The two hundred years that everyone's said might not be the exact timeframe," Devrand added.

Aivean pulled out the map scroll from Rashean and unrolled it. She studied it and Shyvoan saw her lips move. *Counting, probably.*

"Rashean drew thirty-three more islands after the one we're on now," Aivean told them after a couple of minutes. "We must have lived on many of those longer than just a few seasons or even a year. Otherwise, we're missing a lot of islands."

"An average of nearly four years per island," Jarthan murmured.

Shyvoan studied everyone while they guessed at which island would bring them to a dragon. The other warriors looked worn, but still steady, capable of going on yet a long while, she judged. Devrand too looked worn. *And is that a hint of frustration in his expression? Probably he'd thought to be done with this long before now.* She somewhat agreed with that sentiment.

Both Aivean and Jarthan looked worse than the others, weary and drained. Shyvoan hoped the day's rest would see improvements for both. Aivean, at least, still kept her cheerful outlook. Jarthan seemed to have sunk into a dull endurance for the most part. Although that tea of Aivean's did seem to help.

The rest of that day they spent mostly idle. The four warriors switched off scouting every couple of hours throughout the day and each tried to bring back more of the various leaves and flowers, and anything else edible that they found. No one discovered any sign of any Maheaja-Folk, though when they compared notes, they all agreed that they had a sense that someone or something watched them.

While that feeling clung to them, no one spotted anyone or anything that paid them particular attention. They went about their normal activities in and around the camp.

After their evening meal but before they settled into the nighttime routine, Shyvoan headed south to the shore. Buok decided to accompany her.

They walked in their usual silence for the most part, having scouted like this many times before, and chatted now and then quietly of inconsequential things. They reached the shore after close to half an hour and peered out at the darkened sea from the concealment of some trees and brush.

A surprising amount of light came from the hazy sky above. It did not take Shyvoan long to spot what she had come to see.

Off to the southeast, beyond the shallows, sat the familiar dark blot on the water.

"Still they follow," Buok muttered.

Shyvoan nodded. "And promptly. Kind of makes me wonder if Liphye was right and they *do* know somehow where we're going."

Buok gave that some thought. "They've got some kind of different magic, you think?"

Shyvoan nodded. "Wouldn't surprise me at all. We know Devrand's is different."

Buok nodded too, scrutinized the ship again for a few minutes, and turned to head back to the camp. Shyvoan kept pace with him.

"Tell the others?" he said.

"The warriors, yah," Shyvoan said. "I don't know about the others. Any reason they need to know? It's not like any of us can do anything about it."

Buok shrugged. "I'd say keep it to ourselves. For now. See if Devrand gives anything away. He claims they hunt him, but maybe things aren't as he says."

Shyvoan considered that and nodded.

Back at the camp, she and Buok each found a quick moment to pass along the information to Teigye and Liphye when their actions did not look like anything more than arranging the watches for the night. They opted to double the people on watch again and have only the four warriors watch for the night.

Shyvoan and Teigye took the first half of the night. Shyvoan found it colder than expected, but she and Teigye saw and heard nothing unusual. When they woke the other two warriors for their turn, they seemed to have trouble pulling themselves from their sleep, but then took their places as expected.

Shyvoan wrapped her cloak around her and burrowed into her bedding, grateful that she shared the tent with others. At least that helped ease the chill that had come with the night.

CHAPTER 22

"Shyvoan."

Shyvoan grumbled under her breath and swatted at the hand that shook her shoulder. Not really awake, and with a pounding head, she wanted nothing more than to sleep some more.

"Shyvoan, you need to wake up."

She batted at the hands that gripped both shoulders and slit open her eyes. Everything looked blurry and dim, but she could make out Liphye's face not far from her own.

The thought crossed her mind that Liphye did not look well. It vanished beneath a wave of nausea that gripped her.

"Uh oh."

Shyvoan rolled to one side and was sick. Fortunately, the ground was clear there. In fact, someone had taken down the tent around her. *A lucky thing, that.*

With a groan she rolled back and struggled into a seated position. She peered around and at the same time she tried to will her stomach to settle and her eyesight to clear. She spotted Liphye sitting on her other side. The other woman looked no better than she felt.

"Going to stay awake now?" Liphye said.

"Think so. What's—"

"Don't know. Everyone's sick and those who were asleep have been hard to wake."

Shyvoan groaned again and crawled from her bedding. The air was not as cold as the previous night, but still colder than it had been. It helped a little.

She reached back and grabbed her cloak from the tangle of bedding and fumbled it around her shoulders.

"Everyone?"

Liphye nodded. "The tarandeer, too."

"So maybe it's not something we ate," Teigye said as he shuffled to the low fire.

"Unless it's everything from this island," Buok pointed out. He sat near the fire wrapped in his cloak. "We did have those tubers. And the tarandeer have eaten leaves and grasses here."

"Or the water," Devrand muttered from across the camp. He sat by his pack, which looked ready to go, his expression one of misery. Somehow that made Shyvoan feel slightly better, that it had gotten him, too.

But her next thought wiped away that good feeling. "Could it just be this place?" she said. "This island."

"Now there's a pleasant thought," Teigye muttered and doused the fire.

"I don't know that I can open the gateway," Aivean whined. "I feel horrible."

"You have to," Devrand told her. "We all feel horrible. But if it's this island, staying longer won't make us better."

"And if it's not this island, we probably won't be any worse," Liphye muttered.

Shyvoan gathered her bedding, stuffed it back in its pack, and got the rest of her gear together. By the time she was as ready as she was going to get, the others had everything else gathered and ready to go.

Teigye and Buok handed the leads for all the tarandeer to Aivean, Devrand and Jarthan for the trip to the site for the gateway. The tarandeer had submitted to being loaded with gear with ill grace, but now tolerated the packs on their backs.

Shyvoan exchanged glances with her fellow warriors, and they spread out to keep the other three and the tarandeer in the middle. *If any Maheaja-Folk plan to attack, this would be the perfect time, from their perspective.*

"At least the gateway site's not too far," Teigye said.

Aivean groaned. "Far enough."

They stumbled away from their campsite and headed north to the spot they had found the day before for the gateway. Once there, Aivean needed a few minutes to confirm that the location would serve, then she sang the gateway magic. Her voice cracked the first time she sang so she needed a second try for it to work.

Everyone stumbled through and she closed it behind them, her actions clumsy.

When Shyvoan surveyed their new island, she groaned. She saw no plants anywhere. A black grit that only remotely resembled dirt covered the ground. From where they stood, the ground sloped up to a cone-shaped hill some distance away, from which a plume of smoke drifted.

Her breath burned in her chest and Shyvoan coughed, long and hard, which did not help her affliction in the least.

"We can't stay here," Devrand said. He coughed and nearly doubled over from the spasm.

Jarthan dug in his pack and pulled out a shirt which he tore into strips. He tied one of the strips over his mouth and nose, then handed the rest out the others.

Everyone followed his example. Shyvoan was surprised and pleased to discover that she breathed well enough through the cloth. The air stank, and tasted just as bad, but the fiery sensation in her chest eased enough that she stopped coughing.

"There aren't any trees or bushes to form the gateway," Aivean wailed through the cloth that covered half her face. "How can we make the gateway?"

"First we need to get to the right spot, then we'll figure that out," Shyvoan said. She grabbed the reins of one of the tarandeer and headed the direction they had faced when they arrived through the gateway, since always before that had been at least the rough direction that they needed to go. With no clear sun in the sky, she had no other way to determine direction.

After a few minutes, she heard the others follow her.

The journey was rough and Shyvoan stumbled along, ill and sluggish, wrapped in a haze. *But we need to get away from this place, perhaps even more than the previous one.* So, she trudged forward. The effort took all her attention.

A touch on her arm brought her out of her daze. She stopped and stared at the waterskin that someone held in front of her. With too much effort for the slight motion, Shyvoan reached for the skin and looked to see who held it.

"Drink," Buok said, with an encouraging nod. "It helps some."

"It's not…" Shyvoan croaked.

Buok shook his head. "Threw out the water from that last island. This is from the one before."

"And if you feel anything like the rest of us, you're not interested in any food," Liphye added from beyond him.

Shyvoan managed a nod and took a long drink from the waterskin. Although the water was not at all cool, it did refresh her.

"Any idea how much further we need to go?" she said when she handed the waterskin back. "Or how long we've been walking so far?"

"So far, no idea," Liphye said. "We all lost track of time. A couple of hours maybe?"

"As to how far, Aivean has used some of the herbs and done some magic," Buok said. "We're close, she said."

Shyvoan sighed. "Good." Then she looked at their surroundings.

They looked much like they had when they arrived, but ahead and off to her right she saw something that stuck out of the black grit that formed the ground on this island.

When she looked back and met Buok's gaze, he nodded. "The thought is that will be our gateway. Assuming we can find a second piece to form the other side."

"Another hour, maybe less to get there," Liphye added. "Distances seem deceptive here."

After everyone had a chance to drink what water they wanted, and the tarandeer had gotten some water too, the group set off again. This time Shyvoan took the tail end and kept an eye on the others.

Without exception, and herself included, everyone stumbled more than walked, even the tarandeer. But they made progress. Shyvoan hoped they could hold out until they got there and through to the next island.

When they hiked close enough to the object that stuck out of the ever-present grit, Shyvoan saw it was a rock, a rather tall one. *Just hope we'll find another one close to it, maybe one not yet visible.* As Liphye had estimated, it took them close to an hour to reach it where it sat partway up the slope of the hill. An irregularity on the uphill side hinted at another rock, covered by grit.

Teigye stepped close to the irregularity, which reached to his waist, and brushed at it with gloved hands, moving the grit aside to reveal another rock. He frowned at its base.

"We'll have to dig to clear enough height for the gateway," he said.

Aivean groaned and nodded. "Unfortunately, yah. But at least this spot is good enough for the gateway. I don't see another that's close to likely."

Shyvoan followed the other woman's gaze along the gritty hillside where no other rocks close to tall enough were visible.

"This one is far enough out of the grit," Aivean continued and turned back to the taller rock. "But with that one shorter, we'll need to duck, after digging. And clear the grit off the sides of the rocks that face each other."

"And hurry," Devrand said, his attention on the smoke from the mountain. Shyvoan followed the direction of his gaze. *Has the smoke gotten thicker?*

She dropped her pack where she stood and dug out one of their shovels. Sudden fear gave her a burst of energy against the lingering illness.

Liphye and Buok followed her example, while Teigye handed Devrand a spare set of gloves.

"Get busy," Teigye told the other man and started on the taller rock.

Devrand sneered at him and looked ready to refuse, then met Shyvoan's glare. They stared at each other until Devrand gave her a mocking smile and turned to brush grit from the rocks.

Shyvoan lost track of the time as she continued to dig with what speed she could manage. They discovered they needed to make the hole wider than they had first thought because the grit tended to slide back into the spot they dug out. Finally, Aivean said they had enough grit cleared for the gateway.

Weary, aching, and still sick, everyone gathered the packs and the tarandeer while Aivean, Devrand and Jarthan made the gateway.

With a ducking, shuffling run, they passed through the narrow space between the rocks to a much more pleasant island, not unlike where they had made the first gateway on this unusual journey. Although this island was more open, with fewer trees and more short grasses and shrubs.

After a short pause to close the gateway and get their bearings—the sun actually shone here—they headed toward the location for the next gateway. They planned to camp near it as long as they could, to recover in time to open the next gateway the next morning.

The journey to the next gateway site was short and uneventful, a bit of a surprise to all. Again, the area lacked bird and insect sounds. As they set up a quick camp, the others shared their observations: no signs of any other life, either. Just the group and the widely spaced trees with bushes and grasses interspersed.

"Are any of the trees close enough together for the gateway?" Shyvoan said after they had all settled in to rest. No one yet seemed interested in eating, but they had set water to boil for more drinking water.

Aivean shrugged, her expression disinterested. "There are a couple closer to each other than any others near the right spot," she told them. "But they still stand at the limit of what I can manage." She closed her eyes and lay back on her cloak in the warm sunshine.

"We'll make it work," Devrand said. He glanced at Jarthan and Aivean, his look assessing, then he too stretched out and closed his eyes.

Teigye shifted closer to Shyvoan, and the other warriors leaned in at a gesture from him.

"I get the strong impression that we're the unnecessary members of this little trip," he muttered.

Murmured agreements went around the group.

"Except for protection," Buok said when the murmurs died down.

"Servants," Liphye said.

Shyvoan shrugged. "Does it matter? He wants to be able to make a passage himself. He'll not get that chance without us."

"Especially if his hunter catches up to him," Buok agreed.

"As long as we're alerted that danger might not just come from outside the group," Teigye said.

"Sad to think of it, though," Liphye said. "Among our people, we've got squabbles and disagreements and such, and certainly some people who plain don't like each other, but nothing so extreme. I'm not sure we ever have."

"If we ever did, it's long buried in our past," Shyvoan said. She glanced at the other three across the fire. "They do have the right idea."

With a nod and a slight sigh, Teigye stretched out atop his cloak.

"Wake us to trade watches in a couple of hours," Shyvoan told Buok and Liphye before she followed Teigye's example.

By evening, everyone had recovered enough to eat a little. They kept the meal bland, and rested and watched again for the night.

Although not much better the next morning, they managed the gateway. Aivean had to use more of the herbs than usual to make the gate stretch between the two trees they chose.

They again fell into their pattern of two gateways each day, one in the morning right after their first meal and one later in the day. After the second gateway of the day, they traveled to the site for the next one, and rested there for the night.

They decided to push as far as they could following this pattern. As they traveled, the islands each became less and less hospitable to them again, the air thicker and harder to breath, the light dimmer. But none of them was as bad as the one where they took sick and the one that followed it.

They struggled on against lingering aches and fatigue as they tried to recover from the illness. After several islands on which they found nothing they considered safe to eat, they had butchered the weakest of the remaining tarandeer and smoked all the meat they could carry. That helped sustain them when they found more islands with inedible offerings.

This took them to the fifteenth day straight of traveling in this fashion when they passed through the morning gateway. After Aivean closed the gateway behind them, they all huddled close in the cold dimness to discuss their next moves.

"Sixty-three days now, if I count right," Teigye groused and blew on his hands even though he wore gloves.

"Sounds right," Liphye said.

"This is island ninety-eight," Devrand said. "We should slow our gateway travel to take time to investigate each island for signs of that path from the scroll, and dragons, too."

"You don't need to tell us that," Liphye snapped at him. "We know this. We've already agreed to this."

Devrand gave her his bland look, but she did not back down, and he turned away first.

"First a good campsite," Shyvoan reminded them. "Then we can take turns scouting further inland to see if anything looks promising. I hope we can determine that in one day so if we need to travel on, we don't have to make the whole trip too much longer than it's already been."

She looked around at each of her squad-mates and waited for nods or words of acknowledgement. After she had them, she indicated to Buok to go ahead and find the campsite.

They set up a full camp near a stream that held some fish. A small clearing nearby promised ample forage for the three tarandeer. Buok had taken them a little south of the direct line between the gateway they had used and the location for the next one, closer to the shore. He gave Shyvoan a look full of significance when he saw she noticed this.

She nodded acknowledgement. It would make it easier to check for the hunter's ship, assuming it still followed. It *had* been, a few islands previously, so no compelling reason to think it had stopped since then.

Teigye set off further inland after he unpacked all his gear into the tent he shared with Buok. Shyvoan set off for the southern coast. It seemed unlikely that the ship would be visible yet, if it *had* still followed. But that the ship had followed them this long and far was unlikely in itself.

She reached the coast much sooner than she had expected. It was narrower than any she had seen before, the tree line little more than two steps from the water's edge.

She crouched within the cover of the trees and eyed the water, starting south of where she lurked and moving her gaze slowly east. *Nothing there.*

Good news, so far. Nevertheless, she expected to see that ship before they left the island again. Assuming this island was not the one they wanted.

She lingered about a quarter of an hour and watched the water. She spotted some ripples several paces out from the shore that looked like something moving beneath the surface. They were not as far out as she would have liked.

Looked like the shallows did not extend as far from this island as others. *Good to know, if unnerving. Hope no moaras decide to come ashore.* She had not encountered any moaras herself, but the stories she had heard had her hoping those ripples came no closer.

After the ripples vanished, she eased back into the trees again and headed back to the camp.

Teigye returned from his scouting not long after Shyvoan arrived back at camp and much sooner than she had expected.

"Not finding dragons on this island," he said as he walked to the fire to warm himself. "There's not much further that way inland, and it rapidly goes back to a coast. Looks like it doesn't go much further to the sides either than we've already seen."

"Do we linger here longer, then?" Liphye said.

"I'd welcome the rest," Aivean murmured.

Shyvoan looked at the others. Jarthan and Aivean looked bad. Jarthan worse than usual, his gaze on his feet as he sat close to the fire bundled in a heavy cloak and a blanket. The others seemed better than those two. But if they felt anything like she did, they still had not recovered from that illness either. The pace they had traveled the last many days had been hard on everyone, including the tarandeer.

"Let's stay here the full day, as we originally planned," Shyvoan said. "Explore the island more. Thoroughly."

Devrand frowned but did not disagree.

"Stock up on some food," Buok said.

"Give the tarandeer a chance to recover better," Liphye added.

It was Shyvoan and Teigye's turn to stay at the camp. Rather than scouting further, Buok and Liphye chose to fish. To everyone's surprise, Jarthan accompanied them. He even took a line that Liphye offered him.

Although he stayed close and within Shyvoan's sight, for the most part, Teigye ranged around the camp and gathered tubers and late berries that he found. When he finished, he decided to range further out around the camp, to see if he might discover anything they needed to know about.

Devrand pulled out the scroll map from Rashean and studied it again. What he hoped to find, Shyvoan could not guess. They all had gone over the drawing many, many times. Nothing else was there.

Aivean made herself a mug of her chathea tea and dozed near the fire after she drank it.

For the evening meal, they had fish and tubers, a pleasant change from the dried meat that had comprised most of their recent meals.

"I was able to investigate pretty much the entire island." Teigye said around bites of food. "Although I looked over some parts from a little distance. It's as small as I thought. I also think I found a reasonable spot for the gateway for tomorrow."

Shyvoan nodded. "We'll take a look at it then in the morning."

After an uneventful night, they packed their camp in the dim light of dawn and followed Teigye to the two trees he had found for the next gateway. Aivean took one look at them and shook her head.

"Not the right spot," she said, and turned south.

The others followed her for close to a quarter of an hour to a spot almost at the shoreline. "This is the proper spot, and these will do." She pointed to two slender trees that had grown in such a way that they resembled a doorway from the forest to the beach.

The three created the gateway and everyone stepped through. Shyvoan glanced back before she crossed and saw Devrand look out at the water and stiffen. Jarthan followed his gaze, his own expression one of sorrow and longing. Then she passed through the gate.

CHAPTER 23

On the other side of the gate, Shyvoan stopped in her tracks, her attention captured by her surroundings. When she remembered to move out of the way to give the last three room to cross, she stumbled a couple of steps to one side while she continued to gaze around.

All around them stood ruins, old stone structures, the stone a nearly uniform light gray that almost shone in the diffuse light from the sky. The gateway that they had come through was a crumbling stone opening, a doorway of some kind that still stood somewhat intact, although whatever wall it had been part of was not much more than a pile of broken rocks around it.

Teigye whistled as Devrand came through the gateway, the last one through. Aivean closed the gateway and looked around, her attention as captivated as the others'.

"What is this place?" she murmured.

"Has to be a former town of the people's," Liphye pointed out in a matter-of-fact tone. "Before we took to tents and lodgments."

"Looks more like a city," Jarthan muttered. "Wonder

if—" He subsided at a look from Devrand.

"Not even a whisper of something like this in all the tales," Buok said.

"Why would they ever leave such a grand place as this?" Aivean said.

"Same reason we've always left places," Teigye muttered as he poked around the ruins.

"This place is huge," Aivean said and spun around to take in her surroundings. "We must have lived here longer than just a couple of years."

Shyvoan tore her attention from the intriguing surroundings. "Let's find a place for the camp. Then we can explore."

They headed into the ruins and took a rough bearing based on the line drawn for this island to connect to the next on Rashean's map.

Buok leaned close as they walked. "Too many places here for enemies to hide," he whispered.

Shyvoan nodded. "But that also means many places for *us* to hide," she whispered back. "Pick us a good spot."

Buok nodded and caught up with Aivean to guide their direction while staying close to where she wanted to go.

Shyvoan stayed alert as they picked their way along what must have been a main path. At least most of the rubble and ruins sat far to either side of the space they walked.

She also speculated on what the place had been like back when people lived there. *How many could have lived here?* Many more than now made up the people, she guessed. *Were we really once so many more than we are now?* That thought did not sit well with her, and her spirits sank. *This passage idea of Devrand's might be our people's last chance. Otherwise, the Maheaja-Folk will hound us to extinction.*

An hour of scrambling over broken bits and around larger ruins brought them to a central, open area.

"We'll need to set the next gateway near here," Aivean said.

"*If* we need to set a next gateway," Devrand said. "All this could mean this is the island we've been heading for."

Shyvoan had that feeling, too, but did not want to say it out loud. "Camp setup first," she said. "Before we jump to conclusions. After we have our spot, we can investigate."

Devrand met her gaze, and she had the feeling that he somehow knew that she also thought this might be the island they sought. He smirked at her but said nothing.

"This way," Buok said.

He led them a short distance from the central area to a place of fewer ruins and more trees. Shyvoan heard water nearby.

They poked around and found a spot with two low ruined walls that could shield two sides of the campsite. They set up their camp, tents included, and prepared the spot for the fire but did not light it yet.

They left what they could at the camp, made sure the tarandeer were within reach of food and the stream, and split into two groups to start learning about the place. Shyvoan and Teigye headed north with Devrand and Jarthan, while the others headed south.

Both Shyvoan and Teigye stayed alert and flanked the other two. For the most part, they walked in silence. They found more ruins, still the same stone, but Shyvoan got the impression that these structures had been smaller than the others they had seen.

She shook her head at herself when her thoughts wandered too much. Fantasies and imaginings. How could she guess what might have been here from these random clumps of broken rock?

"There's something odd about these ruins, this section…" Jarthan said as he stopped to peer around.

With an irritated expression, Devrand stopped too, but only watched Jarthan.

Teigye and Shyvoan paused and exchanged hand signals communicating that neither had seen any signs that anything else lived there. So Shyvoan watched Jarthan as

Devrand did. What was he talking about?

After a few minutes, Jarthan moved to the most intact structure near them and beckoned the others over.

"What do you see?" he said.

"Bunch of broken rocks and buildings," Devrand replied.

Teigye nodded agreement but peered closer. Shyvoan eyed that ruin for several minutes, then spotted it.

"I don't believe it," she muttered as she approached a doorway that still stood, with part of its lintel intact.

The lintel was too short. It only reached the height of her chest.

When she stopped right next to it, Teigye looked from her to the ruined door and his eyes widened.

"That's the right height for hobs," he breathed and looked from Shyvoan to Jarthan. "Could it have been a home for them?"

Shyvoan nodded. "Looks that way."

"What difference does it make?" Devrand demanded, impatience clear in his tone.

"Seems like I remember seeing a couple other doorways as intact as this one," Teigye said. "I didn't pay them particular attention because they were normal size."

"Looks like the past is a bit more complex than you had thought," Jarthan murmured.

"But… hobs living here with the people? How can that be?" Teigye demanded.

Jarthan shrugged and winced slightly when Devrand grabbed his arm.

"Maybe your dragons can tell us," Devrand said. "That assumes we can ever make it to them. Come on."

He marched away the direction they had been heading and pulled Jarthan with him. Shyvoan and Teigye exchanged glances and resumed their flanking positions.

As they continued their exploration, they found more of the same… piles of broken gray rocks that once formed buildings, most too ruined to guess their purpose. They spotted a few more of the intact doorways, both their own size and the smaller version.

After they reached the apparent edge of the city, they explored it a short distance both directions before they headed out into the wilderness that surrounded it, trying to stay on a direct heading inland. The ground rose some as they traveled, but not anything close to what Shyvoan expected for it to match the writing in the scroll. They continued further and searched through the woods, but she was beginning to doubt this was the island they wanted after all.

After several hours, Shyvoan was ready to head back to the camp. *If only the last lingering effects of that illness will ease.* A chance to rest again sounded appealing, as did regrouping with the others, if they had returned, to compare impressions and thoughts.

Devrand argued against heading back so soon, as he put it. But when he uncharacteristically stumbled, not once but a couple of times over the next several minutes, he admitted that rest would be a good idea. By that time, Jarthan barely managed to put one foot in front of the other and Shyvoan feared they might have to find a way to carry him back.

But they turned back, and without all the side trips, managed to return to camp before another two hours had passed.

The others stumbled in not long after they did the same. Everyone took some time to make themselves comfortable and grab some food and drink – Aivean and Jarthan drinking that tea of theirs. Then they gathered around their small fire.

"The city isn't quite what we thought," Shyvoan said as she pulled a second cloak around her shoulders against the deepening evening chill. "We found doors that are too short for any of the people."

"Too short? You mean they were for hobs?" Aivean said, her expression incredulous.

"Hob-sized, anyway," Teigye said.

"The city is large," Buok observed after a moment. "Too large, I believe, to have been built in just a year. People must have lived here much longer than we have in the individual lodgments."

"More of them, too, I'd think. From the number of structures," Liphye said. "But with hobs?"

"We weren't always at war with the Maheaja-Folk," Buok said. "We know this."

Devrand waved a hand in dismissal. "Interesting. Maybe. But this has no bearing on why we've come here."

After he finished the last of his food and drink, he and Aivean exchanged long looks and they both stood. When Jarthan started to stand as well, Devrand met his gaze and he subsided.

Devrand walked off to the tent he and Jarthan slept in, Aivean next to him. The others exchanged glances.

"You can sleep in our tent if you want," Liphye said.

Jarthan glanced at her, his eyebrows raised.

"Just looks like you'll need a place to sleep," Liphye said with a slight smile. "Although if you *are* interested in something else—"

He held up a hand against her suggestion. "It's nothing at all against you, either of you." He glanced from Liphye to Shyvoan and back. Shyvoan thought his face reddened slightly.

"But I've got a life partner," Jarthan continued and ducked his head. "She might not be here, but even so…." He shrugged and looked at the ground between his feet.

Again, the others exchanged looks.

"Is she back on the other side of that passage you two came through?" Teigye said. "Back at home on some distant island?"

Jarthan shook his head and avoided meeting any of their gazes. "Alorsha's on that ship that follows us. She's the one 'hunting' us."

After that pronouncement, the conversation died for

the evening.

Jarthan did end up sleeping in the tent with Liphye and Shyvoan, as the other tent was too small to sleep three. He used Aivean's bedding and scrunched himself far to one side of the tent to give the two women plenty of room. Shyvoan piled an extra blanket atop him when she saw him shiver along the cold tent wall and left to join Liphye on first watch.

Later, when they returned to the tent, he seemed deeply asleep. They soon joined him in slumber.

~ ~ ~

The cold deepened further during the night. Shyvoan noticed it in half-awake moments when she burrowed further into her bedding. At some point half-awake turned into too awake in the dim early morning light that came through the walls of the tent. She pulled herself from her blankets with a groan of complaint and struggled into as many layers of clothing as she could manage. A glance at her tent-mates showed both Jarthan and Liphye burrowed into their respective blankets.

Shyvoan wrapped her cloak close around her and slipped out of the tent into the frigid outside air. Underfoot a dusting of snow covered the ground.

As she looked around, she spotted Teigye at the far side of the camp. He raised a hand in greeting, but continued his perusal of the area, still on watch. It must be earlier than Shyvoan had thought. *Hard to tell with the gray sky.*

She turned to look the other direction, behind her and her tent. Buok scouted around out there somewhere but she did not see him.

An irregularity on the ground near the back corner of the tent caught her attention. She sidled along that side of the tent, hand on her sword and the cold forgotten for the moment.

Yah, what I thought. A footprint in the light snow. And more, that both came to and went from their tent. Looked like one set, too small to be from a human, and they passed right across the ward-ring around the camp.

Minutes later, they all gathered at the edge of the tent and scrutinized the tracks.

"I'm sorry," Teigye said. "I ought to have noticed—"

Shyvoan broke into his most recent apology. "Teigye, it crossed the ward-ring. If it could do that, it could make it so you'd never notice it."

"Let's track it down," Liphye said.

"Before breakfast?" Teigye complained, but with a grin.

"Do we all have to go?" Aivean said. When the others all turned to look at her, she flushed. "I should see if I can figure out how it crossed the ward-ring," she added.

With exchanged looks, Shyvoan took a silent assessment of the other warriors' expressions as clues to what they thought. She nodded.

"We don't want to leave the camp deserted anyway," she said.

"I'll go," Devrand said. "And Jarthan will stay and help Aivean."

Jarthan did not look up at this preemptive order, just nodded.

"I'll stay as well," Liphye said. "Let me just get my bow and such." She disappeared back into the tent.

"I'd like to go. To make up for earlier." Teigye looked from Shyvoan to Buok. At that moment he looked so very young.

Shyvoan reminded herself he was only a couple of years younger than her, but his far fewer years of experience in the warriors made him seem much younger right then.

"Nothing to make up for," Buok told him and clapped him on the shoulder. "It happens. At least it seems the hob only looked. Nothing bad came of it."

Aivean nodded vigorously. "I can't see yet how it got

past the ward-ring, but I *can* tell none of its magic is on us or any part of the camp. It *must've* just been looking."

Shyvoan looked from Buok to Teigye. "Ready to go, then?"

Liphye rejoined them and handed a bow and arrows to Teigye. "Take these, too, just in case," she said with a smile and moved off to pace the camp on watch.

Buok, Teigye and Shyvoan set off and followed the tracks away from the camp. They carried some dried food and ate as they went. Buok led as the best tracker, although in the snow, for now, Shyvoan spotted the tracks with no difficulty. Devrand tailed right at her heels.

The trail remained easy to follow, so the three warriors spread out a little. Devrand stuck with Shyvoan, to her annoyance, but at least he stayed quiet. He had improved at moving quietly and disturbed little around him compared to when they first met. Shyvoan was somewhat impressed, and annoyed that she felt that way.

The tracks led them deeper into the city ruins, in a direction none of them had investigated the previous day. They headed roughly back the way they had come when they arrived.

The day brightened around them as they continued but grew no warmer. The tracks stood out; the hob had made no attempt to hide them.

Further and further from their camp they walked. After close to two hours of quiet following, Buok gave the hand-sign to stop. He pointed ahead at a small structure that looked more intact than most they had seen. When Shyvoan nodded her understanding, Buok headed to the right to circle the place.

Shyvoan and Teigye exchanged looks and he headed to the left.

Shyvoan glanced at Devrand and placed a finger on his lips to indicate silence when he looked like he might say something. She then edged toward the structure and counted to herself as she drew her sword. She waved

Devrand back when he would have followed her.

When she reached the count of thirty, she stood to one side of the doorway on that side of the structure, her back to the wall. Buok and Teigye eased around the corners of the building and joined her, Teigye flanking the doorway on the other side.

Buok raised a hand with three fingers up and counted down by lowering a finger at a time. When he lowered the last finger, they charged inside.

Shyvoan's first impression of the interior was that it was small, clean, dim, and mostly empty. Movement drew her attention to a far corner where a small figure pulled itself from a bed that sat on a frame that raised it slightly above the floor. With a small shriek, it backed into the wall behind it and froze there, its horrified expression focused on Shyvoan's sword.

Then it jabbered something at them. Most of what it said sounded like what Shyvoan had heard of the Maheaja-Folk's language, but she picked up some words in her own language, too.

"What do you mean 'came back' and 'shouldn't be here'?" she demanded.

The hob jabbered faster and Shyvoan made nothing of it.

"No weapons here," Teigye said after he looked through the small room while Shyvoan and Buok watched the hob.

"No weapons," the hob agreed. "We talk?"

"Outside where we can see," Shyvoan said and backed out of the building. She almost tripped over Devrand who had moved close.

"What've you found?" he said.

Without answering, she grabbed his arm and pulled him with her away from the entrance. A moment later the hob emerged—she now saw it was a male—followed by Teigye and Buok.

The hob studied them all through eyes squeezed almost

shut, as they in turn studied him. He stood shorter than the hobs Shyvoan had seen before, and he seemed much older than any she had ever seen. His scraggly hair and wrinkled skin both were pale gray. His simple clothing looked well-worn but not worn through, and the cold did not seem to bother him.

"So, talk," Teigye said and stood back and to one side behind the hob.

"Yah," the hob agreed. "But fast. You shouldn't be here. Why you came back?"

"Came back?" Shyvoan repeated.

The hob waved his hands around him, seeming to indicate the ruined structures all around them, and edged sideways into a shadow. "Long years back. You left. Hunted by wrong-minded-we. Wrong to return."

"The Maheaja-Folk who hunt us are wrong?" Buok said.

"Yah. Wrong. But wrong-minded-we hunt all you. You left. Some of we stay. Not *all* you fault. Wrong-minded-you fault."

Shyvoan backed up and found a large rock to sit on. The hob plopped down on the ground. "What's not our fault?" she said.

"Dragons. Not *all* you fault. But yah, wrong-minded-you fault."

"What about dragons?" Buok said.

"Gone. Not left like you. Gone."

Devrand lunged for the hob, hands clawed to grab him. Buok's quick action in snagging the man prevented him from reaching the hob.

"You're telling us the dragons are dead?" Devrand shouted at the hob. "All of them?"

The hob cringed away from him. "Yah. Gone. Fault of wrong-minded-you."

"But we need one!" Devrand struggled to free himself from Buok's grasp. "We've got to get more magic."

The hob frowned. "And so, dragons gone."

CHAPTER 24

They took the hob with them back to their camp. He seemed resigned to the trek and squinted his eyes almost shut again as they walked in the diffuse light of day that was still dimmer than what Shyvoan was used to. His vertical slit pupils had contracted to the narrowest of lines. *If this little bit of light bothers the hob, no wonder they almost always attack at night.*

When they reached the small camp, she saw that Aivean had renewed the ward-circle. Regardless, the hob crossed it with no more difficulty than the rest of them. Shyvoan almost laughed at the astonished expression on the mage's face. Her mirth died as the possible ramifications struck her.

"That's not possible," Aivean muttered. She approached the hob, who watched her, his expression curious. "I'll need to take a look…."

"Me too," Devrand said. He glared when Shyvoan grabbed his arm to stop him from getting closer.

"Not like with the unicorn," she told him. "I'll put an arrow in you myself."

"Then you'll doom your people to being hunted to extinction by this creature's fellows," Devrand snarled, but turned away and stalked to the other side of the camp.

Aivean shooed Shyvoan away so she could see what she might learn of the hob. Shyvoan did not go far, and kept watch on their visitor, as Teigye and Buok did also. After several minutes, though, during which she watched Aivean do little else but sing and scrutinize the hob, Shyvoan sidled over to Buok and Teigye.

Teigye cast a glance Devrand's direction. "Seems like a rather extreme reaction at hearing about the dragons," he commented in a quiet voice.

"He's got magic different from what we're used to, but I wonder if he really has very much," Shyvoan said. "He needs the magic as much as we do, it looks like."

"True, that. But to what end?" Buok said. "And if he gets the magic he seeks, will he really open one of those passages to save our people? I don't get a feeling that he cares."

Shyvoan cast her own glance at Devrand. "Good questions."

"Still, I can sort of understand his reaction, too," Teigye said. "If there are really no more dragons, we're in trouble."

"Hm, not really any more than before," Shyvoan said.

"Do we believe the hob? That the dragons are gone?" Teigye looked from the hob to Shyvoan.

"I don't think we can take him at his word," Buok said. "Sounds like the Maheaja-Folk don't want us getting to a dragon, so he'd probably say whatever he thought would keep us away."

Shyvoan nodded slightly and, after another glance at Devrand, then Aivean—who was absorbed in her own magic—hauled out some food. Breakfast had been too little and too long ago.

After she finished a quick meal, she pulled out the map. Three more islands after this one, that was it. *Could it be that this hob speaks truly, and the dragons are all dead? Or maybe that only holds true for this island.* Maheaja-Folk *were* supposedly unable to cross the moving water between the islands so this hob might not know anything about those last islands.

But then what of what he said about the "wrong-minded" of his people? Could those still be here? From some of what the hob said, it sounded like the Maheaja-Folk *had* hunted them, followed them, somehow, *across* the water that they were not supposed to be able to cross.

She frowned and stood abruptly as she shoved the map away.

She heard Teigye mutter to Buok, "I know that look." She ignored the comment and descended on Aivean and the hob.

"What've you learned?" she said to the mage.

Aivean flicked an uncertain glance at the hob, but Shyvoan ignored the implication to talk elsewhere. "Well?"

"It seems our ward-circles are very specific," Aivean said. "The way to create them has been passed down to us. Our hob here could cross mine because he has no ill intent toward us. I think the magic was deliberately set that way."

"So, our ancestors knew some Maheaja-Folk weren't out to kill us," Teigye said as he joined them.

"Bring everyone," Shyvoan told Teigye and waited until the others had joined them and Aivean had shared what she had discovered.

Shyvoan then glowered at the hob who returned her look with a concerned one of his own. "So where are the Maheaja-Folk who hunt us?"

"They follow you away. Maybe they follow you back."

"But your folk can't cross the moving water," Liphye said.

The hob shrugged. "Difficult. Takes time."

"Might explain how we've been able to move to a new island and have peace there for a while, but then they always find us," Buok said.

"Yah. This," the hob said.

"But some of you don't hunt us," Shyvoan said.

"Yah. Me. Others. Stay home."

"And all the dragons are gone. Dead," Devrand said, his tone flat.

Aivean gave him a worried look.

"Yah," the hob said. "No dragons on mist isle. So go back. Wrong to be here. Go before others come."

The hob seemed nervous, his eyes shifting, and he shuffled his feet. Shyvoan tried to engage him with a slight smile, but he seemed unaware of her attempt. *Not surprising that he'd be nervous, surrounded as he is.*

"What others? The ones who don't blame us for the dragons?" Liphye said.

The hob became more agitated. "Others who *do*. Go back."

Shyvoan exchanged glances with her companions. She saw worry in the expressions of most of them, but irritation in Devrand's. The irritation vanished when he met her gaze.

"Doesn't seem to be anything else to learn from this creature," he said with a grimace.

"How do the others cross the moving water?" Buok said to the hob. "If we know, maybe we can stop them."

With a fearful glance at Buok, the hob shuffled his feet even more. "No say if can or can't," he said.

"I doubt he knows," Devrand said, his tone one of disgust. "If he did, wouldn't he have gone with them, too? Rather than stay in these ruins?"

"No ruins here then. Nice place. Long years break them," the hob said.

Jarthan frowned. "You sound like you remember the city the way it used to be. How long do hobs live anyway?"

"Longer than you," the hob shrieked, then fled for the ruins, ducking under both Buok's and Teigye's attempts to catch him.

He vanished when they gave chase, and not as if he

ducked into a hiding spot within the ruins. They all saw him plainly in an open area, then they did not see him. Nevertheless, Buok and Teigye headed into the ruins.

"I don't like the sound that there might be others," Liphye muttered.

"Agreed," Shyvoan said. "Let's pack and be ready to move out when Buok and Teigye get back."

"We can't go to another island yet," Devrand said. "We're not certain that the path isn't on this one."

"I didn't say we were going to another island," Shyvoan snapped and turned her back on him to help Liphye collect their gear. She heard Devrand, Jarthan and Aivean walk away. *Hopefully to collect their own gear.*

Teigye and Buok returned before Shyvoan and Liphye finished packing everything and jumped in to help.

"Couldn't track the hob this time," Buok reported.

"Must have used his magic to get away," Teigye said.

Shyvoan nodded absently, not much interested in the hob any longer.

"We're leaving this site," she said. "The hob knows it and could bring others here."

"We need to finish exploring this island," Devrand said as he joined them. Jarthan followed him and carried the bulk of their packs. "We can't believe that the hob would tell us the truth about the dragons. He's hiding something."

"True, that," Buok said. "So, we make a new camp at some distance, and we finish discovering what we might about the island. Then leave tomorrow morning if this isn't the place."

Because the hob's dwelling had been to the south and east of their camp, they chose to move north and a little west, best they could tell with the haze in the sky.

They chose a new campsite, still within the ruins, near a stream, and set up a rough camp. When they had the camp in decent shape, they separated to finish their explorations of the island, leaving Jarthan, Aivean and Liphye to watch the camp. Shyvoan again found herself paired with Devrand.

They headed north and a bit east and spoke little as they walked. Plant life overran this area of ruins that they traversed more than where they had camped the previous night. Before long, they reached what seemed to be the edge of the city and faced a thick forest with no apparent path through.

Shyvoan took a drink from her waterskin while she eyed the plants. They looked healthy and oddly green for the snow that lingered on the ground. She heard a few birds; calls she did not recognize. *What's that low murmur, just noticeable behind the bird calls?* She frowned when she realized what she heard.

"Is that the sea?" Devrand said.

"I think it is," Shyvoan said. She tucked away her waterskin and drew her sword to hack a path through the dense plants. Devrand followed on her heels.

Less than a quarter-hour of this and she broke through the edge of the foliage to a narrow, rocky shore. The small waves that came ashore crossed the entire shoreline and almost wet the toes of her boots.

"Nothing mountainous enough on this island after all," Devrand commented. Then he murmured, "Wonder what the hob's hiding, then."

They followed the shore to their right for almost half an hour before they headed back into the trees and returned to the ruined city. They saw no signs of any other hobs, or even of the one hob they knew about. Midafternoon brought them back to the camp.

Devrand immediately pulled Jarthan aside for a heated, whispered discussion.

Shyvoan watched them as her curiosity fought with languor. *Wonder what that's about….*

Languor won and left her unconcerned enough to stay where she lounged near the small fire, resting from the day's exertions. Liphye kept watch and circled the camp from time to time. Devrand and Jarthan fell silent when Liphye approached. Shyvoan met Liphye's gaze when that happened a second time and shrugged, and the other woman continued her circuit with just a slight nod for the two men.

Aivean slept wrapped in blankets near the fire. Shyvoan studied the mage as she slept. The woman looked pale and drawn. *Have we been asking too much of her with the gateways so close together in time?* She could still be suffering lingering effects from that illness, too. Shyvoan still tired easier than she should have. *Well, just a couple of islands to go. We have to find what we need on the next islands.*

~ ~ ~

Voices drew Shyvoan from a peaceful nap. Teigye and Buok had returned, and twilight was upon them – not much different from the daylight hazy light, just darker. Something cooking over the fire smelled wonderful.

"Nothing that looks like that path described in the scroll," Teigye reported. "Seems like the city pretty much fills the whole island." He rolled a rock close to the fire to use as a seat.

"That's what we found, too," Shyvoan said. She dished herself some of the stew that Liphye and Jarthan had prepared for everyone's evening meal and perched on another block of stone nearby.

"We could do the gateway to the next island then tonight," Liphye said after she finished her stew. "Wouldn't take too long to pack again."

"Wouldn't have to worry then about any friends our local hob might have," Teigye agreed.

Shyvoan studied Aivean as she tried to judge whether the mage might be ready to make another gateway.

"Why rush it?" Devrand said. Shyvoan gave him a surprised look, and she was not the only one. Devrand smiled in the face of their surprise.

"I've a feeling that next island is the one we want. Why not be as rested as we can manage before we go? I'm certain Aivean would benefit from the extra rest."

Shyvoan glanced at her fellow warriors and read the same astonishment and suspicion in their expressions that she had at this sudden solicitude on Devrand's part. *What's the man up to now?*

Aivean nodded, with a grateful and adoring smile for Devrand. "I'd most certainly feel better for it." She looked to the others. "Who knows what we'll face, beyond what sounds like an arduous hike and perhaps a troublesome meeting with a dragon. Shouldn't we be at the best we can manage?"

Shyvoan took a silent assessment of the others' opinions and nodded. "I've no objection to staying the night here and going through the gate in the morning. Double watches again tonight."

"I can help with watching this night," Jarthan spoke up. "Might help you warriors be at your best tomorrow."

"We can stagger them," Teigye said. "And still have at least two people on watch."

After they agreed to the order of watches, they cleaned up from the meal and Aivean renewed the ward-ring around the camp. She did the ward-ring a little differently from previous ones.

"What did you change?" Shyvoan said to the mage when she finished the warding.

"I added something that will keep our hob 'friend' away now, too," Aivean said. "At least, I think it will." She yawned and curled up with Devrand in a collection of cloaks and blankets at the edge of the firelight.

Shyvoan settled herself similarly, but alone, on the opposite side of the fire. She had taken one of the middle-of-the-night watches and so planned to catch what sleep she could before then, although she had already gotten a couple of hours before the evening meal.

~ ~ ~

In the morning, they followed their usual pattern of food first then packing to move on. Everyone seemed better for the extra rest. Shyvoan certainly felt better for it, even with a middle of the night watch that interrupted her sleep. *An uneventful watch, at least.*

"We're going to need to go back a little south and west to at least the edge of the city ruins," Aivean told them as they loaded the last of their gear on the tarandeer.

"At least?" Shyvoan repeated. "You don't know for sure?"

Aivean shook her head with a frown. "Not from this distance, for some reason. The sense of where our next gateway needs to be is much less clear than it's been before."

"Then let's get going. We don't want to linger in case that hob's got something planned for us." Devrand grabbed the lead of one of the tarandeer and headed out.

Aivean hurried to join Devrand. Jarthan followed and the others fell into a rough line behind them.

"What makes you think the hob's got something planned for us?" Liphye called to Devrand.

For answer, she received a shrug and a quick glance. "Nothing in particular," Devrand said. "But we agreed he was hiding something. What else would it be?"

"What else indeed?" Buok muttered to Shyvoan as they took spots at the end of the line.

Perhaps an hour of walking brought them to the western edge of the city ruins and the tangled forest that formed the border there. Shyvoan shot Aivean a questioning look and received as her response a shake of the head and a finger that pointed into the growth. So, Shyvoan drew her sword and attacked the plants to cut a path for them. The other warriors joined her and widened the space to allow the others to lead the tarandeer through.

An hour of this work had them drained and sweaty, but

they broke through to the shore on that side of the island.

"Look," Teigye breathed.

Shyvoan looked up from cleaning her blade of sticky saps and plant bits. Beyond the narrow rocky shore was the sea but at the edge stood some kind of stone structure. It extended both into the sea and back across the shore, almost to the tree line. It looked as ruined as the city and Shyvoan guessed it was from that same time. Then what lay beyond caught her attention.

Across a wide expanse of the Shallow Sea stood the shoreline of the next island. It seemed to have a rock structure like the one a few feet from where she sat.

What could they be?

Beyond that, Shyvoan saw the island – a lush, bright place, thick with grasses that blended into forest. Further away stood what looked like a rock wall, but not like the broken bits of walls they had seen in the city. *Doesn't look like anyone made that.*

And even further beyond that.... Were those mountains with clouds wreathing their peaks?

That had to be the right place.

Shyvoan glanced at the sky above her. *Unchanged. Still gray and hazy.* But over the other island the sun shone, and she swore she saw flowers in the grasses beyond the shore. No sign of any snow on that island. She exchanged incredulous looks with the others.

"We've found it," Aivean proclaimed.

CHAPTER 25

"Didn't see any of this for the haze yesterday," Teigye muttered, his tone disgruntled. Shyvoan doubted anyone else heard him as everyone stepped with exaggerated care through the rocks, and pulled the tarandeer behind them, to reach the stone structure at the edge of the sea. Even almost on top of it, Shyvoan could not guess its purpose.

What still stood was rectangular, with rounded corners on the two corners on the end of the structure that extended into the water. It looked to be solid, stones fitted snugly together like the remnants of the buildings in the city. Shyvoan stepped onto it. *Sturdy.* She paced its length and stopped at the end to look across the channel to the matching structure on the other island.

"Maybe a bridge used to stand here?" she called back to the others.

"A dock, I'd think," Jarthan said and ignored the glower Devrand gave him.

Shyvoan returned to the others, none of whom had followed her. She eyed the structure a few minutes longer from that angle.

"I suppose it could be," she said.

"Yes, yes. No doubt in the past your people used boats to travel between these islands," Devrand said, his tone impatient.

"The water looks deep enough for small ones," Jarthan said.

"We have no tales that our people used to use boats," Liphye said.

"And yet you people have the words for boats and docks and the like." Devrand shrugged and turned to Aivean. "Where do we need to place the gateway?"

"It feels like right here," she said and looked around with a puzzled expression. "But there's nothing here to hold the sides."

"You came through a gateway that didn't have tangible sides," Buok said to Devrand.

"The magic's not the same," Devrand muttered as he looked around. "One like that takes a lot more to open and hold."

"Can't we just walk across when the tide is low?" Jarthan said. "Like your people did days ago to that new island?"

Shyvoan scrutinized the sea between the two islands. "Can't tell how deep it is. It might not get shallow enough to be safe from moaras."

Teigye frowned at the end of the dock closest to them. "Maybe stack rocks to make the sides?"

Devrand gave him a disgusted look, but Aivean and Jarthan looked thoughtful.

"We could make that work," Jarthan said.

"It only has to hold until we're all through the gateway," Aivean added. "And I think the magic tends to help hold the sides up once it's active. But can we make them tall enough?"

"If it doesn't need to be too sturdy, maybe just lash some branches together instead," Liphye said. "Might be easier and faster."

"Using a doorway back in the ruins would be easier than that," Devrand said.

"But the magic connection is best here," Aivean argued. "By far. Trying to use a doorway in the ruins would take more magic and might not open to an ideal spot on that island." Aivean pointed across the water. "Right here has a good feel to it."

She and Devrand glared at each other several long minutes, while Shyvoan exchanged bemused glances with her fellows. Perhaps their mage was no longer as enamored of the man as she had been.

With a dismissive wave, Devrand turned away. "Do as you think best, then." He grabbed the leads for the tarandeer and settled himself on a large rock nearby in a clear indication that he planned to have no part in constructing the sides for the gateway.

"I'll see what I can find to lash the branches together," Jarthan muttered and dug through packs.

Shyvoan and the other warriors again exchanged glances and headed back to the forest's edge to collect branches. Aivean worked to clear the largest rocks from the spot for the gateway and marked where the sides needed to be.

Under Devrand's disapproving glare, they cobbled together two long bundles of branches to form the sides of the gateway. Liphye found some tall dry grasses that she twisted into narrow ropes to use as ties, so Jarthan did not need to rip strips from the old shirt he had pulled from his pack.

After they tied the branches together into two thin bundles longer than Buok was tall—by a little—Teigye and Buok stood them upright in the spots Aivean indicated. They piled rocks around the bottoms to hold them in place.

As they finished that, Devrand deigned to join them and looked over the makeshift sides. To Shyvoan's eye, they looked like a gentle breeze might knock them over.

Fortunately, the air was still.

Aivean gave a single nod at their work and pulled out the herbs she needed. She crushed a few, blew them between the makeshift sides, and sang the wordless song to open the gateway. As usual, Devrand stood with her, one hand touching her, and his other hand clasped around Jarthan's wrist.

After she sang for close to twice as long as she had needed for any of the previous gateways' sonant magic, Aivean pulled out more of the herbs. She added their crushed remnants to what hung already in the opening without stopping her song. A flicker of the magic formed, then it faded again.

Aivean shot Devrand a pleading look without breaking the rhythm of her song. Devrand nodded with a frown and his grip on Jarthan's wrist tightened. Strain appeared on all their faces and after a couple of minutes, Jarthan dropped to his knees with a groan, Devrand still clasping his wrist. Many long minutes later, the gateway finally formed.

"Hurry," Aivean hissed as she wobbled from the strain.

Shyvoan urged everyone through ahead of her, including Devrand and Jarthan. She pulled Aivean through with her and supported the other woman when she collapsed on the other side. Unlike all the previous gateways, this one did not need Aivean to close it. It collapsed when the mage did.

Shyvoan eased her to the cracked paving stones beneath their feet and sank down beside her. Her own head pounded, her legs felt weak, and she wanted nothing more than to slip into an oblivious sleep.

"We have to move," she muttered and fought to dredge up enough energy to do so.

"Come on." Buok grabbed her arm and hauled her to her feet. Then he lifted Aivean, staggered a couple of steps, and led the way to one side of the archway their gateway had brought them through.

Shyvoan stumbled after him and tried to pay attention

to their surroundings. Looked like more ruins, in worse shape than the previous ones. Much more broken and overgrown. Only the paving stones underfoot approached anything like intact and even they were rough and fragmented. The others stumbled along with her, vague shapes at either side.

Buok took them a short distance into a clump of trees and found a small clearing with a stream flowing through it. He set Aivean on the grass and almost fell in the process. Devrand and Jarthan collapsed next to her. They looked almost as drained as she did.

The warriors stumbled around doing the bare minimum—such as making sure they tied the tarandeer where they could reach the water—before they collapsed. Cool darkness engulfed Shyvoan. A restful daze swallowed her hint of worry that they had set no ward-ring.

~ ~ ~

Minutes—or maybe hours—later, Shyvoan startled from her daze. She had dozed lightly, and it seemed enough to renew her somewhat. What had penetrated her daze?

She sat up and looked over the others. All seemed asleep in the warm sunshine. The tarandeer dozed too, so nothing too alarming could be nearby.

A motion at the edge of her vision caught her attention and drew her gaze to the sky. Something flew high in the deep blue off to her left. West, if she judged the direction right. Something very large.

She shivered in a combination of awe and apprehension. *Could that be a dragon?*

She watched it make lazy circles in the sky. It barely moved its wings and iridescent light flashed sometimes off it. After several minutes, it flew out of sight, headed in the direction that she thought was west, angling a little south of that.

A bird called nearby—*that* was what had pulled Shyvoan from her doze—and her companions stirred. She hauled herself upright and studied their surroundings.

Everything looked peaceful. No sign that anything had come upon them while they had all been dazed or unconscious. The trees that surrounded their small glade had large leaves unlike any Shyvoan had seen before. The small stream looked clear and the tarandeer showed no ill effects from their drinks earlier. A strange aroma hung in the air, a sort of floral, peppery odor. Not unpleasant, but strong. *Will probably grow tired of the scent before long.*

She paced around their clearing in an attempt to clear her head. Oddly, while sunlight bathed them, she could not spot the sun itself. Also, its color seemed different. A bit redder. Even so, she threw a definite shadow on the ground, unlike the previous many islands with their bright haze for daylight.

Shyvoan set her concerns aside for the moment as she helped her fellow warriors set up camp. Jarthan steadied Aivean while she set the ward-rings. Devrand did as little as possible, only pulling out some food and refilling his waterskin at the stream.

Those minimal tasks completed, everyone gathered around the spot Buok had created for a fire—no fire burned there yet—and ate and drank. Shyvoan drew out the scroll that described the path to the dragon. She reread that section and passed the scroll to Buok when he held out a hand for it.

"Followed the path for six days," Buok muttered as he passed the scroll to Liphye.

"And that's after we find the beginning of it," Liphye said.

Teigye glanced at the scroll and passed it to Aivean who did not look at it before she passed it to Devrand. "Is the island even that big?" Teigye said. "I wouldn't have thought so from what we saw back on the other island."

"Could be long and narrow, at least compared to the

other islands," Buok said, "and we've seen just one narrow end."

Devrand studied the scroll several minutes and handed it back to Shyvoan, bypassing Jarthan. When she offered it to Jarthan, Devrand glared at her, then Jarthan. Jarthan shook his head under the weight of Devrand's glare, so Shyvoan tucked the scroll away again.

"If the path was hard to find, as the scroll says, and that was something like two hundred years ago, how can we have any chance to find it now?" Teigye complained.

"All we can do is look," Shyvoan said. "We've made it this far. We're here. We'll rest some more before we explore."

Then the significance of what she had seen earlier struck her. "And I think I've already seen a dragon," she said in a low voice.

"What?!" Teigye lowered his voice at the frantic gestures from the others. "You couldn't have said that from the start?"

"It was when I just woke up. I was still hazy. Still am a little."

"Understandable that it slipped your mind and such," Liphye said, with a glare for Teigye. "But tell us now."

Shyvoan described what she had seen and finished by pointing the direction the supposed dragon had flown.

"So, we might at least have a direction to start," she concluded.

Buok leaned close and whispered for Shyvoan's ears only. "Could be your luck at work for us, too," he said.

With a sharp glance for him, she shrugged.

"I can't go on right now," Aivean said. "That last gateway was much more difficult than any of the others."

Shyvoan nodded. "We'll rest here at least the rest of today. See how we are in the morning. Usual arrangements otherwise."

The other warriors groaned but set about deciding on watches for the rest of the day and for the night, then finished getting the camp set. Shyvoan let them settle things themselves for the most part – everyone knew what needed doing. She jumped when a touch on her hand pulled her from the doze she had fallen into again.

"We need to move around, if only for a little while," Devrand said, his hand still on hers. "We can do one of your scouting trips around our camp."

Shyvoan stared at him a moment, nodded, and scrambled to her feet with his help. He kept her hand in his with his fingers laced through hers. She looked at his hand then at his expression. *Something about his touch*…. But its import slipped away from her.

She waved at the others to get their attention. "Going to take a quick look around us," she said.

After the others waved languid acknowledgement, and Jarthan gave her and Devrand a strange look, she grabbed two waterskins and led the way into the surrounding foliage.

Speckled light broke the shade under the trees, as if the bright sun shone above. The aroma that had permeated the clearing was less intense here. Something Shyvoan appreciated. She shook her hand free of Devrand's grasp and he grinned at her.

"So, what do you want this time?" she growled at him as she absently rubbed her hand. The sensation of his grip lingered, although he had not gripped her at all tightly.

"Want? Many things. But at the moment what I mainly want is to not fall victim to some magic trap. Didn't you notice the scent back in the clearing? Something there—that scent perhaps—worked to make us all complacent and dull-witted."

Shyvoan frowned at him. Sure, the scent was heavy, but not unpleasant.

Devrand grabbed her by the shoulders and gave her a hard shake. Her anger flared and she broke free of his grasp, perhaps hurting him in the process, judging by the way he winced.

But her anger cleared her head. "Each island has had something bad for us. Not counting the first few islands we traveled," she said. She looked back the direction of the clearing. "It's too perfect. We need to move."

"Exactly," Devrand said. "But I think the others won't want to."

"You've never been reluctant to use your magical persuasion before," Shyvoan said. "Just now, even."

Devrand frowned at her but said nothing.

She studied his expression for several minutes. "Aha! I'd wager you can't use it on all of us at the same time."

Devrand's frown deepened, but he did not deny her assertion.

"So, you need me to help."

"You're rather resistant to persuasion," Devrand muttered.

"Fine." Shyvoan grabbed his arm. "Let's get us to a new camp site. And I'll have my eye on you."

"I'm surprised," Devrand muttered in a tone of voice that indicated anything but.

When they returned to the campsite, Shyvoan hurried to haul the other warriors to their feet and attempted to break them out of their stupor, while Devrand worked with Aivean and Jarthan. Shyvoan saw that those two were slower to respond. *Maybe because of the draining of their magic?* She smiled to herself. *Serves Devrand right.* Although she then felt bad about the other two.

Shyvoan prodded and pushed, and did most of the packing herself, but she got the warriors to load the tarandeer and lead them away from the clearing. She chose the direction she had seen the supposed dragon fly. Perhaps that might make their further travels easier.

Devrand's magical persuasion seemed of little use with Aivean and Jarthan, so Shyvoan draped Aivean's arm over her shoulder and walked her after the others. Devrand did the same with Jarthan.

Shyvoan frowned at the slow progress they made

through the thick trees. *Hope we're still traveling the direction we'd intended.* The further from the clearing they got, the better Shyvoan felt. The others seemed to recover some of their animation, too, and Aivean managed to walk on her own, although she stumbled over roots every few steps.

After Shyvoan no longer smelled the suspicious odor, she called a halt and shared what she and Devrand suspected. After a short rest, they headed out again and searched for another stream to camp near.

A few minutes into the search, they stepped out of the trees into another area of ruins. The paving stones looked much like the ones where they came through the gateway. Plants overran the ruins on this island more than they had the ruins on the previous island. Everyone paused to look around.

"Where's the sun?" Teigye said.

Shyvoan looked to the sky and saw the same clear blue she had seen before. They seemed to stand in sunshine, and they threw shadows, but Shyvoan saw no sun where it should have been.

"It feels like spring," Aivean said. "Have we been traveling so long?"

"Should still be plenty of winter left," Buok said after a minute.

Shyvoan mentally added up the days they had traveled. Buok was right.

"We've suspected that the Maheaja-Folk change things on other islands," Liphye said. "Probably the same thing here."

"Have to wait until we see the stars to pick our direction," Buok muttered.

"I'd be happy with a place to camp with a decent stream and no smelly flowers, or whatever it was," Aivean said.

"Let's go, then," Shyvoan said. "This area looks like mainly ruins."

After they looked for a couple of hours, the best they

found was some not-too-stagnant water that had collected in what looked like a large broken bowl in the middle of an open area of the ruins. They found shelter near the edge of that area, tucked in the remnants of one of the nearby broken buildings.

While Shyvoan boiled some of the water they had found, the others got the camp set up. Aivean drew the ward-rings, and this time she needed Devrand's help to manage it. Shyvoan kept an eye on the two of them. The last gate had taken a lot out of their mage and her two helpers. Even then, Jarthan lay asleep in a corner of the camp, too exhausted to stay awake once he stopped moving.

~ ~ ~

That night, Shyvoan shared a watch with Buok. After they made a circuit of the camp to ensure everything was as it should be, they met at the most-shadowed edge and scrutinized the sky. A lot of clouds, but they were on the move and Shyvoan saw stars in their midst. Buok was the best of the group at picking out directions from the stars, but Shyvoan had been learning.

"They're all wrong for winter," Shyvoan said in a low voice after a few minutes.

"Yah. Mid-spring, by their positions," Buok said. "Regardless, there's south."

Shyvoan nodded. "That's good anyway. I don't like the thought that we've lost something like ninety days though, if it's really spring now."

Buok shrugged. "Maheaja-Folk magic. Who knows what they've done to these places they've driven us from."

"True. I just hope our people are all right."

"Yah."

After he studied the sky a few minutes more, he turned to her with a serious expression. "Be cautious around Devrand," he urged her. "He's got some plan and I'd say it's close to fruition. I'd say it involves you somehow."

"He's got Aivean," Shyvoan protested. "He's got no need for me. I'm not magical anyway."

Buok shrugged. "Might be something else. Still…." He drove a branch into the ground on the southern side of the camp to mark that direction for the next day.

Shyvoan sighed. "Yah, I hear you. And I do agree. I feel he's planning something more than just making one of those passages that brought him and Jarthan here. I wish I knew what."

CHAPTER 26

The next day, both Jarthan and Aivean had improved, but not enough to continue on yet. So, they rested in the camp while the others took turns venturing out to hunt for the start of the path that the scroll described. On one of the trips, Buok paired with Devrand to see if they could find the shoreline to the east or south.

They gathered for the evening meal of some fish that Teigye had caught and finished the last of the kuchal.

"Now we have to hurry," Liphye said, with a mournful look for the empty skin. "We can't get any more until we get back to the denizens."

Shyvoan chuckled. "A very good reason."

"Any sign of the path?" Aivean said.

After exchanged glances, the others shook their heads. Jarthan stared at his feet as he seemed to ignore the conversation. He had only eaten half of his meal, too.

"We did find the shore to our southeast," Buok said, working on another wood carving, this one a tarandeer. "Closer than I had thought it would be."

"The city runs almost to the edges of cliffs there,"

Devrand said. "You can see a good distance. No sign of our pursuers."

Jarthan seemed to shrink at that announcement and picked at the rest of his meal.

"And the shore curves far south from there, it looked like," Buok added.

"If you two, Aivean and Jarthan, are up for it, let's move out tomorrow," Shyvoan said.

"Follow your dragon?" Teigye said with a grin.

Shyvoan shrugged but grinned back at him. "I *think* it was a dragon. Not like I've seen one before, but it seemed to fit the tales."

"Aivean and Jarthan will be fine to head out tomorrow," Devrand said.

Shyvoan and Buok exchanged glances at his assertion. Liphye frowned. Neither Aivean nor Jarthan met anyone's gaze.

"Well, then," Shyvoan said, breaking the uncomfortable silence, "usual arrangements and let's plan to leave after our morning meal."

~ ~ ~

In the morning, an exuberant Teigye woke Shyvoan much earlier than she had planned. The pre-dawn glow, barely enough light to see, lit Teigye's broad grin.

"I saw it. I saw it!" Teigye crowed.

The others grumbled as they pulled themselves from their blankets. They turned to the usual morning activities and left Teigye to Shyvoan.

"Saw what?" she said.

"The dragon. I saw it fly over there a few minutes ago." He pointed a direction to the right of the marking stick Buok had placed in the ground earlier.

"We have a direction then," Shyvoan mumbled as she struggled to wake fully.

They hurried through their meal and the packing and

headed the direction Teigye had indicated.

They traveled that day through the broken, overgrown ruins. As before, they never saw the sun, although everything threw enough of a shadow that they could judge their direction without much difficulty.

Sounds of birds surrounded them, although Shyvoan never spotted one. She did not recognize any of the bird calls. Other sounds harmonized with them, likely insects, but she did not recognize any of them either. The plants, too, were unfamiliar, most with multiple stems or trunks and large, oddly shaped leaves. She spotted a few flowers, none of them vesnaflurs.

"I wish we could get somewhere we can see further," Aivean complained as the light dimmed and they looked for a good place to camp for the night.

"Seems like this city's bigger than the one on the previous island," Teigye said.

"Are we still headed the right direction?" Devrand said.

Shyvoan shrugged. "Best we can tell in the weird daylight. We'll check the stars again tonight to make sure and make any changes for tomorrow."

After an uneventful night, the next day passed much the same as the previous. They altered their direction and kept to that heading the best they could. Shyvoan kept an eye on both Jarthan and Aivean. Jarthan had withdrawn to the way he had been when they first met. Aivean was subdued and quiet. Both looked tired, more so than the rest of them, not that anyone seemed fully rested. Weariness certainly bothered Shyvoan, even after what should have been a couple of restful nights.

Worry washed over her that something lurked in the air of this place, as they had encountered before, that sapped their strength even more than the gateways did.

Evening found them in a spot that held more vegetation than ruins. Shyvoan hoped that meant they might soon leave the city behind. The trees grew taller here than they had seen before, but were further apart, which gave better views of the sky.

Again that night, Buok checked and marked their direction for the next day's travel.

The next day, Shyvoan woke to a strange humming sound near her ear. She turned her head, her motion slow and smooth, and saw the tiniest bird she had ever seen hovering in the air not a foot away from her. It was brightly colored, red and orange, and its wings moved so fast she saw nothing more than a blur. For a minute she and the bird stared at each other. In the next instant, the bird was gone, flying so fast she again only saw a blur, headed the direction they planned to go.

Wondering at it, she got ready for the day.

"We'll need to get more food soon," Liphye said as they headed out.

"Probably going to be fish," Buok said. "I haven't seen signs of any other creatures other than the birds. And the birds I've seen are far too small for any kind of meal for us."

"At least the tarandeer are well fed," Teigye said with a gentle tug on the reins of one of them to lead it away from the shrub it had been munching.

"Wonder if there are any berries that we can eat," Aivean said in a low voice.

"If this really is spring here, it'd be too early for berries and such." Liphye waved an arm at all the plant life around them.

"Maybe some of those spring tubers or root vegetables, then," Aivean said. "Leafy greens."

"Haven't seen anything I recognize here," Teigye said. "But maybe we ought to try the plants the tarandeer have been going after. They've shown no ill effects from them."

So that day they gathered what they could of the plants the tarandeer had been eating and stopped in the late afternoon at a promising stream, wider and deeper than any they had seen so far on the island. After everyone helped set up the camp, Buok and Liphye settled in to fish, while Shyvoan and Teigye washed the plants everyone had gathered and tentatively tasted them. Jarthan joined them. Aivean and Devrand settled in a shady spot and watched the others.

"Oh, that's awful!" Teigye spat out a bite of the large leaf he held, the last of his pile. "I don't think this one's for us."

"Probably for the best," Shyvoan said. "The tarandeer seem to enjoy that one and we won't have to fight them for it." She waved a hand at the tarandeer off to the side of the camp munching happily on the big leaves.

"Bleh," Teigye said. "Fine with me." He rinsed his mouth out with a sip from a waterskin.

"So that leaves us with these." He indicated the small pile of variously colored and shaped leaves that sat between the three of them.

Shyvoan and Jarthan nodded. "I like the flavor of this one," Jarthan lifted a narrow, pale-green leaf.

Shyvoan nodded and grabbed several other leaves from the pile. "I believe we can try these cooked, too," she said and set them aside.

"And what of these?" Jarthan held up the last few leaves.

"They're not too bad raw," Teigye said. "But let's dry some and see if we can make teas from them. I think they'll work for that. I just wish we had found more of the chathea for your tea."

Jarthan nodded. "Aivean and I have little left. Although those other plants you've collected have worked too. Just not quite as well. Anla, heagyn, and rastenye are the plants, right?"

Teigye nodded. "And we've still got a fair supply of those."

"Now that we're out of the ruined city, I'm hoping we find the path soon, or something else to help us along," Shyvoan said. "And you two won't need the teas much longer."

Teigye left to gather more of the leaves they had decided were edible, and to see if they might find any tubers or root vegetables. Shyvoan set the leaves they wanted to dry in a patch of bright light and retreated to her own patch of shade across the camp from Aivean and Devrand. Jarthan settled in another bright area and closed his eyes.

For several minutes, Shyvoan watched Aivean and Devrand talk, their voices too quiet to carry. They seemed at odds without really arguing. *Wonder what that's about.* She felt too lazy to move closer to find out.

The smell of something good cooking woke her. She frowned at herself. *Hadn't meant to nap.* But she did feel better for it.

Teigye had not found any edible roots but had brought plenty of the edible leaves back. The cooked ones were tolerable and the few fish Buok and Liphye had caught were delicious. After the meal, Buok and Teigye returned to the stream, hopeful they would catch more fish in the dusk.

As darkness engulfed the small camp, they returned with a respectable number of fish, which they cleaned and set to smoke over the low fire.

~ ~ ~

In the morning, the smoked fish and some of the raw leaves made a tasty breakfast.

They stayed another day there to replenish their food supplies and headed out again the next morning.

As they had traveled, the ground had gradually sloped up. That day, the slope became much more noticeable and around midday they moved out of the tall trees into an area of shrubs and grasses. Teigye continued to collect leaves, with help from Jarthan and Liphye. Shyvoan also gathered a few when she spotted them, but she kept most of her attention on their surroundings, as did Buok. The land continued to rise more sharply ahead of them, leading into those mountains Shyvoan had spotted from the other island.

The mountains looked rugged, from what Shyvoan saw. As often as she scrutinized them during the day, she saw nothing that looked like a path. With the distance—hard to judge—and the abundant plant life, she reminded herself that it might be unreasonable to expect to see any sort of path yet.

In the afternoon, they again traveled through plants that blocked their view, although these trees grew much shorter, with much smaller leaves, still unfamiliar. They stopped at another large stream for the night and added to their food stores. Teigye grabbed some of the leaves they had been trying and attempted a tea. He scrunched up his face when he tasted it but finished the cup. "Let them dry some more and they should be good," he told them.

"Nice to have something other than water," Liphye said with a grin. "Even if it has to be tea."

~ ~ ~

Roughly midafternoon the next day they broke free of the trees into a broad area of tall grass that covered steep slopes that rose ahead of them and to their left. Mixed in with the grass, nearly as numerous as the grass blades themselves, small white flowers grew.

Vesnaflurs.

"There must be thousands of them." Aivean groaned and sank to her knees. "How are we to find the path in that?"

CHAPTER 27

They decided to make camp there at the forest's edge. A stream nearby provided clear water and the tarandeer seemed thrilled to feast on the grasses and flowers beyond the tree line, especially the flowers. As Shyvoan and the others ate their evening meal, they considered the field of vesnaflurs. The sharp, spicy scent that wafted from the flowers in the slight breeze made the inside of Shyvoan's nose tingle. *That'll likely get annoying before very long.* She wrinkled her nose, but it made no difference.

"I've never heard of so many growing in one place," Liphye murmured.

"Is this the path?" Aivean said.

Shyvoan pulled out the scroll and reread the pertinent section aloud. "I doubt it," she concluded. She waved a hand at the field. "Not exactly hard to find."

"Could be the path is there," Jarthan said. "Maybe it begins out there somewhere. That part would be hard to find."

"Especially after so long," Buok said with a nod of agreement.

"Two hundred years," Devrand murmured.

"Best we can tell," Shyvoan said. She stared at the field in the fading light. "At least we're closer to the mountains. I can picture a path starting here and leading into them. We can begin scouting for it tomorrow, I think."

She caught a look exchanged between Jarthan and Devrand. "Unless you have a better idea?" she said.

Jarthan dropped his gaze to his feet. Devrand met hers with a challenging look of his own, then grinned. "Of course not. It's a good idea. And that will let these two rest some more." He gestured to Aivean and Jarthan. "I wouldn't expect a mountain path that's two hundred years old to be an easy one, even if it had been to begin with. And we might need magic when we finally find the dragon."

"We're going to talk to it," Shyvoan said. "Not magic it."

Devrand shrugged. "What if it doesn't want to talk. We might need a magical defense."

Shyvoan frowned but admitted the truth of his words, to herself.

They tossed around some speculations on the path, how long it would take to find it, and the need to stock up on more food before they traveled it when they did find it. When they ran out of ideas to discuss, they settled in for the night.

Their second day at that campsite, Shyvoan stayed in camp as camp guard, and Aivean and Jarthan continued to rest, while the others scouted and gathered food. Shyvoan occupied herself with trying various plant combinations with some mostly dried vesnaflurs to make a tea. The tarandeer liked the flowers so much, and seemed livelier since eating them, so maybe the flowers might help the people of the group, too. She managed a combination of some vesnaflurs and a pinch of one of the large leaves the tarandeer liked so much. It was not too bad.

That afternoon, Buok returned early from his scouting

expedition with a pleased expression and a load of the plants they had found edible. He waited until everyone returned to share his news.

"Might've found something," he said around a bite of fish stew. "Takes almost half a day to get there but could be the path." He waved an arm toward the opposite side of the field of flowers to the southwest. "After so many years, the plants have overgrown the path, or what looks like it could have been a path."

Devrand had given the warrior his full attention while he ignored his own meal. "Finally," he said. "Now we can get moving again."

"In the morning," Shyvoan said.

"We might as well pack the camp," Teigye said. "We've got plenty of food stashed."

"And if it's that far, we'd do well to go from there," Liphye said.

Shyvoan nodded her agreement. "I don't think we should travel at night anyway. Just because we've yet to see any Maheaja-Folk on this island doesn't mean they aren't here. And if they're like all the others we know, they'll prefer the night."

With that decided, they finished their meal. With no need to consult together, everyone prepared the camp as much as possible for departure the next day. They left little that would need to be finished in the morning.

The next morning, they grabbed food they could eat as they walked and set out early. Shyvoan had left the scouting the past days to the others and so had not realized how rugged the ground was under the even-looking blanket of flowers. *No wonder the path had been hard to find, if the plants had overgrown it.* At least that's what she assumed had happened.

About midday—the best Shyvoan could tell from their hazy shadows and no direct sight of the sun—Buok stopped.

"Here, I believe."

Shyvoan looked around, as did the others, and saw no difference in the blanketing flowers. From where they stood, a deceptive rise, one that had not been obvious before, hid their camp of the night before.

Buok waved Shyvoan close and positioned her right in front of him, facing toward a steep rise that led to the mountains.

"Crouch down," he instructed. "Put your eyes at the level of the flowers and see if I'm right."

Shyvoan followed his instructions. When she placed her eyes at the same level as the flowers, she saw that where she and Buok crouched the flowers grew shorter than those to either side. The lower plant growth extended toward the steep rise and looked like an overgrown path. She stood upright again.

"Looks like it to me," she said with a smile.

The others took turns looking at what Buok had discovered. Liphye even placed both hands on the ground under the shorter flowers and compared it to the ground around the edges of the area.

"In this lower area, the ground feels more packed," she said.

"Like it was a regularly used path," Teigye said.

"I thought it sounded like this path was supposed to be a secret," Aivean said.

Shyvoan shrugged. "Maybe a secret only held by you mages. And we know there were far more of you in the past. Who can say how many there were two hundred years ago."

"Maybe they had regular appointments to visit the dragons and have tea with them or something," Teigye teased.

Jarthan chortled, then subsided under Devrand's glare.

"So now that we have our path, we should go," Devrand said.

Shyvoan gave him an absent nod but did not move. She turned, her motion unhurried, and scanned their surroundings. After she had made a complete circle, she crouched in the depression and looked the opposite direction along the hidden path.

"It extends that way, too," she said.

"Of course, it has to come from somewhere," Devrand said. He waved a hand toward the rising ground the other direction. "But there are the mountains. No question of which way to go."

"The scroll said they started at dawn each day and the sun was always at their backs," Shyvoan muttered.

"And didn't it say something about a stream?" Liphye said, with a pointed look for their surroundings. "Anyone see a stream?"

"Could've dried up over the years," Devrand said.

"True. But there could still be signs."

"Seems like we should look," Teigye said.

Devrand started to object, but Jarthan gripped his arm and stopped him. Devrand gave the other man a hostile look but followed him a short distance away. They engaged in a whispered, heated discussion while the others looked on, bemused.

After some debate, Devrand threw his hands up and turned away. Jarthan looked back to the others. "So, what should we look for?" he said.

While Buok explained the subtle and not so subtle signs that could mean an old stream bed, Shyvoan watched Devrand. Something in his stance spoke to her of tension, urgency, perhaps some fear.

When he turned around, she saw all of those in his expression. The next moment they vanished, replaced by his normal semblance of nonchalance.

"What did you see on your scouting trips these past days?" Shyvoan said as a thought came to her.

Unease flashed across his expression. He shrugged and turned away.

She edged closer. "You went east, right? It wouldn't happen to have been that ship, would it? They're close enough to see again, aren't they?"

After several long minutes, and without looking at her, Devrand nodded.

"So that's why the push to go," Shyvoan murmured. "All right, then."

She raised her voice for everyone's ears. "So, let's find this stream, shall we? Where shall we start?" She looked to Buok for an answer.

After he scrutinized their surroundings, he gestured along the supposed path, the opposite direction they had been facing. "I think there is most likely. Might as well follow this 'path' we've found, too."

They followed the hidden depression, with pauses from time to time to crouch and determine its course. It did not run straight but curved, with flower-disguised hillocks that grew more obvious as they found themselves turned around and closer to the edge of the field from which they had started.

As dusk descended and Shyvoan considered calling it time to set up the night's camp, Buok suddenly stopped. He held a hand up for silence and crouched in the knee-high flowers.

The other three warriors stopped at his signal and dropped down into the flowers. Devrand, Jarthan and Aivean followed their example a few seconds later.

Shyvoan edged toward Buok, her attention more on their surroundings than on him. She did not detect anything.

When she stopped next to Buok, he pointed off to one side and readied his bow. Shyvoan eased her sword from its scabbard and glanced at the others. They too readied weapons.

Shyvoan tapped the back of Buok's hand to get his attention and used hand signals to ask what he detected.

He gave her an uncharacteristic shrug, with hand signals that indicated Maheaja-Folk and uncertainty.

An uncanny shriek from the shadows around them sent

chills down Shyvoan's back. In the next instant, a swarm of farliths rushed them from all sides. The creatures flowed over and around them and deafened them with their near-constant shrieks.

Shyvoan scrambled to keep them from touching her, vaguely aware that the others did too.

Except for Devrand and Jarthan, who seemed embroiled in an argument.

"You have to." Devrand's voice rose over the noise from the farliths. "I'm not falling here to these *things*."

Shyvoan swung her sword at one of the shadowy creatures and caught it with the tip of the blade. Its shrieks escalated and sent pain stabbing into her ears. Her sword turned icy cold, but she kept her grip on it.

She caught a glimpse of Jarthan shaking his head. Then Devrand grabbed the other man by the back of the neck.

"Do it," he ordered. Jarthan stiffened and his expression settled into fierce resolve.

With a sound that seemed half growl and half moan, Jarthan stood and closed his eyes. Devrand stood with him and maintained his grip.

Shyvoan called out a warning as the farliths swarmed toward the two men.

Then the Maheaja-Folk stopped.

Silence gripped the area, broken only by a faint whimper from Aivean.

Shyvoan held herself still, afraid of what was happening and afraid to disturb it. *If those farliths get free…. We have no chance against that many.*

The tableau held a few seconds longer. Then with howls louder than their shrieks, the farliths stretched into long shadowy ribbons that gave the impression they tried to claw their way away as they were drawn toward Devrand and disappeared into his body.

When the last farlith was gone, Jarthan's knees buckled. As Devrand eased him to the ground, Shyvoan saw a shadowy wisp wrap around his hand—the hand that touched Jarthan's neck—and twine up his arm before it faded away into his skin.

His gaze met hers and for a moment an odd glow lit his eyes. Then it vanished.

Shyvoan and the others exchanged stunned looks. Devrand broke the spell that held them when he stood again and spun around, one arm outstretched. Dark wisps flowed out from him into the night.

"There aren't any more of them," he said. "And the stream's that way." He pointed north, hauled Jarthan to his feet, and led the way that direction.

~ ~ ~

Shyvoan stumbled in Devrand's wake, aware the others moved likewise. A fog hung around her, not unlike back in that clearing in which they had camped when they first arrived on the island. She shook her head to try to clear her thoughts and glared at Devrand's back. Almost as if he felt her regard, he shot her a glance over his shoulder, then turned back to watch where he stepped.

Close to an hour after the encounter with the farliths, Devrand stopped and eased a groggy Jarthan to the ground.

"There's a stream there," Devrand said with a nod to his right. He dug into Jarthan's pack where it sat atop the back of one of the tarandeer.

Buok headed the direction Devrand indicated and stopped a few steps away.

"There is," he confirmed. "Not much more than a trickle."

"Think it's the one we want?" Aivean said.

"Camp here?" Liphye said at the same time.

The two women exchanged looks and both looked to Shyvoan.

She took a visual assessment of everyone and nodded to Liphye. "Camp here."

Then she shrugged at Aivean. "Hopefully."

Teigye rose from a crouch. "The path we think we've found is here, anyway," he said. He turned his attention to camp setup.

Shyvoan and Buok helped while Liphye stood watch and Devrand and Aivean made a small cup of that bolstering tea for Jarthan.

Shyvoan waited for Devrand to hand Jarthan the cup, and for Jarthan to drink, then she grabbed Devrand's arm, making certain to only touch his sleeve. She spun him around to face her.

"And just what was that back there?" she demanded. "We *all* saw it this time, so you can't just pass it off."

Devrand glanced around the small group with a slight smile.

"What was it that you saw?" he said.

Shyvoan growled, fists clenched. At a light touch from Buok, she subsided. A little.

"You using your magic," Teigye said into the tense silence. "You sucked in the farliths somehow."

"Their magic," Jarthan said, to Shyvoan's surprise.

"Apparently they don't exist without their magic," Devrand said with a shrug and turned his back. "Worked out well for us."

Shyvoan reached out to grab his arm again but hesitated when Jarthan caught her gaze and shook his head.

With a frown, she instead joined Liphye at the edge of their camp and watched Aivean set the ward-ring.

"We'll want to look it over again in the daylight," Liphye said after several minutes. "But I think this *is* the stream we want."

Shyvoan gave her a nod of acknowledgement.

"I'm beginning to believe this might be worse than if we just kept fleeing from island to island like always," she murmured for Liphye's ears alone.

"Could be," Liphye muttered, with a sidelong look at

Devrand. She tapped the hilt of Shyvoan's sword, sheathed at her side. "That affects the farliths better than any other weapon I've seen. Maybe it would be better against other threats and such, too, if needed."

Shyvoan shared a thoughtful look with Liphye and nodded her understanding.

"I'll take first watch," Liphye said then and nudged her back the direction of the camp. "Rest while you can."

~ ~ ~

Did I really see what I think I did last night? One look at Devrand's smug expression in the dim light before dawn the next morning told Shyvoan that she had.

With little conversation, they packed their camp. Devrand atypically grabbed Jarthan's pack and his own and loaded them on a tarandeer himself, before everyone followed Buok to the stream and along it to investigate it in the light of day.

Shyvoan eyed Jarthan as they walked the short distance and saw why Devrand had taken his burden. Jarthan stumbled several times and barely kept himself up and going. Doubtful that he would have been able to lift the pack and secure it.

Shyvoan also saw that Liphye had taken a place behind Devrand. She walked with a hand on the hilt of her sword, with her attention almost as much on Devrand as on their surroundings.

After Shyvoan saw Jarthan stumble a second time, she almost called a halt. But a look from Devrand stopped her somehow. Then Devrand offered Jarthan the support of his shoulder.

Shyvoan wondered how long that would last, but again an odd compulsion to keep her thoughts to herself kept her from doing anything.

Less than a quarter of an hour brought them to a spot Buok identified as likely. He and Teigye poked around and examined the flowers that still blanketed the area. Shyvoan took the time to unload one of the tarandeer—with Devrand's unexpected help—and redistribute those packs to allow Jarthan to ride. After she helped Jarthan mount the tarandeer, Shyvoan turned back to see what Buok and Teigye might have found.

"Here, we think," Teigye said as he waved her closer.

Shyvoan joined them and repeated their actions, crouching to check the flower heights and feeling the packed ground. She stood to get a look at her shadow and turned until it stretched ahead of her. She crouched again and saw that the shorter plants they believed marked the path did run that direction.

"Looks like it," she said and began to follow the path, her shadow stretching in front of her.

She heard the others take positions behind her. She glanced back to check on them and the sudden appearance of the sun blinded her.

"Now that all of us stand on the path," Devrand murmured.

"Must be the right way," Liphye said and urged everyone forward. She clasped Shyvoan's arm to guide her while her vision cleared.

After several minutes, Shyvoan could see again and shook free of Liphye's hand with a smile of thanks. The other warrior dropped back again to follow behind Devrand.

Buok moved to take the lead, with Teigye close behind. With a slight smile for Shyvoan, Aivean moved past her on the path and joined Teigye.

"I can feel a hint of magic now that we're on the right path," Aivean confided over her shoulder. "If it holds, we won't have to pause and crouch down to the flowers' level every so often to keep to the path."

Shyvoan nodded in agreement. "Good to hear," she murmured. She dropped back to join Liphye at the back of their little group.

Liphye nodded to her, and kept her attention divided between their surroundings and Devrand's back. Jarthan rode at the middle of the group and led their two pack tarandeer.

Buok set a brisk pace, but not the rapid one the warriors used when they needed to cover ground as fast as possible. Even so, Shyvoan judged this pace should help them make timely progress. She found she wanted to get there without further delay.

So much time to get to this point, and still six days, counting this one, to get to the dragon. What might have happened to everyone they had left behind in all this time? *And what of Jarthan?* Even riding the tarandeer, he looked drained, and he never once looked up to meet anyone's gaze.

At midday they stopped for a rest and meal. The last half of the morning, the path had begun to climb into the low hills that edged the mountains. When they stepped off the path for their meal, the sun vanished again, although Shyvoan still saw their shadows, minimal at midday.

Everyone exchanged looks and stepped back onto the path. And the sun was visible again.

By mutual unspoken agreement, they all settled on the path to eat. Jarthan only nibbled at his food before he stretched out and closed his eyes.

Shyvoan gave Devrand a questioning look.

"He'll be fine," Devrand assured her. "This isn't unusual."

When he offered no further explanation, Shyvoan turned to scan their surroundings while she ate. A sense of being watched pressed on her, but nothing moved, not even a breeze fluttered the grasses and flowers.

With a hand signal to the other warriors that she would return before long, she strolled along the path the way they had come. She kept her motion deliberately casual but stayed alert to anything different in their surroundings.

At a point where she could just make out the others

behind her, she crouched to hide in the flowers. As she did so, her hand brushed the hilt of her sword, and an odd zing went through her from the contact.

When she drew the sword, it looked as it always had, yet the zing pulsed through her from where she gripped it. She sheathed it and still the sensation tickled her hand whenever she touched the hilt.

She kept hold of it as she slowly scanned a half-circle back the way they had come.

Nothing to see. But the sensation stayed with her, even when she returned to the others.

"Nothing," she said to their questioning looks, and shrugged.

The other warriors situated themselves this time to keep the other three in the center of the group. A subtle tension hung around the group as they set off again.

After about an hour, Shyvoan chuckled softly and pointed to her small shadow that stretched in front of her. "The path turns so that the sun is always at our backs," she said, now understanding that part of the scroll.

As the meaning came to the others, they smiled and nodded.

They continued on, Buok still in the lead.

Buok kept the pace the same for most of the afternoon as the path took them further into the hills and climbed steadily. It also narrowed until it formed a flat ledge not quite wide enough for two people to walk side by side, with increasingly steep slopes up on one side and down on the other. The tarandeer became more skittish as the way became steeper and they often stumbled on large rocks embedded in the path and hidden beneath the flowers. Devrand and Aivean each took a lead from Jarthan, so he only had to deal with the tarandeer he rode.

The afternoon wore on into evening and Jarthan slumped more and more atop his tarandeer, but he waved away offers to stop early. Shyvoan did not like the idea of trying to sleep on the sloped path. *Hopefully, we'll find someplace to make a decent camp.*

As darkness stretched out to cover them, the moon not in the sky yet, they came to a wider area on their left that would make a good spot to camp for the night. A trickle of water ran down the hill at its far edge and curved to run further downhill alongside the path. Shyvoan had not even noticed the water at the side of the path beneath the still dense but shorter flowers.

"Almost as if planned," Liphye murmured as they left the path to make camp.

When she stepped off the path, Shyvoan no longer felt the zings from her sword. She stepped back on the path and the zings returned, although fainter than earlier in the day. *Interesting.* Another way to tell the path's location, assuming the sensation did not fade away completely.

After their evening meal, Teigye used the last of the dried leaves that made that bolstering tea. Jarthan drank it eagerly and fell asleep soon after.

"Care to explain this?" Shyvoan waved a hand at Jarthan.

Devrand shrugged. "It's much as you saw when we first arrived. The magic is taxing, and it takes some time for him to recover."

Liphye frowned at him. "I'd think you'd want to help him better."

"I do what I can."

Liphye snorted her opinion of that. Shyvoan was inclined to agree with her but kept her thoughts to herself. She had to grin, though, when Devrand cast a questioning look in Aivean's direction and she turned her back on him, grabbed a blanket and settled on the far side of their small fire from him.

Shyvoan ducked her head to hide her grin when Devrand glared around at everyone, and shared it with her fellow warriors when he no longer watched. Devrand grabbed a blanket, hunched down next to Jarthan, and periodically glared at Aivean. But he made no move to talk with her.

The warriors settled the watches for the night, and they followed their usual camping pattern.

~ ~ ~

The next morning, Aivean and Devrand engaged in a whispered, heated discussion at the edge of the camp. After they pretended to ignore the tiff for several minutes, Shyvoan and the other warriors dropped the pretense and turned to watch the altercation while they continued to work on their own tasks. Jarthan ignored the conflict.

After another couple of minutes, Devrand reached toward Aivean, and she swatted his hand away.

"No, I *don't* need to," she said and turned away from him to pack her blanket.

Devrand watched her for a moment, before he glanced at Jarthan, then the others, his expression more frustrated than anything else. Then he too turned to get ready to go.

The rest of the day matched the previous in most respects, but with more tension. After their morning spat, Aivean and Devrand avoided each other as much as they could in the small group. The other warriors seemed more alert than usual and on edge, as Shyvoan herself was. But when they all compared notes, none of them had anything more substantial to explain their unease than the sense of being watched. No one saw anything to explain the feeling, though.

Jarthan kept to himself, but his eyes and expression were more alert than the previous day as he rode the tarandeer.

The path continued to curve so the sun always sat at their backs as it took them further into the hills. The slopes on either side grew steeper yet and they made their evening camp in another area that looked designed for it, in what had to be true mountains.

~ ~ ~

When Teigye woke her, Shyvoan felt like she had just gone to sleep. His next words confirmed the truth of that.

"Sorry to wake you so long before your watch," he said in a low voice. "Spotted something you should see."

Shyvoan stifled a groan as she hauled herself to her feet and noted their tiny campfire had not burned down much at all. She truly *had* just gone to sleep.

With a wave in the dim light to Liphye across the camp, Teigye led the way back along the path. As they approached one of the steeper sections closest to their camp, a sharp curve, he dropped to the ground and motioned for Shyvoan to do the same.

They eased over to the edge and Teigye pointed to a tiny spot of brightness in the dark below and some distance off. Somewhere in that field of vesnaflurs, Shyvoan estimated.

"Look like a campfire to you?" he murmured.

Shyvoan nodded, before she realized he might not be able to see her motion. "Looks like it."

"Not Maheaja-Folk, then. Devrand and Jarthan's pursuers, maybe?"

"Can't think who else it'd be."

They saw motion in front of the distant fire and watched for close to a quarter-hour before they returned to their own camp.

"Get the camp ready to leave without delay in the morning," Shyvoan instructed as she returned to her blanket. "Buok and I'll finish anything needed when it's our watch."

Shyvoan fell asleep to a quiet bustle as Liphye and Teigye packed up some of the camp.

266

CHAPTER 28

When the first hint of dawn colored the sky, Shyvoan and Buok woke the others. Teigye told the three who had not had watches about the distant campfire.

"Just an hour ago, I saw no sign of movement where it is," Buok added.

At the news, Jarthan took a step in that direction but Devrand's grip on his arm stopped him. The two men glared at each other, then Jarthan bent to gather his blanket and pack it.

Buok handed out food to eat as they traveled, and a brief time later, they were on the path again. Their barely visible shadows stretched before them. Jarthan again rode one of the tarandeer. Shyvoan watched him and while he did not look happy, he did look like he was recovering.

That day saw them move into true mountains. The path became rockier and more uneven underfoot, still hidden under the vesnaflurs which grew to half the height they had in the field below. Their way grew steeper, and the path no longer held level from one side to the other, which caused the tarandeer difficulty with the steepest of the sections.

Throughout the morning, they encountered places where the path branched, and the flowers covered both possible paths. A check of where their shadows lay helped them differentiate between the paths and keep to the one they needed.

Devrand kept glancing behind them and urging speed. They traveled the path as fast as they could, although their progress felt little greater than that of the previous day.

When they paused around midday, in a spot that had another trickle of water that ran down the hill—this time crossing the path—Buok grabbed some food to carry with him and backtracked along their path. He returned while they packed again.

"No sign of any followers," he said. "But we're leaving quite the trail, the tarandeer in particular."

Shyvoan studied the path they had already traveled. Distinct hoof marks, crushed flowers and plants, and places where the tarandeer had grabbed flowers to eat – all very clear to see.

She scrutinized the tarandeer then.

"They're having more and more difficulty following this path," Jarthan said in a low voice. "It's mountains, so it'll probably get worse. I can walk."

Shyvoan peered at him. He still looked wan but acted more alert and moved without any wobbling.

"We probably should have left them back at the field to begin with," Devrand muttered.

"Can't change that now," Shyvoan snapped.

Devrand scowled at her and glared at Jarthan. "You can't slow us down. You'll have to keep the pace."

Jarthan scowled right back. "I know that." he said with an edge to his voice.

"Won't we be helping your pursuers if we leave the tarandeer, or send them back down to the field?" Aivean said.

Devrand shook his head. "They'd have the same

problem that we do with the tarandeer and this path. And I doubt they've ever ridden tarandeer, or have even seen them before. They won't give them any help."

"Can the tarandeer still manage?" Shyvoan said to the other warriors.

"For now. Perhaps for a while yet," Liphye said. "They're uneasy on this path, don't seem to like the hills, but haven't yet balked."

Shyvoan glanced back down the path.

"Let's keep the tarandeer as long as we can," she said. "Jarthan, you ride. Recover as much as possible before you have to walk."

With nods all around, they resettled packs on the tarandeer, Jarthan mounted his, and they returned to their trek.

~ ~ ~

As the afternoon progressed and their path grew ever steeper, the air grew cooler, with a hint of dampness. The sun still threw their shadows on the ground before them, but Shyvoan kept an eye on the sky. Nothing indicated that a storm approached, but something told her there might be one.

The path narrowed until Jarthan's leg on the uphill side brushed the slope and plants next to him as he rode as far from the steep drop on the other side of the path as he could. Trees grew close to the path on both sides and clung to the steep hillsides, their trunks twisted and bent. They reached perhaps twice as tall as Buok. The vesnaflurs still covered the path and extended beyond it to either side, even under the trees.

The day wore away and Shyvoan peered ahead, through the others in the group, hoping to spot a place for their nighttime camp. The path had become twisty throughout the afternoon, though, and she could not see any great distance in front of Buok, who still let the way.

S. Lynn Helton

A sudden chittering sound from the side startled everyone. The increased tension in the air had them peering into the shadows under the trees around them.

Buok increased their pace and held his bow nocked and ready. Shyvoan rested her hand on the hilt of her sheathed sword. Only faint zings from the sword now. Maybe they had just been to make sure whoever carried the dragon-scale sword was able to get far enough along the path. Still, would have been nice if they'd stayed for the whole way. The tarandeer, too, seemed more jittery and they startled randomly at nothing anyone spotted.

Around several more twisty curves, Shyvoan saw a wider area ahead of them. Buok glanced back at her with a questioning look.

Their shadows stretched long in front of them, and the sky had yet to take on the colors of sunset, but Shyvoan had a feeling they should stop there, so she nodded to Buok.

They had stretched out while they walked but they all clumped together as they reached the wider area because the tarandeer refused to leave the path. Shyvoan exchanged looks with the others and eased off the path, sword drawn.

In that one step, the sunlight vanished. Gusts of frigid wind buffeted her, and cold slivers of ice pelted her. The sky was dark with a storm, and lightning flashed somewhere off to her right.

She jumped back onto the path, into the sunshine. The others stared at her.

"What?" she said to their astonished looks.

"You look like you just came out of a spring storm," Teigye said after a minute.

"I did."

They exchanged looks.

"But how?" Liphye said. "You stepped off the path for a minute and came right back."

Shyvoan frowned and took a good look around them.

No sign of the storm from where she stood. No trees bent in the wind; no sleet sliced through the air. The sky above showed the colors of sunset and their shadows had grown less distinct.

She waved a hand at the open area beyond the edge of the path. "Well, there's an impressive storm out there. Can't blame the tarandeer for not wanting to go into that."

"Looks like we're camping on the path tonight," Devrand said and dug in one of the packs.

"We'll need to keep track of the storm," Buok said and stepped off the path.

Shyvoan watched as he stood there and slowly turned a complete circle. He braced himself against a wind she could not see.

"Can you hear me?" he yelled.

She nodded, reluctant to yell back. Her voice likely would not carry into the storm but might carry down the mountains. She made the hand gesture that indicated quiet, and he nodded his understanding. While the others worked to set up their camp, stretched along the path, Shyvoan continued to watch Buok.

He staggered across the small level area and knelt at the slope on the far side. Trees smaller than the ones nearby clung to that slope and small bushes hid the areas not covered by trees. Buok glanced at the sky from time to time, at lightning flashes she thought. After several minutes he staggered back to the path.

He stepped onto the path with a small sigh and wiped water and ice crystals from his face and hair.

"Nasty," he said with a slight smile. "But I found a small stream, so we can refresh our water stores."

She nodded. "Hopefully, the storm won't last too long. Let's check out there every half hour or so, until the storm dies down, since we can't tell what's happening here." She waved a hand at the path.

So, they worked that into their normal watches for the night.

When Teigye woke her for her watch not long after midnight, Shyvoan ventured off the path into the wind and sleet. It seemed somewhat diminished from earlier. *Perhaps the storm is dissipating? Or moving off?* She could hope.

The next time she checked the area off the path, a half-hour later, the night was quiet there, matching the peace of the night on the path. Thin clouds scudded across what sky she saw through the trees and the dim moon did little to light the area. Rumbles of thunder boomed in the distance and a faint murmur—*a breeze, perhaps*—whispered around the small area.

She ventured further into the level area, with a sense of something imminent that drew her.

Squelch.

Her boot sank into slippery mud. As she caught her balance, she realized the faint murmur she had been hearing was the trickle of water from the stream, louder than it had been before.

She shuffled and slid through the mud for the few steps back to the path. The path itself was dry when she stepped on it, but she did not trust that.

She did not see Liphye, who shared this watch, so she whistled the danger signal and hurried to wake the others.

Buok woke immediately. He jumped up when he placed a hand on the path to rise and it sank into marshy ground that had not been like that a minute earlier.

"We have to go," he shouted. That finished waking the others, confusion clear on their faces, followed by alarm when they discovered the increasingly wet ground beneath them. Buok stepped off the path, looked around, and pointed at the hill to their left. "This way."

None of the usual sounds of night creatures drifted through the air, and the murmur Shyvoan had heard had morphed into a strange rustle. Liphye returned, coming from further down the path.

Everyone snatched at packs as they urged each other to hurry. They scattered in their scramble for the hillside. As he passed the tarandeer, Teigye cut the ropes that they had used to secure them, which freed them to flee on their own.

The morass underfoot had become at least half water, the footing treacherous. The rustle deepened into a rumble.

Then the sound of rushing water overrode any other sounds. Watery mud burst from the former stream on the other side of the small open area and raced for the path. It washed over their feet and ankles.

Shyvoan slipped as the force of the deluge tried to take her feet from under her. Unseen rocks and other debris pelted her lower legs within the mudflow. She cried out as a sharp rock slammed into her right ankle and that leg collapsed beneath her. She fought to regain her feet but could not get any purchase in the slick quagmire.

The rumble grew to a roar as a torrent of muddy water overwhelmed the small stream. Rocks the size of Shyvoan's hands rode the raging water, which tore bark from the trees it roared around. The muck raced across the flat area toward the path and swept Shyvoan with it.

She yelled for help and flailed as she tried to dig her hands into the mire beneath her or grasp anything solid to keep from being hurtled across and down the path.

Someone's hand clamped around one wrist and jerked her to a painful halt. A glance showed her Jarthan had caught her.

Beyond him, Devrand gripped Jarthan's other arm and clung to a tree with his free arm. Shyvoan clasped Jarthan's wrist in turn to help hold his grip and fought again to get her feet under. At the same time, the two men strained to help pull her from the treacherous mudflow.

A scream pierced the roar of the mudslide, coming from somewhere behind her. Shyvoan tried to twist to look, but Jarthan's grasp prevented it, as did the deluge that pushed against her. She did look up and caught the expression on Devrand's face.

He had paused in his efforts, his gaze fixed behind her and his features twisted in torment. His mouth moved but she heard no sound from him. Still, she could tell what he said.

"Aivean!"

He took one step, his gaze focused somewhere beyond her, and his grip on Jarthan slackened. A moment later, he glanced at her, and their gazes locked. His expression of torment flickered into one of indecision. Then that bland look crossed his features and covered what he had so briefly let be seen.

He hauled on Jarthan's arm with renewed strength. The efforts of all three slowly drew Shyvoan from the mudflow's grasp and up the nearby slope into the trees.

Shyvoan grasped a sodden tree to help her climb to her feet. A piercing pain from her ankle let her know she would not be going anywhere soon.

"Go help her," she yelled at Devrand, who only shook his head.

"No point. The flood carried her over the side." He sank down on the ground and rested his arms on his knees as he stared into the distance.

Shyvoan looked around but could not spot the others. She stepped away from her supporting tree to call for them, and the pain that shot up her leg from her ankle dropped her to the ground. A touch on her shoulder startled her.

"I'll look for them," Jarthan said in a low voice, with a glance at Devrand.

"Are you up to it?" she said.

Jarthan shrugged and headed across the slope into the trees, roughly along the mudflow's path.

Shyvoan scooted over to lean against a tree in a position from which she could keep an eye on Devrand. He glanced at her once and returned to his blank staring.

With a shrug, she rummaged for something to wrap her ankle in the pack she had grabbed. All she found were some of their food supplies. *At least we still have some food.*

Cold and drenched, she propped her injured ankle atop her other leg and settled in to wait. She slipped into a daze as she tried to ignore the continued pain, her worry about the others, and the water that dripped on her from the trees.

After an interminable time, Shyvoan heard some movement in the trees. The roar of the mudslide had diminished to a trickle of water again. She pulled herself upright, gripping a tree again, and drew her sword. Devrand did not move.

At the distinct whistle of the Nightsinger, Shyvoan relaxed slightly. *That's Buok, at least.*

Sounds came from the other direction too, along with another Nightsinger whistle. *That sounds like Liphye.*

Then the other warriors, along with Jarthan, came close enough for her to see them in the cloud-filtered moonlight. Mud caked all of them, as Shyvoan realized it did both her and Devrand. She had to smile at that as she pictured his irritation when he discovered it. She sobered again when she saw that the others did not have Aivean with them.

She exchanged a look with Jarthan. He shook his head, a slight motion, and plopped down on the ground.

"The tarandeer are long gone," Teigye said. He looked from Shyvoan's face to the foot she held off the ground. "Need me to take a look at that?"

Shyvoan nodded and sat again. "I don't have any of the bandages in this pack," she told him.

"Couldn't see any sign of Aivean," Liphye said as she sank to the ground nearby. She dug through the pack she carried and pulled out a bandage, which she passed to Teigye. "And she didn't answer when we shouted for her."

"We'll look again at sunrise. Too treacherous right now in the uncertain light." Buok found a spot to crouch at the base of a tree.

Liphye set a pack on the ground next to Shyvoan.

"That's the gateways herbs and such."

Shyvoan nodded and caught her breath as Teigye worked her boot and sock off her foot. Her ankle was swollen and already sported an assortment of colors, visible even in the dim moonlight.

Teigye pressed on it and moved it around slightly, with a gentle touch. Shyvoan hissed at each touch and motion.

"Doesn't seem like anything's broken," Teigye reported. He wrapped the bandage around it and grinned at her when she hissed yet again at the pain as he pulled it tight. "Sorry about that. If someone's got my pack and some water, I've got herbs that can help with the pain and swelling."

A search of what the others had managed to grab revealed another couple of packs of food, and packs with clothing and blankets and some of the cooking gear, but not Teigye's pack.

"Something else to try to find when it's daytime again," Shyvoan said.

Another rumble heralded yet more mud rushing past below them. By mutual agreement, they gathered everything and moved higher up the slope to wait for dawn.

Shyvoan managed to doze a little, as did the others, but no one slept much the rest of the night. Morning's light revealed an expanse of mud that covered the small clearing and ran both along the path they had followed and across it, down the hill.

Everyone made a quick meal of food from the packs, then eased down the slope closer to the quagmire. Shyvoan's ankle pained her, but she managed to slip her boot back on. She hobbled behind the others and joined them at the edge of the mire.

"We need to keep going," Devrand said as he glanced first down the muddied path then further up, past the place they had stopped, to a mud-free area above the path. "We just have the six days. We can't lose the clues of the shadows."

"We'll look for Aivean today," Shyvoan snapped. "Nothing said we had *only* six days. We can catch up with the clues tomorrow."

Devrand scowled at her then glared down the path.

"Worried that your hunter will catch us if we pause?" Teigye challenged him.

Devrand turned his glare on the warrior. "Not particularly. Although I'd prefer she not catch us."

"If she does, she does," Shyvoan said. "We'll see if we can find Aivean."

"*We'll* look for her." Buok waved his hand at himself and the other warriors. "You stay off that foot while you can." He smiled, but she heard the resolve behind his words.

With a nod, Shyvoan hobbled into a spot of sunshine to try to warm up while the others spread out and eased into the marshy areas with an abundance of caution. Jarthan opted to stay with Shyvoan and dug out some more dried meat to share between them.

Devrand looked disgruntled about the whole activity but went with the others after a glare at Jarthan, who glared right back.

~ ~ ~

Before Shyvoan finished her second strip of meat, a call came from the direction of the path. She and Jarthan exchanged glances. She forced her boot over her bandages, and he helped her hobble toward the sound.

They met the others at the edge of a narrower section of the flow. Buok carried Aivean, with Liphye and Teigye on either side to steady them both in the still-slippery mud. Devrand stalked behind them, scowling.

Shyvoan and Jarthan stepped out of their way. Shyvoan studied Aivean as Buok passed. *She breathed!*

With a sigh of relief, Shyvoan followed the others back

up the hillside into thicker trees.

The disaster had not taken Aivean, but how badly was she hurt? They had limited means with them, even more so after the flood. How would they care for her?

A light touch on her sword brought her out of her bleak thoughts. Liphye touched the fingers of one hand to the sword's pommel and brought them to her forehead. With a slight smile for Shyvoan when their gazes met, she hurried to help Buok ease Aivean to the ground.

"What was that about?" Devrand said from right behind her.

Shyvoan squelched her startled jump and glared at him over her shoulder.

But it was Teigye who answered him. "Appreciating the luck that Shyvoan brings to her companions in the warriors. Aivean survived. We all survived."

The young warrior then joined the others around the wounded mage to see what could be done for her.

Shyvoan hobbled closer but stayed out of the way as Teigye and Liphye tended to Aivean. Like them all, the mage was muddied. From the way Teigye wrapped one leg and one arm, Shyvoan surmised that both had broken. Aivean moaned under the young warrior's ministrations but did not wake. *Might she have hit her head, too?*

"We need to get going soon," Devrand muttered in her ear as he stood too close. "We can't miss out on the signs to follow the path."

"She's not going to be able to travel anytime soon." Shyvoan took a deliberate step away from him and matched his scowl with one of her own. "We know what to look for to follow the path. We'll pick it up again."

"The scroll said six days to reach the dragon," Devrand said.

"Sure, if we continue uninterrupted—"

"But what if it means you have only six days to get there, once you've started along the path? We must go."

"It didn't say anything like that."

"But it could be read that way. We can't chance it."

Shyvoan turned to face him and studied his expression. "Why the urgency?"

"Why is it *not* urgent for you? Don't you want to see your people safely away as soon as possible?"

"Of course I do. But not at the cost of Aivean's life because she did not get the rest she needed."

"And what of all the others of your denizens? It's been how many days we've taken already to reach this point? Anything could have happened to them. What of their lives?"

"Of course I'm concerned about them. But there's nothing I can do from here—"

"Except get this magic as fast as possible to be able to use it."

"What do you care? I can't believe after what I've seen that you really care about us, our denizens. You're after the dragon for your own purposes. Don't try to use our people's plight to make us do what you want. I wager you're most afraid your hunter will catch you. That's it, isn't it?"

"Not afraid. But I'd rather not see that happen, certainly. Our purposes coincide, yours and mine. We shouldn't delay in achieving them."

Shyvoan glared at him, tempted to try to break through that bland expression that he again wore. *But what will that accomplish?* Still, the temptation was hard to resist.

She turned away. "You could certainly go ahead, if you want. But you need us, too. And we won't go until everyone is up for it again."

She held herself rigid against the growl of exasperation Devrand made and sighed in relief when he stalked off to one side. Jarthan followed in his wake.

She sank to the ground and motioned Liphye close. "Tell me."

While attempting to brush dried mud from her leathers, Liphye crouched next to Shyvoan. "We found Aivean not far off the path, down the slope some, where it looked like the flood had carried her. A clump of bushes caught her. Her leg is broken, but Teigye's got it well wrapped. He thinks her arm is badly bruised, worse than your ankle, rather than broken. Of course, Aivean's cold and wet, like we all are. She's got a bad bruise on the right side of her face. She slammed into something, or something hit her."

Liphye looked up from her attempts to clean off the drying mud. "Neither of you should travel soon. But we'll try to find the tarandeer and we can maybe continue."

"You heard what Devrand said?"

A smile flitted across her lips. "We *all* heard both of you. Doesn't matter what he thinks. We can't go on right now as we are."

Shyvoan nodded. "And we can't go back either."

"As Buok would say… true, that."

CHAPTER 29

Shyvoan dozed most of the day with her foot propped up. She woke periodically to check on Aivean who slept fitfully under the influence of some herbs that Teigye had found tucked in the bottom of one of the food packs and had given her for the pain. The other warriors set up a rough camp where they had all settled among the trees and hunted for any more of their goods that they could find, as well as the tarandeer.

As afternoon wore toward evening, Aivean stirred and looked around. Shyvoan gave her a slight smile when the mage spotted her where she leaned against a nearby tree. Aivean returned the smile with a slight wince.

"Do you need more of those herbs?" Shyvoan said.

Aivean shook her head. "Not yet. The pain isn't too bad right now, and I'd like to stay awake for a bit. I *am* thirsty though. But first, can you help me up?" She waved a hand toward a cluster of bushes nearby.

With a nod, Shyvoan slipped her boot back on over the wrapping on her ankle, pleased to find the boot fit much better again. The swelling had diminished and left the ankle more stiff than sore. She limped the couple of steps to Aivean and helped the other woman to her feet and into the privacy of the bushes, then back after she was done. She settled Aivean in a more comfortable spot, propped against a tree with a cloak to cushion her back, grabbed a waterskin, and exchanged a nod with Liphye who was on watch.

"Are we the only two hurt? How bad is your injury?" Aivean took the waterskin with a slight smile and drank long and deeply.

"Everyone's got scrapes and bruises. This is a nasty bruise, but it's already feeling better. Some." Shyvoan waved a hand at her ankle and found a spot against a tree near Aivean's. "You got the worst of it. Although Teigye thinks your arm's only badly bruised, not broken. The leg, however…."

Aivean winced. "Yah." She stoppered the waterskin and set it aside. "You're going to have to go on without me."

"What? No."

"Yah. I can't walk on this as it is. Even if I could, I wouldn't be able to keep the pace we need to follow the guide, to keep from losing the path. I won't be healed enough for weeks, I'd guess."

Shyvoan nodded. "I know," she admitted. "But I don't like leaving anyone. Maybe the others will find the tarandeer."

After a long look for Shyvoan, Aivean shrugged. "Maybe. Even so, watch out for Devrand. He's charming but quite focused on getting what he wants. I wouldn't trust his actions if something stood in his way. But I think you've already figured that out."

Shyvoan nodded. "If we didn't need his type of gateway to get our people to true safety, I'd be willing to consider leaving him."

Aivean chuckled softly. "Yah."

"I don't suppose he's taught you how to do that kind

of gateway?"

Aivean frowned and shook her head. "I wish. He's very good at turning the subject aside. But I haven't seen any plants among his things, nothing like what Rashean gave us to make the gateways. I believe his magic works differently somehow. And so, we'll need him to do it."

"I'd suspected that was going to be the case."

They slipped into a companionable silence then and dozed again while they waited for the others' return.

~ ~ ~

When the others *did* return, it was without the tarandeer. Both Buok and Liphye had managed to catch some rodents, though, so they cooked those for the evening meal. Everyone enjoyed the warmth of the small fire as they ate.

"With the tarandeer long gone, or dead, Aivean can't maintain the pace we need to stay to the path," Devrand said as he wiped greasy fingers on some leaves. "She'll have to stay behind."

"That's not your decision to make," Buok said.

"But it should be mine," Aivean said. "This is too important for our denizens to risk it failing. We find a good place for me to stay for the time you need to get there and come back. Just leave enough of the food with me since I can't hunt. Not that I'd know how to even if I could."

"You've thought this through," Shyvoan said. "But we're expecting, hoping for, magic from the dragon somehow. You should be there."

"As you said, I've thought this through. Much as I'd like to have more magic myself, I don't think we should wait until I can go, too. You've got the family background of magic. You've got that." She waved a hand at Shyvoan's sword. "You can get the magic for us."

"Me? I'm no mage."

"But the magic was in your family so probably you could be," Liphye said. "Aivean's right. We shouldn't wait the time she'll need to heal enough to follow the path again. We have no way of knowing what the rest of it will be like. But she shouldn't stay alone."

"I'll stay with her," Teigye said.

"But what if they need a mender?" Aivean protested.

"Warriors all learn basic care for injuries we might encounter," Teigye said. "They'll be fine."

"And what of your knowledge of the various plants?" Liphye said.

"I can divide what we have left. Keep some in case Aivean and I need them and send the rest with you with descriptions for any that none of you recognize. For the few days it'll be, it'll work fine."

"It seems I should be the one to stay with Aivean," Shyvoan said. "I'm injured, too, and moving slower than my usual pace. That could cause us to miss the shadow clues at the right times."

"No, you've got to go," Devrand said, a sharp note to his voice.

"Why? From what we've heard in our stories pretty much anyone could get magic from a dragon. Doesn't seem that it *has* to be someone from one of the families who got it before."

"But there's your sword." Devrand waved a hand toward the weapon. "It's got something to do with dragons, right. I've a feeling it needs to be there when we meet the creature."

Shyvoan looked at her sheathed sword and took a visual survey of the others' expressions.

"I hate to agree, but he's likely right," Liphye said.

Teigye nodded. "Remember what happened when you tried to loan it to another? We know that's not an option."

Shyvoan sighed. The poor warrior who had tried to borrow her blade had then spent the next few weeks nursing burns on his hand from the hilt. She gave a slight nod. *But why is Devrand so insistent I go? He can't have known about that incident, so why does he want to make sure I'm there when we met the dragon?*

"Sounds like it's all settled then," Devrand stated with a satisfied smile.

"It's not all settled." Jarthan's words drew looks of surprise from the others and a glare from Devrand. Jarthan glared right back. "Shyvoan has not agreed and she's the one their Troop-Lead put in charge. Not you."

Rage suffused Devrand's features, and he lunged at Jarthan, but Buok yanked him back and pushed him to the edge of the firelight. Devrand remained there as his customary bland expression wiped the rage from his expression. Then he grabbed a blanket from the ground nearby, wrapped it around himself, and plopped down against a tree. "In that case, I'm sure you'll tell me what to do and when to do it when you've all decided," he snarled and turned his back.

"I'd like to tell him what to do," Liphye muttered, just loud enough for those still by the fire to hear her.

"Why do you stay with him?" Shyvoan said to Jarthan.

He directed a sad look at Devrand and sighed. "I've no choice; he's seen to that. I can't so easily be rid of him. He's got me bound to him so. Magically." He ducked his head then, avoided meeting anyone's gaze, and grabbed a blanket himself.

After he settled on the ground not too far from Devrand, the others drew closer around the fire.

"This *is* the best course of action." Buok rested a hand on Shyvoan's shoulder.

She nodded. "I can see that. I just don't like leaving anyone behind."

"You'll be back for us before long at all," Aivean said, "bringing magic again for our people and a way to get to true safety from the Maheaja-Folk."

Shyvoan sighed. *Hope that's true.*

~ ~ ~

Early the next morning, after a hasty breakfast, the warriors divided the supplies and packs the mudslide had left them: some cooking utensils with a couple of pots, about half the food they had with them, enough blankets for each of them to have one, a few of the herbs that they had gathered and that Teigye had brought, and a random assortment of various clothing items. They left most of the food with Aivean and Teigye, divided the herbs, and made their way back to stand uphill of the mire on the vesnaflur path as the rising sun touched that spot.

They turned to face their shadows and trekked along the increasingly steep path, making appropriate turns to follow side paths when their shadows no longer stretched in front of them as they should. The stiffness in Shyvoan's ankle lingered, as well as a dull ache, but her limp had nearly vanished. Those complaints worsened only a little as she walked, even keeping close to the pace that they had maintained before the mudslide.

Buok led the way with Devrand and Jarthan behind him. Liphye and Shyvoan brought up the rear. All three warriors kept alert for any further mudslides and for rodents or other creatures they could use for food.

The bright sun shone on them. It warmed the crisp air and made the mudslide seem a bad dream. The group spoke little and mostly about practical things.

"Hold a moment," Buok said at one point about midafternoon and eased off the path into the trees that bordered it. Soon he returned with a brace of large rodents, and they moved ahead again. Liphye did something similar a couple of hours later. The creature she brought back was larger than Buok's rodents, but otherwise of a similar shape. It had much longer ears, though, and a shorter tail, not much more than a stub. Liphye shrugged at the curious looks she caught from the others.

"We'll see. No idea what it is, but it looks meaty enough." With murmurs of agreement, they again followed the path.

Shyvoan counted six splits in the path throughout the afternoon and as the day wore on into evening. As before, they paused at each to examine the direction their shadows pointed before they proceeded. She did not recall that there had been as many splits the previous days on the path. But then again, she had not counted them either.

At dusk, as they had the previous days, they found a wider area off to one side of the path. A stream burbled at the far side of the small clearing there, which let them refresh their water.

The meal was hot and Shyvoan found the taste of the other creature's meat acceptable although stronger than the rodents they had been eating. With little to say, they automatically set up a camp, positioning it some distance along the path from the stream, and above the stream. While there had been no storms off the path the past day, no one wanted to take any chances on another streambed mudslide.

"Can you set up a warding circle for us?" Shyvoan asked Devrand.

He shook his head. "I've no way to duplicate Aivean's work."

When Shyvoan looked to Jarthan, he also shook his head. So she spent an uneasy night as her worry about the lack of a warding circle kept her from getting any good sleep. She did manage to doze, with her ankle again propped on her other leg, and was up at dawn with the others.

It took them little time to pack the camp. With much of their supplies gone, they had little to gather. The morning meal consisted of the remnants left from the previous night's meal.

Buok crouched near Shyvoan as he finished his meal. "No predators seem to have sniffed around during the night."

"Odd. Without the ward circle, I wouldn't have been surprised to have some come by."

"I'd find it odder if they had," Devrand said. Shyvoan had not realized he had overheard them. "I'd think a dragon, or more than one, would encourage other predators to find better hunting grounds."

"And yet here you are," Liphye muttered.

Shyvoan squelched her reaction to the comment. She could not tell if Devrand had heard it, but he acted like he had not.

"Possibly," Shyvoan responded to Devrand's comment. "We still don't know that there *is* a dragon."

"Better hope there is," Devrand said and stuffed his blanket in his pack. "Shouldn't we be going?"

Shyvoan scowled at his presumption but finished her last bite as she stood. The group headed along the vesnaflur path, in the same order as the day before.

"At least we should be there tomorrow," Liphye murmured to Shyvoan. "Getting closer to being done with his presence in our lives."

Shyvoan nodded.

~ ~ ~

The path that day differed from the previous day's stretch – they encountered only two splits before dusk approached. As the light faded, they came to a third split and struggled to see their shadows well enough to determine which one to follow. Shyvoan stepped off the path to see if perhaps they had arrived at another of those wider spots, but all she found were trees that grew close to the path on all sides.

After several minutes of debate—both paths headed roughly the same direction—they agreed on the best one and headed along it, with frequent forays to the sides to find the wider area for the night's camp.

When they still had not found the camping area and before the dark of night completely enveloped them, they paused.

"Someone should go back and take a look at that other split," Devrand said.

"Why don't you then?" Liphye said.

Devrand glowered at her.

"I'll go," Jarthan spoke into the tense silence.

"We'll all go," Shyvoan said before Jarthan had taken more than a step. "We've already split the group once. I don't want to do that any further."

They followed the path back the way they had come, careful of their footing in the growing darkness. Shyvoan hoped the moon would rise soon to give them light to work with.

"We've come further than where the split was," Buok said when he stopped in the middle of the path some time later.

Shyvoan turned and surveyed the surroundings. "Well, that makes it easy. Somehow, we must have moved slower than before and so we haven't made the full day's travel yet. Back to where we were, and we'll keep on until we find that wider area."

They continued on and periodically one of them stepped off the path to one side or the other. Off the path, dim moonlight lit the area, filtered through the trees. But on the path, the darkness deepened. Shyvoan and the other warriors grabbed dry sticks from off the path and created crude torches to use. While dim and smoky, the torches let them at least see the vesnaflurs.

Perhaps an hour after darkness engulfed them, Liphye called out from where she scouted a short distance ahead.

"Come slowly," she instructed. "We've got a problem."

At the rear again, Shyvoan joined the others where Liphye had stopped. In front of them, nearly at Liphye's toes, extended a wide section of what looked like another mudflow. An older one, Shyvoan judged, long dried out but not yet covered by regrowth. The path had been obliterated as far as she saw in the torchlight.

She had not noticed that Devrand had stepped to one side until he returned to the path.

"Looks like that area's our wider spot," he reported.

"Wonderful," Liphye said. Her tone indicated she believed it anything but.

"At least we've found our camping spot," Shyvoan said. "We'll look this over again tomorrow. For now, we'll settle in for the night."

CHAPTER 30

In the pre-dawn light, at the end of her watch for the night, Shyvoan stood at the edge of the destroyed section of the path and scrutinized the rough area ahead. The trees had been swept away on both sides and that bare section of the mountainside was steep.

"That doesn't look like it's safe to cross," a soft voice came from behind her. Jarthan eased closer to stand next to her and also surveyed the broken hillside.

"Agreed. Looks like it could shift far too easily underfoot and send us rolling down there." Shyvoan waved an arm at the long hillside below them.

She turned to Jarthan. "Would you please see what ropes we have left to us?"

With a dubious look for the broken hillside, Jarthan nodded and returned to their meager camp.

Shyvoan followed and built up the fire a little. She grabbed the rodents she had caught and prepared earlier and set them to cook for the morning meal.

After everyone woke and ate and finished the preparations to continue, they gathered at the broken edge of the path.

"We can't take too long to cross that," Devrand said. "This is the day. We don't want to linger and mess up following the correct side paths."

"And how do we cross that?" Liphye said. "Will the ropes reach?"

Buok held the two ropes that the group had left and eyed the broken hillside.

"The way the slope curves here, I can't see anything on the far side to tie to." Buok handed Liphye the end of one rope and tied the two ropes together. "You get the honors. You're the lightest. With two undamaged ankles, anyway." He grinned at the look she gave him and at Shyvoan's glower. "Tie it around your waist."

"We'll all hold this end," Shyvoan assured Liphye.

With a frown, Liphye tied the rope to herself as Buok instructed and eased out onto the broken section. As she put her weight down, the earth and rocks underfoot slid, and she flailed to catch her balance. When she did, she glared at the others over a shoulder.

"Thank you so very much for volunteering me for this."

"We've got you," Buok said and gave the rope a slight shake. "Slow and easy."

"Easy for you to say," Liphye shot back but continued to ease forward, barely lifting each foot before she placed it again. A couple of steps held, then the ground shifted again under her, and this time dropped her to one knee.

Devrand sighed, his expression frustrated. "We don't have the time for this."

"We don't have the time to lose anyone," Shyvoan snapped at him.

He glared and turned away. Jarthan grabbed his arm, and they leaned close and whispered. Shyvoan kept most of her attention on Liphye and the rope but watched the two men from the corner of her eye. *Are they arguing?*

Liphye sidled a half-pace forward and the dirt and

rocks beneath her feet shifted again. This time more shifted further up the hill, too, and swept her feet from under her. She grabbed the rope and held on while Buok and Shyvoan hauled her back to safety through a torrent of dirt that slid down the slope.

More dirt slipped past as they backed away from the crumbled edge.

Liphye braced herself hands on knees as she caught her breath. "That's a scare I could've done without. So, what other ideas do we have?"

A sharp voice drew the three warriors' attention to their two charges. Devrand gripped Jarthan's shoulders and spoke directly into the other man's face. Shyvoan could not make out what he said, but Jarthan wilted briefly under the verbal barrage before he straightened his shoulders and nodded.

"So, you'll have to be sure you do your part," he snapped and shrugged out of Devrand's grip.

Shyvoan passed her rope to Buok—who rolled it with the other one—and squared off in front of Devrand and Jarthan. "What's this all about?"

The two men exchanged glances and Jarthan sighed. "I think I have a way to get us across. It'll mean using my magic."

The three warriors stared at him in a silence that stretched.

"You didn't think to mention before now that you have such magic?" Liphye broke the tense silence.

"It wasn't necessary," Devrand stated. "And now that you know, he should be about it." He shoved Jarthan toward the broken edge of the path.

Shyvoan and the other warriors stepped back to give Jarthan room. "Can we help?" she whispered to him as he stopped near her.

He shook his head and glared over his shoulder at Devrand. "Well? You're the one who's made it so I can't do this sort of thing alone."

His bland expression firmly in place, Devrand stepped up next to Jarthan and brushed Shyvoan aside in the process. She directed a glare at his back and eased to the side to be able to see what they did.

Devrand placed his hand on Jarthan's shoulder, his fingers brushing the side of the other man's neck. Both men closed their eyes and Jarthan held his hands out in front of him, palms down.

Shyvoan saw nothing else for several minutes but gradually became aware of a warmth that emanated from her sword sheathed at her side. She slipped the weapon from its scabbard. *Looks no different.*

But the warmth from the blade increased, although the hilt held no warmth other than that from her hand. She held the blade out away from herself, in perhaps an excess of caution, and returned her attention to Jarthan and Devrand.

An oddly rectangular haze formed and hovered over the damaged section of hillside, no wider than the width of Buok's shoulders. As she watched, the haze grew less and less transparent, until it formed a narrow walkway that extended out several paces from the path's broken edge.

Shyvoan glanced at the two men doing this magic without the wordless singing that she was accustomed to. *What else might they be capable of?*

Both men's expressions showed signs of strain.

"I can't extend it any further." Jarthan's voice reflected the strain in his expression. He turned his head to look at Shyvoan through nearly closed eyes. "Have to get all of us on it and close to the other end. I'll have to let the walkway go behind us to be able to create more in front of us."

Shyvoan exchanged quick glances with the other warriors. Were they as uncertain about this as she was? They'd be at Jarthan and Devrand's mercy. While she had little trouble believing benign intentions of Jarthan, Devrand was a different matter.

"Hurry!" Devrand's voice broke into her thoughts. If anything, his voice held more strain than Jarthan's. "We have to bring up the rear."

"Your magic can just make something out of nothing?" Liphye said as she peered at Jarthan.

"Essentially. But it doesn't last long."

With a shrug of his shoulders, Buok led the way onto the walkway, with Liphye on his heals. Shyvoan followed close behind her, and Jarthan followed her so closely she felt his breath on the back of her neck.

Buok stopped when he reached the far end.

"Can you see how much further we need?" Jarthan called to him.

"Not yet," Buok called back. "The slide goes around the curve of the hillside. It's about three paces to as far as I can see around the curve."

They waited there in their precarious line as Jarthan did whatever it was he needed to let the walkway go behind them and extend it further ahead. Buok moved forward again when the walkway became opaque.

In this stuttering manner, they balanced their way on the narrow walkway around the curve of the hill and across the slide to reach the broken edge of the path on the other side. Shyvoan estimated they had traversed fully twenty paces of damaged hillside to regain the vesnaflur path.

After they reached the other side and moved a safe distance back from the broken edge, Jarthan sank to his knees.

Devrand wobbled but remained upright. He pointed to their shadows, which had begun to veer off the center of the path. "We've got to keep going."

Liphye handed Jarthan a waterskin and some herbs. "We can take a few minutes," she told Devrand over her shoulder.

With a nod to Shyvoan, Buok headed along the path to scout ahead beyond the small section they currently saw amid the trees. Liphye offered the waterskin and herbs to

Devrand when Jarthan finished, but he waved them off.

When Buok returned a few minutes later, Jarthan hauled himself to his feet with Devrand's help.

"There's a split in the path ahead. I checked the shadow and know which one we need to take. And we're still in plenty of time. The shadow lined up fine with one of the paths, as we've seen before."

With nods of acknowledgement, the group resumed their trek up the path, steeper than it had been before but still passable. At the split, they took the shadow-designated path, which grew steeper yet as they followed it. Their pace necessarily slowed, with Jarthan's ongoing fatigue and as the footing beneath the flowers grew more uncertain. Still, they pushed on.

As the day wore on, they saw no signs of the path reaching anything that would fit the description of the dragon's location in the scroll. Just more trees and ever-steeper going. The warriors walked with hands close to weapons, by mutual unspoken agreement, and everyone kept watch all around them.

Except for the breeze that whooshed through the trees from time to time, silence enveloped the woods. Shyvoan did not worry over much at the quiet. *Likely their passage silenced any animals in the vicinity.* From time to time a faint sound came from behind them. But glances that direction showed nothing. Even so, she kept at least part of her attention on the path they had already traversed and worked to ignore the lingering ache in her ankle.

Afternoon edged toward evening with still no sign of anything that resembled what the scroll had described. For hours, they had followed a single path, no branches. Liphye eased close to Shyvoan but kept her attention on the surroundings.

"Could we have somehow gotten on the wrong path?" the other warrior voiced a concern that had nagged Shyvoan as the day passed.

"I worry that it's so, but I don't see how."

Liphye nodded. "Agreed. And yet, shouldn't we be there already?"

"I'd expected to be, but it's not much more than guesswork. The scroll was not particularly clear on details."

A few paces ahead of them Buok came to a stop. "Something here."

The rest of the group crowded around him to study what seemed to be the end of the path. Amid dense trees, the flower path, not more than half a pace wide at that point, ended at what looked like a rockfall.

Shyvoan walked close to it and placed her hand on a rock the size of her head.

"Now what?" Liphye said in unconscious echo of Shyvoan's thoughts.

Jarthan sat on a fallen tree off to the side and stared at the rocks, then looked back down the path. "This has to be it."

Devrand turned his head, and his gaze followed the direction of Jarthan's. "There weren't any other ways to go," he muttered. "The shadows were clear."

Buok paced to one side and eyed the rocks, then paced to the other.

"Here," he called from the other side of a large evergreen tree.

Shyvoan and the others circled the tree as Buok had and learned what he had found: an opening in the rocks. It was tall enough for Buok to walk through without the need to bend, but only wide enough for one person at a time.

"Could this be the threshold?" Shyvoan exchanged glances with each of the others, all of whom shrugged.

"Some of those flowers are here." Jarthan pointed at the ground where indeed a few scraggly vesnaflurs grew to either side inside the opening.

With looks again exchanged among them, they eased into the opening. Buok led the way, and Devrand, Jarthan, Liphye and Shyvoan followed, in that order. Shyvoan drew her sword, to have it ready. *Just in case.*

The other warriors readied weapons, too.

"Don't believe a dragon would get through there," Liphye quipped, her voice low.

"How big are these dragons?" Devrand whispered.

"That's the question," Shyvoan said. "As we've said before, no one alive has seen one. All we have are a few old tales. What I saw flying looked pretty big, but who can say."

"Big enough to eat us in one gulp, I'm guessing," Liphye said.

"Wonderful," Devrand muttered.

Uneven rock covered with a scattering of dirt formed the floor of the passage, which meant they kept their attention at least somewhat on their footing. A couple of steps beyond the opening, the passage widened enough to allow them to walk two abreast. Only Devrand and Jarthan did so, and the former supported the latter. Shyvoan saw no tracks in the dirt. A cool breeze came from further ahead and brushed her face. What she saw of the place beyond Buok looked no darker than the area where she stood, lit from the opening behind her. A good sign that they'd find another opening ahead, and not too far.

Buok made the hand motion for the others to stay back while he continued ahead.

Liphye whispered to Devrand and Jarthan what that meant and clasped their arms to hold them back when Devrand looked like he intended to go ahead.

"Are we really trying to sneak up on a dragon?" Devrand's whisper had a hiss to it.

"Don't want to charge one, that's for certain," Liphye hissed back.

Buok disappeared around a curve and returned minutes later. "The other end's a few paces further along. Nothing to see out the opening. It's in a clump of brush and trees. I'll scout further." He headed back the way he had come, and the others followed at a slower pace.

They paused at the opening while Buok eased into the surrounding brush. Shyvoan peered after him in the fading light. *Not perhaps the best time of day to be approaching a dragon. If, in fact, one is there.*

A strange cough-like sound came from somewhere beyond the brush. From their right.

Buok had gone to the left.

Shyvoan exchanged looks with Liphye and pulled Devrand and Jarthan back from the entrance. "Wait here," she whispered.

She and Liphye then eased out the opening into the brush and sidled to the right along what seemed to be a natural rock wall. Shyvoan glanced up and saw a bit of sky through the branches of the surrounding plants, and also what looked like the edges of rocks that partially extended over them.

Another cough came from beyond the blocking plants, followed by a deep voice. "While I appreciate your attempts to be quiet—so as not to disturb me, I prefer to assume, rather than for any nefarious purpose—I must inform you that you have not succeeded. My hearing is still rather good, so you might as well come on out."

Shyvoan and Liphye froze and Liphye gave Shyvoan a wide-eyed look. With a shrug, Shyvoan indicated that they should proceed and pushed through the brush with no attempt at silence as she led the way, holding her sword in a nonthreatening position. The crackling of branches behind her let her know that Liphye followed, and likely Devrand and Jarthan, too.

When she stepped out of the clutching bushes, she pulled up short and stared, only peripherally aware that her companions did likewise, including Buok who had come from a different direction.

A large clearing extended in front of her, easily half the size of the denizen's latest lodgment. Short grasses carpeted the near half, interspersed with rocky areas, and surrounded by more of the thick bushes Shyvoan had fought through. Above, a gap of darkening sky showed through what looked like a massive hole in the center of a dome shape of rock that formed a rough circle around the area.

The far side of the clearing was obscured by the large reptilian shape that lay there, most of its side and part of a long tail visible. Its long neck and head rested on the ground. One pale-yellow eye regarded the small group. The top of the creature's head and the top of Buok's were nearly at the same height, and if its tail was as long as its neck, the dragon stretched close to a hundred feet.

The dragon's large head, long snout, and somewhat bulbous eyes with vertical slit pupils reminded Shyvoan of lizards she had seen in various streams. Large scales covered its body, legs, and feet, even the long toes. The one folded wing she saw seemed covered with much smaller scales. The scales were a brilliant blue and green, and the colors formed wide stripes that ran the length of the dragon's body. A frill around the dragon's neck near its head looked to be made of feathers, rather than hide with scales. Its colors shimmered in the fading light and ranged from blue to purple. As Shyvoan eyed it, the dragon's gaze moved from one to another of the group before it settled on Shyvoan.

"Ah, you carry gift-scales."

While the voice remained deep, it sounded feminine. Shyvoan took a step toward it but stopped when the dragon lifted its head from the ground.

"It's been passed down in my family," Shyvoan said. She turned her sword sideways, the hilt lightly gripped in her left hand, and rested the blade against the palm of her other hand.

"A sword. Of course, they made them into a sword." The dragon's voice carried a sense of sadness in its tone.

Devrand stepped forward and stopped right next to Shyvoan, close enough that she felt the warmth from his body. "Yes, it's a nice sword. But we've come for the magic."

Why's he standing so close? Perhaps he's more afraid than he's let on? Shyvoan glanced at his expression but saw no sign of any fear there. She sidled a step to the side to put more space between them.

"Ah, yes. Of course. Always for the magic. Perhaps things might not have turned out the way they did if not for the Human-Folk's thirst to retain the magic." The dragon turned its head aside and coughed, a deep, rough sound.

Shyvoan frowned. That cough didn't sound good.

"What do you mean?" Buok said.

"What does it matter what it means?" Devrand said.

"She," the dragon rumbled.

Devrand stared at the dragon. "What?"

"She, not 'it'. I am Tinanay."

"Ah, fine then, Tinanay." Devrand scowled at the dragon, something Shyvoan did not think a wise move.

"What do you mean about our thirst to retain the magic?" Liphye said.

Tinanay dipped her head and turned to focus on Liphye with both eyes, her neck arching up behind her lowered head and back down to her shoulders. "When your kind came here to our world, in your flight from whatever you fled, you naturally brought much with you… your herds of animals, your way of doing things… your magic, too. But it soon became clear that your magic wasn't accordant with this place, and it began to fail your people. In their struggle to still have magic to use, your ancestors turned to the Maheaja-Folk for answers. Lamentably, there's been no lasting solution."

"We were running from something and came to your world?" Shyvoan murmured.

"But we did get magic from you," Liphye said at the same time. "What must we do to get magic again?"

Tinanay nodded in response to Shyvoan's question and tiled her head toward Devrand. "One of you at least has obtained the knowledge about the magic."

As the warriors all turned to look at him, he brushed his hand across Shyvoan's neck. A burnt-wood scent engulfed her, and her knees buckled under a sudden wave of exhaustion. While she staggered, Devrand snatched the hilt of her sword. He swung the weapon away from her and sliced her hand in the process. He winced even as his hand reddened but did not stop or let go of the sword.

Devrand charged the few steps that separated them from Tinanay and plunged the blade into the dragon's side, just behind her foreleg. Oblivious to the others' yells and the dragon's low groan of pain, he plunged the sword in again before anyone could reach him and left it there. Then he placed both hands against the dragon's side.

"No!" A voice Shyvoan had never heard before came from behind her. She glanced back and saw a woman, a stranger, running toward them. From the corner of her eye, Shyvoan also saw Devrand turn to Jarthan with an exultant grin and beckon him forward.

Jarthan shook his head yet moved toward Devrand in a fitful motion that looked like he was pulled against his will. Devrand grabbed his arm when he drew close and yanked him against his side.

Devrand held his other arm up and a shimmery vertical line formed in the air next to him. The line grew wider and split into two to create an oval in the air. Through it, Shyvoan saw a place that looked nothing like where they stood.

He's going to leave us? Along with the other warriors, and the stranger, she ran toward Devrand, stumbling from the aftermath of what he had done to her. *He can't go without helping our people!*

But none of them was fast enough to catch Devrand before he stepped into the oval and dragged Jarthan with him. The opening snapped shut as the others reached it and they all collided next to the dragon.

CHAPTER 31

After some confusion, as they grabbed each other to stay on their feet, they sorted themselves out. Shyvoan studied the newcomer while Liphye cursed Devrand, long and with much creativity.

The newcomer stood about Shyvoan's height and had golden-brown skin, dark eyes, and straight black hair. Her expression showed anger, with perhaps disappointment mixed in, but when her gaze met Shyvoan's, her expression smoothed out into one of inquiry and interest.

At a wheezing groan from Tinanay, Shyvoan lost interest in the woman. She stepped closer to the dragon and reached toward the sword still stuck in Tinanay's side. "Can we help? What can we do?"

Tinanay shook her head. "He struck true, and my time was slipping away anyway. I thank you for your solicitude, but I've an egg that already waits for me. Soon I'll be back as a new youngling." Tinanay coughed and looked at the newcomer.

"My apologies that I could not delay until your arrival. I'd heard on the wind that you were coming, but he proved just too avaricious. Nonetheless, I held back enough of the magic to share with you for your need and for you to uphold your part of the pact."

Tinanay stretched out her neck and touched the tip of her chin to the top of the woman's head.

"I don't understand," Shyvoan said.

The woman sank to her knees, shuddering, but otherwise looked unharmed.

"Your original Human-Folk magic… both deleterious and largely ineffectual here. And you cannot remain here." Tinanay paused to draw in a quivery breath. She winced and continued, rushing her words. "All Maheaja-Folk have some magic. The largest portion of this place's magic is shared from dragon to dragon, or to someone else, like some of you Human-Folk, when dragons die. The magic slowly returns to the dragons as they grow in their new lives, over the course of those very long lives, as compared to yours."

"No wonder magic faded from our families," Shyvoan murmured.

With a slight nod, Tinanay drew another shuddering breath, and her words came faster and fainter and with a clear note of disappointment. "That man with you had learned he could seize control of some magic by killing a dragon near her end. I'd have willingly shared with him if he'd *truly* intended to take you Human-Folk from this place."

She coughed again, longer and harder. "But I triumphed and held some from his greedy grasp…."

She laid her head on the ground. "Hold to your promise."

Then Tinanay's focus slid away to something distant, and her eyes dulled as her breathing stopped.

Shyvoan drew a shaky breath, surprised at the sense of loss that swept over her. She reached to draw the sword from the dragon's body but pulled back when the dragon began to glow a brilliant blue-green. As the glow intensified, Shyvoan squinted against the glare and finally had to shut her eyes altogether. Even then, she saw the glow through her eyelids, until it dimmed after a few minutes.

She opened her eyes, ready to close them at the slightest hint of another painful glow. A faint reddish-gold glow hugged her sword, while the glow of Tinanay's body had softened. As Shyvoan watched, the dragon faded.

Then her scales twinkled like sparks that rose from a fire, blinking points of light that drifted into the air and swirled above the dragon. Perhaps half of them stretched from the main flurry to swirl around the stranger and settle on her skin before they vanished. Tinanay's fading body shrank to the length of Shyvoan's arm and the sword dropped to the ground, its glow extinguished. Still diaphanous, the small, wispy dragon then lifted its head and stretched its wings.

With a shake of its head, it launched into the air and flew through the opening far above, headed toward the setting sun. The remaining sparks followed it and were gone.

Shyvoan's attention returned to her sword, unchanged and lying there. But now it wasn't a proud link to ancient magic. It had been used not to defend but deliberately murder. She frowned. Maybe she shouldn't keep it any longer. Maybe just leave it here.

"What promise?" Liphye said after the silence had stretched many long minutes.

"That was directed at me," the stranger said as she stood. She wobbled and Shyvoan turned from her tainted sword, reached out to steady the other woman. With a smile, the woman nodded her thanks.

"I'd better sit for a bit," she said as she made her way to a nearby rock. "I've not absorbed magic like that before. Feels strange."

"Alorsha!" A voice called out from near the entrance as a man ran to the stranger. Another man followed him, and behind him came the hob that Shyvoan and her companions had met earlier.

Buok and Liphye both stepped back to a position from which they could watch everyone. Shyvoan scrutinized the newcomers. They all wore hip-length shirts, belted over loose trousers, and solid shoes. The man who had called out—and even then fussed over the woman Alorsha— seemed near Shyvoan's age. He looked to be a little taller than her, stocky and strongly built, with skin a lovely shade of dark brown and hair, beard, and mustache all a pale yellow and close cut. His shirt was much more brightly colored than his companions' and he wore the sleeves pushed above his elbows, baring solid forearms.

The other man, who stood apart as Buok and Liphye did, stood taller than Buok. His long, brown hair hung in two plaits over his shoulders and his weathered skin was a lighter brown than the woman's.

Dark blotches marked the hob's skin. Bruises, Shyvoan judged. She had a horrid suspicion that they had come from Devrand.

After Alorsha assured the man who hovered near her of her fitness and health, she met Shyvoan's gaze. "Please, sit, if you wish. I suspect we've got a few things to talk about."

Shyvoan found a rock for herself, as did the newcomers.

"You're Devrand's hunters," Liphye said as she found a fallen log to perch on, still in a position to see everyone.

"Yes, I suppose you could call us that. And I can only imagine how he presented us to you."

"What little we know we had to drag out of him," Shyvoan said. "And it sounded less than half the truth."

"Not that we really believed him much anyway," Liphye muttered.

"I'm glad to hear that. But introductions first? I'm Alorsha Tavano." She gestured to the man closest to her, then the tall one who stood somewhat behind her. "Gyasi

K'rond and Mikolus Ludek." Last, she gestured to the hob. "I believe you've met Ezei before."

Shyvoan nodded to the hob. "Yah, but not by name, nor under the best of circumstances."

Ezei returned her nod.

"Liphye Maivschld, Buok Daheaschld, and I'm Shyvoan Naivaschld." While she introduced herself and the others, Shyvoan's gaze was drawn to the one called Gyasi. Everyone murmured words of greeting, and he smiled at her before he glanced away, looking unsure of himself.

"So, what's this promise?" Buok said.

"It's a promise to take your people from this world to another," Alorsha said.

Shyvoan exchanged glances with the other warriors. "That's like what your Devrand said he would do for us. But he didn't say another world. He said someplace safe far away. But why should we trust again?"

Alorsha nodded. "He *would* say whatever he needed to, to get what he wanted. More magic to escape again. But let me try to explain better."

She folded her hands in her lap and looked from each one to the next. "You *do* know we—and Devrand and Jarthan—aren't from this world?"

"Another world…" Liphye murmured and shook her head.

"As Tinanay said about our ancestors," Buok said. "The same world?"

Alorsha shrugged. "I don't know. But I doubt it, since until we left ours, we'd never heard of anyone traveling to another world. Also, the moaras said that our magic felt different from 'the others who have lingered so long', as they put it. Your people."

"You met the moaras and lived to tell of it?" Liphye said.

Alorsha nodded, with a hint of a smile.

"Wasn't a comfortable thing," Gyasi said.

Shyvoan frowned. "Devrand only told us he – they – came from very far away."

"Suppose it explains some things," Liphye added after some thought. "The clothes they came in, them not knowing our language, the different magic, and such. And what we just saw."

"Still hard to believe," Shyvoan said.

Alorsha nodded, her expression sympathetic. "We came to your world aboard our ship, the *Deliberia*, in pursuit of Devrand and my life-partner Jarthan, who's held captive by Devrand. We arrived far out at sea and encountered the magic people who live in the waters, those moaras."

"More like 'were caught by them'," Gyasi muttered.

Alorsha nodded. "Yes, certainly a more accurate way to put it."

"Can't imagine they were too happy to have you and your ship on their water," Liphye said.

Alorsha smiled slightly. "They weren't. After they held us trapped for a long while, they took us to meet with what I have to assume are their leaders. They called themselves the conclave."

Liphye, Buok and Shyvoan exchanged looks. "Like our Elders Council, perhaps," Buok murmured.

"The conclave wanted to know what purpose brought us to again invade their world. Their words," Alorsha said. "After we explained how and why we were here, they told us your magic and the world's magic were unsuited to each other. They said that your people came here from another world originally and that your presence is problematic both for you and them. They emphasized that you don't belong here and that you face your end. That there are few of you, and you're growing fewer."

Again, Shyvoan and the other two warriors exchanged looks.

"We'd never heard tell of coming from another world until today," Liphye said, an edge of uneasiness in her voice. Buok gave her shoulder a gentle squeeze.

"Well, *we* are from here," he murmured to her. "Just not our ancestors, if all this is to be believed."

"That does explain the little bits of oddness we've all noticed and then passed off," Shyvoan said. "Things like why the magic slips away from us. Why we and our goats and tarandeer seem different from all the other island life, with their slit pupils and preference for little to no light."

"And carrying their own magic," Liphye said.

"True, that," Buok said.

"To get free of the moaras," Alorsha continued, "and to have a chance of catching Devrand, we had to reach an agreement with them. They offered a pact to us. Again, their words. That's the promise the dragon mentioned. The moaras put some of their magic into our ship for a short time, to give it additional speed to get us closer to the two we follow. They also bolstered our magic some, to help with the wayfinding magic that I use to find the direction to Devrand. In exchange for this help, they want us to take all of your people with us when we leave this world."

"We saw you sometimes, your ship. From various islands," Liphye said. "How have you only now caught up to us?"

Alorsha sighed and glanced at Ezei. "Not *all* the moaras agreed with the pact. And so we encountered several difficulties with getting from the ship to any islands."

"And then you'd move," Gyasi said.

Shyvoan leaned forward. "So, you *can* leave here? Go to yet another world?"

Alorsha nodded. "Even if we had managed to catch Devrand here, we had never planned to stay in this world. We have our own. And so, we agreed to provide passage for your people away from here."

"And what say do we get in this?" Liphye's tone was heated.

"Say of live or die," Ezei spoke up. "Strong wrong-minded-we hunt to kill you if you stay. You die. Or you go. You live."

"You told us the dragons were all dead," Shyvoan accused.

"Yah. Told you. Protect ones left. Tinanay had different idea."

"So, you'll just take us all away out of the goodness of your heart?" Liphye said to Alorsha.

Alorsha shared a pained look with Mikolus. "I can only tell you that we aren't like Devrand. We'd like to help. Ezei's people helped us get here and didn't attack us at any time. Although we didn't catch Devrand—"

"Again," Gyasi interjected.

"This time," Mikolus said at the same time.

"Yes. We'd like to help you, since we can. We must leave this world anyway. We can offer you a way to go to a new place. But we won't force you onto our ship, force you to leave," Alorsha said.

She gave the hob a glare, then muttered, "I'll not become like Devrand that way."

"That *was* why we made this excursion," Buok said. "Does it matter who makes the gateway to take us?"

Shyvoan and Liphye shrugged, almost in unison. "You can and will take us?" Shyvoan said to Alorsha.

She nodded. "We can and will. Although we'll take you back to the rest of your people first, of course. We have one chance at the passage."

Liphye sighed. "Right, the trip back. Another long slog?"

Alorsha stood. "Only a little bit of one to collect your two friends further down the trail. After that comes a boat ride out to the *Deliberia*."

"Water-we promise a swift boat trip," Ezei said.

After they exchanged nods amongst themselves, Shyvoan and her squad-mates stood again.

"We should get going, then," Shyvoan said, after a last

look at where Tinanay had been. A large, flattened area in the sparse grass was the only sign left that the dragon had been there. And the murdering sword lay there.

Ezei walked over to it, lifted it, and carried it to Shyvoan. "Gift-scales belong with you."

"I don't know—"

"Yah. Take."

With a sigh, Shyvoan took her sword and sheathed it. *Don't know that I can use it ever again.*

They all headed back to the rock tunnel that served as entrance to the dragon's place.

"Will we have to return again then, to make the passage?" Gyasi said to Alorsha. "Won't their people be too far from here for the magic to work?"

Alorsha shook her head as she followed Mikolus into the bushes. "As I've mentioned before, distance hasn't been an issue. I was close enough when Devrand created his passage. Once I share the magic from the dragon with the *Deliberia*, then with my ring and the ship's own magic, we can open the passage to where he went. It won't matter where we are in this world, so we'll just open it from near where their people are. The true concern is time. I've noticed the more time that passes between when he creates his passage and we do ours, the more difficult it is and often the rougher the actual passage."

"Right-minded-we, water-we can help you move fast," Ezei said.

Alorsha nodded. "You'll have our thanks. That'll make a difference."

After they all passed through the rock tunnel and headed down the path again, Shyvoan found herself walking with the hob. She glanced at him and winced at the bruises she saw on his face and arms, lit by the last remnants of sunset.

"I apologize for the rough treatment you got from Devrand," she said. She kept her voice quiet, for his ears alone.

The hob glanced at her and tilted his head. "Kind of you, but right-minded-you did no wrong. No sorry needed." He nodded firmly and waved a hand over the vesnaflurs on the path while he made a chattering sound, much like the small tree rodents Shyvoan remembered from her childhood. After a few seconds, the flowers let off a soft glow, enough for them to see by. He smiled at Shyvoan.

"Better now."

Shyvoan agreed and pondered how to ask something she needed to understand.

"About my sword," she said.

The hob bobbed his head. "Yah, the gift-scales. A trust-sign between Human-Folk families and dragons. Once. Also, in sadness, most effective weapon against dragons."

"Then why would they have allowed them to be made into a weapon? Did they agree to let their scales become part of the weapon?"

Ezei shrugged. "Dragons always keep counsel with themselves. Don't think agreed or allowed. Don't think said *what* to do with gift-scales."

At a sudden thought, Shyvoan peered at the hob. "How are you here? On this island? I thought you said it takes time for the Maheaja-Folk to find a way to cross the water between islands."

Ezei grinned. "Said is difficult. Takes time. Not to find way, to make new connection. Magic is connection. Why Human-Folk have trouble. Only connection to where lived long. Weak connection to rest." He waved his hand at the landscape around them, hidden in the night. "Weak connection to places lived short, too."

"So how *are* you here? In so short a time? And what of the arcasi? Can't they just fly over the water?"

Ezei chuckled, a sound Shyvoan had never heard from any of the Maheaja-Folk. "Water magic block flying. For arcasi. Dragons…." He shrugged. "Dragons go own way.

For me… rode boat." He pointed at Alorsha and chuckled again, then sobered as he looked ahead. "Ah, must help now."

They had come to the section of the path that was destroyed. Ezei wound through the people ahead and stopped near the edge of the broken section. He walked a few feet into the trees uphill of the path and made the chattering sound again, a different rhythm from before. A shimmer formed on the hillside next to him, turned foggy, and cleared to reveal a hole.

"That's how he brought us past the damage before," Alorsha said to a questioning look from Shyvoan.

"Faster. Safer," Ezei said and led the way into the hole, a tunnel Shyvoan discovered when she followed.

"Did any of you see loose tarandeer as you followed us?" Liphye said, her voice echoing slightly in the tunnel. "Our pack animals. Big enough and sturdy enough to ride. With short brown hair, cloven hooves, and small antlers."

"We've seen no large animals on this island," Mikolus said.

"Hope they just ran off and found some good plants to eat somewhere," Liphye murmured.

Shyvoan patted her shoulder. "We'll watch for them on our way back, but I'd imagine that's exactly what they did. I've a feeling we won't see them."

"Yah, probably."

The tunnel seemed no longer than the one they had traversed to reach Tinanay, but when they exited the other end, Shyvoan saw they had almost reached the spot where they had left Aivean and Teigye.

"Your companions are not too far," Mikolus said. "Our healer stayed with them while we came on ahead."

Within minutes, they rejoined their squad-mates. While they gathered everything to leave, Shyvoan and Alorsha covered the introductions and Buok told Aivean and Teigye what had happened. Shyvoan learned the mender's name, the 'healer' as they called him, was Taesen Bashiad.

He was an older man—his hair and mustache more than half white—but with a wiry strength: he hefted a pack easily as heavy as the ones they had started the journey with.

Teigye and Gyasi, who were of a height with each other, took places at Aivean's sides with her arms over their shoulders to help her along. Her injured leg and arm had been wrapped with new bandages—lumpy ones. Shyvoan smiled to see her able to move much easier and with little apparent pain. *The newcomers' mender must be truly accomplished.*

The next several hours passed in a blur. Shyvoan was tired already, her ankle still ached, and something about the hob's magic made everything flow together. He opened tunnel after tunnel for their use and they traveled swiftly down the mountains, back the way that had taken them so many days to travel originally. Then they traveled further, with not tunnels but some Maheaja-Folk magic that moved them far with each step. A cloudy dawn found them at the shore south of the ruins, bleary, but at the same time exhilarated from the speed of their journey.

Ezei eased as close to the waterline as he could get without getting wet and pursed his lips. He looked like he was whistling, but Shyvoan heard no sound. The hob paused, head cocked like he listened to something the others did not hear, then he jogged back to where they waited near the edge of the shore. He waved a hand at two boats that sat some distance from them on the sandy shore above the high-tide mark.

"Back home now for me. Others, right-minded water-we, meet you a little out from shore. Take you back to your floating home."

"Aren't you riding a boat back to your own island?" Shyvoan said.

Ezei shook his head. "Faster on own. Already connection to home. Easy to go back." He bowed and ran back into the trees before anyone could react.

Shyvoan eyed the two boats. *Will we all fit? Do I trust these newcomers to take us safely to this ship of theirs?* She felt inclined to trust Ezei, at least, that the others he mentioned would help them as he had. She sighed and approached one of the boats.

"What do we need to do?"

The group divided into two and Alorsha's people helped Shyvoan and her squad-mates into the boats. With everyone aboard, and all their gear, even as little as remained, it was a tight squeeze. Shyvoan shared a boat with Mikolus, Gyasi, Aivean and Taesen. The others took the other boat. Mikolus and Gyasi showed her how to row, and she helped as she could while she fought fatigue at the same time.

About a quarter hour out from the shore, the boat jerked unexpectedly and picked up speed.

"You can stow your oars, now," Mikolus said. He stowed his own as he showed her how it was done. Shyvoan looked over the side but only saw long, sleek shapes in the dark water. She counted four of them as they brought the boats to a surprising speed.

The cold spray flung in the air from their passage caught her in the face, and in the middle of a yawn. It chased away her drowsiness as she sputtered in surprise then laughed. The boat turned. She lost her balance and leaned too far toward the edge. Gyasi caught her hand and helped steady her.

For a moment, their gazes caught. He smiled shyly and quickly released her hand. More spray drenched them and Shyvoan laughed again in delight. *Who knew traveling on the water could be so fun!* Gyasi's laughter joined hers.

Too soon, the small boats came alongside the huge ship that could only be the *Deliberia*. Shyvoan's mouth dropped open when they eased alongside and she saw how far above them it rose.

"We're like a large town aboard," Gyasi told her as a rope ladder dropped over the side for them. "It's that big.

We'll be able to take your people without too much crowding."

"I can see that," Shyvoan murmured.

One at a time, they climbed the ladder to the main level of the ship, called the deck, Shyvoan learned. Her warriors gathered with her, and they looked around.

The place bustled with activity. So many people doing things about which Shyvoan had no clue. She did see them secure ropes to the two small boats and haul them out of the water. She tried to make sense of what she saw, but her eyelids drooped. She wanted to know, but she decided right then she wanted sleep more.

A light touch on her arm startled her out of her fight with fatigue.

"A few last things to do and we'll get underway," Alorsha told her and her squad-mates. "You'll have time to learn more as we sail, if you wish. But looking at you, I'd think you might be interested in beds right now?"

At their nods she smiled and beckoned a couple of her people close, a man and a woman, the woman clearly pregnant.

"Kluir and Hali will show you places to sleep for now. And we can make more long-term arrangements when you are up to it." She turned away as someone called her name.

With gentle smiles, Kluir and Hali ushered them across the deck to an opening that led below. Down a steep stair, they showed them to three rooms next to each other along one side of a narrow hall. Within were two beds each, strange beds suspended from ropes, but inviting, nonetheless.

Shyvoan did not even kick off her boots before she clambered into a lower one and let sleep claim her.

CHAPTER 32

The sounds of battle woke Shyvoan. She tumbled out of the hanging bed and reached for her sword before she remembered what had happened, what it had done. She would need to find another one, if she was not going to use that one anymore, and quickly, judging from the sounds she heard.

But when she scrambled onto the deck, and cleared the bleariness of sleep from her eyes, she discovered that no battle raged, but rather sparring, from the look of it. Although some of the techniques were unlike any she had seen before.

She found a space off to the side out of the way and settled in to watch and see what she might learn.

One of the people they had met the previous day—Mikolus—led the session. He spotted her off to the side and, after he made a small correction to one woman's stance, wound his way through the combatants and joined her.

"We do this every morning. You and your companions are welcome to join in."

"I don't recognize a lot of the techniques you're showing them," Shyvoan said.

"Join in then and learn some. I'd imagine you might have things to show us, too."

Shyvoan yawned and stretched, and hitched her breath at unexpected aches.

"Tomorrow, if that's all right."

"Whenever you'd like." With a slight smile, he returned to the others.

After the sparring session ended, Shyvoan found her squad-mates and, with Gyasi as a willing guide, they began to explore the ship and learn about the people who called it home.

The rest of the journey back to the island where they had left the denizens passed in a similar fashion, and smoothly. No storms, no trouble from the moaras.

At least a dozen moaras at a time gathered around the *Deliberia* to speed it on its way. Shyvoan counted them. They ignored her.

A haze hung around the ship and blocked the direct sunlight. *Probably the moaras' doing.* So Shyvoan assumed.

Shyvoan did take part a couple of mornings—along with her fellow warriors—in the regular sparring sessions Mikolus ran. But most of the time she perched in various places around the ship, out of the way, as she continued to learn about the ship – the place she would likely call home soon. *At least for the time it takes to find a new place for the people to settle, anyway.*

The ship's healers, in particular, fascinated her. Spouses, Taesen and Naltha Bashiad allowed her, with Aivean's agreement, to watch as they worked to heal the mage's injuries.

Their healing magic seemed to reside in what they called charms: small flat carvings of glinting curves and swirls, no longer than the joint of one finger and made of some shiny substance. The healers put two each within the wrappings around Aivean's arm and leg whenever they changed the wrappings, replacing the charms they had placed there previously.

The charms created odd bumps under the wrappings, but Aivean became more mobile each day. She confided in Shyvoan that since Taesen had put the first charms in the wrappings, back on the dragon's island, little pain had bothered her.

When Shyvoan lurked and watched the ship's people, Gyasi often lingered nearby, willing to answer her questions and show her things she might not have noticed on her own. She learned that he preferred to be called Gya and that many of the people on the ship had come from vastly different worlds, him included.

That last intrigued her. They allowed people to stay with them, to travel with them. What places might she see if she dared ask to stay on the ship?

Mid-morning of the eighth day of the journey from Tinanay's island, as the ship slowed then stopped, Shyvoan and the other warriors joined Alorsha at the rail. Heavy clouds hung in the sky, but no rain had fallen, although it looked like it could at any time.

"Here *Deliberia* must stop," one of the moaras called from the water. "We'll speed your small boats close to the isle as we can and speed them back again with the Human-Folk."

"You have our thanks," Alorsha called to them and sent her people to lower three of the ship's four small tenders.

"Not all four of the boats?" Teigye said.

"We'll keep the last with the ship, in case they need to communicate with us," she explained. "I'd thought to have all of you come with us this first time. I'm sure you're eager to see your people again."

"And we can smooth over any difficulties with your arrival," Buok added.

"And explain what's going on and such," Liphye said.

"Those, too," Alorsha agreed.

"It's probably going to take some time to convince everyone to go," Teigye said. "And that's if we assume they already know of the idea, that anything's been said to more than a handful about the gateway that Devrand had promised. If everyone doesn't already know about that, seems like this won't go smoothly."

"True, that," Buok said.

"And once we *do* have everyone behind the idea, it's going to take a lot of back and forth to get everyone here," Liphye said.

"Then we'd better get started," Shyvoan said.

She headed for one of the tenders, Buok with her, while Liphye and Teigye took a second. Aivean chose to stay behind, so the remaining tender held only Mikolus and Alorsha.

As promised, the moaras sped the small tenders from the *Deliberia* to the shallows not far offshore from the island. Then those in the tenders rowed the rest of the way.

As they approached the island, Shyvoan heard shouts and screams and the distinct sounds of battle. People surged on the shore, close to the waterline. She and Buok exchanged looks and pulled harder on the oars.

They landed amid chaos. Drawing her sword, a new one she had acquired from the Ship's Captain, Shyvoan plunged into the mess. She shoved her way through, headed for the sounds of fighting, and discovered that the people she passed were denizens.

Why weren't they at the new lodgment? What had happened that they were backed up to the sea here?

When she spotted Troop-Lead Meara, Shyvoan headed to her and called out.

The Troop-Lead turned, and surprise and relief crossed her face. She shouted encouragement to the warriors who battled Maheaja-Folk just steps away from her and hurried to Shyvoan.

"Just in time." She clasped Shyvoan's arm and

squeezed. "Have that Devrand make his gateway. We've got to get out of here."

"What happened?"

"It's like all the Maheaja-Folk on this island just went berserk. All at once. Eight days ago, they suddenly attacked, in these numbers. Like something set them off, but we don't know what." She waved a hand at the seething fight mere steps from where they stood. "They've been whittling us down since then. We're all that's left."

Shyvoan frowned. Eight days before, Devrand had used her heirloom sword to stab the dragon before he made his escape. *Could the Maheaja-Folk here have somehow known of that attack when it happened?* From what Meara had said, it seemed so.

Shyvoan took a moment to look around. *Looked like only half the denizens are here.* They had little with them beyond the clothes they wore and bordered on hysterical, crowded against the waterline with nowhere else to go. Too few warriors stood defending them.

"Leader Finnschld?" she said when she couldn't spot the Shield-Lead.

"They got her a couple of days ago. She saved Rashean and the menders, but we couldn't save her." Meara's voice shook as she gazed into the distance.

Shyvoan sighed and closed her eyes as she absorbed the news. Then she gave herself a little shake. *Too much to do to dwell on it right now.*

"No Devrand to make the gateway, but we have another solution," she told the Troop-Lead.

"Whatever it is, do it."

The Troop-Lead turned back to the fight and plunged into it herself, leading a few warriors who had been catching some rest.

Shyvoan raced back to the denizens and looked for anyone in charge. But she found no Elders among the frightened younger men, women and children who clung to each other. She whistled the bird call to bring her squad to her and shouted to get the denizen's attention.

"We've got a way to get away," she told them and pointed to the tenders and Alorsha, who had lingered near them.

"You'd just take us to the water Maheaja-Folk," someone shouted. After a moment, she realized it was Neasha's voice. Shyvoan spotted her sister toward the side of the group, with Glin and their two children. *At least they're safe.*

"No," Shyvoan shouted back. She pointed to some of the denizens who had been at the waterline when they landed. "You saw us come ashore. We have a way back out. Away from here. To safety. Don't you want to escape that?" She pointed to the frenzied fight that had crept closer.

With shouts of agreement, denizens surged toward the boats. Shyvoan worked to maintain order, and despaired when it became clear that even with their diminished numbers, still too many people needed to escape for the tenders to take everyone at once.

When Liphye charged up to her in response to her summons, she sent her to find the Troop-Lead to let her know the situation. Buok and Teigye joined her as Liphye ran off. The two men grasped the frantic denizens' situation at a glance.

"The warriors can hold for now," Buok told her.

"Fill the boats as full as we can?" Teigye said. "We only have to get them out to the moaras."

"Do it. And if any warriors can be spared to help keep order here, please bring them. Buok, please show them how to row."

While frantic to get away, most of the denizens willingly helped matters along without further complications. A few of the adults supported the warriors and kept the tenders from being overloaded. Many hefted makeshift weapons and formed a line in front of the tenders, between those small boats and the warriors and the fight, to give the others time to get away. Among those, Shyvoan spotted Buok's spouse and Rashean.

Soon the first tender was in the water and, with several people trying to row, it made its way out to where the moaras waited to speed it to the *Deliberia*. When they saw how the tenders and oars worked, the other denizens managed better. While they waited for the tenders to return, Shyvoan and her fellow warriors helped the others hold the raging Maheaja-folk back, helped pull injured warriors from the conflict.

Soon the tenders returned, with some of the *Deliberia's* warriors aboard to help the beleaguered people ashore.

Loading the tenders took less time that second time and soon they headed across the water. Shyvoan estimated at least two more trips to get the rest of the denizens and the remaining warriors off the island.

As the Maheaja-Folk pressed the defenders and pushed them step by step toward the water, she hoped they had the time.

While the tenders sailed from the island on their third trip, taking the last of the denizens and as many of the wounded as possible—Renan among them, sorely injured but alive Shyvoan was glad to see—those who remained fought with their feet in the water.

Mikolus and the other ship's warriors showed themselves fierce allies as they helped hold the line from moving further. Alorsha had helped earlier with the wounded and returned with the third wave of tenders, to help explain everything to the displaced denizens who now crowded her ship.

When the tenders returned, the warriors fought their way backwards to board, and even from aboard the small craft. One of the last to scramble into a tender, Shyvoan watched as the Maheaja-Folk charged right to the water's edge, but no further. They howled and screamed at the departing boats but did not send any ranged attacks after them.

The moaras met the tenders at the limit of their tolerance for shallow water and took over moving them from the wearied occupants. The quick journey back to the *Deliberia* and up the ladder to the deck passed in a fog for Shyvoan. She could not remember fighting so fiercely before with the Maheaja-Folk. *They'd truly wanted to wipe out our people.*

Aboard the ship someone handed her something to drink and chuckled softly when she gagged on the taste.

"Sorry about that," Alorsha said. "But it'll help revive you. I assume you'd rather not sleep through our passage to another world."

Shyvoan smiled. "Too true." She downed the rest of the awful drink. "So how do you do this?"

Alorsha gave her a slight smile. "Come forward and you can watch."

She waved a hand to one side to beckon Gya to join them. With a shy smile for Shyvoan, he led the way to the raised deck at the front of the ship. The bow, Shyvoan reminded herself. They stepped around denizens and warriors who seemed to have collapsed to the deck right where they were after they boarded the ship. Members of the ship's crew moved among them to see what they could do for them.

While Shyvoan hung back, Gya joined Alorsha at the forward rail. Alorsha removed something from a pendant she wore and placed it on a ring on her thumb. She then clasped the rail with both hands. Gya also clasped the rail with both hands, one of his right next to Alorsha's hand, sides touching. They both looked ahead.

At first, Shyvoan saw nothing different, just the water of the Shallow Sea, a few moaras within who apparently watched the ship. Then the moaras rose to the surface and held their arms up from the water. Above them, the air shimmered, like a heat shimmer. The shimmering grew agitated, and a vertical line formed, like Shyvoan had seen before. The line extended far above the water's surface, much longer than the one Devrand had created.

The line split open to reveal a sea of a different color, darker, more purple, and light brighter than any Shyvoan had ever seen before. What looked like a shoreline drew a dark line across the new sea, off in the distance. The *Deliberia* eased toward the passageway. Shyvoan smiled as she eagerly studied what she saw of the new world they sailed toward. *Hopefully, a place of safety for the denizens.*

And what wonders might be there for her to discover?

$\sim$

PRONUNCIATIONS

Aivean – ay VEEN
aliso – AH lih soh
Alorsha – uh LOHR shuh
anla – AHN luh
Anyeschld – AHN yuhs chuhld
arcasi – AHR kuh see

Bashiad – BAHSH ee ahd
berevo – buh REH voh
Breanschld – BREENS chuhld
Buok – BOO uhk

cadno – KAHD noh
Charnov – CHAHR nawf
chathea – CHAH thee

Daheaschld – DAH hees chuhld
Darreschld – DAH ruhs chuhld
Deliberia – dehl ih BAYR ee uh
Devrand – DEHV ruhnd
Duveasa – duh VEE suh

Eadaschld – EE duhs chuhld
Earlu – EER loo
Ezei – ehz EYE
Eztevo – EHZ teh voh

farlith – FAHR lihth
Finnschld – FIHNS chuhld
Feayon – FEE yohn

Glin – GLIHN
Grannye – GRAH nyuh
Gya – G-EYE uh

Gyasi – g-eye AH see

hob - HAHB
Hali – hah LEE
heagyn – HEE gihn

Jarthan – JAHR thuhn
jerffu – JEHR foo

kalsh – KAHLSH
Keavye – KEE vyuh
Klaidschld – KLAYDS chuhld
Kluir – KLOOR
K'rond – kuh RAHND
kuchal – koo CHAHL

Liphye – LIHF yeh
Ludek – LOO dehk
Lusaschld – LOO suhs chuhld

Maheaja-Folk – mah HEE juh fohk
Maivschld – MAYVS chuhld
Meara – MEE ruh
Mikolus – MIH koh luhs
moara – MOH ruh

Naivaschld – NAY vuhs chuhld
Naltha – NAHL thuh
Neasha – NEE shuh

Orinschld – OH rihns chuhld
Oshean – oh SHEEN

Padrigean – PAH drih geen

Rashean – rah SHEEN
rastenye – ruhs TEHN yuh

Renan – REHN uhn

Saevalde – say VAHL deh
Saivschld – SAYVS chuhld
Shyvoan – shih VOHN

Taesen – TAY sehn
taiawood – TAY uh wood
tarandeer – TAHR uhn deer
Tavano – tuh VAH noh
Teigye – T-EYE gyuh
Tinanay – TIH nuh nay
Turea – TOO ree

Uasal – oo AH suhl

vesnaflur – VEHS nuh floor

~

TITLES BY S. LYNN HELTON

Wild Heritance fantasy series

Duplicity of Power
Power Awry
Power Redeemed

Trial Run (prequel novella)
Trial and Tribulation (prequel novella)

The Deliberia Chronicles fantasy trilogy

Crystalborne Sigils
Songborne Gates
A Galeborne Resolve

AUTHOR'S NOTE

Thank you for reading my book. I hope you enjoyed it!

Please consider leaving an honest review on the book's
product page at your favorite online bookstore
and on Goodreads. Reviews from readers like you are
powerful and greatly help other readers
discover books they might enjoy.

-Lynn

ABOUT THE AUTHOR

S. Lynn Helton lives in the foothills of the Rocky
Mountains, U.S.A., with her family and a couple of crazy
cats. Lynn enjoys camping and hiking, playing games,
crafting, reading (a lot) and, of course, writing.

Read more about her books on her website:
www.slynnhelton.com